The Wanderer

The Wanderer

Fritz Leiber

VICTOR GOLLANCZ
LONDON

Copyright © Fritz Leiber 1964
All rights reserved

The right of Fritz Leiber to be identified as the author
of this work has been asserted by him in accordance with
the Copyright, Designs and Patents Act 1988.

This edition published in Great Britain in 2000 by
Victor Gollancz
An imprint of Orion Books Ltd
Orion House, 5 Upper St Martin's Lane,
London WC2H 9EA

To receive information on the Millennium list, e-mail us at:
smy@orionbooks.co.uk

A CIP catalogue record for this book
is available from the British Library

ISBN 0 57507 112 5

Printed in Great Britain by
The Guernsey Press Co. Ltd, Guernsey, C.I.

'How about a hyperspatial tube?'
'Um . . . m. Distinctly a possibility . . .'
One instant space was empty; the next it was full of warships . . .
Planets. Seven of them. Armed and powered as only a planet can be armed and powered.

EDWARD E. SMITH, PH.D., in
Second Stage Lensmen

Tiger! tiger! burning bright
In the forests of the night,
What immortal hand or eye
Could frame thy fearful symmetry?

In what distant deeps or skies
Burnt the fire of thine eyes? . . .

In what furnace was thy brain? . . .

WILLIAM BLAKE

And I beheld when he had opened the sixth seal, and lo, there was a great earthquake; and the sun became black as sackcloth of hair, and the moon became as blood;

And the stars of heaven fell unto the earth, even as a fig tree casteth her untimely figs, when she is shaken of a mighty wind.

And the heavens departed as a scroll when it is rolled together; and every mountain and island were moved out of their places . . .

And the third angel sounded, and there fell a great star from heaven, burning as it were a lamp, and it fell upon the third part of the rivers, and upon the fountains of waters.

The Revelation of St John the Divine

Actual interstellar voyaging was first effected by detaching a planet from its natural orbit by a series of well-timed and well-placed rocket impulsions, and thus projecting it into outer space at a speed far greater than the normal planetary and stellar speeds . . .

Then followed wars such as had never before occurred in our galaxy. Fleets of worlds, natural and artificial, manoeuvred among the stars to outwit one another, and destroyed one another with long-range jets of sub-atomic energy. As the tides of battle swept hither and thither through space, whole planetary systems were annihilated.

OLAF STAPLEDON in *The Star Maker*

Chapter 1

Some stories of terror and the supernormal start with a moonlit face at a diamond-paned window, or an old document in spidery handwriting, or the baying of a hound across lonely moors. But this one began with an eclipse of the moon and with four glisteningly new astronomical photographs, each showing star-fields and a planatary object. Only . . . something had happened to the stars.

The oldest of the photographs was only seven days out of the developer at the time of the eclipse. They came from three widely separated observatories and one came from a telescope on a satellite. They were the star-graven runes of purest science, at the opposite extreme from matters of superstition, yet each photograph struck a twinge of uneasiness in the young scientist first to see it.

As he looked at the black dots that should have been there . . . and at the faint black curlicues that shouldn't . . . he felt the barest touch of a strangeness that for a moment made him kin to the caveman and the devil-worshipper and the witch-haunted Middle Ages.

Passing along priority channels, the four photographs came together at the Los Angeles Area Headquarters of the Moon Project of the U.S. Space Force – the American Moon Project that was barely abreast of the Russian one, and far behind the Soviet Mars Project. And so at Moon Project, U.S., the sense of strangeness and unease was sharpest, though expressed in sardonic laughter and a bouncy imaginativeness, as is the way with scientists faced with the weird.

In the end the four photographs – or rather, what they heralded – starkly affected every human being on Earth, every atom of our planet. They opened deep fissures in the human soul.

They cost thousands their sanity and millions their lives. They did something to the moon, too.

So we might begin this story anywhere – with Wolf Loner in the mid-Atlantic, or Fritz Scher in Germany, or Richard Hillary in Somerset, or Arab Jones smoking weed in Harlem, or Barbara Katz sneaking around Palm Beach in a black playsuit, or Sally Harris hunting her excitement in the environs of New York, or Doc Brecht selling pianos in L.A., or Charlie Fulby lecturing about flying saucers, or General Spike Stevens understudying the top role in the U.S. Space Force, or Rama Joan Huntington interpreting Buddhism, or with Bagong Bung in the South China Sea, or with Don Merriam at Moonbase, U.S., or even with Tigran Biryuzov orbiting Mars. Or we could begin it with Tigerishka or Miaow or Ragnarok or the President of the United States.

But because they were close to that first centre of unease near Los Angeles, and because of the crucial part they were to play in the story, we will begin with Paul Hagbolt, a publicist employed by Moon Project; and with Margo Gelhorn, fiancée of one of the four young Americans who had soared to Moonbase, U.S., and with Margo's cat Miaow, who had a very strange journey ahead of her; and with the four photographs, though they were then only an eerie, top-secret mystery rather than a trumpeting menace; and with the moon, which was about to slide into the ambiguous gleam-haunted darkness of eclipse.

Margo Gelhorn, coming out on the lawn, saw the full moon half-way up the sky. Earth's satellite was as vividly three-dimensional as a mottled marble basketball. Its pale gold hue fitted the weather rarity of a balmy Pacific Coast evening.

'There's the bitch up there now,' Margo said.

Paul Hagbolt, emerging through the door behind her, laughed uneasily. 'You really do think of the moon as a rival.'

'Rival, hell. She's *got* Don,' the blonde girl said flatly. 'She's even got Miaow here hypnotized.' She was holding in her arms a tranquil grey cat, in whose green eyes the moon was two smudged pearls.

Paul too turned his gaze on the moon, or rather towards a point near its top, above the Mare Imbrium shadow. He couldn't distinguish the crater Plato holding Moonbase, U.S., but he knew it was in view.

Margo said bitterly: 'It's bad enough to have to look up at that graveyard monstrosity, knowing Don's there, exposed to all the dangers of a graveyard planet. But now that we have to think about this other thing that's shown up in the astronomical photographs –'

'Margo!' Paul said sharply, automatically flashing a look around. 'That's still classified information. We shouldn't be talking about it – not here.'

'The Project's turning you into an old auntie! Besides, you've given me no more than a hint –'

'I shouldn't have given you even that.'

'Well, what *are* we going to talk about, then?'

Paul let off a sigh. 'Look,' he said, 'I thought we came outside to watch the eclipse, maybe take a drive, too –'

'Oh, I forgot the eclipse! The moon's turned a little smoky, don't you think? Has it started?'

'Looks like it,' Paul said. 'It's time for first contact.'

'What'll the eclipse do to Don?'

'Nothing much. It'll get dark up there for a while. That's all. Oh yes, and the temperature outside Moonbase will drop 250 degrees or so.'

'A blast from the seventh circle of Hell and he says, "That's all"!'

'Not as bad as it sounds. You see, the temperature will be about 150 degrees above zero to start with,' Paul explained.

'A Siberian cold wave cubed on top of scalding heat and he says, "That's ducky"! And when I think of this other, unknown horror creeping towards the moon from outer space –'

'Drop it, Margo!' The smile left Paul's face. 'You're talking strictly off the top of your imagination.'

'Imagination? Did you or did you not tell me about four star photos that showed –'

'I told you nothing – nothing that you didn't completely misinterpret. No, Margo, I refuse to say another word about that. Or listen to you over-rev your mind. Let's go inside.'

'Go inside? With Don up there? I'm going to watch this eclipse through – from the coast road, if it lasts that long.'

9

'In that case,' Paul said quietly, 'you'd better get something more than that jacket. I know it seems warm now, but California nights are treacherous.'

'And nights on the moon aren't? Here, hold Miaow.'

'Why? If you think I'm going to travel a loose cat –'

'Because this jacket is too hot! Here, take it and give me Miaow back. Why not travel a cat? They're people, same as we are. Aren't you, Miaow?'

'They are not. They're simply beautiful animals.'

'They are so people. Even your great god Heinlein admits they're second-class citizens, every bit as good as aborigines or fellahin.'

'I don't care about the theory of it, Margo. I'm simply refusing to travel a nervous cat in my convertible with the top down.'

'Miaow's not nervous. She's a girl.'

'Females are calm? Look at yourself!'

'You won't take her?'

'No!'

A paltry quarter million miles starwards of Earth, the moon turned from ghostly gold to pale bronze as it slowly coasted into the fringe of the larger orb's shadow. Sun, Earth, and Moon were lining up. It was the moon's ten billionth eclipse, or thereabouts. Nothing extraordinary, really, yet from under the snug blanket of Earth's atmosphere hundreds of thousands of people were already watching the sight from Earth's night side, which now stretched across the Atlantic and the Americas from the North Sea to California and from Ghana to Pitcairn Island.

The other planets were mostly on the other side of the sun, as far away as people at the other end of a big house.

The stars were frosty, dimensionless eyes in the dark, as distant as bright-windowed houses across the ocean.

The Earth–Moon pair, huddling by the solar fire, were almost alone in a black forest twenty million million miles across. A frighteningly lonely situation, especially if you imagined something wholly unknown stirring in the forest, creeping closer, shaking the starlight here and there as it bent the black twigs of space.

Far out in the North Atlantic, a dash of dark spray in his eyes roused Wolf Loner from a chilly dream of fear in time to see the last ragged window high in the thickening black cloud-bank to the west close on the coppery moon. He knew it was the eclipse that made the orb look smoky, yet in the after-glisten of his dream the moon seemed to be calling for help from a burning building – Diana in peril. The shouldering black waves and the wind on the curved drum of the sail soon rocked and harshly crooned away the disturbing vision.

'Sanity is rhythm,' Wolf Loner said loudly to no one within five miles, or, for all he knew, two hundred – the latter being the distance he reckoned he was from Boston in his one-man, east–west passage begun at Bristol.

He checked the link between mainsheet and tiller that kept the twenty-foot sailing dory slanting into the west, then slid himself feet first into the coffin-wide cabin for a warmer and longer nap.

Three thousand miles south of the dory, the atomic luxury liner *Prince Charles* raced like a seagoing mesa towards George-town and the Antilles through an invisible mist of converging radio waves. In the air-conditioned and darkened astrodome a few older people, yawning at the post-midnight hour, watched the eclipse, and a few younger couples necked discreetly or played footsies, which the foot-glove fad facilitated, while from the main ballroom there rumbled faintly, like distant thunder, the Wagnerian strains of neojazz. Captain Sithwise tallied the number of known Brazilian fascists of the unpredictable new sort on the passenger list, and guessed that a revolution had been scheduled.

At Coney Island, in the heavy shadow of the new boardwalk, Sally Harris, her hands clasped back of her neck under the sunburst of her permanent-static-charge explosion hair-do, held herself humorously still as Jake Lesher tugged crosswise at the backstrap of her bra through the silky black fabric of her Gimbel's Scaasi Size 8 frock. 'Have a good time,' she said, 'but remember we're seeing the eclipse from the top of the Ten-Stage Rocket. All ten tops.'

11

'Aw, who wants to gawk at a moon that's sick, sick, sick,' Jake retorted a bit breathlessly. 'Sal, where the hell are the hooks and eyes?'

'In the bottom of your grandmother's trunk,' she informed him, and ran a silver-nailed thumb and forefinger down the self-sealing, mood-responsive V of her frock. 'The magnetic quick-release gear is forward, not aft, you Second Avenue sailor,' she said and gave a deft twist. 'There! See why it's called the Vanishing Bra?'

'Christ!' he said, 'they're like hot popovers. Oh Sal . . .'

'Amuse yourself,' she told him coolly, her nostrils flaring, 'but remember you're not getting out of taking me for my roller-coaster ride. And kindly handle the bakery goods with reverence.'

Don Guillermo Walker, straining to see, through the dull black Nicaraguan cloud-jungle, the inky gleam of Lake Managua, decided that bombing *el presidente*'s stronghold in the dark of the eclipse had been a purely theatric idea, a third-act improvisation from desperation, like having Jean wear nothing under her negligée in *Algiers Decision*, which hadn't saved that drama from a turkey's fate.

Eclipses weren't at all dark, it turned out, and *el presidente*'s three jet fighters could chop up this ancient Seabee in seconds, ending the Revolution of the Best, or at least the contribution to it of the self-proclaimed lineal descendant of the original William Walker who had filibustered in Nicaragua in the 1850s.

If he did manage to bale out, they would capture him. He didn't think he could stand an electric bull prod except by turning into a three-year-old.

Too much light, too much light! 'You're a typical lousy bit-player,' Don Guillermo shouted up at the brazen moon. 'You don't know how to efface yourself!'

Two thousand miles east of Wolf Loner and his cloudbank, Dai Davies, Welsh poet, vigorous and drunk, waved good night from near the dark loom of the Severn Experimental Tidal Power Station to the sooty moon sinking into the cloudless Bristol Channel beyond Portishead Point, while the spreading glow of dawn erased the stars behind him.

12

'Sleep well, Cinderella,' he called. 'Wash your face now, but be sure to come back.'

Richard Hillary, English novelist, sickish and sober, observed finically, 'Dai, you say that as if you were afraid she wouldn't.'

'There's a first time for everything, Ricky-bach,' Dai told him darkly. 'We don't worry enough about the moon.'

'You worry about her too much,' Richard countered sharply, 'reading a veritable vomit of science fiction.'

'Ah, science fiction's my food and drink – well, anyhow my food. Vomit, now – you were maybe thinking of the book-vomiting dragon Error in *The Faerie Queene* and fancying her spewing up, after all of Spenser's musty hates, the collected works of H. G. Wells, Arthur C. Clarke, and Edgar Rice Burroughs?'

Hillary's voice grew astringent. 'Science fiction is as trivial as all artistic forms that deal with phenomena rather than people. You should know that, Dai. Aren't the Welsh warm-hearted?'

'Cold as fish,' the poet replied proudly. 'Cold as the moon herself, who is a far greater power in life than you sentimental, sacrilegious, pub-snoozing, humanity-besotted, degenerate Saxo-Normans will ever realize.' He indicated the Station with a sweep of his arm. 'Power from Mona!'

'David,' the novelist exploded. 'You know perfectly well that this tidal power toy is merely a sop to people like myself who are against atomic power because of the weapons aspect. And please don't call the moon Mona – that's folk etymology. Mona's a Welsh island, if you will – Anglesey – but not a Welsh planet!'

Dai shrugged, peering west at the dim, vanishing moon-bump. 'Mona sounds right to me and that's all that counts. All culture is but a sop to infant humanity. And in any case,' he added with a mocking grin, 'there are men on the moon.'

'Yes,' Hillary agreed coldly, 'four Americans and an indeterminate but small number of Soviets. We ought to have cured human poverty and suffering before wasting milliards on space.'

'Still, there are men on Mona, on their way to the stars.'

'Four Americans. I have more respect for that New Englander Wolf Loner who sailed from Bristol last month in his dory. At

13

least he wasn't staking the world's wealth on his adventurous whim.'

Dai grinned, without taking his eyes off the west.

'Be damned to Loner, that Yankee anachronism! He's most likely drowned and feeding the fishes. But the Americans write fine science fiction and make moon-ships almost as good as the Russkies'. Good night, Mona-bach! Come back dirty-faced or clean, but come back.'

Chapter 2

Through his mushroom helmet's kingsize view window, still polarized at half max to guard his eyes from solar glare, Lieutenant Don Merriam, U.S.S.F., watched the last curved sliver of solid sun, already blurred by Earth's atmosphere, edge behind the solid bulk of the mother planet.

The last twinges of orange light reproduced with frightening exactitude the winter sun setting through the black tangle of leafless trees a quarter mile west of the Minnesota farmhouse where Don Merriam had spent his childhood.

Twisting his head towards the right-hand mini-console, he tongued a key to cut polarization. ('The airless planets will be pioneered by men with long, active tongues,' Commander Gompert had summed it up. 'Frogmen?' Dufresne had suggested.)

The stars sprang out in their multitudes – a desert night squared, a night with sequins. The pearly shock of Sol's corona blended with the Milky Way.

Earth was ringed by a ruddy glow – sunlight bent by the planet's thick atmosphere – and would remain so throughout the eclipse. The ring was brightest near the planet's crust, fading out a quarter diameter away, and brightest of all along the left-hand rim behind which the sun had just vanished.

Don noted without surprise that the central bulk of Earth was the blackest he had ever seen it. Because of the eclipse, it was no longer brushed with the ghostly glow of moonlight.

He had been half crouched in his suit, leaning back and supporting himself on one arm to get an easy view of Earth, which was half-way to its zenith. Now with a wrist-flick nicely gauged to the moon's dreamy gravitation, he came fully to his feet and looked around him.

Starlight and ring-glow tinged with bronze the dark grey plain of dust, mouse-soft, a mixture of powdered pumice and magnetic iron oxide.

Back when Cromwell's New Model Army ruled England, Hevelius had named this crater the Great Black Lake. But even in bright sunlight Don could not have seen the wall of Plato. That near-mile-high, circular rampart, thirty miles away from him moon-east, north, south, and west, was hidden by the curve of the moon's surface, sharper than the earth's.

The same close horizon hid the bottom half of the Hut, only three hundred yards away. It was good to see those five little glowing portholes at the margin between the dark plain and the starfield – and near them, silhouetted by starlight, the truncated cones of the base's three rocket ships, each standing high on its three landing legs.

'How's the dark dark?' Johannsen's voice softly asked in his ear. 'Roger and over.'

'Warm and spicy. Suzie sends love,' Don responded. 'Roger to you.'

'Outside temperature?'

Don glanced down at the magnified fluorescent dials beneath the view window. 'Dropping past 200 Kelvin,' he replied, giving the absolute equivalent of a temperature of almost exactly 100 degrees below zero on the Fahrenheit scale still widely used in Earth's English-speaking areas.

'Your SOS working?' Johannsen continued.

Don tongued a key and a faint musical ululation filled his helmet. 'Loud and clear, my captain,' he said with a flourish.

'I can hear it,' Johannsen assured him sourly. Don tongued it off.

'Have you harvested our cans?' Johannsen next asked, refer-ring to the tiny, rod-supported canisters regularly put out and collected to check on the movements of moon dust and other materials, including radioactively tagged atoms planted at various distances from the Hut.

'I haven't sharpened my scythe yet,' Don told him.

'Take your time,' Johannsen advised with a knowing snort as he signed off. He and Don were well aware that planting and harvesting the cans was mostly an excuse to get a man suited up and out of the Hut as a safety measure during times of greatest danger from moonquakes – when Earth and Sun were dragging at the moon from the same side, as now, or from opposite sides, as would happen in two weeks. Gravitational traction has been thought to trigger earthquakes, and so, possibly, moonquakes. Moonbase had not yet experienced anything beyond the mildest temblor – the pen of the seismograph keyed to the solid rock below the dust cushioning the Hut had hardly quivered; just the same, Gompert made a point of having a man outside for several hours each fortnight – at 'new earth' and 'full earth' (or full moon and new moon, if you stayed with the groundster lingo, or simply the spring tides). Thus if the unexpected did occur and the Hut sustained serious damage, Gompert would have one egg outside his basket.

It was just another of the many fine-drawn precautions Moonbase took for its safety. Besides, it provided a tough regular check on the efficiency of spacesuits and of personnel working solo.

Don looked up again at the Earth. The ring was glowing less lop-sidedly now. He couldn't make out a single feature of the inky circle inside, though he knew the eastern Pacific and the Americas were to the left and the Atlantic and the western tips of Africa and Europe to the right. He thought of dear, slightly hysterical Margo and good old neurotic Paul, and truly even they seemed to him rather trivial at the moment – nice little beetles scuttling under the bark of Earth's atmosphere.

He looked down again, and he was standing on glittering whiteness. Not whiteness literally, yet the effect of a new-fallen Minnesota snow by starlight had been duplicated with devilish precision. Carbon dioxide gas, seeping steadily up through the pumice and oxide of Plato's floor, had suddenly crystallized throughout into dry-ice flakes forming directly on the dust floor or falling on to it almost instantly.

Don smiled, feeling less inhumanly distant from life. The moon had not become a Mother to him yet, not by a long shot,

16

but she was getting to seem just a little like a chilly Older Sister.

Balmy air sluiced the convertible carrying Paul Hagbolt and Margo Gelhorn and the cat Miaow along the Pacific Coast Highway. At almost regular intervals a weathered yellow road-sign would grow until it plainly said SLIDE AREA or FALLING ROCK ZONE, and then it would duck out of the headlight beam. The highway travelled a generally narrow strip between the beach and an almost vertical hundred-foot cliff of geologically infantile material – packed silt, sand, gravel, and other sediments, though here and there larger rocks thrust through.

Margo, her hair streaming, sat half switched around with her knees on the seat between her and Paul, so she could watch the smokingly bronzed moon. She had her jacket spread on her lap. On it was Miaow, curled up in a grey doughnut and fast asleep, or giving a good imitation.

'We're getting near Vandenberg Two,' Paul said. 'We could look at the moon through one of the Project 'scopes.'

'Will Morton Opperly be there?' Margo asked.

'No,' Paul replied, smiling faintly. 'He's over in the Valley these days, at Vandenberg Three, playing master sorcerer to all the other theory boys.'

Margo shrugged and looked sideways up. 'Doesn't the moon ever black out?' she wondered. 'It's still sooty copper.'

Paul explained to her about the ring-glow.

'How long does the eclipse last, anyway?' she asked, and when he said, 'Two hours,' she objected: 'I thought eclipses were over in seconds, with everybody getting excited and dropping their cameras.'

'Those are the eclipses of the sun – the totality part.'

Margo smiled and leaned back. 'Now tell me about the star photographs,' she said. 'You can't possibly be overheard in a moving car. And I'm not so worked up about them now. I've stopped worrying about Don – the eclipse is just a bronze blanket for him.'

Paul hesitated.

She smiled again. 'I promise not to rev my mind at all. I'd just like to understand them.'

Paul said: 'I can't promise you any understanding. Even the astro big-wigs only made profound noises. Including Opperly.'

'Well?'

Paul wove the tyres around a tiny scatter of gravel. Then he began. 'Well, ordinarily, star photos don't get seen around for years, if ever, but the astro boys on the Project have a standing request out with their pals at the observatories to be shown anything unusual. We've even had star pix the day after they were taken.'

Margo laughed. 'Late Sports Final of the Stellar Atlas?'

'Exactly! Well, the first photo came in a week ago. It showed a starfield with the planet Pluto in it. But something had happened during the exposure so that the stars around Pluto had blanked out or shifted position. I got to look at it myself – there were three very faint squiggles where the brightest stars near Pluto had shifted. Black-on-white squiggles – in real astronomy you look at the negatives.'

'Inside stuff,' Margo said solemnly. Then, 'Paul,' she cried. 'There was a newspaper story this morning about a man who claimed to have seen some stars twirl! I remember the headline: STARS MOVED, SAYS WRONG-WAY DRIVER.'

'I saw it, too,' Paul said a bit sourly. 'He was driving an open-top car at the time, and had an accident – because he was so fascinated by the stars, he said. Turned out he'd been drinking.'

'Yes, but the people with him in the car backed him up. And later there were phone calls to the planetarium, reporting the same thing.'

'I know, we had some at the Moon Project,' Paul said. 'Just the usual business of mass suggestion. Look, Margo, the photo I was telling you about was taken a week ago, and it was of something only a powerful telescope could see. Let's not get it mixed up with flying-saucer-type nonsense. I'm saying, we got a photo of Pluto showing three faint star-squiggles. But get this – Pluto hadn't shifted at all! Its image was a black dot.'

'What's so astonishing about that?'

'Ordinarily you don't get startled at starlight or even star images wavering. Earth's atmosphere does it, same as it makes hills waver on a hot day – in fact, that's what makes the stars twinkle. But in this case, whatever was twisting the starlight had to be out beyond Pluto. This side of the stars, but beyond Pluto.'

'How far away is Pluto?'

'Almost forty times as far as the sun.'

'What would twist starlight way out in space?'

'That's what puzzles the big boys. Some special sort of electric or magnetic field, maybe, though it would have to be very strong.'

'How about the other photos?' Margo prompted.

Paul paused while he pulled around a deep-growling truck. 'The second, taken four nights ago by our astro satellite and TV'ed down, was the same story, except that the planet involved was Jupiter, and the area of the twist was larger.'

'So that whatever made the twist must have been nearer?' Margo suggested.

'Perhaps. Incidentally, Jupiter's moons hadn't wavered either. The third photo, which I saw day before yesterday, showed a still larger area of twist with Venus in it. Only this time Venus had made a squiggle – a big one.'

'As if the light had been twisted this side of Venus?'

'Yes, between Venus and Earth. Of course it could have been atmosphere-waver this time, but the boys didn't think so.'

Then Paul grew silent.

'Well?' Margo prodded him. 'You said there were four photos.'

'I saw the fourth today,' he told her guardedly. 'Taken last night. Still larger areas of twist. This time the edge of the moon was in it. The moon's image hadn't wavered.'

'Paul! That must have been what the man who was driving saw. The same night.'

'I don't think so,' he told her. 'You can hardly see any stars near the moon with the naked eye. Besides, these reports by laymen just don't mean anything.'

'Well,' she countered, 'it certainly *does* sound as if something were creeping up on the moon. First Pluto, then Jupiter, then Venus, getting closer each time.'

The road curved south and the darkly bronzed moon came swinging out over the Pacific as it rode along with them.

'Now, wait a minute, Margo,' Paul protested, lifting his left hand for a moment from the wheel. 'I got the same idea myself, so I asked Van Bruster about it. He says it's completely unlikely that one single field, travelling through space, was responsible for the four twists. He thinks there were four different twist fields involved, not connected in any way – so there can't be any question of something creeping up on the moon. What's more, he says he's not too surprised at the photos. He says astronomers have known the theoretical possibility of such fields for years, and that evidence for them is beginning to show up now, not by chance, but because of the electronically amplified 'scopes and superfast photographic emulsions that have just gone into use this year. The twists show up in star snapshots where they wouldn't in long exposures.'

'What did Morton Opperly think of the photos?' Margo asked.

'He didn't . . . No, wait, he was the one who insisted on plotting the course of the twist fields from Pluto to the moon. Say, we just passed Monica Mountainway! That's the fancy new road across the mountains to Vandenberg Three where Opperly is right now.'

'Was the Pluto–moon course a straight one?' Margo asked, refusing to be deflected.

'No, the darnedest zig-zag imaginable.'

'But did Opperly say anything?' Margo insisted.

Paul hesitated, then said, 'Oh, he chuckled, and said something like, "Well, if Earth or Moon is their target, they're getting closer with each shot." '

'You see?' Margo said with satisfaction. 'You see? Whatever it is, it's aiming at planets!'

Barbara Katz, self-styled Girl Adventurer and long-time science-fiction fan, faded back across the lawn, away from the street-globes and the Palm Beach policeman's flashlight, and slipped behind the thick jagged bole of a cabbage palmetto before the cold bright beam swung her way. She thanked Mentor, her science-fiction god, that the long-hoarded, thirty-inch nylon foot-gloves she was wearing below her black playsuit were black, too – one of the popular pastel shades would have shown up even without the flash. The bag dangling from her shoulder was a black one, of the Black Ball Jetline. She didn't worry about her face and arms, they were dark enough to melt with the night – and get her mistaken for coloured by day. Barbara was willing to do her bit for integration, but just the same she sometimes resented it that she tanned so dark so fast.

Another burden for Jews to bear bravely, her father might have told her, though her father wouldn't have approved of stouthearted girls hunting millionaires in their home lair in Florida, which they shared with the alligators. Or of such girls carrying bikinis in their swiped shoulder bags, either.

The policeman's flash was prodding the shrubs across the street now, so she continued across the lawn springy as foam rubber. She decided that this was certainly the house from beside which she'd seen a lens flashing while she'd sneaked her swim at sunset.

It got very dark around her as she advanced. As she rounded another palmetto, she heard the whisper of a tiny electric motor, and she almost overran a white suit that was seated at the eyepiece of a big white telescope supported on a white-legged tripod and directed at the western sky.

The suit got up with a kind of lurch that showed it was helped by a cane, and a voice quavered from atop it. 'Who's that?'

'Good evening,' Barbara Katz responded in her warmest, politest voice. 'I believe you know me – I'm the girl who was changing into the black-and-yellow striped bikini. May I watch the eclipse with you?'

Chapter 3

Paul Hagbolt looked at the heights ahead, where the Pacific Coast Highway swung inland and began to climb. Beyond this approaching bend, between the road and the sea, loomed the three-hundred-foot plateau on which stood Vandenberg Two, home of the Moon Project and the U.S. Space Force's newest base and rocket launching and landing area. Gleamingly wire-fenced around its foot and showing only a few dark red lights

21

along its crest which stretched off endlessly, the space base towered mysteriously between the diverging highway and ocean – an ominous baronial stronghold of the future.

The highway hummed more hollowly as the convertible crossed a flat concrete bridge over a wash and Margo Gelhorn sat up sharply beside him. Miaow flinched. The girl's gaze swung back past Paul. 'Hey, wait a minute.'

'What is it?' Paul asked, not slowing down. The highway had begun its climb.

'I'd almost swear,' Margo said, staring back down the road, 'that I saw a sign with the words "Flying Saucer" on it.'

'Flying Saucer-Burgers?' Paul suggested. 'Same shape, you know.'

'No, there wasn't a café or anything like that. Just one little white sign. Right before the wash. I want to go back and have a look at it.'

'But we're almost to V-2,' Paul objected. 'Don't you want to see the moon through a 'scope while the eclipse is still on? You'll be able to see Plato, only we'll have to put up the top and leave Miaow locked in the car. You can't take pets into Vandenberg.'

'No, I don't,' Margo said. 'I'm sick of being given the slick Project treatment. What's more, I abominate any organization that denies cats are people!'

'All right, all right,' Paul chuckled.

'So let's turn back right now. We'll be able to see the moon better facing that way.'

Paul did his best to drive past the little white sign, but Margo brought him up short. 'There! Where the green lantern is! Stop there!' As the car bumped on the uneven shoulder, Miaow sat up and stretched and then looked around with no great interest.

There was a dirt road going down beside the beach, along the foot of the headland the highway had swung inland to climb – a lesser bump before the big plateau of Vandenberg Two.

On one side of the dirt road there hung a flickering kerosene lantern with green glass around the flame. To the other side, standing out sharply in the convertible's headlights, was a rather small white sign. The black lettering on it, not at all crudely

drawn, read: THIS WAY TO THE FLYING SAUCER SYM-
POSIUM.

'Only in Southern California,' Paul said, shaking his head.

Margo said, 'Let's drive in and see what's going on.'

'Not on your life!' Paul assured her loudly. 'If you can't stand Vandenberg, I can't stand saucer maniacs.'

'But they don't sound like maniacs, Paul,' Margo said. 'The whole thing has tone. Take that lettering – it's pure Baskerville.'

Snatching up Miaow, she clambered out of the car for a closer look.

'Besides, we don't know if the meeting's tonight,' he called after her. 'It was probably earlier today, or even last week. Who knows?' He stood up too. 'I don't see any lights or signs of life.'

'The green lantern proves it must be tonight,' Margo called back from where she stood by the sign. 'Let's go, Paul.'

'The green lantern probably has nothing to do with the sign.'

Margo turned towards him, holding up a black finger in the headlight's glare.

'The paint's still wet,' she said.

The moon burrowed deeper into the earth's shadow, nearing that central point where the three bodies would be lined up. As always the moon – and much less strongly in its effects, the sun – plucked at the planet between them with invisible gravitational fingers, straining earth's rock crust and steel-strong inner parts, lightly brushing the triggers of immense or tiny earthquakes, and setting the ponderous film of Earth's oceans and seas, gulfs and channels, straits and sounds, lakes and bays resonating in the slow and various music of the tides, whose single vibrations are a little longer than a night or day.

On the other side of the earth from Southern California, swart Bagong Bung, sweat dropping from under his splotched yellow turban on to his bare shoulders and chest, called to his naked Australian mate to cut the engine of the *Machan Lumpur*. If they didn't lose any time, they'd be getting to the little inlet south of Do-Son before the ten-foot tide could lift them over the bar, and here in the Gulf of Tonkin the demon-controlled high tide came only once every twenty-four hours. A patrolling helicopter might take note if they hung about outside the inlet before slipping in to deliver the arms and drugs to the North Vietnam anti-Communist Underground – afterwards proceeding to Hanoi to deliver the main cargo (also arms and drugs) to the Communists.

As the bow-ripples died, the two-hundred-mile-wide gulf around the tiny rusty steamer glowed like a lake of molten brass. Bagong Bung, squinting about at the shimmering horizon, hand resting on the brass spyglass thrust in his belt, had no thought for the eclipse which noon and the globe hid from him. For that matter, the little Malay, his tired ship (mortgaged to Chinese bankers), and the lukewarm sea were all standing on their heads in relation to the Americas, and the sun baking his turban would have been toasting the soles of a billion Occidental feet, could it have shone through the planet between.

Bagong Bung was dreaming of the host of wrecked ships under the shallow waters around him and south and east away, and of the treasure he would win from them when he had accumulated enough money from this accursed smuggling to pay for the equipment and the divers he'd need.

Don Guillermo Walker told himself that the cluster of feeble lights he'd just droned past must be Metapa. But – his celestial navigation being as much boast as his European Shakespearian career – what if they were Zapata or La Libertad? Better, perhaps: in widely missing his target he'd miss the torture. Sweat itched on his chin and cheeks. He should have shaved his beard, he told himself. His captors would say, jiggling the bull prod in the steaming cell, that the beard proved he was a Castro-inspired Communist and his cards of the John Birch Society forgeries or worse. Burn *la barba* off his face with *la electricidad*!

'Damn you for getting me into this, you whore in black underwear, you nigger-Indian bitch!' Don Guillermo yelled at the sooty orange moon.

The *Prince Charles* and the dory *Endurance* went their diverging ways across the dark Atlantic. Most of the nylon-shod ones had gone to their rendezvous with sleep or each other, but

Captain Sithwise was taking a turn on the bridge. He felt strangely uneasy. It was having those Brazilian insurgents aboard, he told himself: this new lot of empire-snatchers did such unaccountably crazy things – as if they lived on ether.

Wolf Loner rocked in the arms of the sea, cushioned by a mile of salt water. The cloudbank under whose eastern verge the *Endurance* had entered was a vast one, trailing veils of fog and stretching to Edmonton and the Great Slave Lake, and from Boston north to Hudson Strait.

Sally Harris granted Jake Lesher another burst of hand-clutching at a dark turn in the House of Horror, but, 'Hey, don't ruck up my skirt – use the auxiliary hip placket,' she admonished.

'Are your pants magnetically hung too?' Jake demanded.

'No, just Goodyear, but there's a vanishing gadget. Easy there – and for God's sake don't tell me they're like the big round loaves of good homemade bread Mama Lesher used to bake. That's enough now, or the Rocket'll close down before we've seen the eclipse.'

'Sal, you were never astronomical like this before and we don't need that kind of roller-ride. You got the key to Hasseltine's place, don't you, and he's away, isn't he? – and besides, you've never taken me there. If that skyscraper isn't high enough for you –'

'The roller coaster's my skyscraper tonight,' she told him. 'That's enough, I said!'

She twisted away from him and ran off, past an eight-foot-tall grey Saturn-man who reared out of a wall, gripping a yard-long ray-gun and peppering her with sizzling blue light.

Asa Holcomb, puffing a bit, surmounted the top of the little mesa west of Arizona's Superstition Mountains. Just at that moment the wall of his aorta tore a little, and blood began to seep into his chest. There was no pain, but he felt a weakness and sensed a strangeness, and he quietly lay down on the flat rock, which still had a little heat in it from the day of sun.

He was neither particularly startled nor very afraid. Either the weakness would pass, or it would not. He'd known this little climb to a good spot to watch the eclipse was a dangerous thing. After all, his mother had warned him against climbing by himself in the rocks, seventy years ago. Doubly dangerous, with an aorta paper-thin. But it was always worth everything to get away by himself, climb a bit, and study the heavens.

His eyes had been resting, a little wistfully, on the lights of Mesa, but now he lifted them. This was about the fiftieth time he had seen Luna shrouded, but tonight she seemed more beautiful in her bronze phase than ever before, more like the pomegranate Proserpine plucked in the Garden of the Dead. His weakness wasn't passing.

Chapter 4

The convertible carrying Paul Hagbolt and Margo Gelhorn and her cat softly jounced along the rutted trail, raw cliff again to the right, beach sand to the left, both now only a yard or so off. Away from the big highway, the night pressed in. The three wayfarers shared more fully the lonely obscurity of the eclipsed moon climbing the starry sky. Even Miaow sat up to peer ahead.

'Among other things, this road probably leads to the back door of Vandenberg Two,' Paul ruminated. 'The beach gate, they call it. Of course I'm supposed to use the main gate, but in a pinch . . .' Then after a bit: 'It's really funny how these saucer maniacs are always holding their meetings next door to missile bases or atomic installations. Hoping a little glamour will leak their way, I guess. Did you know that at one time the Space Force was really suspicious about it?'

The headlights picked up an earth-fall blocking more than half the road. It was as high as the hood of the car, and recent, judging by the damp look of the granulated dirt. Paul let the car stop.

'End of saucer expedition,' he announced cheerfully.

'But the others have gone on,' Margo said, standing up again. 'You can see where they've gone around the fall.'

'O.K.,' Paul said mock-doomfully. 'But if we get stuck in the sand, you're going to have to hunt drift-boards to put under the tyres.'

The wheels spun twice, but the convertible had no real trouble getting traction. A little beyond, they came to a shallow pocket in the cliff, where the road expanded to thrice its width. A dozen cars had used the extra space to park side by side, their rear bumpers snug to the cliff. The first-comers included a red sedan, a microbus, and a white, open-back pickup truck.

Beyond the last car was another green lantern and an elegantly lettered sign: PARK HERE. THEN FOLLOW THE GREEN LIGHTS.

'Just like the Times Square subway station,' Margo exclaimed delightedly. 'I'll bet there are New Yorkers in this crowd.'

'Newly arrived,' Paul agreed, eyeing the cliff distrustfully as he parked beside the last car. 'They haven't had time to find out about California slides.'

Margo jumped out carrying Miaow. Paul followed, handing her her jacket.

'I don't need it,' she told him. He folded it over his arm without comment.

The third green lantern was out on the beach, by a stand of tall sea-grass. The beach was very level. They could at last hear the hiss of tiny breakers – little more than wavelets, from the sound. Miaow mewed anxiously. Margo talked to her softly.

Just beyond the cars, the cliffs swung sharply to the right and the level beach followed them inland. Paul realized they must be at the mouth of the wash they'd crossed and re-crossed back on the highway. Some distance beyond the wash, the ground began to rise again. Still farther off he could see a red light blinking high up and, much lower down, the glint of a mesh fence. He found these evidences of Vandenberg Two obscurely reassuring.

They headed oceanward past the sea-grass towards the green spark of the fourth lantern, tiny almost as a planet. The crusted sand sang faintly as they scuffed it. Margo took Paul's arm.

'Do you realize the eclipse is still going on?' she whispered. He nodded. She said, 'Paul, what if the stars around it should squiggle now?'

Paul said, 'I think I can see a white light beyond the fourth green one. And figures. And some sort of low building.'

They kept on. The low building looked as if it had once been someone's large beach house, or else a small beach club. The windows were boarded up. On this side of it was a rather large floor, unsided and unroofed, about two feet above the sand, that could hardly be anything else but an old dance floor. On it had been set about a hundred folding chairs, of which only the front twenty or so were occupied. The chairs faced the sea and a long table, slightly elevated on what had once been the orchestra's platform. Behind the table sat three persons with a little white light shining on their faces – the only illumination besides the green lantern at the back of the audience.

One of the three persons had a beard; another was bald and wore glasses; the third was in evening dress with a white tie and wore a green turban.

Beardy was speaking, but they weren't yet near enough to hear him distinctly.

Margo clutched Paul's arm. 'The one with the turban is a woman,' she whispered loudly.

A tiny figure got up from the sand near the lantern and approached them. A small white light blinked on, and they saw it was a narrow-faced girl with pale reddish braids. She couldn't have been more than ten. She had some sheets of paper in one hand and she held the forefinger of the other across her lips. The white light was that of a small battery lamp hanging against her chest by a cord around her neck. As she came close she lifted the sheets to them, whispering, 'We've got to be quiet. It's started. Take a programme.'

Her eyes lit up when she saw Miaow. 'Oh, you've got a cat,' she whispered. 'I don't think Ragnarok will mind.'

After Margo and Paul had each taken a sheet, she led them to a central step going up to the floor and gestured that they should sit down in front. When Margo and Paul, smiling but shaking their heads, sat down in the back row instead, she shrugged and started to go away.

Margo felt Miaow stiffen. The cat was staring at something lying across two end chairs in the front row.

Ragnarok was a large German police dog.

The moment of first crisis passed. Miaow relaxed a little, though continuing to stare unblinkingly with ears laid back.

The little girl came behind them. 'I'm Ann,' she whispered. 'The one with the turban is my mother. We're from New York.'

Then she went back to her vigil beside the green lantern.

General Spike Stevens and three of his staff sat close-crowded in a dimmed room of the Reserve Headquarters of the U.S. Space Force. They were watching two large television screens set side by side. Each screen showed the same area of darkened moon, an area which took in Plato. The image on the right-hand screen was relayed from an unmanned communication-and-observation satellite hanging 23,000 miles above Christmas Island, 20 degrees south of Hawaii, while the one on the left-hand screen came from a similar equatorial satellite over a point in the Atlantic off the coast of Brazil where the *Prince Charles* was atom-steaming south.

The four viewers crossed their eyes with practised skill, fusing the images which had originated 30,000 miles apart out in space. The effect was exaggeratedly three-dimensional, with the moon section bumping out solidly. 'We can give the new electroamplif a limited O.K.,' the General said. 'I'd say that's adequate crater definition now Christmas has got rid of its herringbone. Jimmy, let's have an unmagnified view of the whole moonward space sector.'

Colonel Mabel Wallingford studied the General covertly, knitting together her long, strong fingers. Someone had once told her that she had a strangler's hands, and she never looked at the General without remembering that. It gave her a bitter satisfaction that Spike should sound as casually confident as might Odin surveying the Nine Worlds from Hlithskjalf tower in Asgard, yet that he knew no more of where they now were than did she: that they were within fifty miles of the White House and at least two hundred feet underground. They had all been driven here, and had entered the elevator hooded, and they had not met the staff they had relieved.

Arab Jones and High Bundy and Pepe Martinez sipped at their fourth stick of tea, passing the potent thin reefer from fingers to fingers and holding the piney smoke long in their lungs. They sat on cushions and a carpet in front of a little tent with strings of wooden beads for a door, pitched on a rooftop in Harlem, not far from Lenox and 125th Street. Their eyes sought each other's with the friendly watchfulness of weed-brothers, then moved together towards the eclipsed moon.

'Man, I bet she on pot too,' High said. 'See that bronzy smoke? Those lunar spacemen gonna get *high*.'

Pepe said, 'We're gonna be way out there ourselves. You planning to eclipse, Arab?'

Arab said, 'The astronomical kick is the most.'

Chapter 5

Paul Hagbolt and Margo Gelhorn began to listen to what the man with the beard was saying: 'A human being's hopes and fears, his deepest agitations, will always colour what he sees in the skies – whether it's a plane or a planet or a ship from another world, or only a corpuscle of his own blood. Put it this way: every saucer is also a sign.'

Beardy's voice was mellow yet youthfully intense. Doc – the big bald man with thick glasses – and the She-Turban listened inscrutably. (It hadn't taken Margo two minutes to nickname all three panellists and several members of the audience.)

Beardy continued: 'The late Dr Jung has explored this aspect of saucer sightings thoroughly in his book, *Ein Moderner Mythus von Dingen die am Himmel gesehen werden*.' His German was authentically gargled. He immediately translated: '*A Modern Myth of Things Seen in the Skies*.'

'Who *is* Beardy?' Margo demanded of Paul. He started to study his programme, but that was useless in the back-row darkness.

Beardy went on, 'Dr Jung was particularly interested in saucers with the appearance of a circle divided into four parts. He relates such shapes to what Mahayana Buddhism calls mandalas. A mandala is a symbol of psychic unity – the individual mind is embattled against insanity. It is apt to appear at times of great stress and danger, as today, when the individual is torn and shaken by his horror of atomic destruction, his dread of being depersonalized, made into one more soldier-slave or consumer-robot in a totalitarian horde, and his fear of completely losing touch with his own culture as it goes chasing off into ten thousand difficult yet crucial specializations.'

Paul found himself going through one of his usual guilt spasms. Not five minutes ago he'd been calling these people saucer maniacs, and here was the first one he heard sounding sensible and civilized.

A little man, sitting at the same end of the first row as the dog Ragnarok, now stood up.

'Excuse me, Professor,' the Little Man said, 'but according to my watch there are only fifteen minutes of full eclipse left. I want to remind everyone to keep up the watch, while paying attention of course to what our interesting speakers have to say. Rama Joan has told us of cosmic beings able to attend to a dozen lines of thought at once. Surely we can manage two! After all, we did hold this meeting because of the unusual opportunity for sightings, especially of the less bold saucers that shun the light. Let's not lose what's left of this precious opportunity to see Bashful Saucers, as Ann calls them.'

Several heads in the front row dutifully swivelled this way and that, showing profiles with unlifted chins.

Margo nudged Paul. 'Do your duty,' she whispered gruffly, peering about fiercely.

'Good hunting, everybody,' the Little Man said. 'Excuse me, Professor.' He sat down.

But before Beardy could continue, he was challenged by a man with high shoulders and folded arms who sat tall in his seat – Margo tagged him the Ramrod.

'Professor, you've given us a lot of fancy double talk,' the Ramrod began, 'but it still seems to me to be about saucers that people imagine. I'm not interested in those, even if Mr Jung was. I'm only interested in real saucers, like the one I talked to and travelled in.'

Paul felt his spirits lift. Now these people were starting to behave as saucer maniacs should!

Beardy seemed somewhat flustered by the challenge. He said, 'I'm very sorry if I gave that impression. I thought I made it clear that –'

Doc lifted his bald head and cut short Beardy's defence by laying a hand on his arm, as if to say, 'Let me handle this character.' The She-Turban glanced at him with a faint smile and touched the tie of her evening clothes.

Doc leaned forward and bent his gleaming dome and glittering glasses down towards the Ramrod, as if the latter were some sort of insect.

'Excuse me, sir,' he said with an edge to his voice, 'but I believe you also claim to have visited other planets by flying saucer – planets unrecognized by astronomy.'

'That's right,' the Ramrod replied, sitting an inch taller.

'Just where are those other planets?'

'Oh, they're . . . places,' the Ramrod replied, winning a few chuckles by adding: 'Real planets don't let themselves be bossed around by a pack of astronomers.'

Ignoring the chuckles, Doc continued, 'Are those planets off at the edge of nowhere – the planets of another star, many light-years away?' His voice was gentle now. His thick glasses seemed to beam benignly.

'No, they're not that,' the Ramrod said. 'Why, I visited Arletta just a week ago and the trip only took two days.'

Doc was not to be diverted. 'Are they little tiny planets that are hiding behind the sun or the moon or perhaps Jupiter, in a sort of permanent eclipse, like people hiding behind trees in a forest?'

'No, they're not that either,' the Ramrod asserted, squaring his shoulders afresh, but nevertheless beginning to sound a shade defensive. 'They don't hide behind anybody's skirts – not them. They're just . . . out there. And they're big, you can bet – as big as Earth. I've visited six of them.'

'Humph,' Doc grunted. 'Are they by any chance planets that are concealed in hyperspace and that pop out conveniently once in a blue moon – say, when you come visiting?'

Now it was Doc who was getting the chuckles, though he ignored those, too.

'You're being negativistic,' the Ramrod said accusingly, 'and a darn sight too theoretical. Those other planets are just *out there,* I tell you.'

'Well, if they're just out there,' Doc roared softly, 'why can't we just see them?' His head was thrown back in triumph, or perhaps it was only that his glasses had slipped down his nose a bit.

There was quite a pause. Then: 'Black-negativistic,' the Ramrod amended loftily. 'Be a waste of time to tell you how some planets have invisibility screens to make starlight curve round them. I don't care to talk to you any longer.'

'Let me make my position clear,' Doc said hotly, addressing the whole audience. 'I am willing to consider any idea whatsoever – even that there's an alien planet lurking in our solar system. But I want *some* hint of a rational explanation, even if it's that the planet exists in hyperspace. I give Charles Fulby' – he waved towards the Ramrod – 'a fractional plus score for his screens notion.'

He subsided, breathing victoriously. The Little Man took this opportunity to pop up from beside the big dog Ragnarok at the end of the front row and say: 'Only ten minutes left. I know this argument is interesting, but keep watching, please. Remember, we're first and foremost saucer students. Flying planets are exciting, but just one little saucer, witnessed by a whole symposium, would be a real triumph for us. Thank you.'

Asa Holcomb had been blinking his flashlight towards town from the mesa top near the Superstition Mountains. After all, he was supposed to try to save his own life. But now, growing tired of that duty, he looked up again at the stars, diamond-bright during the full eclipse, and he named them without effort, and then lost himself once more in the earth-shadowed moon, standing there in the foreground like some great Hopi emblem hammered out of age-blackened silver. There was always something new to be seen in the unchanging night sky. He could easily lie here and watch all night without a moment of boredom. But the weakness and the strangeness were growing greater, and the rock beneath him had become very cold.

Pepe Martinez and High Bundy rose from their cushions and

drifted like leaves towards the grimed brick wall of the roof in Harlem. Pepe said, waving towards the moon: 'One more puff and then – poof! I'll be there, just like John Carter.'

High said: 'Don't forget your spacesuit.'

Pepe said: 'I'll take a big lungful of pot and live on that.' He waved towards the stars. 'What's all that black billboard of jewellery advertising say, High?'

High said: 'Billboard! That's motor-sickles, man, every one of them with a diamond headlight, going every way there is.'

Arab, still on his cushion before the tent, and now trickling down his gullet a few drops of muscatel from a thin liqueur glass, called: 'What of the night, oh my sons?'

Pepe called back: 'Beautiful as a silken serpent, oh my Daddy-o.'

The moon continued to swing through Earth's cold silent shadow at her sedate pace of forty miles a minute, as irrevocably as the blood leaking into Asa Holcomb's chest, or the spermatozoa lashing their tails in Jake Lesher's loins, or the hormones streaming from Don Guillermo's adrenal glands, or the atoms splitting to heat the boilers of the *Prince Charles*, or the wavicles carrying their coded pictures to Spike Stevens' cave, or Wolf Loner's unconscious mind opening and shutting its windows in the rhythm he called sanity. Luna had been doing it a billion years ago; she would be doing it a billion years hence. Some day, astronomers said, obscure tidal forces would draw her so close to earth that racking internal tides would shatter her, turning her into something like the rings of Saturn. But that, astronomers said, was still a hundred billion years away.

Chapter 6

Paul Hagbolt nervously nudged Margo Gelhorn, warning her to stop giggling as a woman in the second row called to Doc: 'What's that hyperspace you were saying planets could come out of?'

'Yes, why not give us a run-down?' Beardy suggested like a veteran panellist, turning to Doc.

'It's a notion that's turned up in theoretical physics and any number of science-fiction stories.' Doc launched out, adjusting his glasses and then running his hands back across his bald head.

'As you all know, the speed of light is generally accepted as the fastest possible. One hundred and eighty-six thousand miles a second sounds like a lot, but it's snail slow when it comes to the vast distances between the stars and within the galaxies – a dismal prospect for space travellers.

'However,' Doc continued, 'it's theoretically possible that space-time may be so warped or crumpled that distant parts of our cosmos touch in a higher dimension – in hyperspace, which is where the word comes in. Or even that every part touches every other part. If that is the case, then faster-than-light travel would be theoretically possible by somehow blasting out of our universe into hyperspace and then back in again at the desired point. Of course, hyperspace travel has been suggested only for spaceships, but I don't know why a properly equipped planet couldn't manage it, too – theoretically. Professional scientists like Bernal and philosophers such as Stapledon have theorized about travelling planets, not to mention authors like Stuart and Smith.'

'Theory!' the Ramrod snorted, adding *sotto voce*: 'Hot air!'

'How about that?' Beardy asked Doc, bringing the question on to the platform with a fine impartiality. 'Is there any concrete evidence for the existence of hyperspace or hyperspace travel?'

From beyond Doc, the She-Turban glanced towards him and Beardy curiously.

'Not one shred,' Doc said, with a grin. 'I've tried to goose my astronomer friends into hunting for clues, but they don't take me very seriously.'

'You interest me,' Beardy said. 'Just what form might such clues take?'

'I've thought about that,' Doc admitted with relish. 'One idea I've come up with is that the thrust necessary to get a ship into and out of hyperspace might involve the creation of momentary artificial gravitational fields – fields so intense that they would visibly distort the starlight passing through that volume of space. So I've suggested to my astronomer friends that they watch for the stars to waver on clear nights of good seeing – and especially from satellite 'scopes – and that they hunt through short-exposure star photographs for evidence of the same thing happening – stars blanking out briefly or moving twistedly.'

The thin woman in the second row said: 'I saw a story in the papers about a man seeing the stars twirl. Would that be evidence?'

Doc chuckled. 'I'm afraid not. Wasn't he drunk? We mustn't take these silly-season items too seriously.'

Paul simultaneously felt a shiver hug his chest and Margo clutch his arm.

'Paul,' she whispered urgently. 'Isn't Doc describing exactly what you saw in those four photographs?'

'It sounds similar,' he temporized, trying to straighten it out in his own mind. 'Very similar.' Then, wonderingly: 'He used the word "twist".'

'Well, how about it?' Margo demanded. 'Has Doc got something or hasn't he?'

'Opperly said –' Paul began . . . and realized that Doc was speaking to him.

'Excuse me, you two in the back row – sorry, I don't know your names – do you have a contribution to make?'

'Why, no. No, sir,' Paul called rapidly. 'We were simply very much impressed by your presentation.'

Doc waved his hand once in a good-natured acknowledgement.

'Liar,' Margo breathed at Paul with a smile. 'I've half a mind to tell him all about it.'

Paul hadn't the heart to say no, which was probably a good thing. He was having another guilt attack, unlocalized but acute. Certainly, he told himself, he couldn't spill inside Project information – to saucerites, to boot. Still, there was something wrong with a set-up in which someone like Doc couldn't know about those photographs.

But then he started thinking about the point at issue, and

the shiver returned. Damn it, there was something devilish about the way Doc's guesswork fitted with those photographs. He looked up uneasily at the dark moon. Margo's words resounded thinly in his memory: 'What if the stars around it should squiggle now?'

The moon-dust canisters hanging on their thin metal stalks above the dimly glittering film of carbon dioxide snow looked like the weirdly mechanistic fruits of an ice garden. Moving in his helmet's headlight beam, Don Merriam stepped towards the nearest one as gently as he could, so as to kick up a minimum of contaminating dust. In spite of his caution, some dry-ice crystals arched up in the path of his metal boots and fell back abruptly, as is the way of dust and 'snow' on the airless moon. He touched the trigger on the canister which sealed it hermetically and then he plucked it from its stalk and dropped it in his pouch.

'Highest-paid fruit picker this side of Mars,' he told himself judicially. 'And even at that I'm finishing this job too fast to suit Union Czar Gompert, the Slow-Down King.'

He looked back up at the black earth inside the bronze ring. 'Ninety-nine and nine-tenths per cent of *them*,' he told himself, 'would agree I'm featherbedding. They think all space exploration is the biggest featherbed since the Pyramids. Or the railroads, anyhow. Air-clams! Troposphere-barnacles!' He grinned. 'They've heard about space but they still don't believe in it. They haven't been out here to see for themselves that there isn't any giant elephant under the earth, holding it up, and a giant tortoise holding up the elephant. If I say "planet" and "spaceship" to them, they still think "horoscope" and "flying saucer".'

As he turned towards the next canister-bearing reed, his boot scuffed the crystal film, and a faint creaky whir travelled up the leg of his suit. It was an echo, from across the years, of his galoshes singing against the crusty Minnesota snow on a zero day.

Barbara Katz said, 'Hey, check me, Mr Kettering – I see a white light flashing near Copernicus.'

Knolls Kettering III, creaking a bit at the joints, took her place at the eyepiece. 'You're right, Miss Katz,' he said. 'The Soviets must be testing signal flares, I imagine.'

'Thanks,' she said. 'I never trust myself on moon-stuff – I keep seeing the lights of Luna City and Leyport and all the other science-fiction places.'

'Confidentially, Miss Katz, so do I! Now there's a red flare.'

'Oh, could I see it? But I hate making you get up and down. I could sit on your lap, if you wouldn't mind – and if the stool would stand it.'

Knolls Kettering III chuckled regretfully. 'I wouldn't mind, and the stool might stand it, but I'm afraid the bone-plastic splice in my hip mightn't.'

'Oh, gee, I'm sorry.'

'Forget it, Miss Katz – we're fellow lensmen. And don't feel sorry for me.'

'I won't,' she assured him. 'Why, I think it's romantic being patched up that way, just like the old soldiers that run the space academies in the Heinlein and E. E. Smith stories.'

Don Guillermo Walker finally had to admit to himself that the black glisten ahead was water – and the little lake, rather than the big one, for there at last were the lights of Managua twinkling no more than ten miles away. A new worry struck him: that he had cut his timing too fine. What if the moon came out of eclipse right now, pinpointing him for *el presidente*'s jet and A.A. guns, like a premature spotlight catching a stage-hand in overalls making a dark-stage scenery change? He wished he were back doing second-rate summer stock near Chicago, or haranguing a 'guns-south' Birch splinter group; or ten years old and putting on a back-yard circus in Milwaukee, defying death by sliding down a slanting rusty wire from a height of nineteen feet.

That second memory gave him courage. Dead for a back-yard circus ... dead for a greaser city bombed! He revved the motor to its top speed, and the prop behind him drummed the lukewarm air a shade less feebly. 'Guil-*ler*-mo ge-*ron*-imo!' Don Guillermo yelled. 'La Loma, here I come!'

Chapter 7

Paul Hagbolt was paying only half attention to the speakers on the platform. The coincidence of the star photos and Doc's notion about planets travelling through hyperspace had distracted him and set his imagination drifting. As if a big clock, that only he could hear, had just now begun to tick (once a second, not five times like wrist-watches and many spring clocks), he found himself becoming acutely aware of time and of everything around him – the huddled group of people, the level sand, the faint rattle of the toppling wavelets just beyond the speakers, the old, boarded-up beach houses, the hooded and red-blinking installations of Vandenberg Two thrusting up behind him, the dirt cliffs beyond the sea-grass, above all the mild night pressing in from the ends of space and making tiny everything but the globe of Earth and the dark moon and the glittering stars.

Someone addressed a question to Rama Joan. She smiled with her teeth at Beardy and then looked down at her audience, her gaze moving to each member in turn. The bulging green turban hid her hair, though she had the same pale complexion as Ann, and it emphasized the tapering of her thin face. She looked like a half-starved child herself.

Still without speaking, she gazed across the heavens and above her shoulder at the dark moon, then back at her audience.

Then she said very quietly, yet harshly: 'What do any of us *really* know about what is out there? Far less than a man imprisoned from birth in a cell under the city would know of the millions in Calcutta or Hong Kong or Moscow or New York. I know some of you think advanced races will love and cherish us, but I judge the attitude of more advanced races towards man on the basis of man's attitude towards the ant. On that basis I can tell you this much: there are devils out there. Devils.'

There was a low, grinding sound like steel clockwork being wound. Miaow stiffened in Margo's arms, and the short hairs rose along her spine. Ragnarok had growled.

Rama Joan continued: 'Among the stars, out there, there may be Hindus who won't kill a cow and even Jains who whisk off whatever they sit on for fear of crushing an ant and who wear gauze over their lips to keep from swallowing a gnat, but those will be at most the rare exceptions. The rest will not strain at gnats. To us, they will be devils.'

Weirdness engulfed Paul. Everything around him seemed much too real, yet on the verge of dissolution – frozen, phantasmal. He looked towards the stars and the moon for support, telling himself that the heavens were the one thing that hadn't changed through all history, but then a demon voice deep in his mind said: *'But what if the stars should move? They moved, in the photographs.'*

Sally Harris led Jake Lesher across the worn wood platform to the fifth and last car of the Rocket train. The only other passengers this trip were a rather timid-looking Puerto Rican couple, sitting in the first car and already gripping the safety bar with all four hands.

'My God, Sal, the waits I put up with,' Jake said. 'And the sidetracks I go down – I mean up! – to humour you. Hasseltine's penthouse –'

'Shh, this ain't no sidetrack, lover boy,' she whispered as the launcher hurried past, making the last quick check. 'Now listen hard: as soon as we start to climb, slide forward about a foot and grab on to the back of the seat for all you're worth with your left hand, because with your other arm you're going to be holding me.'

'But that's the arm away from you, Sal.'

'Now it is,' she told him and touched him intimately.

He goggled at her, then smirked incredulously.

'Just you follow directions,' she told him. With a creak and a clicking the train started its steep climb. A dozen yards from the top, she stood up lightly, swung her leg in a gleaming arc and straddled his waist. One hand gripped his neck, the other swiftly fitted things.

'Jesus, Sal,' he gasped. 'I bet we make the earth move like in *For Whom the Bell*.'

'Earth, hell!' she told him, grinning bare-fanged down at

him like a Valkyrie, as the train poised for its swoop and the tow let go. 'I'll make the stars move!'

Rama Joan said: 'Oh, the star people would be awesomely beautiful to us, I imagine, and as endlessly fascinating as a hunter is to a wild animal that hasn't yet been shot at. I'm dreadfully interested in speculating about them myself – but to us they would still be as cruel and distant as ninety-nine per cent of our own gods. And what are man's gods except his imaginings of a more advanced race? Take the testimony of ten thousand years, if you won't take mine, and you will realize that out there . . . up there . . . there are devils.'

Ragnarok growled again. Miaow flattened herself against Margo's shoulder, digging in with her claws.

The Little Man said: 'End of totality.'

Doc said: 'Really, Rama Joan, you surprise me.'

Margo said: 'Miaow, *it's all right.*'

Paul looked up and saw the eastern rim of the moon lighten, and it was like a reprieve from prison. He suddenly knew that his incomprehensible fears would lift with the ending of the eclipse.

A half-dozen moon-diameters east of the moon, a squad of stars spun in tight little curlicues, like ghostly white fireworks erupting, squibs and pinwheels . . . and then blacked out.

From his lonely mesa, Asa Holcomb saw the stars near the moon shake, as if a fanfare were being blown through the cosmos. Then a great golden and purple gateway four times as wide as the moon opened in the heavens there, pushing the blackness aside; and Asa strained eagerly towards it, and his heart swelled with the wonder and majesty of it, and his aorta tore all the way, and he died.

Sally Harris saw the stars squiggle just as she and Jake, momentarily shedding thirty pounds of weight apiece, started to come atop the sixth summit of the Ten-Stage Rocket at Coney Island. In the blind egoistic world of sexual fulfilment that lies exactly on the boundary between the conscious and unconscious regions of the mind, she knew that the stars were a provincial district of herself – the Marches of Sally Harris – and so she merely chortled throatily: 'I did it, Christ! I said I'd do it and I did it!'

And even when atop the next summit, after a choking, pulsing plunge to the nadir and back up, she saw the squiggling stars replaced by a yellow and purplish disc twenty times the size of the moon and bright enough to show up the pinstripe in the shoulders of Jake's suit as his face pressed between her breasts, she leaned back, like a Valkyrie, the safety bar cold across her rump, and cried triumphantly to the heavens: 'Jesus, a bonus!'

High Bundy said: 'Oh, what a kick! Listen, Pepe, there's this crazy old Chinaman, bigger than King Kong, on the other side of the world kicking his legs up at us, and he's painting golden plates with grenadine so they look like two raindrops making love, and he's skimming them off to the moon with a reverse twist as he finishes them, and one of them sticks there.'

'Reet-reet,' Pepe cooed. 'It's lighting all New York. Plate lightning.'

'I'm getting it, too,' Arab said, floating up behind them. 'Man, what great tea!'

Knolls Kettering III, eye glued to the eyepiece in the Palm Beach dark, was saying a bit stuffily: 'The noun "planet", Miss Katz, is derived from the Greek verb *planasthai*, to wander. Originally it meant simply "Wanderer": a body that roves here and there among the fixed stars.' His voice tightened. 'Hello, the moon is lightening, and not just along the limb coming out of eclipse. Yes, definitely. And there are colours.'

A hand curved over his shoulder protectively, and just about the littlest voice he'd ever heard – it was as if Barbara Katz had turned into a grasshopper – said, 'Dad, *please* don't look away from the eyepiece now. You've got to prepare yourself for a big shock.'

'A shock? What is it, Miss Katz?' he asked nervously, though following instructions.

'I'm not quite sure,' the microscopic voice continued. 'It looks like an old *Amazing* cover. Dad, I think your Wanderer's roved this way – only the Greeks didn't grow 'em this big. I think it's a planet.'

Paul, flinching, had shut his eyes for at most two seconds.

When he opened them, the Wanderer was there, streaming with bloody and golden light.

The Wanderer was there, four times the diameter of the moon and at least that far east of the moon in the sky, sixteen times the moon's area, wavily split by one ragged, reverse-S curve into golden and maroon halves, looking softer than velvet yet with a clear-cut, unhazed rim.

That much Paul saw as a visual pattern, saw in a flash without analysis. The next moment he had thrown himself to the floor, shoulders hunched and head down, away from the Wanderer. For the first, dominating impression was of something gigantic and flaming overhead, something intimidatingly massive, about to crash to earth and crush him.

Margo, clutching Miaow, was on the floor beside him.

Purely by happenstance, Paul's eyes were directed at the programme he was holding. He automatically read a line: 'Our bearded panellist is Ross Hunter, Professor of Sociology, Reed College, Portland, Oregon' – before he realized he was reading easily by the light of the Wanderer.

To Don Guillermo, approaching the hill with its huddle of official buildings, his eyes on 'the Palace', his left hand gripping the cross-stick handle on the bomb-release wire, the Wanderer was a Nicaraguan loyalist jet materialized on his tail and erupting a volcano of silent tracer bullets. He ducked in his seat, squinted his eyes, and tightened his neck and shoulders against the slugs. They didn't come and they didn't come – the bastard must be a sadist, prolonging the agony.

He banked left towards the big lake, according to plan, then made himself look up and back. Why, the damn thing was just a big barrage balloon, somehow suddenly illuminated. To think they'd tricked him with a carnival gadget like that into not dropping his egg. He'd swing back and show 'em!

At that moment a dazzling pink volcano erupted from La Loma, and he saw that his left hand gripped the cross-stick that was now trailing a length of broken wire. The next second, a blast boxed his ears and shuddered the plane. He righted it and automatically kept on towards Lake Nicaragua.

But, he asked himself, how was a balloon like that keeping exact pace with his old crate? And why was the whole landscape glowing, as if the ambers had come up in the universal theatre?

Bagong Bung, the sun baking his brains as he leaned on the paintless rail of the bridge, but with his brains visualizing a weed-veiled, gold-hearted wreck not twenty leagues away, was utterly unaware and felt not one iota of strangeness as the gravitational front of an unknown body struck upward through him from below, locking on to every atom of him. Since it clutched with proportional force at the *Machan Lumpur*, the Gulf of Tonkin, and the whole planet, the gust of cosmic power did not so much as jostle one of Bagong Bung's cool green thoughts.

If Bagong Bung had been looking at the compass of the *Machan Lumpur*, he would have seen its needle swing wildly and then come tremblingly to rest in a new direction a shade east of north, but the little Malay seldom looked into the binnacle – he knew these shallow seas too well. And he had dealt so long with turncoats and time-servers on both communist and capitalist sides, that even if he had seen the compass veer, he might merely have felt that it was, at last, showing its own natural degree of political unreliability.

Wolf Loner frowned in his chilly sleep as, half-way around the world, the tiny compass of the *Endurance* swung and resettled in an identical manner as the *Machan Lumpur*'s, and as a blue finger of St Elmo's fire flickered briefly at the top of the dory's mast. He stirred and almost woke, then slept again.

General Spike Stevens snapped: 'Jimmy, get that big burn out of there before we lose a screen.'

'Yes, sir,' Captain James Kidley responded. 'But which screen is it? I keep seeing it in both.'

'It *is* in both screens,' Colonel Willard Griswold cut in

hoarsely. 'Uncross your eyes, Spike. It's *out there* – as big as the Earth.'

'Excuse me, Spike,' Colonel Mabel Wallingford put in, her blood racing, 'but mightn't it be a *problem*? H.Q. One can switch our input-output to test conditions any time they want.'

'Right,' the General said, snatching at the out she'd handed him; and this made her smile fiercely: Spike had been *scared*. He continued: 'If it's a problem – and I think it is – they've thrown us a doozie. In five seconds our communications will be jumping with simulated crisis data. O.K., then, everybody, we pretend it's a problem.'

Forcing himself to squint upward, Paul saw that the Wanderer, so far as he could estimate, was not moving or changing. Helping Margo at the same time, he scrambled to his feet, though still hunched away from the Wanderer, as a man would hunch under a hanging block of concrete or away from a lifted fist.

Apparently the hit-the-dirt reaction had been universal. Chairs were scattered; the people in the front rows and the panellists were out of sight.

Not quite universal, though. The Ramrod was standing up straight and saying in a strangely even, high-pitched voice: 'Don't panic, folks. Can't you see it's just a big fire balloon? Manufactured in Japan, I'll bet from that design.'

A woman brayed from the floor: 'I saw it rise up from Vandenberg! Why's it stopped? It's still firing! Why doesn't it keep on going?'

From under the table came a still louder bellow from Doc. 'Stay down, you fools! Don't you know the atomic fireball's a sphere in outer space?' Then, not quite as loudly: 'Find my glasses, Rama Joan.'

Ragnarok, tail between his legs, came circling back to almost the exact centre of the floor, stopped there among the empty chairs, lifted his muzzle towards the Wanderer and began to howl. Paul and Margo, moving forward towards the others, veered around him.

Ann came up behind them. 'Why's everybody scared?' she asked Paul, gaily. 'That must be the biggest saucer ever.' She switched off her chest lamp. 'I won't need this.'

The Ramrod took up again in an emotionless, squeaky monotone. 'The Jap fire balloon is moving very slowly, folks. It's passing close overhead, but don't worry, it's going to miss us.'

The Little Man walked over to the Ramrod, reached up and shook his arm.

'Would a fire balloon dim the stars down to a half dozen?' he demanded. 'Would it show up the colours of our cars over there? Would it turn Vandenberg green and light up the Pacific out to the Santa Barbara Islands? God damn it, answer me, Charlie Fulby!'

The Ramrod looked around. Then the pupils of his eyes rolled up out of sight, he slowly crumpled against a chair and slid limply to the floor. The Little Man looked down at him thoughtfully, and said: 'Whatever *it* is, it's not Arletta.'

Simultaneously, Doc's shining dome and gleaming glasses and the shaggy face of Hunter – the Reed College professor they'd thought of as Beardy – rose from behind the table. For a moment the impression was of two stalwart dwarfs. Then, 'That's no atomic fireball,' he announced, 'or it would keep on expanding. And it would have been one hell of a lot brighter to start with.' He helped Rama Joan to her feet. A green edge dangled loose from her turban. Her white shirt was crumpled.

Hunter stood up too.

Ann reached up and touched Miaow. 'Your cat's purring and she's looking at the big saucer,' the little red-headed girl told Margo. 'I think she wants to stroke it.'

The Wanderer continued to hang in the heavens, velvet soft yet sharply defined, incontrovertible, its maroon and golden markings raggedly approximating the yin-yang symbol of bright and dark, male and female, good and evil.

While the others stared and imagined, the Little Man took a small notebook from his breast pocket and made a neat diagrammatic sketch on one of the unruled pages, smoothing the ragged boundary line on the new heavenly body and indicating the purple with a shading of parallel lines.

Don Merriam harvested the last canister and started back to the Hut. He looked up at the eclipse. The ring was very bright to the right now. In a matter of seconds the sun's disc would

46

begin to emerge, bringing hot day back to the moon and softening Earth's inky disc with moon-reflected sunlight.

Then he stopped in his tracks. The sun's disc still hadn't showed, but earth's disc, inky a second ago, was now glowing twenty times more brightly than he'd ever seen it by moonlight. He could readily make out both Americas, and upon the right-hand rim the tiny soft gleam of the Greenland icecap.

'Look at Earth, Don.' Johannsen's voice was crisp in his ear.

'I'm doing that, Yo. What is it?'

'We don't know. One guess: there's a burst of light somewhere else on the moon. Total flame-out at Soviet base – all their rocket fuel going.'

'Wouldn't make that much light, Yo. Still, maybe Ambartsumian has invented a twenty-moon-power flare.'

'Atomic limelight?' Johannsen laughed bleakly. 'Dufresne's just made Guess Three: All the stars back of us have novaed.'

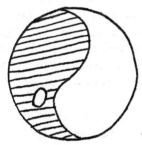

The Little Man's Sketch

'That might do it,' Don agreed. 'But, Yo, what's that spot in the Atlantic?'

The spot he referred to was a bright yellow and purple highlight on the pallid waters.

Richard Hillary pulled the shade beside his seat against the low, stabbing morning sun and settled back comfortably as the London clipper gathered speed on the way to Bath. It was a pleasant contrast to the ratty little bus that had carried him from Portishead to Bristol. At last he felt his sickishness begin to moderate, as though his guts, madly convulsed an hour ago, were settling into a smooth coil.

And see what only one night with a beery Welsh poet does

to one's mental images, he thought wryly. *Snakes in my belly indeed! No more of that for a long while now.*

Dai Davies had been particularly boisterous at parting, loudly chanting fragments of a *Farewell to Mona* he'd been alcoholically extemporizing. The fragments had been full of horrid neologisms such as 'moondark' and 'manshine', and to cap that, 'girl glow'; and Richard's relief at getting rid of Dai was genuine and profound. It didn't even bother him, at least for the moment, that the bus driver had the wireless turned on softly, inflicting the half-dozen passengers with American neojazz, pretentious as the Republican Party.

He gave a silent but heartfelt sigh. *Yes, no more Dai for a while now, no more science fiction, no more moon. Yes, particularly no more moon.*

The wireless said, 'We interrupt this programme to relay to you a puzzling news flash from the United States.'

Chapter 8

Hunter and Doc were jabbering together as they watched the Wanderer. Doc's bald dome had a weird magenta glow as Hunter's shaggy head and bearded face momentarily cut him off from the golden half of the body in the sky.

Paul, suddenly flooded by a strange, reckless energy, sprang up on the platform beside them and said loudly: 'Look here, I've got some inside information on star photos showing areas of twist that completely confirm what you –'

'Shut up! I've got no time to listen to the crackpot claims of you saucer bugs,' Doc roared at him, not unkindly, and instantly went on: 'Ross, I'll grant you that if that thing is as far away as the moon, then it's as big as the earth. Has to be. But –'

'Provided it's a sphere,' Hunter put in sharply. 'Could be flat like a plate.'

'Sure, provided it's a sphere. But that's a natural, sane assumption, don't you think? I was going to say that if it's only a thousand miles up, then it's only' – he shut his eyes for two seconds – 'thirty miles across. You follow me?'

'Sure,' Hunter told him. 'Similar triangles and eight thousand miles divided by 250.'

Doc nodded so violently he almost lost his glasses and had to grab at them to steady them. 'And if it's only a hundred miles up – that's still high enough for it to give a general illumination, though not from reflected sunlight –'

'Then it's only three miles across,' Hunter finished for him.

'Yes,' Paul agreed loudly, 'but in that case it'll be moving in a ninety-minute orbit. That's four degrees a minute – enough so we'll notice it pretty quickly, even without stars to judge it by.'

'You're absolutely right,' Doc said, turning to him now as if Paul were an old colleague. 'Four degrees is as long as Orion's Belt. We'll see that much movement pretty fast.'

'But how do you know it's in any kind of orbit?' Hunter asked. 'How do we know anything like that?'

'It's just another natural, sane assumption,' Doc told him, rather bitterly and roaring a little. 'Like we assume the thing's reflecting sunlight. Wherever it came from, it's in space now, so we assume it obeys the laws of space until we know different.' He switched to Paul. 'What were you saying about star photos?'

Paul began to tell them.

Margo hadn't followed Paul on to the platform. People were pushing and jabbering around her, two women were kneeling by the Ramrod and rubbing his wrists, the Little Man was hunting behind chairs for something, but Margo was staring across the dun sand at the eerie amethyst and topaz wake of the Wanderer in the waters of the Pacific. The fancy came to her that all the ghosts in her past, or perhaps it was the world's past, were going to come marching towards her along that jewelled highway.

The She-Turban's face came in the way and said to her accusingly, 'I know you – you're the girl friend of that spaceman. I saw your picture in *Life*.'

'You're right, Rama Joan,' a woman in a pale grey sweater and slacks said to the She-Turban. 'I must have seen the same picture.'

'She came with a man,' Ann volunteered from Rama Joan's

49

side. 'But they're nice people; they brought a cat. See how it stares at the big velvet saucer, Mommy?'

'Yes, dear,' Rama Joan agreed, smiling twistedly. 'It's seeing devils. Cats like them.'

'Please don't try to scare us any more than we are,' Margo said sharply. 'It's stupid and childish.'

'Oh, you think there won't be devils?' Rama Joan asked, quite conversationally. 'Don't worry about Ann. She loves everything.'

Ragnarok, slinking by, reared at Miaow with a snarl. The Little Man, still feeling under chairs, snapped out: 'Down, sir!' Margo fought to hold on to the cat and minimize scratches. Rama Joan turned her back and looked up at the Wanderer and then at the moon emerging from eclipse. The Little Man found what he'd been hunting for and he sat down and settled it on his knees – something the size of a briefcase but with sharper edges.

On the platform Doc was saying to Paul: 'Well, yes, those photos sound pretty suggestive of emergences from hyperspace, but –' His thick glasses magnified his frown. 'I don't see how they're going to solve any problems here and now. Especially the one of how far away the damn thing is.' The frown deepened.

Hunter said loudly to Doc: 'Rudolf! Listen to me!'

Doc grabbed up a furled umbrella, saying: 'Sorry, Ross, I've got to do something else,' and jumped rather clumsily off the platform into the sand.

Paul realized what the strange energy flooding him was, because he could see now that it possessed everyone else: plain exhilaration.

'But this is important,' Hunter went on, loudly speaking half to Paul and half past Paul down to Doc kneeling in the sand. 'If that thing's just a hundred miles up, it's in Earth's shadow and can't be reflecting sunlight. So suppose we figure it's just ten miles up. That's altitude enough for illumination of a wide area. And then it would be just three-tenths of a mile across – only five hundred yards. Rudolf, listen – I know we all laughed at old Charlie Fulby's idea of a fire balloon, but balloons over a hundred yards in diameter have been flown to altitudes of twenty miles and more. If we assume a gigantic balloon carrying

50

inside itself a tremendous light source, which perhaps adds to the lift by heating the balloon's gas . . .' He broke off. 'Rudolf, what the hell are you doing down there?'

Doc had thrust the furled umbrella deep into the sand and was crouched behind it, peering up towards them through the curve of the umbrella's handle. The Wanderer was reflected fantastically in his thick lenses.

'I'm checking that damn thing's orbit,' Doc called up. 'I'm lining it up with the corner of the big table and this umbrella. Don't anybody move that table!'

'Well, I'm telling you,' Hunter called back, 'that it may not have an orbit at all, but simply be floating. I'm telling you it may be nothing but a balloon as big as five football fields.'

'Ross Hunter!' Rama Joan's voice was ringing and carried the hint of a laugh. The bearded man looked around. So did the others.

'Ross Hunter!' Rama Joan repeated. 'Twenty minutes ago you were telling us of great symbols in the sky and now you're willing to settle for a big red and yellow balloon. Oh, you children, look at the moon!'

Paul copied those who held up a hand to blank out the Wanderer. The eastern rim of the moon glowed whitely, almost one-third out of eclipse, but even that area had coloured flecks on it, while the brownishly shadowed margin around it was full of purple and golden gleams. Unquestionably, the light of the Wanderer was falling at least as fiercely on that side of the moon as on the Earth.

The silence was broken by a sudden *rat-a-tat-tat*. The Little Man had unfolded a collapsible portable typewriter on his knees and was pecking away at it. To Margo, that irregular clicking sounded as lonely and incongruous as a tap dance on a tomb in a graveyard.

General Spike Stevens snapped: 'O.K., since H.Q. One isn't taking it, we are. Jimmy, crash this order through to Moonbase: LIFT A SHIP AND SCOUT THE NEW PLANET BEHIND YOU. ESTIMATED DISTANCE FROM YOU 25,000 MILES. (Add the lunacentric spatial co-ordinates there!) VITAL WE HAVE IN-TELLIGENCE. SEND DATA DIRECT.'

Colonel Griswold said: 'Spike, their ship senders haven't the power to reach us.'

'They'll relay through Moonbase.'

'Not through the thickness of the moon they won't.'

Spike snapped his fingers. 'O.K., tell 'em to lift two ships. One to reconnoitre, the other – after a suitable interval – to relay to Moonbase. Hold that. They're supposed to have three ships operational, aren't they? Good, make it two to scout the new planet, north and south, and one to orbit the moon as cover point and relay. Yes, Will, I know that just leaves 'em one man and no ship to hold down home, but we've got to get intelligence even if we strip the base.'

Colonel Mabel Wallingford, shivering in the electric atmosphere of the buried room, suddenly wondered: *What if it's not a problem? Spike won't be able to handle it then. I'll have given him his little victory and I'll see it taken away!*

Margo Gelhorn heard one of the women say: 'Don't try to get up yet, Charlie.' The Ramrod lay back in her arms and watched the Wanderer quite tranquilly, a faint smile playing around his lips.

On an impulse Margo leaned over. So did Rama Joan, mechanically tucking in the trailing end of her green turban.

'Ispan,' the gaunt man said faintly. 'Oh, Ispan, how did I not know thee? Guess I must have never thought about this side of you.' Then, more loudly: 'Ispan, all purple and gold. Ispan, the Imperial Planet.'

'Ispan-Dishpan,' the Little Man said without emotion, continuing to type.

'Charlie Fulby, you old liar,' Rama Joan said almost tenderly, 'why do you keep it up? You know you never set foot on another planet in your whole life.'

The woman glared but the Ramrod looked up without rancour at the green-turbaned one above him. 'Not in the body, no, that's quite true, Rama,' he said. 'But I've visited them for years in my thoughts. I'm as sure of their reality as Plato was of universals or Euclid of infinity. Ispan and Arletta and Brima *have to exist*, just like God. I *know*. But to make people under-

52

stand in this materialistic age, I had to pretend I'd visited them in the flesh.'

'Why do you drop the pretence now?' Rama Joan pressed lightly, as if she already knew the answer.

'Now no one needs to pretend anything,' the Ramrod said quietly. 'Ispan is here.'

The Little Man spun the sheet out of his typewriter, stuck it in a clipboard, stepped on to the platform, and rapped on the table for attention.

Reading from the sheet, he said: 'After the place, date, hour and minute I've got: WE THE UNDERSIGNED SAW A CIRCU-LAR OBJECT IN THE SKY NEAR THE MOON. ITS APPARENT DIAMETER WAS FOUR TIMES THAT OF THE MOON. ITS TWO HALVES WERE PURPLE AND YELLOW AND RESEMBLED A YIN-YANG OR THE MIRROR IMAGE OF A SOLID SIXTY-NINE. IT GAVE ENOUGH LIGHT TO READ NEWSPRINT BY AND IT MAINTAINED THE SAME APPEARANCE FOR AT LEAST 20 MINUTES. Any emendations? Very well, I'll circulate this for signatures as read. I'll want your addresses, too.'

Somebody groaned but Doc called from his post in the sand: 'That's right, Doddsy, nail it down!' The Little Man presented his clipboard to the two women nearest him. One giggled hysterically, the other grabbed his pen and signed.

Paul called down to Doc: 'Are you getting any movement yet?'

'Not anything I can be sure of,' the latter said, standing up carefully so as not to disturb the deep-thrust umbrella. 'It's certainly not anything in a nearby orbit.' He climbed back on the platform. 'Anybody here got a telescope or binoculars?' he asked loudly but not very hopefully. 'Opera glasses?' He waited a moment longer, then shrugged. 'That's typical,' he said to Paul, removing his glasses to polish them and to massage around his eyes. 'What a bunch of greenhorns!'

Hunter's bearded face brightened. 'Anybody here got a *radio*?' he called out.

'I have,' said the thin woman sitting on the floor with the Ramrod.

'Good, then get us a news station,' Hunter told her.

She said, 'I'll get KFAC – that's got classical music with regular traffic bulletins and news flashes.'

He commented, 'If they're seeing it in New York or Buenos Aires, say, we'll know it has to be high.'

Margo was studying the Wanderer again when someone jogged her elbow, the one away from the cat. The Little Man said to her pleasantly: 'My name is Clarence Dodd. You are . . . ?'

'Margo Gelhorn,' she told him. 'Is that huge beast your dog, Mr Dodd?'

'Yes, he is,' he said quickly, with a bright smile. 'May I have your signature on this document?'

'Oh, please!' she said sourly, looking up again at the Wanderer overhead.

'You'll be sorry,' the Little Man assured her peaceably. 'The one time I saw a plausible saucer I omitted to get signed statements from the four people in the car with me. A week later they were all saying it was something else.'

Margo shrugged, then went to the edge of the platform and said: 'Paul, I think the purple half is getting smaller and there's a purple streak down the outside edge of the yellow half that wasn't there before.'

'She's right,' several people said. Doc fumbled at his slipping glasses, but before he could get a word out Hunter said: '*It's rotating*. It must be a sphere!'

Suddenly the Wanderer, which Paul had been seeing as flat, rounded itself out. There was something unspeakably strange about the hidden and utterly unknown other side crawling into view.

Doc raised a hand. 'It's rotating towards the east,' he asserted. 'That is, this side of it is – which means that it is rotating *retrograde* to Earth and most of the other planets of our solar system.'

'My God, Bill, now we get astronomy lessons,' the woman in pale grey carped in a low, sardonic voice to the man beside her.

The thin woman's portable radio came on, quite weakly except for the static. The music, what there was of it, had a galloping, surging rhythm. After a moment Paul recognized

Wagner's 'The Ride of the Valkyries', sounding, out here in the great open, as if it were being played by an orchestra of mice.

Don Merriam was almost half-way back to the Hut, his boots kicking up dust as he hurried with care across the lightening plain, when Johannsen's voice sounded crisply by his ear. He stopped.

Johannsen said: 'Get this, Don. You are not to re-enter the Hut. You are to board Ship One and prepare for solo take-off.'

Don suppressed the impulse to say: 'But Yo –'

The other chuckled approvingly at his silence and continued: 'I know we've never flown them solo except in practice on the mock-up, but this is orders from the top. Dufresne's suited up. He'll join you in Ship Two. I'll be in Baba Yaga Three to relay back to Gompert at base, who'll relay to H.Q. Earth. On order you and Dufresne will take off. You will reconnoitre the northern half, and he, the southern, of the object behind Luna that's making the yellow and purple light. It's hard to believe, but H.Q. Earth says it's a –'

The voice was lost in a ponderous, almost subsonic, grinding roar coming through Don's boots and up his legs. The moon moved sideways a foot or more under Don's feet, throwing him down. In the two seconds he was falling his only active thought was to lift his arms bent-elbowed to make a cage around his helmet, but he could see the grey dust rippling and lifting a little here and there like a thick rug with wind under it, as inertia held it back while the solid moon moved beneath it.

He crashed hollowly on his back. The roaring multiplied, coming in everywhere through the underside of his suit. Gouts of dust skimmed off around him in low parabolas. His helmet hadn't cracked.

The roaring faded. He said: 'Yo!' and 'Yo!' again, and then with his tongue he triggered the Hut whistle.

The purple-and-yellow highlight glared down at him from the western edge of the Atlantic, touching Florida.

There was no answer from the Hut.

Chapter 9

Paul and Margo started out after the main body of saucer students heading back to the cars. They couldn't recall now who had first said: 'We'd better be getting out of here,' but once the words had been spoken, agreement and reaction had been swift and almost universal. Doc had wanted to stick with his umbrella-and-table-corner astrolabe, and had tried to browbeat a nucleus of informed observers to stay with him, but he finally had been dissuaded.

'Rudy's a bachelor,' Hunter explained to Margo as a few of them waited for Doc to gather his things. 'He's willing to stay up all night making observations or chess moves, *or trying to make burlesque babes*' – he shouted the last back towards Doc – 'but the rest of us have got families.'

As soon as the idea of leaving had been proposed, Paul had been in a sweat to get to Moon Project headquarters. He and Margo would swing around direct to Vandenberg Two, he decided; in fact, he had been about to suggest to her that they tramp to the beach gate – it might be quicker – when he remembered that admission clearance would be delayed there.

Then just as they had been setting out, among the first to leave, Miaow, perhaps encouraged by seeing Ragnarok put on leash, had sprung from Margo's arms to investigate the under parts of the dance floor. Ann had stayed to witness the recovery of Miaow, and Rama Joan with her daughter. The last two made a queer sight: the calm-eyed little girl with her pale red braids and the mannish woman in her rumpled evening clothes.

When Doc came bustling along, the six of them set out, stepping briskly along to catch up with the others.

Doc jerked a thumb at the bearded man. 'Has this character been daggering my reputation?' he demanded of Margo.

'No, Professor Hunter has been building it up,' she told him with a grin. 'I gather your name is Rudolf Valentino.'

'No, just Rudolf Brecht,' Doc chortled, 'but the Brechts are a sensuous clan, too, heigh-ho!'

'I see you forgot your umbrella,' Hunter told him, instantly clamping a hand on Doc's elbow. 'Not that I'm going to let you go back for it.'

'No, Ross,' Doc told Hunter, 'I deliberately left it stuck there – that bumbershoot is already a kind of monument. Incidentally, I want to go on record that we're all being fools. Now we'll be fighting traffic the whole night, whereas we could have employed it in fruitful observation at an ideal location – and I'd have treated you all to a big farm breakfast!'

'I'm not at all sure about that ideal location part,' Hunter began sombrely, but Doc cut him off by pointing up at the Wanderer as he strode along and demanding: 'Hey, granting that thing's a genuine planet, what do you think the yellow and maroon areas are? I'll plump for yellow desert and oceans full of purple algae and kelp.'

'Arid flats of sublimated iodine and sulphur,' Hunter hazarded wildly.

'With a border patrol of Maxwell's demons to keep them separate, I suppose?' Doc challenged amiably.

Paul looked up. The purple margin-band was wider now and the yellow area, moving towards the centre, was almost like a fat crescent.

Ann spoke up, 'I think it's oceans of golden water and lands of thick purple forest.'

'No, young lady, you got to stick to the rules of the game,' Doc admonished, leaning down towards her as he still strode on. 'Which is that you can't have anything up there that you don't know about down here.'

'Is that your formula for approaching the unknown, Mr Brecht?' Rama Joan asked with a suggestion of laughter. 'Would it even work for Russia?'

'Well, I myself think it's a darn good formula for approaching Russia,' Doc replied. 'Hey, young lady,' he continued, speaking to Ann, 'what's the best way of getting on the good side of your mother? I never wooed a Rama yet and the idea intrigues me.'

Ann shrugged, switching her red braids, and Rama Joan answered for her. 'Don't begin by expecting to find only reflections of yourself,' she said tartly. Suddenly she jerked off her turban, releasing a cloud of red-gold hair which at last made her seem plausible as Ann's mother, though rendering her male evening dress doubly incongruous.

They were catching up with the others now, threading past the sea-grass. Paul was intrigued by the number who were walking with a permanent hunch away from the Wanderer, then realized that he was walking that way, too. They overtook the Ramrod and the two women with him, the thin one of them carrying the radio, which was now playing tinnily the Greig A minor Concerto, sandwiched between thick static.

'I tried other stations,' the woman told Hunter, 'but the static was even worse.'

Abruptly the music broke off. As one, they stopped, and several of the people ahead of them did, too.

The radio said, quite clearly: 'This is a Sigalert Bulletin. The Hollywood and Santa Monica Freeways – no, change that – the Hollywood, Santa Monica and Ventura Freeways are closed by congestion. Motorists are requested to use *none* of the freeways until further notice. Please stay home. The appearance in the sky is not an atomic attack. Repeat: *not* an atomic attack. We've just been talking over the phone with Professor Humason Kirk, noted Tarzana College astronomer, and he tells us that the appearance in the sky is unquestionably – get that, folks, unquestionably – an orbiting cloud of metallic powders reflecting sunlight. He tentatively identifies the powders as gold and roseate bronze. The total weight of the powders can be no more than a few pounds, Professor Kirk assures us, and they can't hurt –'

'Oh, the stupid ass!' Doc broke in. 'Powders! *Puffballs!*'

Several people shushed him, but by the time they could listen again, there was only the sound of the piano rippling through A minor runs.

Don Merriam figured he had to be within a hundred yards of the Hut when the second big moonquake came, a vertical one this time, but heralded by the same horrible grinding roar, as if Luna were tearing her guts out. His teeth stung and the metal of his suit vibrated fiercely, as if resonating a cosmic piano note.

Solid moon dropped from under his boots, then smashed up against their corrugated soles, then dropped away and smashed again. The dust carpet fell and lifted with him. Here and there bushels of it shot up a dozen feet or more, then fell back, abruptly compared with dust on Earth.

The jolts went on. Don fought to keep his footing as if he were standing on the back of a bucking horse, his hands ready to move to whichever side towards which he should overbalance. The jumping dust made bright vertical scrawls – thick, hairpin brushstrokes – against the starfields. Some solid sunlight was once more bathing Plato's plain.

The jolts subsided. Don upped the polarization of his helmet window to four-fifths max and scanned for the Hut. He'd quit trying to raise them by suit radio. He couldn't make out the portholes, but that was always harder in sunlight. He figured the right direction from the stars and started out. He thought he saw the gleam-edged, long-legged trapezoids of two of the Baba Yagas.

A second horizontal moonquake threw him on his face. He got his forearms raised in time to catch the impact. This ground-parallel temblor was protracted. There were a half-dozen sideways surges. Plato's grey dust-lake rippled to the horizon. Dust spray rose and fell. The stuff really did behave more like water (on Earth) than like dust. Rock knobs thrusting up through it made dust wakes. Dust squirts peppered Don's helmet.

A vertical component added itself to the horizontal quake. The roar dazed him. Don's suit shook like an empty tin can in a paint-mixer.

He gave up waiting and began to crawl towards the ships like a dust-drenched silver beetle. He wished he had a beetle's two extra legs.

The saucer students were sorting themselves out as they headed for their cars, which showed up colourfully at the base of the brown cliffs. The general effect of the Wanderer's light, mixing complementary yellow and violet, was yellowish white, except where mirror surfaces such as water reflected the entire orb, or in the edges of shadows where one colour was cut off.

Hunter said to Paul, a shade enviously, 'I suppose you Moon Project people already have this thing a lot more thoroughly comprehended than we do. More data, for one thing. Satellite 'scopes, radar, all the rest.'

'I'm not so sure of that, Ross,' Paul replied. 'On the Project you develop a kind of tunnel vision.'

The Little Man came back towards them with Ragnarok on short leash and his clipboard in the other hand.

'Remember me? – I'm Clarence Dodd. Mayn't I have your signature now, Miss Gelhorn?' he said winningly, holding out the clipboard to Margo. 'Tomorrow a lot of people are going to be saying: "Why didn't we sign it?" But then it'll be too late.'

Margo, struggling to contain Miaow, snarled: 'Oh, get away, you idiot!'

'I'll sign it for you, Doddsy,' Doc called cheerfully. 'Only, come on over here and quit trying to provoke felino-doggy war.'

Ann giggled. 'I like Mr Brecht, Mummy.' The red-haired woman in evening clothes smiled down at her faintly.

'That's what I like to hear,' Doc called. 'Keep on propagandizing your mother.'

Paul took Margo's elbow to guide her to his car, but then something made him stop and look up at the Wanderer. The purple-bordered yellow figure had rotated completely into view now and stood out sharply, thick at the base, thinner and sharply bent at the top. It teased Paul's imagination.

Clarence Dodd – or the Little Man, as Paul still called him in his mind – gave Ragnarok's leash to Doc and made another quick simplified sketch, using criss-cross lines to show the purple. He labelled it 'After One Hour'.

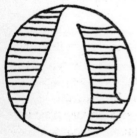

After One Hour

One of the cars, a red sedan, backed and took off, far ahead of any of the others.

From ahead the thin woman called: 'Please help us, someone. I think Wanda's having a heart attack.'

Ragnarok whimpered. Miaow hissed.

Suddenly Paul realized what the yellow figure reminded him of: a dinosaur. A long-jawed dinosaur rearing on its great thick hind legs. His skin prickled. Then he was trembling and there was a faint low roaring in his body.

When Paul was a little boy, he had liked to stand on the middle of the porch swing, a cushioned, solid seat for three hanging from the ceiling by chains at the four corners. It had seemed at the time a daring feat of equilibrium. Now, all at once, he was standing on that swing again, for the ground under his feet moved, gently but solidly with a ponderous muffled thud, a few inches back, a few inches forward, and then back again, and he was swaying his body to keep balanced, just as he'd used to do on the swing.

Over inarticulate exclamations and calls, Hunter shouted with strident anxiety: *'Come away from the cars!'*

Margo clung to Paul. Miaow, squeezed between them, squeaked.

People were whirling and running. The brown cliff appeared to swell; cracks opened in it all over; and then it sank, slowly, it looked, but with shuddering sledge strokes at the end. Gravel pattered. A grain stung Paul's cheek. There was a puff of gritty air. Suddenly the smell of raw earth was very strong.

'Come on!' Hunter yelled. 'Some of them were caught!'

But Paul first looked upward again at the uprearing yellow figure on the purple orb now perceptibly nearer the moon.

Tyrannosaurus Rex!

Pershing Square is a block of little fountains and neatly manicured greenery roofing a municipal garage and atomic shelter in the heart of old Los Angeles, where the signs read 'Su crédito es bueno' more often than 'Your credit is good'.

Tonight the winos and weirdies and anonymous wayfarers who, next to the furred squirrels and feathered pigeons, are the Square's most persistent inhabitants, had something more exciting to observe than the beards of Second Coming preachers and the manic gesticulations of threadbare lecturers.

Tonight the inhabitants of Pershing Square spilled into Olive Street at the corner of Fifth, where a bronze statue of Beethoven broodingly faces the Biltmore Hotel, Bunker Hill, and the Baptist Auditorium which serves as one of the city's chief theatres. Their lifted faces were bright with Wanderer-light as they silently stared south at the monstrous sign in the heavens, but Beethoven's visage remained introspectively in the shadow of its great brow and hair-mop as he peered down at his half-buttoned vest whitened with pigeon droppings.

There was a momentary intensification of the awed silence, then a faint distant roaring. A woman screamed, and the watchers dropped their gaze. For a long moment it looked to them as if a black ocean were coming towards them up Olive in great waves crested with yellow and violet foam – great black waves that had travelled all the twenty miles north from San Pedro along the Harbour and Long Beach Freeways.

Then they saw that the waves were not black water but cold black asphalt, that the street itself was surging as great earthquake shocks travelled north along it. In the next instant the roaring became that of a hundred jets, and the asphalt waves tossed the watchers and broke up the walls of the buildings around them in a stone and concrete surf.

For a second an infinitely sinister violet light flashed from the deep eyesockets of the giant metal Beethoven, as he slowly toppled over backwards.

The saucer students had trouble enough coping with the results of the fringe reverberation of the big Los Angeles–Long Beach quake. After the thin woman and two others had been half dug, half pulled out of their light entombment in the edge of the landfall, a hurried count showed three others still missing. There followed a frantic ten minutes of digging, mostly with two bright-bladed shovels that the Little Man had produced from the back of his station wagon, which was solidly buried only as far as the rear wheels and its top dented in only about a foot. Then someone remembered the red sedan that had left ahead of the rest; and someone else, that it had been the one in which the three missing people had arrived.

While the diggers caught their breath, Paul, whose convertible was hopelessly buried, explained his connection with the Moon Project and his intention of making with Margo for the beach gate of Vandenberg Two, and he offered to take anyone along with him who wanted to come and to vouch for them to the guards – their obvious distress in any case ensuring admission.

Doc enthusiastically endorsed this suggestion, but it was opposed by a thick-armed man wearing a leather windbreaker and named Rivis, who had a very low opinion of all military forces and the degree of helpfulness to be expected of them – and whose car had only its radiator and front wheels dirt-encumbered. Rivis, who also had four cute kids, a swell little wife, and an hysterical mother-in-law – all of them in Santa Barbara – was for digging out and getting home.

Rivis was seconded by the owners of the microbus and the white pickup truck, both only lightly buried vehicles. The truck's people, a trimly handsome couple named Hixon wearing matching pale grey slacks and sweaters, were particularly insistent on getting out quickly.

There followed a progressively more embittered argument involving such points as: Would the Pacific Coast Highway be traffic-jammed and/or quake-blocked? Was Paul what he claimed? Would the motors of the buried cars start when dug out? (Rivis proved something by starting his, though his car radio got only the howlingest static.) Was Wanda's heart attack genuine? Finally, weren't the panellists and their dubious new friends a bunch of oyster-brained intellectuals scared of getting a few blisters on their hands?

In the end, half the saucer students, most of them with cars rather lightly buried, stuck with Rivis and the Hixons and, in a burst of hard feelings, even refused to promise to care for the fat woman who had had the heart attack until Paul could send a balloon-tyred sand jeep from Vandenberg Two to pick her up.

The other half set off for the beach gate.

Don Guillermo Walker knew the Wanderer had to be something like a planet, for it and its glaring image in black Lake Nicaragua below had followed him sixty miles southeast now without shifting position – except that it was nearer the western horizon and maybe nearer the moon. And now there was showing on the thing what looked like a golden cock crowing to wake Simon Bolivár. *I once played in* Le Coq d'Or, *didn't I?* the lonely bomb-raider asked himself. *No, it's an opera, or a ballet.*

The general glare had turned pinkish here and there along the western horizon; he didn't know why. Skirting the long ridgy island of Ometepe, he saw more lights at Alta Gracia than you'd ever expect after midnight. Everybody up and gawking at it and going ape or diving into churches, he supposed.

Suddenly red glare and rocks erupted from beyond the town and for an instant he thought he'd dropped a bomb he didn't know about. Then he realized it had to be one of Ometepe's volcanoes letting go. He banked east – get away, get away from the blast! Those pink glares – why, the whole Pacific Coast must be in eruption, from the Gulf of Fonseca to the Gulf of Nicoya.

Don Merriam, a battered and grievously weak-legged beetle, pushed himself up on his arms beside the Hut's proud magnesium flagpole and saw, where the Hut should be, a raw-walled chasm twenty feet across with little waterfalls of dust trickling down its farther lip.

One of the ships was gone with the Hut, one was lying on its side across the chasm with two of its three shock-absorbing legs sticking up like the legs of a dead chicken, while he'd almost crawled under the third Baba Yaga without seeing it.

They called the little moon-type rocket ships 'Baba Yagas' because – Dufresne had first thought of it – they suggested the witch's hut on legs that figures in a couple of popular bits of classical Russian music and that, in the underlying folklore, runs about by night on those legs. It was rumoured that the Soviet moonmen called their ships 'Jeeps'.

But now the walking-hut comparison was getting altogether too close, for the continuing vertical moonquake, which Don hardly noticed any more, was making the last Baba Yaga step about on its plate-shod legs as it rocked this way and that. One of the shoes was only a yard from the chasm and as Don watched, it tramped six inches closer.

Don carefully pushed himself into a wide-based crouch. He

told himself Dufresne might have taken off in the missing rocket, though he'd seen no jet flare. And Yo might be alive or dead in the ship across the chasm. Gompert . . .

The Baba Yaga took another step towards the gulf. Don took a couple of quick ones himself across the jolting surface and then straightened and grabbed the last rung of the ladder down from the body of the ship midway between the three legs.

He chinned himself and climbed towards the hatch, set ominously between the five trumpetlike tubes of the jet. The Baba Yaga rocked. Don told himself that his weight lowered its centre of gravity a little, making its steps a little shorter.

Chapter 10

Sally Harris and Jake Lesher were on one of the subway trains to be halted and emptied at 42nd Street. The traffic jams had been hopeless and Jake's car was parked in Flatbush. Police helped the guards clear the subway cars and hurry the passengers topside.

'But why, but why?' Jake was demanding. 'It looks bad.'

'No, good,' Sally told him. 'Bombs, and they'd be herding us *down*. Besides, here we're near Hugo's penthouse. This is exciting, Jake!'

Emerging, they found Times Square more packed than they'd ever known it to be at three a.m.

Looking west on 42nd Street, they could see the Wanderer still quite high in the sky, with the moon so close they almost touched. On the south side of the street the shadow edge made a swath of motionless yellow people and on their side a swath of purple ones. The electric ads were all going full blast, but paled way down by the supermoonlight.

The Square was quieter than they'd ever known, too, except that just now a man emerged from behind them crying: 'Extra! Read all about it! Read all about the new planet!'

Jake traded two bits for a *Daily Orbit*. Its tabloid front page was a pic of the Wanderer in wet, acrid red and yellow inks and six lines of information anyone could have got by looking at the sky and his watch. The headline was: STRANGE ORB BAFFLES MAN.

'Doesn't baffle me,' Sally said in the highest spirits and then, grinning at Jake, 'I created it. I put it up there.'

'Don't be blasphemous, young woman,' a lantern-jawed man admonished her sourly.

'Ha, you think I didn't do it, huh?' she demanded. 'I'll show you!' She cleared a place around her with her elbows and tossed Jake her jacket. Then, stabbing a finger successively at Lantern Jaw and at the Wanderer, and next snapping her fingers as she swayed provocatively, she began to sing, in an electrifying contralto and a melody borrowed half-and-half from 'Green Door' and 'Strange Fruit':

> Strange orb! . . . in the western sky . . .
> Strange light! . . . streaming from on high . . .

Don Merriam had ignited the Baba Yaga's jet before he'd strapped down and when the aniline and nitric pumps had barely started to spin. The reason was simple enough: he'd felt the jouncing ship step off the edge.

He'd done everything he could to cut time. He'd blown the ship, letting its air escape in a great puff to clear a direct entry for himself, rather than waiting for the airlock between the fuel and oxidizer tanks to empty and fill. He'd barely dogged the hatches behind him and made only the most perfunctory swipe at the oxygen release lever although he knew his suit oxy was running out – and he'd been almost too late at that.

The cold jet fired strongly, however. Lemon-hot molecules streamed out of the Baba Yaga's tail at almost two miles a second, and after a sticky moment she lifted, but sideways rather than up – like an old airplane taking off.

Perhaps Don's mistake was in trying to correct at all – his present vector would likely have got him into some sort of orbit, perhaps quite efficiently. But he was flying by eye and he didn't like the way white moon crossed by cracks kept bulking so large in the spacescreen, and he knew that the sooner you corrected the less power it took, and he wasn't sure how much fuel and oxidizer he had – in fact, he still wasn't quite sure which of the three sister ships he was in – and, besides all that, he was probably already quite giddy and illogical from oxygen-lack.

So, careless of the gravity-and-a-half dragging at him, he reached out sideways – it was quite a reach: normally it would have been a robot's or co-pilot's job – and slapped the keys to fire three solid-fuel rockets on the side of the ship towards the moon.

The sudden extra jolt they gave the Baba Yaga was enough to unseat him. Inexorably, but with agonizing slowness, the stick slipped out of his hand and he fell heavily – a lot more heavily than he would have on the moon – to the floor a dozen feet below, and his helmet smashed against the back of his head, knocking him out.

Ten seconds later, the aniline-nitric jet died, as was the automatic way in these ships when you let go the stick. The solid-fuel rockets had burnt out a fractional second earlier. The correction had been calculated with remarkable accuracy, under the circumstances. The Baba Yaga was mounting almost straight up from Luna with nearly enough kinetic energy to kick free. But now, Luna's mild gravity was slowing the ship second by second, although the ship was still rising swiftly in free fall and would continue to do so for some time.

Don's helmet lay across the lightly-dogged hatch. A tiny flat jet of white vapour about the size and shape of a calling card was escaping through a fine slit in the view window. Frost formed along the crack.

Barbara Katz said to Knolls Kettering III: 'Less than a minute now until contact, Dad.' She meant by 'contact' the moment the Wanderer would overlap the moon, or the moon the Wanderer, or –

'Excuse me, suh,' came a soft deep voice from behind them, 'but what's going to happen when they hit?'

Barbara turned. Some light was on at the back of the big house now: it silhouetted a big man in a chauffeur's uniform and two women grouped tightly together. They must have come out very quietly.

From beside her Mr Kettering said with thin exasperation:

'I told you people to go to bed hours ago. You know I don't want you fussing over me.'

Excuse me, suh,' the voice persisted, 'but everybody's up and outside watching it. Everybody in Palm Beach. Please, suh, what's going to happen when it hit the moon?'

Barbara wanted to speak up and tell the chauffeur and maids many things: that it was the moon that was moving towards the Wanderer, because the telescope's electrically-driven mounting had been set to track the moon across the sky and the moon was now running five diameters ahead of its normal course; that they still didn't know the distance of the Wanderer – for one thing, its surface showed no sharp details except its rim, just a velvety yellow or maroon under all magnifications; that bodies in the heavens mostly didn't hit but went into orbit around each other.

But she knew that men – even millionaires, presumably – like to do the scientific talking; and, besides that, she disliked having to fool around with Palm Beach interracial etiquette.

Then she looked up and saw that the problem had solved itself.

'They're not hitting,' she said. 'The moon is passing in front of the Wanderer.' She added impulsively: 'Oh, Dad, I didn't believe it was really out there until now.'

There were little gasps from the women.

'The Wanderer?' the chauffeur asked softly.

Knolls Kettering III took over. He said, a bit primly: 'The Wanderer is the name Miss Katz and I have selected for the strange planet. Now please go to bed.'

Arab Jones called across the roof to Pepe Martinez and High Bundy, who were waltzing together free-style: 'Hey, man, look, they mating now! Old Moon going into her like a sperm into a purple egg.'

The three interracial weed-brothers had smoked four more prime reefers to celebrate the master-kick of the Wanderer's appearance and they were now high as kites – high as orbital radar beacons! But not so high, if one ever is, as to be utterly devoid of reasoning powers, for Pepe exclaimed: 'How those square Mexicans must be crossing themselves south of the border, and the brownies dancing down Rio way,' while High summed it up with: 'Like this, man: kicks has come into the world to stay.'

Arab said, his brown face gleaming in the Wanderer's glow: 'Let us fold our tent and descend, my sons, and mingle with the terrified populace.'

Hunter said to Doc: 'The moon has sure thumbtacked it down out there,' referring to the plaster-white round standing in front of the Wanderer. 'In fact, I'm beginning to wonder – remembering the similar triangles, Rudy – whether it mayn't be two and a half million miles away and eighty thousand miles across.'

'Jupiter come to call, hey?' Doc replied with a chuckle and then immediately demanded of the others: 'Well, can anyone point out Jupiter to me elsewhere in the sky right now? Though,' he added, 'I've got to admit I never heard of a purple aspect for Jupiter or a yellow spot in the form of a giant duck.'

'A penguin!' Ann called from behind them.

The two men were part of the little cortège plodding through sand and sea-grass towards the beach gate of Vandenberg Two. The cortège was led by Paul, Margo with Miaow, and Doc. Then came Hunter, the Ramrod, and two other men lugging by its four corners an aluminium cot with folded legs, on which Wanda – the fat woman – reposed, groaning a little now and then. Beside the cot walked the thin woman, but without her radio, which had been lost in the slide. She talked soothingly to Wanda. The rear guard consisted of Rama Joan, Ann, and Clarence Dodd – the Little Man – with Ragnarok on leash and nervous.

The aluminium cot was another you-name-it-we-got-it item from the Little Man's station wagon. (Margo had asked him if he had a primus stove and fuel. He had replied, without batting an eyelash: 'Yes, I do, but I see no point in taking it with us this time.')

Just after Doc had made his not entirely frivolous suggestion about Jupiter, Rama Joan called out for them all to look at the Wanderer again. They had already noticed considerable changes in the past forty minutes. The duck (or dinosaur) had all its

69

body on the left-hand side of the disc, its head sticking out to the right as if part of a north pole goldcap. In the new purple area swinging into view there had appeared a large central yellow patch, in shape half-way between an equilateral triangle and a solid capital D.

'See, just after the D,' Rama Joan called, 'there's a thin black crescent coming. The moon almost hides it.'

'That's the shadow of the moon on the new planet!' Doc yelled excitedly after a few freezing seconds. 'And if it's any smaller than Luna I can't see the difference. Ross, they can't be more than a few thousand miles apart! Now we know that planet is Earth-size, almost exactly.'

'Mommy, does that mean they almost hit each other?' Ann whispered. 'Why's Mr Brecht so happy? Because they missed?'

'Not exactly, dear. He'd probably have enjoyed the spectacle. Mr Brecht is happy because he likes to know exactly where things are, so he can put his hands on them in the dark.'

'Mr Brecht can't put his hands on the new planet, Mommy.'

'No, dear, but now he can put his thoughts there.'

Oxyhelium mix gradually filled the cabin of the Baba Yaga from the tank Don Merriam had valved open. Its pressure sealed the inner hatch and opened two doors in Don's helmet. Little fans went on around the cabin, keeping the new air moving in spite of it being in free fall. It pushed into Don's helmet, replacing the foul air there. His features twitched and he shuddered a little. His breathing strengthened and he went into a deep, healthy sleep.

The Baba Yaga reached the top of its trajectory, poised there, then began to fall back towards the moon. As it fell, it tumbled slowly. Every thirty seconds, about, its spacescreen looked at the moon, and fifteen seconds later at Earth. As it tumbled, the dust-filmed spacesuit with Don inside began to move across the floor, rolling very slowly.

The Little Man called ahead to Paul: 'I don't mean to impugn your veracity, Mr Hagbolt, but the Vandenberg Two beach gate seems to be a lot farther away than you led us to believe. Easy, Ragnarok!'

70

'It's right in front of the blinking red light,' Paul told him, wishing he were inwardly as sure of that as he tried to make his voice sound. He added, 'I have to admit I underestimated the distance of the light.'

'Don't worry, Doddsy. Paul will get us there,' Doc pronounced confidently.

The three of them were preparing to relieve Hunter, the Ramrod, and one of the two other men at the three corners of the fat woman's stretcher.

'How are you feeling, Wanda?' the thin woman asked, kneeling by the cot in the sand. 'You can have another digitalis.'

'A little better,' the fat woman murmured, fluttering her eyes open. They rested on the Wanderer. 'Oh, my God,' she groaned, turning her head away.

The strange orb, inexorably rotating, presented a new aspect. The remains of the dinosaur, or penguin, made a huge yellow *C* around the left-hand rim of the planet, while the solid yellow *D* had swung to the centre, so that the effect was of *D-in-C*. The Little Man did another quick sketch, labelling it simply, 'Two Hours'.

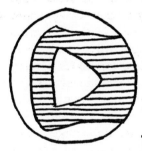

Two Hours

Ann said, 'I think the *C* is a straw basket on its side and the *D* a piece of cake with lemon frosting. And the moon is a honeydew melon!'

'I know who's hungry,' her mother said.

'Or you can think of the *D* as the eye of a giant purple needle,' Ann quickly pointed out.

The Golden Serpent coils around the Broken Egg, the Ramrod thought. *Chaos is hatched.*

The moon and its shadow had moved all the way across the

71

planet. There was a feeling of relief when a thread of night-sky appeared between the two orbs.

The man at the fourth corner of the cot, a heavy-faced welder named Ignace Wojtowicz, perhaps just wanting to prolong the rest period, said: 'There's one thing I don't get at all. If that's a real planet out there big as Earth, how come we don't feel its gravity pulling at us – sort of making us feel lighter, at least.'

'For the same reason we don't feel the gravity of the moon or the sun,' Hunter answered quickly. 'Then, too, although we know the size of the new planet, we have no idea of its mass. Of course,' he added, 'if it did appear out of hyperspace, there must have been an instant when its gravity field didn't exist for us and then an instant when it did – I'm assuming the front of a newly-created gravity field moves out at the speed of light – but apparently there were no transition effects.'

'That we noticed,' Doc amended. 'Incidentally, Ross, what's this casting doubt on my emergence-from-hyperspace theory? Where else could the thing have come from?'

'It might have approached the solar system camouflaged or somehow blacked-out,' Hunter asserted. 'We should consider *all* the improbabilities. Your own philosophy back at you, Rudy.'

'Humph,' Doc commented. 'No, I think what Paul told us about twist fields in the star photos tips the scales towards Brecht's Hyperspace Hypothesis. And it would have had to have its gravity blacked out too, I'd think, by your theory. Incidentally, I imagine we already can deduce something about the planet's mass. It's now seven minutes past one, Pacific Standard Time,' he said, glancing at his wrist. 'About two hours since the new planet appeared.'

'Two hours and five minutes,' the Little Man inserted.

'You're a pearl, Doddsy. Everybody engrave that eleven-oh-two P.S.T. on their memories – some day your grandchildren may ask you to tell them the exact time you saw Mrs Monster pop out of hyperspace. But anyway, at one a.m. the full moon ought to be past her highest in the sky, an hour towards setting. I judge she's definitely east of that point, still near her highest. About three or four degrees east, I'd say –

six or eight moon diameters. Which would mean that the gravitational pull of the emergent planet has speeded up the moon in her orbit. Ergo, the newcomer is no lightweight.'

'Wow,' Wojtowicz said appreciatively. 'Just how much speed-up is that, Doc, figuring like the moon's a rocket?'

'Why, from two-thirds of a mile a second to . . .' Doc hesitated, then said, as if incredulous of his own figures: 'to four or more miles a second.'

He and Hunter looked at each other.

'Wow,' Wojtowicz repeated. 'But now I take it, Doc, the moon keeps on in her old orbit, just speeded up a lot? Maybe a month every week, huh?' The black isthmus between moon and planet had widened a little while they'd been speaking.

'I think we'd better be getting a move on, ourselves,' Doc said in an oddly distant way, stooping for his corner of the cot.

'Right,' Hunter seconded brusquely.

Great rotary pumps surged, moving water to the port side of the *Prince Charles* to compensate for the weight of the passengers and crewmen lining the starboard rails and crowding the starboard portholes to watch the Wanderer and the moon set in the Atlantic, while dawn paled the sky behind them unnoticed. The thickness of Earth's atmosphere had turned the purple of the planet red and its gold orange. Its wake across the calm sea was spectacular.

The radio engineer of the atom-liner reported to Captain Sithwise a very unusual and growing amount of static.

Don Guillermo Walker managed to land his airplane on the south end of Lake Nicaragua near the mouth of the San Juan River, despite the broken left aileron and half-dozen holes struck or burnt through the wings by chunks of red-hot pumice. What the devil, the big rock had missed him!

The volcano on Ometepe was now joined by its brother peak, Madera, and they were sending twin ruddy pillars skyward almost fifty miles northwest. And now, passing all expectation on such a crazy opening night, he saw wink on, scarcely a mile away, the twin red flares the Araiza brothers had promised would guide him to the launch. *Caramba, que fideli-*

dad! He'd never accuse another Latin American of frivolity or faithlessness.

Suddenly the reflection of the Wanderer in the black lake shattered towards him. He saw the sinister water formations, like low wide steps, approaching him. Barely in time, he headed the plane around into them. The old Seabee mounted the first successfully, though with a great heave and splash. Earthquake of landslide waves!

Chapter 11

Doc puffed out rapidly: 'I don't care how near we are to the gate, I got to rest.' He lowered his corner of the cot to the sand and knelt there, arm on knee and with bald head bent, panting.

'Your evil life catching up with you,' Hunter jeered lightly, then muttered to Margo: 'We better go easy on the old goat. He normally gets about as much exercise as a Thuringer sausage.'

'I can take over again,' eagerly volunteered the one who had had Doc's corner earlier – a thin-faced high school student who had ridden to the symposium from Oxnard with Wojtowicz.

'Better we all have a breather, Harry,' the latter said. 'Professor – ' He addressed himself to Hunter. 'It looks to me like the moon's slowed down again. Like back to normal.'

All of them except the fat woman studied the situation in the western sky. Even Doc raised his head while continuing to gasp. Unquestionably the black isthmus between the Wanderer and the moon hadn't widened during the last short march.

'I think the moon's getting smaller,' Ann said.

'So do I,' the Little Man agreed. He squatted on his hams with an arm around Ragnarok and soothingly kneaded the huge dog's black and brown throat while he squinted upward. 'And – I know this is utterly fantastic – but it looks to me as if the moon were becoming oblate, flattening a little from top to bottom, widening from side to side. Maybe it's just eyestrain, but I'll swear the moon's becoming egg-shaped, with one end of the egg pointing at the new planet.'

'Yes,' Ann told him shrilly. 'And now I can see . . . oh, just

74

the teensiest line going from the top of the moon to the bottom.'

'Line?' the Little Man asked.

'Yes, like a crack,' Ann told him.

The Broken Egg and the Dire Hatching, the Ramrod thought. *It comes to pass as I foretold. Ispan-Serpent fecundates and the White Virgin gives birth.*

'I must confess I don't see that,' the Little Man said.

'You've got to look very close,' Ann told him.

'I'll take your word for it,' Wojtowicz said. 'Kid's got sharp eyes.'

Doc gasped excitedly, 'If there's a crack up there that any of us can see, it must be miles across.'

Hunter said slowly and heavily, pushing out the words, 'I think the moon is going into orbit around the new planet . . . and way inside Roche's limit.' He added swiftly, 'Rudy, do solid satellites break up like liquid ones inside Roche's limit?'

'I don't think anybody really knows,' Doc answered.

'They're going to find out,' the bearded man said.

Rama Joan said: 'And we're going to find out what ants feel like when someone steps on their nest.'

Wojtowicz said: 'The moon . . . breaking up?'

Margo clutched Paul. 'Don!' she cried. 'Oh my God, Paul, I'd forgotten Don!'

The Wanderer first appeared twenty-five thousand miles away from the moon, ten times closer to Luna than Earth is. Its deforming or tide-producing effects on the moon were therefore one thousand times greater than those the Earth exerts on Luna, since such effects vary inversely with the cube of the distance between bodies. (If they varied inversely only as the square, the massive sun would exert a tidal effect on Earth many times greater than the moon, instead of being outweighed tidewise by that small body eleven to five.)

When Luna went into orbit around the Wanderer at a distance of twenty-five hundred miles, she was a hundred times closer to that planet than she is to Earth. Accordingly, her whole body, crust and core, was being wrenched by a gravitational grip *one million times stronger.*

75

The Baba Yaga's spacescreen was swinging up towards Earth when the gentle bumping of his spacesuit against the walls of the cabin finally woke Don Merriam, just as he himself was rolling across the inside of the spacescreen. He woke clearheaded and ready for action, refreshed by the extra oxy. Two yanks and a wriggle got him into the pilot's seat. He strapped down.

White moon, jagged with crater walls and with something else, came into view, visibly swelling in size as the screen swung. Then came a vertical precipice of glittering raw rock stretching down, interminably it seemed, towards the moon's core. Then a narrow ribbon of black gulf, bisected along its jet length by a gleaming thread that was mostly violet but bright yellow towards one end. Then another glittering and interminable chasm wall shooting down sheer towards Luna's very centre.

His eyes told Don he was no more than fifteen miles above the moon's surface and hurtling towards it at about a mile a second. There was nowhere near enough time to break fall by swinging ship and main-jetting to cancel the mile-a-second downward velocity.

As those thoughts flashed, Don's fingers flicked the keys of the vernier jets, halting the Baba Yaga's slow tumbling so that the spacescreen – and Don – looked straight down the chasm.

There was one hope, based on nothing more than a matching of colours. There had been something violet and yellow glaring with tremendous brilliance behind the moon. Now there was a violet-and-yellow thread gleaming in the blackness of the moon's core. He might be looking through the moon.

The moon, split like a pebble? Planetary cores should flow, not fracture. But any other theory meant death.

The walls of fresh-riven rock rushed up at him. He was too close to the right-hand one. A baby solid-fuel rocket fired on that side set the Baba Yaga drifting away from it – and started a secondary tumbling which another ripple of the verniers neutralized almost before it manifested itself.

When he was a boy, Don Merriam had read *The Gods of Mars* by Edgar Rice Burroughs. In that romance of science fantasy, John Carter, greatest swordsman of two planets, had escaped with his comrades from the vast, volcanic, subterranean cavern-world of the Black Pirates of Barsoom and their hideous Issus-cult by racing a Martian flyer straight up the miles-long narrow shaft leading to the outer world, instead of rising slowly and cautiously by the buoyancy of the flyer's ray tanks. The latter had been the normal and only sane course, but John Carter had found salvation for himself and his companions in sheer blinding speed, steering vertically for a star visible at the top of the well-like shaft.

Perhaps the Gods of Mars were the arbiters of all Don Merriam's actions at this point. At any rate, he suddenly felt around him in the cabin of the Baba Yaga the ghostly presences, in their jewelled harness, of Xodar the Black renegade, Carthoris the mysterious Red Martian, Matai Shang the sinister Father of Holy Therns, and his brave, beautiful, love-struck infinitely treacherous daughter Phaidor. And it is a fact that as the plummeting Baba Yaga was engulfed between blurs of raw rock touched by sunlight for the first time in billions of years, and as Don fired the G-rich main jet and was pinned by it up against his seat, where he steered by the verniers and the solid-fuel rockets to keep the glitter of the rock walls equal and the violet-and-yellow thread splitting the black ribbon into equal halves, he cried out sharply in the empty cabin: 'Hold on for your lives! I am flying straight down the chasm!'

The saucer students felt sand give way to a stretch of adobe-hard earth sloping sharply up to the high mesh fence ringing the base of the plateau of Vandenberg Two. But here – seaward of the point where the blinking red light sat atop its mast a hundred feet behind the fence and two hundred feet, at least, above it – a broad gully cut through the ridge, gentling the slope. Tyre and caterpillar tracks ran up the gully. There was a big gate in the fence where it crossed the road, and beside the gate, built like it into the fence, a two-storey guard tower. The gate was closed and the tower was lightless, but the small door in the outside of the tower was open.

The sight cheered Paul considerably. He straightened his shoulders and his necktie. The little cortège halted fifty feet in front of the gate and he, Margo, and Doc walked forward, preceded by their inky, purple-and-yellow-edged shadows.

A brazen mechanical voice came out of the box over the door, saying, 'Stop where you are. You are about to trespass on restricted property of the United States Government. You may not pass this gate. Return the way you came. Thank you.'

'Oh, my sainted aunt!' Doc exploded. Since being relieved of cot-lugging by young Harry McHeath, he'd got his bounce back. 'Do you think we're an advance deputation of little green men?' he shouted at the box. 'Can't you see we're human beings?'

Paul touched Doc's arm and shook his head, but continued to advance. He called out in a mellow voice: 'I am Paul Hagbolt, 929-CW, JR, accredited PR captain-equivalent of Project Moon. I am asking admission for myself and eleven distressed persons known to me, and requesting transport for the latter.'

A soldier stepped from the darkness of the doorway out into the light of the Wanderer. There was no mistaking he was a soldier, for he had boots on his feet and a helmet on his head; a pistol, knife, and two grenades hung from his belt; his right arm cradled a submachine gun, and tightly harnessed to his back – Paul noted incredulously – were jump rockets.

The soldier was pokerfaced and he stood stiffly, but his right knee was jouncing up and down a little, rapidly and steadily, as if he were about to go into a stamping native dance or, more reasonably, as if he were trying to control a tic and not succeeding.

'CW *and* JR, eh?' he said to Paul, suspiciously but also respectfully: 'Let's see your ID cards . . . sir.'

There was a faint, acrid odour. Miaow, who had been remarkably calm since the landslide, lifted a little in Margo's arms, looked straight at the soldier, and hissed like a teakettle.

Handing the soldier the cards, which he had ready, Paul caught a sharp tremor.

As the soldier studied the cards, tipping them forward to catch the Wanderer's light, his face stayed expressionless, but Doc noticed that his eyes kept jumping away from the cards to the Wanderer.

Doc asked conversationally, 'Heard anything about *that*?'

The soldier looked Doc straight in the eye and barked: 'Yes, we know all about that and we're not intimidated! But we're not releasing any information, see?'

'Yes, I do,' Doc told him softly.

The soldier looked up from the cards. 'Very well, Mr Hagbolt, sir, I'll phone your request to the main gate.' He backed off towards the doorway.

'You're sure you've got it right?' Paul asked, repeating and amplifying it and mentioning the names of several officers.

'And Professor Morton Opperly,' Margo put in with strong emphasis.

Paul finished: 'And one of our people has had a heart attack. We'll want to bring her in the tower, where it's warmer. And we'd like some water.'

'No, you all stay outside,' the soldier said sharply, raising the muzzle of the submachine gun an inch as he continued to back away. 'Wait,' he called to Paul. 'You come here.' From the darkness inside the tower he handed Paul first a loose blanket, next a half-gallon bottle of water. 'But no paper cups!' he added, choking off what might have become a high-pitched laugh. 'Don't ask me for paper cups!' He drew back into the darkness, and there was the sound of dialling.

Paul returned with his booty, handing the blanket to the thin woman. The water was passed around. They drank from the bottle.

'I expect we'll have to wait a bit,' Paul whispered. 'I'm sure he's O.K., but he's pretty nervous. He looked all set to stand off the new planet singlehanded.'

Margo said: 'Miaow could smell how scared he was.'

'Well,' Doc philosophized softly, 'if I had been all alone when I first saw the thing, but with the hardware handy, I think I'd have switched the lights off and draped myself with the hardware and shook a bit myself. We met the new planet under just about the best circumstances, I'd say – peering around for saucers and talking about hyperspace and all.'

Ann said: 'I'd think if you were scared, Mr Brecht, you'd switch on all the lights you could.'

Doc said, 'My wicked idea, young lady, was that I'd be *so* terrified I wouldn't want something big, black, and hairy able to see where I was, to grab me.'

Ann laughed appreciatively.

The Little Man said to them all in a small, almost unfeeling, far-away voice: 'The moon is swinging behind the new planet. She's . . . going away.'

Eyes confirmed what the words had said. A chunk of the moon's rim was hidden by the purple-and-gold intruder.

Wojtowicz said: 'My God . . . my God.'

The thin woman began to sob shudderingly.

Rama Joan said: 'Give us courage.'

Margo's lips formed the word, 'Don,' and she shivered and hugged Miaow to her. Paul put his arm around her shoulders, but she moved away a little, head bowed.

Hunter said: 'The moon's in a very constricted orbit. There can't be more than three thousand miles between their surfaces.'

The Ramrod thought: *Her birth-pangs upon her, the White Virgin shelters in Ispan's robes.*

The Little Man made a cup of his hands and Rama Joan poured a drink for Ragnarok.

Colonel Mabel Wallingford said stridently: 'Spike, I've been talking with General Vandamme himself and he says that this *isn't* a problem. They've been letting us handle a lot of it because we were faster on the jump. Your orders have gone out approved-and-relayed.'

Spike Stevens, his eyes fixed on the twin screens showing the moon moving behind the Wanderer, bit off the end of a cigar and snarled: 'O.K., tell him to prove it.'

'Jimmy, warm up the inter-H.Q. screen,' Colonel Mabel ordered.

The General lit his cigar.

A third screen glowed on, showing a smiling, distinguished-looking gentleman with a bald head. The General whipped his cigar out of his mouth and stood up. Colonel Mabel felt a surge of hot joy, watching him play the guilty, dutiful schoolboy.

'Mr President,' Spike said.

'I'm not part of a simulated crisis, Spike,' the other responded, 'though it's hard to believe that's been bothering you, considering the masterly way your gang's been operating.'

'Not masterly at all, sir,' the General said. 'I'm afraid we've lost Moonbase. Not a word for over an hour.'

The face on the screen grew grave. 'We must be prepared for losses. I am now leaving Space H.Q. to meet the Coast Guard. My word to you is: Carry on! . . . for the duration of this . . .' You could sense him reaching for one of his famous polished phrases '. . . astronomical emergency.'

The screen faded.

Colonel Willard Griswold, his eyes on the astronomic screens, said: 'Moonbase? Hell, Spike, we've lost the moon.'

Chapter 12

Don Merriam had been fifteen minutes in the body of the moon, doing much of it at two miles a second, and now the violet-and-yellow thread, after widening to a ribbon, was staying the same width, which couldn't be good, but there was nothing to do but bullet towards it through the incredible flaw that split the moon along an almost perfect plane like a diamond tapped just right, and nothing to be but one great piloting eye, and suffer what thoughts to come that would, since he couldn't spare mind to control them.

After the first big shove, he fired the main jet in brief bursts, aiming the Baba Yaga with the verniers.

Don Merriam was making a trip through a planet's core. He had passed through its very centre, and so far the trip had been glitter and blur and blackness and a violet thread halving a spacescreen turned milky in patches. That and an aching throat and smarting eyes and the picture of himself as a glass bee with a Prince Rupert's Drop tail buzzing through a ripple in a stack of metal sheets miles long, or an enchanted prince sprinting down a poisoned corridor wide as his elbows – to brush a wall, what a *faux pas*!

Towards midpassage there had been soot-black streaks and a flash of green fire, but no guessing what made them.

The milkiness in the spacescreen, at any rate, should be

erosion from the fantastic thin-armed dust swirls that at one point had almost lost him the thread.

He had lost the aftward sunlight, too, sooner than he'd hoped, and had to aim the Baba Yaga solely by the fainter purple and golden wall-glimmers, and that was deceptive because the yellow was intrinsically brighter than the purple and tempted him to stay too far away from it.

But now the violet ribbon began to narrow and he knew it was the doom of him, worse than collision course, for there came unbidden to his mind a vision of the riven halves of the moon crashing together behind him, cutting off all sunlight, and then – in ponderous reaction and by the fierce mutual attraction of their masses moving – to crash together ahead of him, swinging through yards while he rocketed through miles, but swiftly enough to beat him to the impact point.

Then, just as he seemed almost to reach it, just as by his rough gauging he'd moon-traversed close to two thousand miles, the violet ribbon blacked out altogether.

And then, as incredible as if he'd found a life after death, he burst out of the blackness into light, with stars showing off to all sides and even old shock-headed Sol shooting his blinding white arrows.

Only then did he take in what lay straight ahead of him.

It was a great round, as big as Earth seen from a two-hour orbit. This vast, mounded disc was all radiantly violet and golden to the right, where Sol lay beyond, but to the left inky black save for three pale greenish oval glow-spots curving off the disc in the distance.

The unblurred night line between the radiant and the inky hemispheres was slowly drifting to the right as he watched, just as Sol was slowly drifting towards the violet horizon. He realized that back there in the moon he had lost sight of the violet ribbon, not because the jaws of the moon had clamped together, but simply because the night side of the planet ahead had moved over and looked down the chasm at him.

He at once accepted the fact that it was a massive planet and that the moon had gone into a tight orbit around it, because that alone, as far as he could reason, could explain the sights and happenings of the past three hours: the light deluging

Earth's night side, the highlight in the Atlantic, and above all the shattering of Luna.

And, beyond reason, there was that inside him – since he was out here and facing it – that cried out to believe it was a planet.

He swung ship, and there, only fifty miles below him, was the moon's vast disc, half inky black, half glaring white with sunlight. He could see where the chasm walls had truly crashed shut behind him by the line of dust-geysers rising gleaming into sunlit vacuum almost along the moon's night line, and by the surrealist, jagged-squared chessboard of lesser cracks marked by lesser geysers radiating outward from the crash line. Monstrous cross-hatching!

He was poised fifty miles – and receding – over what every moment looked more like a rock sea churning.

Then, because he didn't want to plunge – not yet, at least – at a mile a second into the glow-spotted black hemisphere now beneath his jets, he fired the main jet to kill that part of his velocity – at last checking the tank gauges and discovering that there was barely enough fuel and oxidizer for this manoeuver. It should put him into orbit around the strange planet – inside even the tight orbit of the moon.

He knew that the sun would soon sink from view and the metamorphosing moon be blackly eclipsed, as the Baba Yaga and Luna swung together into the shadow-cone – into the night – of a mystery.

Fritz Scher sat stiffly at his desk in the long room at the Tidal Institute at Hamburg, West Germany. He was listening with amusement tending towards exasperation to the demented morning news flash from across the Atlantic. He switched it off with a twist that almost fractured the knob and said to Hans Opfel: 'Those Americans! Their presence is needful to hold the Communist swines in check, but what an intellectual degradation to the Fatherland!'

He stood up from his desk and walked over to the sleekly streamlined, room-long tide-predicting machine. Inside the machine a wire ran through many movable precision pulleys, each pulley representing a factor influencing the tide at the point on Earth's hydrosphere for which the machine was set; at the end of the wire a pen drew on a graph-papered drum a curve giving the exact tides at that point, hour by hour.

At Delft they had a machine that did it all electronically but those were the feckless Hollanders!

Fritz Scher said dramatically: 'The moon in orbit around a planet from nowhere? Hah!' He tapped the shell of the machine beside him significantly. 'Here we have the moon nailed down!'

The *Machan Lumpur*, her rusty prow aimed a little south of the sun sinking over North Vietnam, crossed the bar guarding the tiny inlet south of Do-Son. Bagong Bung noted, by a familiar configuration of mangrove roots and by an old grey piling that was practically a member of his family, that the high tide was perhaps a hand's breadth higher than he'd ever encountered it here. A good omen! Tiny ripples shivered across the inlet mysteriously. A sea hawk screamed.

Richard Hillary watched the sunbeams slowly straighten up as the big air-suspended bus whipped smoothly on towards London. Bath was far behind and they were passing Silbury Hill.

He listened idly to the solemn speculations around him about the nonsensical news items that had been coming over the wireless concerning a flying saucer big as a planet sighted by thousands over the United States. Really, science fiction was corrupting people everywhere.

A coarsely attractive girl from Devizes in slacks, snood, and a sweater, who had transferred aboard at Beckhampton, now dropped into the seat ahead of him and instantly fell into small talk with the woman beside her. She was expatiating, with exactly equal enthusiasm, on the saucer reports – and the little earthquake that had nervously twitched parts of Scotland – and on the egg she'd had for breakfast and the sausage-and-mash she was going to have for lunch. In honour of Edward Lear, Richard offhandedly shaped a limerick about her:

There was a Young Girl of Devizes
Whose thoughts came in two standard sizes:
  While most fitted a spoon,
  Some were big as the moon;
That spacestruck Young Girl of Devizes.

Thinking of it kept him amused all the way to Savernake Forest, where he fell into a doze.

Chapter 13

Times Square at five a.m. was still as packed as it had been on the nights of the moon landing and of the False War With Russia. Traffic had long stopped. The streets were full of people. The Wanderer, now masking half the moon, was still visible down the crosstown streets, including 42nd, but low in the sky, its yellow mellower and its purple turning red.

The advertisements were a bit brighter by contrast, especially the new sixty-foot genie bafflingly juggling the three oranges big as bushel baskets.

But the streets were no longer still. While some people just stood there and stared west, the majority were rhythmically swaying: not a few had joined hands and were snaking about with a compulsive stamp, while here and there young couples danced savagely. And most of them were humming or singing or shouting a song that had several versions, but the newest of these was being sung at the source, where Sally Harris still danced, though now she had acquired a supporting team of half a dozen sharp, aggressive young men besides Jake Lesher. And the song as she sang it now, her contralto more vibrant for its hoarseness, went:

> Strange orb! . . . in the western sky . . .
> Strange light! . . . streaming from on high . . .
>   It's a terrifying sight
>   But we're gonna live tonight,
> Live with a neo-bop beat!

Golden! . . . like treasure ships . . .
Crimson! . . . as sinful lips . . .
  But there'll be no more June
  'Cause there ain't no more moon
      Just a
Planet! . . . on Forty-second Street!

All of a sudden the singing and dancing stopped everywhere at once – because the dance floor had begun to tremble. There was a brief shaking. A few tiles, not many, and other trifles of masonry fell, cracking sharply against the sidewalks. There were screams – not many of those, either. But when the little earthquake was over, it could be seen that the sixty-foot genie had lost his three oranges, though he still kept going through the motions of juggling.

Arab Jones and his weed-brothers walked rapidly, three abreast, along 125th Street away from Lenox, in the direction all the other dark faces were peering: west, where the Wanderer was setting, a great gaudy poker chip – bloated purple *X* on orange field – that almost covered the pale gold-piece of the moon. Soon the heavenly pair would be hidden by the General Grant Houses, which emphasized with their tall, remote bulking the small-town look of Harlem, the two- and three-storey shop-fronted buildings lining 125th.

The three weed-brothers were so loaded that their excitement had only been heightened by the quake, which had brought out on to the street most of those who weren't already watching the Wanderer.

The east was rosy, where the sun, pausing in the horizon wings for his entrance, had washed out all the stars and brought the morning twilight to Manhattan. But no one looked that way, or gave any sign that it might be time to be off and doing or trying to get some sleep. The spires of lower Manhattan were an unwatched fairy-tale city of castles to the south.

Arab and Pepe and High had long since quit trying to push through the staring, mostly silent crowd on the sidewalks and had taken to the street, where no cars moved and fewer people clustered and where the going was easier. It seemed to Pepe that a power came out of the planet ahead, freezing all motors and most people like some combined paralysis-and-motor-stalling ray out of the comic books. He crossed himself.

High Bundy whispered: 'Old moon *really* going into her this time. He circle in front of her, decide he like her, then *whoosh!*'

Arab said, 'Maybe he hiding 'cause he scared. Like we.'

'Scared of what?' asked High.

'The end of the world,' said Pepe Martinez, his voice rising in a soft, high wolf-wail.

Only the rim of the Wanderer showed above the General Grant buildings, which were mounting swiftly up the sky as the weed-brothers approached them.

'Come on!' Arab said suddenly, catching hold of the upper arms of Pepe and High and digging his fingers in. 'World gonna end, I gettin' off. Get away from all these owly-eyed deaders waitin' for the tromp and the trump. One planet go smash, we take another. Come on, before she get away! – We catch her at the river and climb aboard!'

The three began to run.

Paul and Margo and their new friends were sitting on the sand fifty feet in front of the dark gate when the second quake jolted the beach. It did nothing beyond rocking them, and there was nothing they could do about it, so they just gasped and rocked there. The soldier ran out of the tower with his submachine gun, stopped, and after a minute backed inside again. He did not answer when Doc called cheerily: 'Hey, wasn't that a sock-dolager!'

Five minutes later Ann was saying: 'Mummy, I'm really getting hungry now.'

'So am I,' said young Harry McHeath.

The Little Man, diligently soothing a very upset Ragnarok, said: 'Now, that's a funny thing. We were going to serve coffee and sandwiches after the eclipse. The coffee was in four big thermos jugs – I know, because I brought it. It's all still down at the beach.'

Wanda sat up on her cot, despite the thin woman's protests.

'What's all that red glow down the coast?' she demanded crossly.

Hunter started to tell her, not without a touch of sarcasm, that it was merely the light of the new planet, when he saw that there really was another light-source – an ugly red furnace-flaring which the other light had masked.

'Could be brush fires,' Wojtowicz suggested sombrely.

The thin woman said: 'Oh dear, that would have to happen now. As if we didn't have enough trouble.'

Hunter pressed his lips together. He refused to say: 'Or it could be Los Angeles burning.'

The Little Man recalled their attention to the heavens, where the purple-and-yellow intruder now hid the moon completely. He said, 'We ought to have a name for the new planet. You know, it's funny, one minute it's the most important thing in creation to me, but the next minute, it's just a patch of sky I can cover with my outstretched hand.'

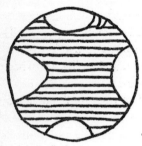

Three Hours

'What's the word "planet" really mean, Mr Brecht?' Ann asked.

' "Wanderer", dear,' Rama Joan told her.

The Ramrod thought: *Ispan is known to man by a thousand names, yet is still Ispan.*

Harry McHeath, who'd just discovered Norse mythology and the Eddas, thought: *Moon-Eater would be a good name – but too menacing for most people today.*

Margo thought: *They could call it Don*, and she bit her lip and hugged Miaow so that the cat protested, and tears lumped hotly under her lower eyelids.

'Wanderer is the right name for it,' the Little Man said.

The yellow marking that was the Broken Egg to the Ramrod and the Needle-Eye to Ann now touched the left-hand rim of

88

the Wanderer as they viewed it. The yellow polar patches remained and a new central yellow spot was crawling into view on the right-hand rim. In all, four yellow rim-spots: north, south, east, and west.

The Little Man got out his notebook and began to sketch it.

'The purple makes a big X,' Wojtowicz said.

'The tilted cross,' the Ramrod said, speaking aloud at last. 'The notched disc. The circle split in four.'

'It's a mandala,' said Rama Joan.

'Oh yeah,' Wojtowicz said. 'Professor, you was telling us about those,' he addressed himself to Hunter. 'Symbols of psychic something-or-other.'

'Psychic unity,' the bearded man said.

'Psychic unity,' Wojtowicz repeated. 'That's good,' he said matter-of-factly. 'We're going to need it.'

'For these we are grateful,' Rama Joan murmured.

Two big yellow eyes peered over the hump of the big gully in Vandenberg Two. There was a growling roar. Then the jeep was careening down towards the gate, its headlights swinging wildly over brush and rutted dry earth.

'Everybody on your feet,' Paul said. 'Now we'll get some action.'

Don Merriam could see a thick-waisted, asymmetric hourglass of stars in the spacescreen of the Baba Yaga. Some of the stars were slightly blurred by the dust-blasting the screen had suffered during his trip through the centre of the moon.

The black bulk shouldering into the hourglass from port was the moon, now totally eclipsed by the vast, newly appeared body.

The Wanderer, shouldering into the starry hourglass from starboard, was not entirely black – Don had in view seven pale green glow spots, each looking about three hundred miles across, the farther ones being ellipses, the nearest, almost circular. They were featureless, though at times there was the suggestion of a phosphorescent pit or funnel. Of what they signified, Don had no more idea than if they had been pale green spots on the black underbelly of a spider.

In company with the moon, the Baba Yaga was orbiting the Wanderer, but slowly gaining on Luna because the little ship, nearer the Wanderer, had the faster orbit.

He warmed the radar. The return signal from the moon showed a surface more irregular than craters and mountains alone could account for, and even in five minutes the patterns had greatly changed: the tidal shattering of Luna was continuing.

The surprisingly strong signal from the intruding planet showed a spherical, matte surface with no indication at all of the greenish glow spots – as if the Wanderer were smooth as an ivory ball.

Intruding planet! – impossible, but there it was. At the top of his mind Don tried to recall the scraps of speculation he'd read and heard about hyperspace: the notion that a body might be able to travel from *there* to *here* without traversing the known continuum between, perhaps by blasting or slipping into some higher-dimensioned continuum of which our universe is only a surface. But where in all the immensity of stars and galaxies might the *there* of this intruding planet be? Why should the *there* even be anywhere in our universe? A higher-dimensioned continuum would have an infinity of three-dimensional surfaces, each one a cosmos.

At the bottom of Don's mind there was only an uneasy voice repeating: 'The earth and sun *are* on the other side of that green-spotted black round to starboard. They set ten minutes ago; they'll rise in twenty. *I* have not travelled through hyperspace, only through the moon. I am *not* in the intergalactic dark, staring at a galaxy shaped like a sheaf or an hourglass, while seven pale green nebulas glow to starboard. . . .'

Don was still in his spacesuit, but now he removed and secured the cracked helmet. There should be a sound one in the locker. 'Make and mend,' he muttered, but his throat closed at the sound of his own voice. He unstrapped himself from the pilot's seat to push as close as he could to the spacescreen. The cabin was chilly and dark, but he turned on neither heat nor light – he even dimmed the control panel. It seemed all-important to *see* as much as possible.

He was gaining on the moon, all right, with his inside orbit; the sheaf of stars ahead was very slowly widening to port, as the black bulk of the eclipsed moon dropped back.

Suddenly he thought he saw, against the star-studded glow of the Milky Way, wraithlike black threads joining the top of the Wanderer – call it its north pole – to the leading rim or nose of the moon. Looping through space, the black strands were so nearly imperceptible that, like faint stars, he could detect them best by looking a little away from them.

It was as if, having snared and maimed the moon, the Wanderer were spinning a black shroud around it, preparatory to sucking it dry.

He shouldn't have started to think about spiders.

The voice kept repeating: 'The sun and Earth *are* beyond the green-spotted black bulge to starboard. I *am* Donald Barnard Merriam, Lieutenant, U.S. Space Force. . . .'

Barbara Katz, her back to the other ocean bordering America three thousand miles east of the saucer students, saw the mandala as a purple-spoked oxcart wheel. The huge wheel seemed to revolve a quarter turn as the planet touched the horizon.

'Gee, Dad, it's as if the Wanderer were lying down,' she said, all at once feeling agonized and desperate because she wouldn't be able to see the next face the Wanderer showed, or to see the moon come out from behind it, either. But it would all be on TV. Or would it? *Will there still be TV?* she asked herself, looking around incredulously. Everywhere the sky was paling with the dawn that would not reach the Pacific Coast for another three hours.

From beside Barbara, Knolls Kettering III said in a groggy voice she hadn't heard before: 'I'm very tired. . . . Please . . .'

She grabbed his arm as he swayed and leaned most of his weight on her – which wasn't a great deal. Inside the white suit his body seemed like the curved, brownish husk of an insect, while his face was as hollow-cheeked and criss-crossed with wrinkles as an Indian great-grandmother's. Barbara was almost shocked, but then she reminded herself that he was her own private millionaire, to preserve and to cherish. She made her

91

grip more delicate on his shoulder, as if it were a shell she might crush.

The older Negro woman, dressed like the younger, in pearl grey with white collar and cuffs, came fussing up and took hold of him on the other side. This seemed to irritate him awake.

'Hester,' he said, leaning away from her towards Barbara. 'I told you and Benjy and Helen to go to bed hours ago.'

'Huh!' she laughed softly. 'As if we would leave you playing around with that telescope in the dark! You watch how you put your weight now, Mister K. Plastic in your hip get tired working all night, it break easy.'

'Plastic can't get tired, Hester,' he argued wearily.

'Huh! It not anywhere as strong as you, Mister K!' she said, putting him off. She looked across him questioningly at Barbara, who nodded firmly. Together they walked him across the thick, weedless carpet of the lawn, up three spotless concrete steps, and through a big cool kitchen with old, nickel-heavy fixtures that seemed to Barbara huge enough for a hotel.

Half-way up a wide stairway, he made them stop. Perhaps the vast, cool, dark living room next to the stairs took him back into the night, for he said: 'Miss Katz, every heavenly body that seems to stand erect when it's high in the sky, appears to lie down when it rises and sets. It's true of constellations, too. I've often thought –'

'Come on now, Mister K, you need your rest,' Hester said, but he fretfully shook the arm she was holding and said insistently: 'I have often thought that the answer to the Sphinx's question of what goes on four legs in the morning, two legs at midday, and three legs at evening was not Man but the constellation Orion walking just ahead of the Dog Star, whose rising signalled the flooding of the Nile.'

His voice wavered on the last words, and his head drooped, and he permitted himself to be led upward again. Barbara, feeling his weight on her arm – more than he was putting on Hester, she was pleased to note – thought: *I guess I can see why you're thinking of three legs at evening, Dad – or four.*

They laid him down on a big bed in a dark bedroom bigger than the kitchen. Hester whisked something from the pillow into a drawer, then changed her mind and let Barbara see it.

It was a slim, black-haired fashion doll about ten inches high, dressed in black lace underwear and black stockings and long black gloves.

Knolls Kettering III muttered thickly: 'For midday, read midnight.'

Hester looked up from the doll to Barbara's long black footgloves and playsuit and black hair, and she grinned.

Barbara couldn't have stopped herself from grinning back, even if she'd wanted to.

Chapter 14

Paul Hagbolt faced Major Buford Humphreys through the beach gate of Vandenberg Two. Margo stood beside him holding Miaow. The ten saucer students were crowded around them. The edges of all their shadows made purple and golden flecks on the silvery mesh of the gate.

There were gold and purple flecks in the Pacific behind them as well, where the Wanderer, still rather high in the sky, had begun a coasting descent towards the placid ocean. It still showed the face Rama Joan had called the mandala, though now the western yellow spot was growing and the eastern one shrinking as the orb rotated. It cast a strong twilight across the scrubby coastal landscape and turned the sky a slate grey through which only five or six stars showed.

The jeep that had brought Major Humphreys down the gully from the heights still growled behind him and stared with its unnecessary headlights. One of the two soldiers with him sat at the wheel, the other stood at his side. The heavily-armed soldier on guard at the gate stood outside the fence in the dark doorway of the guard tower. His eyes were on the major. His submachine gun was in shadow except for the purple ring showing on the muzzle.

Major Humphreys had the thoughtful eyes and downturned mouth of a schoolteacher, but right now his dominant expression was the same as that of the soldier on guard – tension masking dread.

Paul, his soft, handsome face firmed a bit by the responsibility he felt, said: 'I was hoping it would be you, Major. This saves a lot of trouble.'

'You're lucky, because I didn't come on your account,' Major Humphreys retorted sharply, then added in a rush: 'A few others of the L.A. section made it before the Coast Highway went. We're hoping the rest will arrive by the Valley – over Monica Mountainway or through Oxnard. Or we'll lift them out by 'copter – especially Cal. Tech. Pasadena really got it in the second quake.' He checked himself with a frown and a head-shake, as if irritated at having impulsively said that much. Then he continued loudly, speaking over the flurry of exclamations from the saucerites. 'Well, Paul, I haven't got all night – in fact, I haven't got a minute. Why'd you come by the beach gate? I recognize Miss Gelhorn, of course –' he nodded curtly towards Margo – 'but who are the others?' His gaze flickered across the saucer students, pausing doubtfully at Ross Hunter's full brown beard.

Paul hesitated.

Doc, looking like a long-faced, modern-day Socrates with his hairless dome and thick glasses, cleared his throat and prepared to risk all by rumbling: 'We are clerical members of Mr Hagbolt's section.' He suspected that this was one of those moments when a large white bluff is essential.

But Doc had hesitated a fractional second too long. The Little Man, pushing to the front between him and Wojtowicz, fixed the major with a benign stare. A confident smile nestled under his brush moustache as he said with lawyer-like glibness: 'I am secretary and we are all members in good standing of the Southern California Meteor and UFO Students. We were hold-ing an eclipse symposium at the Rodgers beach house, having signed permission from the Rodgers estate and – although it was not strictly needed – approval from your own headquarters.'

Doc groaned, fringe-audibly.

Major Humphreys froze. 'Flying saucer bugs?'

'That's right,' the Little Man retorted sweetly. 'But please – not bugs – students.' His left arm was jerked back and he rocked on to his heels as Ragnarok, in a flurry of uneasy efface-ment, tugged at the leash.

'Students,' Major Humphreys echoed doubtfully, looking them up and down, almost, Paul thought, as if he were going to demand to see their college registration cards.

Paul said earnestly: 'Their cars were buried in a landslide along with mine, Major. Miss Gelhorn and I would hardly have got here without their help. There's nowhere for them to go now. One of them has had a heart attack and one is a child.'

Major Humphreys' gaze hesitated at Rama Joan, who was standing behind Hunter. She stepped forward around him and showed all of herself – her shoulder-length, red-gold hair and her white-tie evening clothes – then smiled gravely and made a little bow. Ann, with her matching red-gold braids, came forward beside her. They looked as strangely beautiful and as insultingly perverse as an Audrey Beardsley illustration for *The Yellow Book*.

'I'm the child,' Ann explained coolly.

'I see,' Major Humphreys said, nodding rapidly as he turned away. 'Look, Paul,' he said hurriedly. 'I'm sorry about this, but Vandenberg Two can't possibly take in quake refugees. That question's already been explored and decided. We have our own vital work, and an emergency only tightens security regulations.'

'Hey,' Wojtowicz broke in. 'You're saying the quakes were really big in L.A. County?'

'You can see the fires, can't you?' Major Humphreys snapped at him. 'No, I can't answer questions. Come in through the tower, Paul. And Miss Gelhorn – by herself.'

'But these people aren't ordinary refugees, Major,' Paul protested. 'They'll be helpful. They've already made some interesting deductions about the Wanderer.'

As soon as he spoke that last word, the gold-and-purple orb, momentarily out of mind, was once again dominating their thoughts.

Major Humphreys' fingers gripped through the mesh as he drew his face close to Paul's. In a voice in which suspicion, curiosity, and fear were oddly mixed, he demanded: 'Wanderer? Where did you get that name? What do you know about the . . . body?'

'Body?' Doc cut in exasperatedly. 'Any fool can see by now it's a planet. Currently the moon's orbiting behind it.'

'We're not responsible for it, if that's what you're thinking,' Rama chimed in lightly. 'We didn't conjure it up there.'

'Yes, and we don't know where the body was buried beforehand, either,' Doc added zestfully. 'Though some of us have notions about a cemetery in hyperspace.'

Hunter kicked him surreptitiously. ' "Wanderer" is simply a name we gave it because it means "planet",' he interposed soothingly to the major.

'Wanderer will do well enough, though the true name be Ispan.' The Ramrod's voice boomed out hollowly from where his angular face, eyesockets and cheeks deep-shadowed, rose over Beardy's shoulder. He added: 'Belike the imperial sages have but now touched down in Washington.'

Major Humphreys' shoulders contracted as if he'd been stung between them. He said curtly: 'I see.' Then, to Paul: 'Come on through. And Miss Gelhorn – without that cat.'

'You mean you're turning these people away?' Paul demanded. 'After I vouch for them? And one of them deathly ill?'

'Professor Opperly will have something to say about your behaviour, Major, I'm sure,' Margo put in sharply.

'Where is the heart case?' Major Humphreys demanded, his knee starting to jump as the guard's had.

Paul looked around for the cot, but just then Wanda pushed her considerable bulk forward between Hunter and Rama Joan. 'I'm she,' she announced importantly.

Doc groaned again. Wojtowicz looked at the fat woman reproachfully, rubbing the shoulder that had taken the strain on the cot corner.

Major Humphreys snorted. 'Come on – the two of you, alone,' he said to Paul, and turned back towards the jeep.

Hunter muttered to Margo: 'Better take him up on it before he changes his mind. It's the best thing for you and Paul.'

'Without Miaow?' Margo said.

'We'll take care of her for you,' Ann volunteered.

That last did something to Paul's churning uncertainties. It might be the sheerest sentimentality to let the last straws of a cat and a child's unthinking generosity weigh down the balance. But: 'I'm not coming!' he heard himself shout.

In a voice that tried not to be waspish, Major Humphreys called back: 'Don't be melodramatic, Paul. You haven't the choice. You can't desert the Project.'

Margo's free arm went around Paul and tightened encouragingly. Doc muttered in his ear: 'I hope you know what you're doing.'

Paul shouted: 'The hell I can't!'

Major Humphreys shrugged and got into the jeep. The guard shut the tower door behind him and moved out towards the twelve standing in front of the gate. 'Get moving, you people,' he said edgily, wagging the muzzle of his gun. A heavy wire looped behind him from his left hand – the controls of his jump rockets.

Except for the Little Man, everyone stepped back from the gun – even Ragnarok, for the Little Man had dropped the leash as he stared through the fence in scandalized amazement.

'Major!' the Little Man called. 'Your conduct is outrageous and inhumane, and I'll see to it that my opinion goes on record! I'll have you know that I'm a taxpayer, sir. My money supports installations like Vandenberg Two and pays the salaries of public servants like yourself whether they're in uniform or not, and no matter how much brass there is on that uniform! You will please reconsider –'

The guard moved towards him. It was clear he wanted this whole problem out of sight before he was alone again. He grated: 'Shut up, you, and get moving!' And he lightly prodded the Little Man in the side with the muzzle of his gun.

With a growl like clockwork going out of control, Ragnarok shot from behind the group, leash flirting behind him, and launched himself at the guard's throat.

The guard's jump rockets blossomed – as if he had grown a second pair of legs, bright orange – and he lifted into the air, up and back. As he did so, he gave a remarkable demonstration of accurate shooting on the rise, sending four slugs crashing into his attacker. The big German police dog flattened and never moved again.

The group started to run, then stopped.

The guard sailed over the fence and dropped inside, his rockets blossoming briefly to cushion his landing.

The Little Man dropped to his knees beside the body of his dog. 'Ragnarok?' He paused, uncertain. Then, 'Why, he's dead,' and his voice was full of bewilderment.

Wojtowicz picked up the aluminium cot and ran forward with it.

'It's too late for anything,' the Little Man murmured.

'You can't leave him here,' said Wojtowicz.

They heaved the dead dog on to the cot. The Wanderer was more than bright enough to show the colour of blood.

Margo gave Miaow to Paul and took off her jacket and laid it over Ragnarok. The Little Man nodded to her dumbly.

Then the little cortège moved off the way it had come, through the twilight that was flecked with purple and gold.

Young Harry McHeath pointed up over the sea. 'Look,' he said. "There's a white sliver. The moon's coming out from behind the Wanderer.'

Donald Merriam shivered as he saw the faint black threads joining the nose of the moon to the top of the Wanderer turn bone white – making them suddenly easy to see and more suggestive than ever of a spiderweb.

Then the nose of the moon turned almost glaringly bone white, too: a tiny white crescent that swiftly lengthened and widened. The white threads came out of the white moon-nose and then looped up.

A profoundly disturbing thing about the crescent: as it grew, it seemed to become too convex, as though the moon were tending towards the shape of a football. And this too-convex leading rim wasn't smooth against black, star-specked space, but just a bit jagged. The boundary between black moon and crescent was a bit jagged, too. Also, there were sharp cracks in the surface of the crescent, as if it were a moon in a Byzantine mosaic.

Suddenly a white glare erupted dazzlingly from starboard into the nose of the Baba Yaga. Reflection from the port rim of the spacescreen almost blinded Don.

He shut his eyes and groped on the rack for a pair of polarizing goggles, put them on, and set them to max. Then, with a double puff of the vernier rockets, he swung the ship a shade to starboard.

There, just risen from behind the Wanderer, was the blazing round of Sol next to the dark circle of Earth – a whitehot dime beside a sooty dollar. Like the moon and the threads, the Baba Yaga had completed its first passage behind the Wanderer and emerged into sunlight again.

Don adjusted the goggle visors to block off the sun, then cut the polarization until he could see Earth's night side by Wanderer-light. The eastern third of North America had slipped around the right-hand rim into day. All of South America was gone. The rest of the globe was Pacific Ocean, except where New Zealand had started to show on the lower left-hand rim – it would be nightfall there.

Don was startled at how much it warmed his heart to see Earth again – not lost on the other side of the cosmos, but a mere quarter of a million miles away!

New Zealanders and Polynesians ran out from their supper-tables and supper-mats to stare at the prodigy rising with the evening. Many of them assumed the Wanderer must be the moon, monstrously disfigured – most likely by American or Soviet atomic experiments gone out of control – the purple and the gold the aura of a moon-wide atomic blast – and they were hours being argued out of this conviction. But most of the inhabitants of Australia, Asia, Europe, and Africa were still going about their daytime business blissfully unaware of the Wanderer, except as a wild, newspaper-reported Yankee phenomenon, to be classified with senators, movie stars, religious fundamentalism, and Coca-Cola. The shrewder souls thought: *Publicity for a new horror film, or – aha – pretext for new demands on China and Russia.* No connexion was seen – except by a few supersubtle psychologists – between the crazy news stories about the moon and the real enough reports of earthquake disasters.

The Atlantic Ocean was also on Earth's day side now, but there it was a different story, since most of the craft plying its shipping lanes and airways had observed the Wanderer during the last hours of the night. These furiously searched the static-disturbed wavebands for news and tried to get off reports and requests for advice to owners and maritime authorities. A few headed for the nearest ports. Others, with a remarkably know-ledgeable prudence, turned towards the open sea.

The *Prince Charles* suffered a drastic transition. A group of fascist Brazilian insurgents, with the help of two officers of Portuguese extraction, seized control of the great luxury liner. Captain Sithwise became a prisoner in his own cabin. The plans of the insurgents had been brilliantly conceived, but would probably never have been successful except for the excitement attendant on the 'astronomical emergency'. With a feeling almost of awe they realized that, at the expense of six men shot and three of their number wounded, they had gained control not only of a ship big as a resort hotel, but of two atomic reactors.

Wolf Loner breakfasted comfortably and went about his small morning chores as the *Endurance* wested steadily beneath the overcast. His thoughts occupied themselves with the great regularities of nature, masked by modern life.

Don Guillermo Walker sped in the Araizas' launch out of Lake Nicaragua into the San Juan River, past the town of San Carlos, as dawn reddened the jungle. Now that the Wanderer was out of the sky, Don Guillermo was less inclined to think about it and about the volcanoes and earthquakes, and more inclined to dwell on his successful bombing of *el presidente*'s stronghold in the tiny plane that now rested in the bottom of the lake. *Sic semper all leftists! At last he had really graduated from the namby-pamby John Birch Society!* . . . or at least that was how Don Guillermo thought of it.

He struck his chest and cried: '*Yo soy un hombre!*' One of the Araiza brothers, squinting against the rising sun, nodded and said: '*Si,*' but rather unenthusiastically, as if being a man were not quite that grand a matter.

Chapter 15

Paul Hagbolt had to admit to himself that walking through sand does get tiring, even when you're with new friends and under a sky bright with a new planet. The exhilaration of defying Colonel Humphreys and the Moon Project had worn off very quickly, and this backbreaking trudge across the beach seemed peculiarly purposeless and depressing.

'It gets lonely, doesn't it?' Rama Joan said softly, 'when you cut yourself off from the big protector and throw in your lot – and your girl friend's – with a bunch of nuts, just to attend a dog's funeral.'

They were walking at the tail end of the procession, well behind the cot borne between Clarence Dodd and Wojtowicz.

Paul had to chuckle. 'You're frank about it,' he said. 'Margo's not my girl friend, though – I mean the feeling's all on my side. We're really just friends.'

Rama Joan looked at him shrewdly. 'So? A man can waste his life on friendship, Paul.'

Paul nodded unhappily. 'Margo's told me that herself,' he said. 'She claims I get my satisfaction out of mother-henning her around and trying to keep other men away from her. Except for Don, of course – and she thinks my interest in him is more than brotherly, even if I don't know it.'

Rama Joan shrugged. 'Could be, I suppose. The set-up of you and Margo and Don does seem unnatural.'

'No, it's perfectly natural in its way,' he assured her with a kind of gloomy satisfaction. 'The three of us went to high school and college together. We were interested in science and things. We meshed. Then Don went on to become an engineer and a spaceman, while I took the turn into journalism and PR work, and Margo into art. But we were determined to stick together, so when Don got into the Moon Project, we managed to, too, or at least I did. By that time Margo had decided she liked him a little better than she did me – or loved him, whatever that means – and they got engaged. So that was settled – maybe simply because our society frowns on triangular living arrangements. Then Don went to the moon. We stayed on Earth. That's all there is to it, until this evening, when I seem to have thrown in with you people.'

'Maybe because you had an explosion overdue. Well, I can tell you why I'm here,' the red-blonde woman continued. 'I could be safe in Manhattan, an advertising executive's wife: Ann going to a fancy school, myself fitting in an occasional lecture on mysticism to a women's club. Instead, I'm divorced, eking out a tiny inherited income with lecture fees, and dressing up the mysticism with all sorts of carnival hokum.' She indicated her white tie and tails with a disparaging laugh. ' "Masculine protest", my friends said. "No, just human protest", I told them. I wanted to be able to say things I really meant and say them to the hilt – things that were mine alone. I wanted Ann to have a real mother, not just a well-dressed statistic.'

'But do you really mean the things you say?' Paul asked. 'Buddhism, I gather – that sort of thing?'

'I don't believe them as much as I'd like to, but I do believe them as much as I can,' she told him. 'Certainty's a luxury. If you say things with gusto and colour, at least you're an individual. And even if you fake it a bit, it's still you, and if you keep trying you may some day come out with a bit of the truth – like Charlie Fulby did, when he told us he knew about his wild planets not by flying-saucer trips, as he'd always claimed, but by pure intuition.'

'He's paranoid,' Paul muttered, gazing ahead at the Ramrod where he marched behind the cot, with Wanda to his right and the thin woman to his left. 'Are those two women his disciples, or patrons, or what?'

'I'm sure he is somewhat paranoid,' Rama Joan said, 'but you surely don't believe, do you, Paul, that sane people have a monopoly of the truth? No, I think they're his wives – he grew up in a complex-marriage sect. Oh, Paul, you do find us alarming, don't you?'

'Not really,' he protested. 'Though there's something reassuring about moving with the majority.'

'And with the money and the power,' Rama Joan agreed. 'Well, cheer up – the majority and the nuts spend most of their time the same way: satisfying basic needs. We're all going back to the pavilion on the beach simply because we think there'll be coffee and sandwiches.'

At the head of the procession, Hunter was telling Margo Gelhorn very much the same sort of thing. 'I started going to flying-saucer meetings as a sociological project,' he confessed to her. 'I went to all kinds: the way-out contactees like Charlie Fulby, the sober-minded ones, and the in-betweeners and free-wheelers, like this group. I wanted to analyse a social syndrome and write a few papers on it. But after a while I had to admit I was keeping on going because I was hooked.'

'Why, Professor Hunter?' Margo asked, hugging Miaow to her. She was cold without her jacket, and the cat was like a hot water bottle. 'Does saucering make you feel bohemian and different, like wearing a beard?'

'Call me Ross. No, I don't think so, though I suppose vanity plays a part.' He touched his beard. 'No, it was simply because I'd found people who had something to follow and be excited about, something to be disinterestedly interested in – and that's not so common any more in our money-and-sales-and-status culture, our don't-give-yourself-away yet sell-yourself-to-every-body society. It got so I wanted to make a contribution of my own – the lecturing and panel bits. Now I do almost as much saucering as Doc, who knocks himself out selling pianos – he's a whiz at that – so he can divide the rest of his time between saucering, chess, and living it up.'

'But Doc's a bachelor, while I believe you implied you had a family . . . Ross?' Margo pointed out with faint malice.

'Oh yes,' Hunter conceded a bit wearily. 'Up in Portland there's a Mrs Hunter and two boys who think Daddy spends altogether too much time consorting with saucer bugs, consider-ing the few papers he's got out of it and the nothing it's done for his academic reputation.'

He was thinking of adding: 'And, right now, they're sitting up asking why Daddy wasn't home the night the heavens changed and saucers came true' – but just then he realized they'd reached the boarded-up beach house and the old dance floor. There was the green lantern, he saw, still burning, and beside it a chair with a little stack of unused programmes, and there were the empty chairs sitting in rows, though with the first rows much disarranged (when would Doddsy ever reclaim the deposit they'd made on them at the Polish funeral parlour in Oxnard?) – and there was a coat someone had forgotten laid over one of the chairs, and there was the panellists' long table and under it some cardboard boxes they'd left in their hurry. And thrust deep into the sand near by there was even the big furled umbrella Doc had used as part of a crude astrolabe when first checking the movement of the Wanderer.

As Ross Hunter saw these things standing out against the purple-gold-speckled, spectrally calm Pacific, he felt a great, unexpected surge of affection and nostalgia and relief, and he suddenly realized why, after being rebuffed by a landslide and a steel mesh fence and a red-tape major, they had trudged back to this spot.

It was simply that it was home to them, the spot where they'd been together in security and where they'd witnessed the change in the heavens, and that each of them knew in his heart that this might be the last home any of them would ever have.

Without haste Wanda and the thin woman and young Harry McHeath made for the boxes under the table.

Wojtowicz and the Little Man set down the cot with Ragnarok on it, half shrouded by Margo's jacket.

Wojtowicz looked around, then pointed at the umbrella and said in a firm voice: 'I somehow think that would be the right spot – that is, if you wouldn't mind?' he added to Doc, who'd walked silently all the way from Vandenberg Two beside the Little Man.

'No, I'd be proud,' Doc answered gruffly.

They lugged the cot up, and Doc recovered his umbrella. Then Wojtowicz took a flat-bladed spade from under the edge of the mattress on the cot and began to dig.

The fat woman noticed and called down from the platform: 'No wonder I felt something sticking in my side all the way.'

Wojtowicz paused to call out: 'You should just be damn thankful you got that free ride when you thought you was having a heart attack.'

Wanda called back angrily: 'Look, when I have a heart attack, it's bad – and there's no thinking about it! But when my heart attack's over, it's over.'

'O.K.,' Wojtowicz told her over his shoulder.

The spade made a faint, clean, rasping thud as he dug. The thin woman and Harry McHeath wiped sand from some cups and set them out. The rest of them watched the moon emerging from behind the Wanderer, which seemed to tip over as it sank towards the Pacific.

Luna looked visibly conical – mashed. And instead of the smooth smudges of 'seas' on her face, there was the faintest tracery of shadow-lines, here and there palely flashing the Wanderer's colours. The effect was horrid, somehow suggesting a sack of spider's eggs.

A forceps birth, the Ramrod thought. *The White Virgin, fecundated by Ispan, bears herself in pain – and must birth herself again and again in torture. I had not thought of that.*

Margo thought, *I'm sorry I called her a bitch. Don . . .*

Rama Joan whispered to Paul: 'Her young man was up there, wasn't he? Then she could be your girl now, Paul.'

Wojtowicz straightened up. 'That's all the deep we can have it,' he told the Little Man huskily. 'Any farther we'd get water.'

They turned towards the cot. Clarence Dodd unsnapped the leash from the heavy collar and lifted the jacket a little from Ragnarok's body, looking at Margo, but she shook her head, and he grimaced a smile at her and let the jacket fall again. He and Wojtowicz and Doc let down the shrouded dog into his shallow grave. Miaow lifted in Margo's arms to watch curiously.

Over the Pacific the Wanderer hung as strangely as if the blind spot had acquired imperial colours, and was as perfectly spherical as the emergent moon was maimed. The western yellow spot had rotated out of sight, so that the face the orb showed had become a Three-Spot; but the most striking impression, with the two thick eastern arms of the purple cross widening above and below the great eastern yellow spot, was of the head of a purple beast with jaws agape.

Fernis Wolf, thought Harry McHeath. *And now it looks like it's really eating the moon, with the moon orbiting around in front between its jaws.*

'It looks like a big dog getting ready to snap,' Ann said thoughtfully. 'Mummy, do you suppose the gods have put

105

Ragnarok up there, like they used to put Greek heroes and nymphs up in the stars?'

'Yes, I think that's happened, dear,' Rama Joan told her.

The Little Man pulled out his notebook and pen automatically and then looked dully at the next empty page. Margo gave Miaow to Paul to hold while she took the things out of the Little Man's hands and sketched the Wanderer for him, imitating his diagrammatic style.

Four Hours

The Serpent gorges on the Egg, thought the Ramrod. *Or is it that roads divide?*

Wojtowicz swiftly spaded first dry, then wet sand back into the grave. Doc took the leash out of the Little Man's fingers and wove it tightly around the head of his furled umbrella and fastened it that way. When Wojtowicz had patted the sand flat with his spade and stepped back, Doc thrust the umbrella deep into the centre of the grave.

'There, Doddsy,' he said, putting an arm around the Little Man's shoulder. 'He's got a marker now. A sort of caduceus.'

From the platform the thin woman called: 'Come and get it, everybody! The coffee stayed real hot.'

Donald Merriam was in darkness again. The Baba Yaga had once more been eclipsed, this time by the moon as it passed in front of the Wanderer. The tiny moon-ship fell free between the two bodies. It was continuing to gain on the moon, but had not yet quite out-nosed it.

The cabin had swiftly warmed from the direct sunlight, but before it had become uncomfortably hot, the moon had swung between the Baba Yaga and the sun.

The darkness of this eclipse was not nearly as great as that of the first, being pervaded by sun-reflected violet and yellow from the Wanderer. This Wanderer-light revealed the continuing rock-churning of the moon's surface, looking like a stormy sea seen from an airplane by brilliant moonlight.

At his altitude above the Wanderer – 1,600 miles now by radar check – Don could see only about a fifth of the planet's disc. Passing across the face variously named on Earth the X, the Notched Disc, the Wheel, St Andrew's Cross, and the Mandala, he saw only the western yellow spot and a rim around it widening ahead – the eastern and two polar yellow spots were out of sight for him around the curve of the Wanderer.

By watching the yellow spot emerge from the Wanderer's night side across the sunrise line, Don had got confirmation that the Wanderer was rotating and that its top and bottom were indeed its poles, its axis being roughly parallel to that of Earth.

By timing the speed of the spot's emergence Don had estimated the Wanderer's period of rotation as six hours – a 'day' only one quarter as long as Earth's. And it was rotating in the same direction as he and the moon were moving in their two-hour orbits – the planet's surface features following, but falling swiftly behind.

The greenish glow-spots on the Wanderer's night side did not seem to show up in any way on the day side – perhaps they were some sort of phosphorescence visible only in the dark. Nor, so far as he could recall, had there been any indication of the distinction between violet and yellow areas on the night side – apparently it took sunlight to bring that out.

A good half of the great yellow spot was occupied by the moon's shadow – inky, and undeniably elliptical and growing more so. Studying it, Don noted a very ghostly pale green round beginning to intrude into its forward edge – apparently the green spots did carry around, though being invisible in sunlight.

The plain weirdness of his situation suddenly hit him – a midge between a black plum and a pink grapefruit, all three careening free.

He fancied himself, a little boy, in the kitchen of the Minnesota farmhouse, with the darkness of early evening pressing on the window, and he, Donnie, saying: 'Ma, I found a deep black hole in the woods, and I know it has to go all the way through to the other side of the earth because I saw a star twinkling at the bottom. I got scared and, Ma, I know you won't believe this, but as I came running home I saw a big yellow and purple planet behind the barn!'

He shook off the pseudomemory. However weird this situation might be, it was a little less so because he had lived a month on the moon and had now driven a spaceship through it.

He turned his attention to the white threads looping up from the nose of the moon. He swung ship to follow with his eyes their curving course against the stars, diverging at first and then beginning to converge again as they vanished north over the horizon of the Wanderer.

Well, if the white threads somehow tied the moon and the Wanderer together, it made sense that they should be tied to a pole of the latter. Attached to a spot on the equator of the Wanderer they'd get stretched and broken, or wound around the Wanderer, since the moon was orbiting three times as fast as the planet was rotating.

Tied together! Wound around! Here he was thinking of them as actual threads, as though the Wanderer and the moon were two Christmas tree ornaments.

Still, the white threads had to be something actual.

He followed them back along their course to the nose of the moon. The Baba Yaga was ahead of the moon now, but still in its shadow because they were both starting to swing behind the Wanderer again – its black sunset line that he had first seen through the moon-chasm was already in sight once more, chopping off the violet horizon.

So the nose of the moon was in shadow, its surface bronze-dim and churning. He took from the rack a pair of binoculars with big objective lenses and carefully focused them.

In the churning nose of the moon were a dozen huge, conical pits, their inner surfaces spinning rapidly clockwise, as though they were maelstroms in the fracturing rock.

Each sleek white thread, turning bronze-dark as it entered the moon's shadow, led to the bottom of one of the whirlpool pits and kept swinging around in a tiny circuit, in pace with its whirling. The threads thickened somewhat down towards their restless roots. They resembled waterspouts or tornado-funnels.

Around each pit were three or four bright violet or lemon dots. He had seen one or two other such dots along the strands. It struck Don that they might be big spaceships, presumably from the Wanderer, and possibly generating gravitational or momentum fields of some kind.

For the inference to be made from the whirlpool pits and the entering strands was clear: somehow, the substance of the moon, in the form of dust and gravel and perhaps larger rocks, was being sucked out and carried looping through space towards the north pole of the Wanderer.

Arab and Pepe and High stood over the Hudson, sharing a stick, ready to shred it into the pale, oil-filmed water if anyone should come.

But no one did. The city was strangely still, even for six in the morning. So High flipped away the half-inch butt, and Arab lit another reefer, and they passed it around.

Their arrival at the river, after slanting north past the General Grant Houses, and under the Henry Hudson Parkway, had been anticlimactic. There had been simply nothing over to the west, but pale sky and distant piers and Edgewater and the southern end of the Palisades.

'She disappear somehow,' High decided. 'Maybe just set.' He laughed. His gaze switched south to Grant's Tomb. 'What you think, General?'

'River look high, Admiral,' Arab adjudged, frowning, as he lit a third reefer for them.

'Sure do,' High agreed. 'See it washin' over that dock!'

'That no dock,' Arab protested scornfully. 'That a sunken barge.'

'Just the same, water's ten feet higher'n when we come.'

'You crazy!'

'I know where *she* disappear to,' Pepe cried suddenly. 'That big purple'n golden thing a amphi-whamf – a balloon-submarine combo! She *submerge*. That why river high – she bulk it up. She lurkin' down there, glowin' in the wet-wet dark.'

As the others quivered at the delicious horror of the thought,

Pepe threw up his spread-fingered hands beside his cheeks and cried again, piling it on: 'No, wait! She not that. She a frozen atomic blast. They start the blast, then freeze the fireball. She float around like a ball lightning, first over the river, then under. When she unfreeze, city go *whish!* Look there!'

Red sun was glinting from banks of windows across the river, so low they looked like part of the water. Suddenly the pretended horror became appallingly real to all of them – the sudden fear against which no weed-smoker can wholly insure himself.

'Come on!' Arab screamed in a whisper.

They turned and ran back towards Harlem.

Jake Lesher curled his lip at the thinning crowd. With the sinking of the Wanderer and the seeping in of grey morning light, the excitement had drained out of Times Square. The earthquake litter now looked merely untidy and gritty – one more Manhattan demolition project.

Incredulously, as if they were something from a musical extravaganza, he remembered Sal's song and the stamping crowd under the vast purple-and-amber floodlight. Then his lip relaxed and his eyes widened a little but stopped watching, as he felt brushing against the edges of his imagination the first tendrils of a dream – or of a scheme, for the two were very close in Jake's universe.

Sally Harris suddenly snaked her arm through his from behind. As she pulled him around, she whispered rapidly in his ear: 'Come on, let's get out of here before those other wolves find me. It's only four blocks.'

'You shouldn't startle me that way, Sal,' Jake complained. 'I was getting a money-making thought. Where to?'

'You were just saying nothing could startle you any more. Ha! I'm taking us to breakfast at Hugo Hasseltine's penthouse – me and my little key. After that quake, the higher I get, the safer I'll feel.'

'You'll have farther to fall,' Jake pointed out.

'Yeah, but things won't fall on me. Come on, you'll scheme better on a full stomach.'

Way up, a little pink was showing in the sky.

Chapter 16

Doc grunted happily and said, 'I could do with another sandwich.'

'We thought we'd better hold back half,' the thin woman told him apologetically from the other side of the long table.

'It was my idea,' young Harry McHeath said, embarrassed.

'And probably a good one,' Doc allowed. 'Straight out of *Swiss Family Robinson*. Anyone care for a taste of Scotch?' He fished a half-pint bottle out of his left-hand coat pocket. The fat woman humphed.

'Better save that for emergencies, Rudy,' Ross Hunter said quietly.

Doc sighed and tucked it away. 'I suppose all second cups of coffee have been interdicted by the Committee of Public Safety, too,' he growled.

Harry McHeath shook his head nervously and hastened to pour one for Doc and then for several of the others.

Rama Joan said: 'Rudolf, ages ago you were wondering what makes the colours of the Wanderer.'

She had had Ann stretch out on two chairs beside her, wrapped in the coat someone had left behind, with the girl's head pillowed on her mother's thigh. Rama Joan was looking at the Wanderer. The eastern yellow spot now had purple all around it, destroying the illusion of the jaws. The two polar yellow spots were shrinking as they rotated out of sight. In fact, the effect was almost that of a purple target with a great yellow bull's-eye. Meanwhile the faintly crack-webbed moon, perceptibly lozenge-shaped, had almost finished a second westward crossing of the Wanderer's face.

Rama Joan said: 'I don't think it's natural features at all. I think it's simply . . . décor.' She paused. 'If beings are able to drive their planet through hyperspace, they'd surely be able to give it an appearance they considered artistic and distinctive. Cavemen didn't paint the outside of their homes, but we do.'

'You know, I like that,' Doc said, smacking his lips. 'A two-tone planet. Impress the neighbours in the next galaxy.'

Wojtowicz and Harry McHeath laughed uneasily. The Ramrod thought: *Unwillingly they grow towards comprehension of Ispan's glory.* Hunter, his voice low but jerky with tension, said: 'If you were that advanced, I don't suppose you'd use natural planets at all. You'd design and build them from scratch. Gosh, this seems crazy!' he finished rapidly.

'Not at all,' Doc assured him. 'Be damned efficient to use all of a planet's volume. You could have storerooms and dormitories and field generators down to the very core. Of course that would require some pretty tremendous beams and bracing –'

'Not if you had antigravity,' said Rama Joan.

'Wow,' Wojtowicz said tonelessly.

'You're clever, Mommy,' Ann observed sleepily.

Hunter said: 'If you cancelled the gravity of a rotating planet, you'd have to have it pretty well tied together, or centrifugal force would tear it apart.'

'Nope,' Doc told him. 'Mass and momentum would disappear together.'

Paul cleared his throat. He was sitting beside Margo and he'd taken off his coat and put it around her. He'd meant to put his arm around her too, if only for the practical purpose of getting some of his body-heat back, but somehow he hadn't yet. He said: 'If beings were that advanced, wouldn't they also be careful not to injure or even disturb any inhabited planets they came near?' He added uncertainly: 'I suppose I'm assuming a benign Galactic Federation, or whatever you'd call it. . . .'

'Cosmic Welfare State,' Doc suggested in faintly sardonic tones.

'No, you're absolutely right, young man,' the fat woman said authoritatively, while the thin woman nodded, her mouth pursed. 'The first law of the Saucerians is to harm no life, but to nurture and protect all.'

'But is it the first law of General Motors?' Hunter wanted to know. 'Or General Mao?'

Rama Joan smiled quizzically and asked Paul: 'When you make an automobile trip, what *special* precautions do you take against running over cats and dogs? Are the anthills all marked in your garden?'

112

'Still hot on your devil-theory, aren't you?' Doc observed.

Rama Joan shrugged. 'Devils may be nothing but beings intent on *their* purpose, which now happens to collide with yours.'

'Then evil's just an auto accident?'

'Perhaps. Remember, there are careless drivers, and even drivers who use a car to express themselves.'

Paul asked: 'Even if the car's a planet?'

Rama Joan nodded.

'Hmm. I just use naked me to express myself,' Doc asserted, chuckling wickedly.

Margo, whose hands were curved around Miaow asleep on her lap, interjected sharply: 'When *I* drive I can see a cat on the sidewalk three blocks ahead. Cats are people. That's why I could never have gone into Vandenberg, even if they'd been more decent about the rest of it.'

'But are people always people?' Hunter asked her with a smile.

'I'm not so sure of that,' she admitted, wrinkling her nose.

The fat woman made a *pshaw*-sound. Rama Joan said sweetly to Margo: 'I hope that when things get . . . well . . . rougher, you never regret passing up Vandenberg and throwing in with us. You had your chance, you know.'

Wojtowicz jumped up: 'Look at that!' he said.

He was pointing across the sand to where a pair of headlights were bobbing up and down. And now there came plainly to their ears the swelling growl of an engine.

Hunter said: 'Paul, looks like Major Humphreys has changed his mind and sent to fetch you.'

Doc said: 'It's coming from the wrong direction.'

Wojtowicz said: 'Yeah, it's from the highway, come around the slide.'

The headlights slewed around, hesitated, then came on bright. Their glare made it hard to see the car, despite the twilight.

Margo said: 'They'll get stuck, whoever they are.'

'Not if they keep up speed they won't,' said Wojtowicz.

The car came on as if it were going to ram the platform and then careened to a stop fifty feet away and doused its headlights.

'It's Hixon's panel truck!' the Little Man said.

'And there's Mrs Hixon,' Doc said, as a figure in pale slacks and sweater dropped from the back of the truck and ran towards them.

Wojtowicz, Ross Hunter, and Harry McHeath hurried towards the truck. As Mrs Hixon passed them, she cried: 'Help Bill look after Ray Hanks. Ray's got a broken leg.' Then she was on the platform.

Earlier in the evening Mrs Hixon had been a handsome-looking woman, but now her hands, face, slacks, and sweater were smeared with dirt, her hair had come unpinned and hung down in strands, her lips were pulled back from her teeth, and her eyes stared. There was blood on her chin. As soon as she stopped moving she started to shake.

'The highway's blocked both ways,' she gasped. 'We lost the others. I think they're dead. I think the whole world's smashed. My God, have you got something to drink?'

Doc said: 'You called it,' to Hunter as he pulled out his half pint, poured a double shot in an empty coffee cup, and started to add water. She clutched it before he could and sucked it down greedily, then shuddered over her shaking. Doc put his arms around her shoulders, hard. 'Now tell us point by point,' he said, 'from the beginning.'

She nodded, closed her eyes a moment. Then: 'We dug out three cars. Rivis', our truck, Wentcher's microbus. The rest were too deep, but that was enough to hold us easy. Just Bill and Ray and me in the truck. When we got to the highway there was no traffic. That should have warned us, but we thought it was great. Christ! Rivis turned north. We headed for L.A., following the microbus. The car radio got two stations through the static. Just snatches. Nothing but the big L.A. quake – do this, do that, don't do it. We had to keep swinging around little falls and rocks. Still no cars. The microbus was way ahead. We were where there was no beach, just a drop into the sea.

'The road heaved – just like that, without warning, my God! It rocked the car like a boat. The door jerked open and Ray Hanks pitched out. I hung on to Bill. He was rammed against the back of the car seat, braking. The cliffs came down. A rock big as a room hit ahead of us and cut a slice out of the

114

road ten feet wide. I remember I bit my tongue. Ray got the car stopped. The road stopped heaving, too. Then I was choking on dust, but then through the dust came a big splash of water where the rock hit the sea. I was tasting salt and blood and dust, and I could still feel my brains shaking.

'It got awful quiet. The road ahead was all blocked, dirt piled against the bumper. I don't know if we could have climbed the fall, but we were going to try, because we didn't know if the microbus got buried, or got away, or what. Just then an after-slide came. A boulder as big as a lion missed me by *that*. Another just exploded. Bill made me get back in the car, while he walked through the new falls, telling me how to cut the wheels as I backed it around rocks and over ridges and angles. In between, he was coughing and cursing that new planet.

'Someone was screaming curses too – at us. It was Ray. We'd forgot him. His leg was broken above the knee, but we got him in the back on a canvas. I stayed beside him. Bill could turn the car now, and we headed back.

'The little slides were bigger but we got around them. We wanted to meet cars now, but there still weren't any. Bill stopped at a roadside phone, but it was dead, and the light in the booth died while he was trying to get a dial tone. The radio was nothing but static now. The only word that ever seemed to get through was *fire*! Ray and I kept yelling at Bill to go slower and faster.

'We passed the turnoff here, but after a quarter of a mile the road was blocked by another slide – not a soul in sight, not a light – except that godawful thing up there. We came back here. There wasn't anywhere else.'

She breathed deeply. Doc asked: 'What about the little roads back across the Santa Monica mountains? Specifically, what about the Monica Mountainway?'

'Little roads?' Mrs Hixon looked up at him wonderingly, then started to laugh and sob together. 'You goddamn fool idiot, those mountains have been stirred like stew!' Her laughter went out of control. Doc clapped his hands over her mouth. She struggled wildly for a moment, then let her head slump. Wanda and the thin woman took over from Doc, walking her away down the platform. Rama Joan followed them, after asking Margo to take her place as a pillow for Ann, who was watchful as a mouse.

Paul said to Doc: 'I wonder why there weren't any other cars trapped in that stretch of the highway? Seems unnatural.'

'They probably got out past the first, smaller slides,' Doc opined. 'The same slides would have turned back any cars trying to come into that stretch. And still, despite all she says, I think some may have escaped over Monica Mountainway.'

Hunter called up: 'Come on down, the rest of you guys, and bring the cot. We've got to get Ray out of the truck, so some of us can go back in it to our cars.'

Trembling and breathless and a little teeter-gaited from their wild run past the mausoleum-like General Grant Houses, Arab and Pepe and High started east along 125th Street with an initial feeling of reassurance at having entered the hallway to their friendly, familiar Afro-Latin home.

But the sidewalks, packed two hours ago, were empty now. Only a scattering of crushed paper cups and bags, empty pop bottles, and half-pint flasks testified to the vanished multitude. No cars moved along the street, though here and there were empty ones parked higgledy-piggledy, two with their motors' exhaust streaming blue from their tail pipes.

The weed-brothers had to squint against the sun when they scanned east, but as far as they could tell the same desertion prevailed all along the crosstown street that led through the heart of Harlem.

The only sounds, at first, besides their own footsteps and the motor chugging, were the sepulchral mouthings of unseen radios, sounding horribly important, by their tone; but the words were uncatchable by reason of static and distance – and drowned out by the excited, equally unintelligible calling to each other of distant sirens and horns.

'Where's everybody?' High whispered.

'Atomic attack,' Pepe affirmed. 'Russia's sent the superdoops. Everybody crouchin' down below in the basements. We gotta get to ours.' Then, a ghost of the wolf-wail returning to his voice: 'Fireball risin' from the river!'

'No!' Arab contradicted, softly. 'While we at the river,

116

Resurrection come and go. Old Preacher-dads right after all. Everybody snatched – no time to turn off their cars or their radios. We the only ones left.'

They took hold of each other and tiptoed, to kill the sound of their footsteps as they went fearfully on.

Sally Harris and Jake Lesher tiptoed out of the tiny aluminium-lined box that had lifted them the last three storeys. Before their eyes was dimness, with gleams highlighting a grand piano. Under their feet was thick carpet, sponge-based.

Sally yoohooed softly. With a whispered sigh the door behind them slid sideways, but Sally caught it and blocked it with a tiny table holding a silver tray.

'What are you trying to do?' Jake asked.

'I don't know,' she said. 'We'll hear the buzzer if anybody else wants in. Come on.'

'Wait a minute,' Jake said. 'You're sure Hasseltine's not home?'

Sally shrugged. 'I'll have a look while you raid the icebox. Just leave the sterling alone. Come on, haven't you a bagel-size hole in your gut?'

Like a mouse with a friend, she led him to the kitchen.

Dai Davies listened with wicked amusement to the weird reports of the Wanderer coming over the wireless to the tiny Severn-shore pub near Portishead, where he'd gone after a two-hour snooze to do his late morning drinking. From time to time he embroidered the reports fancifully for the edification and jollification of his unappreciative fellow-topers: 'Purple and sickly amber, eh? 'Tis a great star-written American advertisement, lads, for grape juice and denatured beer!' and, 'It's a saintly Soviet super-balloon, boys, set to pop over lawless Chicago and strew the Yankee heartland with begemmed copies of Marx's holy Manifesto!'

The reports were coming over an Atlantic cable, the derisive announcer said – extraordinary severe magnetic storms had disordered the radio sky to the west. Dai greatly wished that Dick Hillary were still with him – this lovely nonsense was just the thing to make that hater of spaceflight and space fiction squirm; besides, he'd be a better audience for a Welsh poet's rare wit than these Somerset sobersides.

But when, two mighty drinks later, the wireless reports began to include mention of a cracked and captured moon – the announcer growing still more derisive, yet now with a nervous note in his voice, almost hysterical – Dai's mood changed abruptly, and there was much more drunken emotion than wit in his cry: 'Steal our moon-bach, would they, those damned Yanks! Don't they know Mona belongs to Wales? And they hurt her, we'll swim across and gut Manhattan Isle from the Battery to Hell Gate, will we not, my hearties?'

This met with, 'Shut up, you sot, he's saying more,' 'Wild jabbering Welshman,' 'Bolshy, I'd think,' 'No more for you, you're drunk' – this last from the host.

'Cowardly Somersets!' Dai retorted loudly, grabbing up a mug and brandishing it like a knuckleduster. 'And you follow me not I'll fight you myself, all up and down the Mendip Hills!'

The diamond-paned door was thrown open and a white-eyed scarecrow figure in dungarees and wide-brimmed rain-hat faced them against the light fog outside.

'Is there aught on the wireless or the telly of the tide?' this apparition called to the host. 'Two hours yet till low, and the Channel's ebbing as I've never seen it, even at the equinoctial springs with an east gale blowing. Come, look for yourselves. At this progress a man'll be able to walk on all the Welsh Grounds by noon and an hour after that the Channel'll be near dry!'

'Good!' Dai cried loudly, letting the host take away the mug and leaning hunch-shouldered on the bar as the others made a tentative move towards the door. 'Then I'll walk the five miles back to Wales straight across the Severn sands and be shut of you lily-livered Somersets. By God, I will!'

'And good riddance,' someone muttered loudly, while a hair-splitting jokester pointed out: 'If that's your aim you must walk east aslant, using the Grounds and Usk Patch for stepping stones if you like – and more than twice five miles. Straight across here, man, it's Monmouth, not Wales.'

'Monmouth's still Welsh to me and be damned to the Union of 1535,' Dai retorted, slumping his chin on to the bar. 'Oh, go

118

gawk at this watery prodigy, all of you. It's my guess the Yanks, having broken and chained the moon, are stealing the ocean, too.'

General Spike Stevens snapped: 'Get Christmas Relay, Jimmy! Tell 'em *their* picture's starting to swim, too.'

The watchers in the underground room were grouped in front of the right-hand screen, ignoring the other, which for more than an hour had been nothing but a churning rectangle of visual static.

The picture from the satellite above Christmas Island showed the Wanderer in her target face with Luna swinging behind her, but both planet and moon were bulging and rippling as electronic distortion invaded the screen.

'I've been trying, General, but I can't raise them,' Captain James Kidley responded. 'Radio and shortwave are gone. Ultrashort's going – every kind of communication that isn't by buried wire or wave guide. And even those –'

'But we're a headquarters!'

'I'm sorry, General, but –'

'Get me H.Q. One!'

'General, *they* don't –'

There was a strong vibration from the floor and a sharp crackling sound. The lights flickered, went out, came on again. The buried room rocked. Plaster fell. Once more the lights went out – all except the pale glow of the Christmas Island screen.

Abruptly the wavering astronomic picture on the screen was replaced by the silhouette of a large feline head with pricked ears and grinning jaws. It was as if, out on that unmanned satellite 23,000 miles above the Pacific, a black tiger had peered into the telescope. For a moment the picture held. Then it swam, and the screen blacked out.

'My Christ, what was that?' the General yelled in the dark.

'You saw it, too?' Colonel Mabel Wallingford demanded. A laugh, half hysterical, half exultant, rimmed her question.

'Shut up, you stupid bitch!' the General shrilled. 'Jimmy?'

'It was a chance distortion.' The younger man's voice came shakily through the blackness. 'Inkblot effect. It couldn't have been –'

'Quiet!' Colonel Willard Griswold yelled at all three of them. 'Listen!'

They all heard it: the sound of water gushing and splashing.

Aboard the *Prince Charles* they were especially conscious of the choking radioways.

Both the insurgents now controlling the luxury liner, and also the loyal crew members, using a ham sender, tried unsuccessfully to get off messages of the great *coup*, the one group to their revolutionary leaders, the other to the British Navy. And Wolf Loner, three thousand miles north, was thinking how good it was to be without newspapers and radio – he rather wished he and his dory weren't reaching Boston quite so soon.

The Wanderer's magnetic field, far stronger than Earth's, sprang out through space as swiftly as its gravitational field, almost instantly affecting instruments sensitive to it. But besides this all-pervasive magnetic influence, there were stranger straight-line influences streaming down from the Wanderer and striking the side of the earth facing it. They ripped the van Allen belts and dumped a cloudburst of protons and electrons on Earth.

These powerful straight-line influences were greatly intensified when Luna went into orbit around the Wanderer and began to break up. They produced ionization and other, subtler effects, the chief perceptible result of which was swiftly to unfit Earth's stratosphere and also her lower atmosphere for any sort of electromagnetic communications.

As the First Night of the Wanderer travelled west around the world, or, rather, as the world spun eastwards into it, this poisoning of the radio sky spread to the whole globe, greatly contributing to the fog of catastrophe that was cutting off country from country, city from city, and, ultimately, mind from mind.

Chapter 17

While the oddly-assorted medical team of Doc, Rama Joan, and the Ramrod prepared to set Ray Hanks' broken leg, Clarence Dodd led the rest of the men in an expedition back to the buried cars. With three or four of them to give the truck a running push, it got under way easily enough in the sand, but tended to stall when they all tried to pile in, so Hixon, the Little Man, and young Harry McHeath rode, while Paul, Hunter, and Wojtowicz trudged.

Half-way there, McHeath came loping back past them with splints and tape from Doddsy's first-aid stores.

'Don't strain yourself, kid,' Wojtowicz yelled after him. 'Run it like the two-mile, not the four-forty!'

'The kid overdoes,' he told Paul. 'I'm responsible for him to his aunts, though they are a pair of snooty old dames.'

After the little trek, they helped Doddsy and Bill Hixon unload from the unburied back of his station wagon and on to the truck a formidable assortment of practical equipment, including tins of food and near-beer, blankets, two leather jackets, a small tent, charcoal briquettes and kerosene, and a primus stove – and some seven-power field glasses, which they instantly used to look at the Wanderer, but the lenses only stretched the purple and gold; however, the cracks on the surface of the mashed and ellipsoidal moon, now disappearing on its second time around, became chillingly wide.

Then from Doddsy's car came two machetes (Paul chuckling to himself at the romanticism of it), and two army-surplus rifles with ammunition. Lastly, three five-gallon cans and a length of hose which they used to siphon gas from the tanks of the buried cars to fill the truck's tanks and make a fifteen-gallon reserve.

Wojtowicz shouldered one of the rifles and announced: 'Hey, look, I'm back in the service! Forward . . . *march*! – I got a clownish side,' he explained to Paul.

The loaded truck, though sluggish once or twice in the looser sand, did the return trip readily enough. Hixon even whirled it in for a landing as fancy as a speedboat's with the tailgate abutting the raised platform.

Doc's comment, when he'd surveyed the treasures, was, 'Doddsy, I see everything here for emergencies but hard liquor – or soft, for that matter,' he added, shaking his head incredulously at the label on a near-beer can.

'I have an ample supply of barbiturates and Dexedrine,' the Little Man batted back at him.

'Not the same thing,' Doc mourned. 'I never was partial to goofballs. Now if it were mescaline, say, or peyote, or even a few sticks of marijuana . . .'

Wanda glared. Harry McHeath laughed nervously, and Wojtowicz said solemnly, with a warning glance at Doc: 'He's jokin', kid.'

Doc grinned and said to the thin woman: 'Break out the last of the hot coffee, Ida. The Hixons still haven't had any, or sandwiches either, and we can all do with a bite and a cup. Now we know Doddsy's got jars of the powdered, there's no need to hoard. Besides, we'll need the jug for water from the beach-house tank – I've checked it, and it's drinkable. Some of you may think I'm nothing but a C_2H_5OH maniac, but actually I give an occasional thought to H_2O.'

Agreement on the coffee suggestion was unanimous. Everybody was tired and glad to sit or flop on the platform, up off the gritty sand. In their midst on the cot was Ray Hanks, with his leg wrapped and taped until it looked, in Wojtowicz's words, like a section of sewer pipe. But the injured man was resting tolerably after being dosed with the rest of Doc's whisky – and with the Ramrod keeping a light 'healing touch' on his hip.

Ida poured first for the Hixons, who were sitting side by side now, he with his arm around her. They looked at each other, then touched cups rather solemnly. It set a tone. There was something solemn about them all as they started to sip their last scant cups of brewed coffee. As Hunter had divined earlier, each in his way felt that this place was home and dreaded the moment of departure. Here on the beach there were no hills to fall, no buildings to collapse and burn, no gas pipes to crack and flare hot yellow, or wires to fall and flash blindingly. (True, there was the beach house, looking lopsided now with one wall

122

knocked askew by the quake, but it was dark and low and boarded up, and so could be ignored.) There were no strangers monitoring their actions, no victims to enjoin their aid. Static choked what messages of catastrophe, what do's and dont's, what police and Red Cross and Civilian Defence directives must be crowding the airwaves. It was good to dream of just staying here, a compatible little beach colony – just staying here and watching the Wanderer, which was sinking and leaning towards the ocean, the moon again eclipsed behind it and the planet itself showing a face like that of a bull charging purple head on, the yellow target-centre half out of sight and a larger, lower yellow round creeping into view. By chance, or conceivably by intention, two small yellow ovals made eyes. Doddsy set down his coffee cup to sketch it.

'*El toro*,' Margo said.

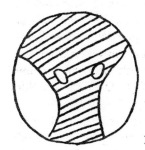

Five Hours

Rama Joan said: 'The head of an octopus. The Cretans drew it just so on their vases.'

'But we're going to have to get out of here – and in three or four hours,' Doc said suddenly, as if aware of the general, unstated dream of staying for ever on the beach. 'The tide.'

Hunter frowned at him warningly and Doc hastened to say: 'Now, don't anybody get me wrong – we're in no danger right now, in fact, just the opposite. The high-water interval here is about ten hours, which means a *low* tide comes about four hours after the moon's at the top of the sky. In other words, in about an hour the tide'll be dead low. See how far away the edge of the surf is? That leaves us ample time for a good rest – which I for one fully intend to take.'

'But whaddya mean, Doc, the tide?' Wojtowicz asked.

Again Hunter frowned and shook his head slightly.

Doc said to Hunter: 'No, Ross, I think we'd better face up to it now we've got a breathing space.' Then, turning towards Wojtowicz: 'You know of course how the moon – the mass of the moon – is the main cause of the tides? Well, now we've got the Wanderer out there. It's about the same place as the moon, so we can expect the tides to have about the same general pattern as before.'

'That's good,' Wojtowicz said. 'For a minute you had me scared.'

But most of the others were looking at Doc now and they weren't smiling. He sighed and said: 'However, judging from the way it's captured the moon, the Wanderer must have a mass about as great as Earth – in other words, a mass eighty times that of the moon.'

There was a rather long silence. The one word 'eighty' hung in the air like a grey rock, getting bigger and solider every second. Only the Ramrod and his two women didn't seem greatly concerned. Hunter was frowning worriedly, watching reactions. Rama Joan, her lap once more a pillow for her sleeping daughter, suddenly smiled at Doc warmly. Mrs Hixon put out her hands a little as if to say, 'But . . .' Her husband drew them down to her lap and hugged her a little tighter as he nodded solemnly at Doc. Paul did the same, at last putting an arm around Margo. The Little Man pocketed his notebook and folded his arms.

Doc looked back at them all with a rather sorrowful, thoughtful grin.

It was young Harry McHeath who finally put it into words.

'You mean, Mr Brecht, that although the tides will be coming at the same times and in the same general way as before, they'll be . . . *eighty times bigger*?'

'He didn't say that!' Hunter interposed hotly. 'Rudy, you're not allowing for the age of the tides. We should have a day's grace in any case. Besides that, tides are a reasonance phenomenon – it should take quite a while for the oceanic tidal bands to get to vibrating in a larger amplitude.'

'That may be true,' Doc said. 'Also there'll be spill-over effects to moderate the factor of eighty. However,' he went on more firmly, 'that two-tone planet is out there, and thinking isn't going to change its mass. You've seen what it's done to the moon. Whether it's going to take seven hours or a week, the big water's coming, and when it does I'm going to feel securer if I've got a couple of hills under me. That's why I inquired about Monica Mountainway,' he explained to the Hixons. '*Nevertheless*' – he continued very loudly, checking the excited flood of talk just beginning – '*before a man makes an effort, he gathers his strength* – as I'm going to do right now. Anyone wants to waste energy jabbering, go ahead. He won't bother me.'

And he stretched out on four chairs, put his arm across his eyes, and, presently, gave out with a large, theatrical snore.

Don Merriam, orbiting for a second time behind the Wanderer, suddenly thought of the menace to Earth which the mere physical presence of the strange planet constituted. Why, there would be earthquakes – possibly – and gigantic ocean tides – certainly, though he wasn't sure how quickly they'd build up – and there might be . . . well, he didn't think the Wanderer could crack the Earth at this distance, but just the same he wished he could look at Terra right now, with his binoculars, and reassure himself.

It was his duty to warn Earth, or at least to try, no matter how hopeless the attempt seemed. He warmed the radio of the Baba Yaga and began alternately to send and listen. Once he thought he heard the beginning of a reply, but it faded.

He wondered if anything down on that green-spotted black hemisphere could be listening in.

Arab Jones and his weed-brothers on Manhattan Island were almost twice as far into the day as the saucer students were still in the night, since the dawn-line at this moment was sweeping west across the Rocky Mountains at its customary seven hundred miles an hour, also bringing rosy daybreak and the buzzards to Asa Holcomb's mesa.

Somewhere near Roosevelt Square Arab pointed up at the roofs and cried: 'There they are!'

High and Pepe looked. The low roofs were lined with people,

125

explaining in part the mystery of deserted 125th Street. Some of the people were looking down at them, and a few were beckoning urgently and calling.

But it was impossible to make out the words because of the loud chugging of an abandoned taxi, skew-parked so close by that High clutched one of its open doors to steady himself.

'They crazy they think they escape the bombs that way,' Pepe said, peering upward. 'Bombs come from space, don't burrow up through the rock from old Pellucidar.'

'You sure of that?' High demanded. 'Maybe that fireball tunnelling from the river!'

'They all awaiting the glorious fireball!' Arab cried loudly, spreading his arms to comprehend the roofs. 'They all dead already. Like Manator! They a rooftop wax museum! All New York!'

Abruptly the fear-kick in that last vision became absolutely real fear, and the thought of being spied upon and chittered at and lured and finally, irresistibly summoned by all those dark, wax-skinned living mummies fifty feet overhead became quite intolerable.

'Let's get out of here!' High yelled. He crouched down and squat-stepped into the front of the taxi. '*I* getting out!'

Arab and Pepe piled into the back. The forward lurch of the taxi slammed the door shut and sent them back against the cold, slick leather cushions as High headed west, gathering speed as he wove around abandoned cars.

The stampede of sections of the New York City Police and Fire Departments, marring the metropolis' relatively swift and sensible preparations for catastrophe, was due to a number of factors: exaggerated reports of the tidal bulge at Hell Gate and the quake damage to the Medical Centre on upper Broadway, scrambled directives sent out by a water-shorted computer in the underground centre of the new inter-departmental co-ordinating system, and false reports of riots around the Polo Grounds.

Yet just plain nerves played their part – naked fear operating alongside the frantic urge to rush out and somehow play the hero. It was as if the Wanderer were finally bringing true the old lunatic superstitions about the moon pouring down rays of madness. All over the Western Hemisphere – in Buenos Aires and Boston, in Valparaiso and Vancouver, there were the same wild, purposeless sorties.

High Bundy was stepping on the gas three blocks west of Lenox when he and Pepe and Arab heard the sirens coming. At first they couldn't tell where they were coming from, only that they were coming, because they were getting louder fast.

Then the cab crossed Eighth Avenue, and as the raucous wailing crescendoed they saw charging towards them up Eighth, not a block away, two squad cars abreast and what looked like more behind them, their red business-lights flashing.

High stepped harder. The sound of the sirens should have cut down for a couple of seconds while there were buildings between the cab and the police cars. But it didn't. It got louder.

There was an old jalopy abandoned smack in the middle of the next intersection. High aimed to pass it to the right. A Black Maria and a fire chief's car hurtled out of Seventh Avenue from the south and swerved around the jalopy to either side. High stepped to the floor and held his course, just missing their tails, and got across Seventh feet ahead of a big, end-swinging fire-truck following the other two cars by hardly a length. Pepe glimpsed the great red hood and the wide-eyed face of the driver and clapped his hands to his eyes, it was so close.

The cab wasn't half-way down the next block when the intersection ahead filled with more red and black cars, racing north on Lenox. The sound of the sirens from behind and ahead was brain-shaking.

If the weed-brothers hadn't been loaded on pot, they might have realized that this stampede of police cars and firetrucks from lower Manhattan had nothing to do with them personally and that the ferocious vehicles weren't converging into 125th Street, but continuing their mad dash north.

But the weed-brothers were loaded, and the master fear-kick of pursuit by police was upon them. Pepe believed they were to be scapegoats for an attempt to destroy Manhattan by suit-case bombs – they'd be frisked for fireballs and convicted on the evidence of a Zippo lighter.

Arab knew it was the purpose of the police to frog-march them to the nearest roof and tie them down among the grinning wax mummies.

High simply thought they'd been spotted smoking weed back at the river – probably by telepathy. He braked the cab to a stop just short of Lenox. They piled out.

The subway entrance yawned with the dark invitation of a cave or den, promising the security all terrified animals crave. There was a white sawhorse half blocking it, but they darted past and clattered down the stairs.

The token booth was empty. They scrambled over the turnstiles. There was a lighted train waiting, its doors open. But there wasn't anybody in it.

The station was lit, but they couldn't see any people anywhere, on this platform or the one across.

The empty train was purring softly and insistently, but after the sirens faded there wasn't another sound.

Chapter 18

Despite Doc's snoring for morale purposes, no one except Rama Joan tried to follow his example, and after a half hour or so Doc himself lifted his head, propping it up on his doubled arm, so as to get into an argument Hunter and Paul were having about the paths in space Earth and the Wanderer would take with respect to each other.

'I've figured it all out in my head – roughly, of course,' Doc told them. 'Granting they're of equal mass, they'll revolve around a point midway between them in a month lasting about nineteen days.'

'Shorter than that, surely,' Paul objected. 'Why, we can see with our own eyes how fast the Wanderer's moving.' He pointed to where the strange planet, maroon and light orange now, was dipping atilt towards the ocean, the blunt yellow spearhead of the moon striking across its front almost from below.

Doc chuckled. '*That* movement's just the Earth turning –

same thing as makes the sun rise.' Then, as Paul grimaced in exasperation at his own stupidity, Doc added: 'Natural enough mistake – I keep making it in my own mind, which I inherited from my cavemen ancestors along with my tail bones! Say, look how far the sea's gone out! Ross, I'm afraid the tidal effects are showing up faster than we hoped.'

Paul, trying to get back into the swing of the discussion, made himself visualize how tides eighty times higher would mean tides eighty times lower too – at six-hour intervals, at most places.

'Incidentally,' Doc added, 'we'll be about ten days getting into that nineteen-day orbit, since Earth's acceleration is only about five-hundredths of an inch a second. That of the moon, also in respect to the Wanderer, must have been about four feet a second, cumulative, of course.'

A chilly land-breeze came sneaking around Paul's neck. He pulled his coat tighter – he'd got it back from Margo when the Little Man had given her one of the leather jackets. In spite of that she had Miaow inside the jacket to make her warmer as she stared out across the long, flat beach.

'Look how the light glistens on the wet gravel,' she said to Paul. 'Like amethysts and topazes shovelled out of trucks.'

'Ssh,' said the fat woman, beside her. '*He's* getting messages.'

Just the other side of Wanda, the Ramrod was gazing at the Wanderer as though hypnotized by it, his chin on his fist, rather in the attitude of 'The Thinker'.

'The Emperor says, "No harm to Terra",' the Ramrod droned just then in a trancelike voice. ' "Her turbulent waters shall be stilled, her oceans withdrawn from her shores".'

'A planetful of King Canutes,' Doc murmured softly.

'Your emperor ought to have got on the ball in time to stop the earthquakes,' Mrs Hixon called tartly. Mr Hixon laid his hand on her arm and whispered to her. She flirted her shoulders, but made no more cracks.

Rama Joan opened her eyes. 'How are your speculations going now, Rudolf?' she challenged Doc. 'Angels? Or devils?'

He replied: 'I'll wait until one flies in close enough for me to see whether his wings are feathery or leathery.' Then, realizing that he'd not necessarily made a joke, he looked quickly towards the Wanderer with a sardonic shudder. Then he stood up and stretched himself and surveyed the platform.

'Ha, I see you loaded the truck while I snoozed,' he commented blandly. 'That was considerate. Didn't even forget the water jugs – I suppose I have you to thank for that, Doddsy.' Then, softly, to Hunter: 'How's Ray Hanks?'

'Hardly woke up when we moved the cot into the truck and guyed it to the sides. Put a blanket around him.'

There was a droning in the sky. Everyone held very still. Several looked apprehensively towards the Wanderer, as if they thought something might be coming from there. Then Harry McHeath called excitedly: 'It's a 'copter from Vandenberg – I think. . . .'

But it looked like a regulation enough little dragonfly of an observation 'copter as it slanted down towards the sea, then swung around and came along the beach, travelling at not much more than fifty feet. Suddenly it swerved towards them and hovered overhead. The drone became a roar. The down-blast from the vanes scattered the pile of unused programmes in a white flutter.

'Is the damn fool trying to land on us?' Doc demanded, crouching and squinting upward like all the others.

A great voice came down through the drone. *'Get out! Get out of here!'*

'Why, the bastards!' Doc roared, so that what the voice said next was lost. 'They're not satisfied with slamming the door in our faces. Now they order us out of the neighbourhood!' Beside him the Little Man lifted and fiercely shook his fist.

'Get off the beach!' the great voice finished as the 'copter tilted over and continued on its course down the coast.

'Hey, Doc!' Wojtowicz yelled, grabbing the bigger man's shoulder. 'Maybe they're trying to warn us about the tides!'

'But that won't be for at least six hours –'

Doc broke off, as it became apparent that the roar wasn't leaving with the 'copter, and as water spurted upward in a dozen places through the cracks between the floorboards.

All around the platform was a pale welter of foam. The wave had come in while all their eyes were on the 'copter and its roar had masked that of the wave.

'But –' Doc demanded, rather like King Canute himself.

'Not tides, but tsunami!' Hunter yelled at him. 'Earthquake waves!'

Doc smote his own forehead.

With a hissing of sand and a hollow clanking of gravel the water receded, leaving behind a ghostly patchwork of spume.

'There's another coming!' Paul cried out, watching a distant pale wall with horror. 'Start the truck!'

The Hixons were already piling into the front seat. The motor coughed and died. The starter whined by itself. Hunter, Doddsy, Doc, and Harry McHeath jumped down and prepared to heave at the truck's sides. Rama Joan half-carried Ann across the platform, pushed her into the truck, and slapped her across the face when she tried to come back. 'Stay there and hold on,' she snarled. Wanda tried to follow Ann, but Wojtowicz grabbed her in a bear-hug, telling her: 'Not this time, Fatty!' Paul lifted and tried to secure the truck's tailgate.

The motor caught. Wojtowicz swung Wanda behind him, and he and Paul pushed at the tailgate, sprawling on the boards when the truck lurched forward a foot or so. Its rear tyres squealed as they spun in the wet sand. A heave from the men below, another forward lurch, a hesitation, another running heave, and suddenly the truck was going away fast, its tailgate swinging, its tail lights shining on the foam-frosted water nipping at its heels.

The second wave was high enough to overrun a corner of the platform and rock it a little, the cracks spouting like a sprinkler system. As it receded, Paul hustled Margo across the slippery boards. She was clutching Miaow. He paused on the back edge of the platform and looked around at the others and at the men struggling to their feet below in the shallow water.

'Come on! Quick, before the third one hits!' he yelled and plunged off with Margo, leading the rush after the truck.

Arab and Pepe and High expected blue floods of police to pour down after them into the Lenox and 125th Street subway station. So they hid in the can, Arab ready to shred their remaining reefers into the toilet and High set to flush it, while Pepe listened at the door. It wasn't very smart but it was done almost instinctively.

But nobody else tried to come in; they didn't hear police tramping and shouting around, in fact they didn't hear anything. Presently they came out.

The empty station was like a haunted house, so for a while they just stuck around. Pepe tried to get some chocolate out of a machine but it stuck. He biffed it once but stopped at the noise. They got on the back end of the empty, waiting train, which was headed downtown, and walked through it all the way to the front. There Arab fingered a lever for a while and then swung it. The doors started to close and he swung it back quick. He moved another lever and the purring got louder, and the train seemed to strain, and he quickly reversed that one, too.

'Better not mess with those,' he said with a giggle.

They studied the black double tunnel through the front door, waiting for a train to come the other way, but none did.

The longer the station stayed empty, the more it felt like a private world of their own. Feeling world-owner wealthy, they lit three sticks and sipped them on the engineer's platform.

Finally Arab said: 'What we think really happen, High?'

High frowned hard. Then, 'Russians land at the Battery from supersubs. Defeat the fuzz at the Battle of Union Square. Fuzz retreat north, fighting a rear-guard action. Russians advance. My orders of the day: lurk below, men, and play deaf and dumb.'

Arab nodded. 'Pepe?'

'That fireball! *She* surface at the Battery and split up without blasting, and then come flowing uptown through the streets. People think she poison gas and go for the roofs, but she really happy smoke, poppy-weed mix. Everybody but us strangle to death. Too scare' to inhale. Arab?'

A warm breeze began to flow past them from the tunnel ahead. It was heavy with subway smell: metal, dry dirt, human staleness, a dash of electricity.

'Come on, Arab, you started this,' Pepe prodded him.

'O.K., I got it now,' Arab said. 'River high, we saw. Keep getting higher. *Water* surface at the Battery, drive ashore and come north. Floods like Noah's! Tell people to take to the roofs and turn to pillars of salt. Clear out the basements and the subways. Fuzz run. Firemen all set with hoses, but water one thing they can't fight. They run too. Water just a-coming and a-coming.'

'Hey, that's good,' High said. 'Ree-alistic.'

The breeze got stronger and so did the subway smell, but now an inappropriate odour was mixed with the latter.

Far down the tunnel there was a blue flash.

'Train coming,' Pepe said.

There was another blue flash, and another. The breeze became a wind, and now the inappropriate odour came clear: it was the smell you got near the river. And there was a roaring growing louder.

'Dark train coming on both tracks!' Arab screeched.

The blue flashes came closer, closer, became brighter, brighter. The salty, sour wind was a gale; papers and dust were flying; the roaring was that of a thousand lions.

For a moment, clutching each other on the platform, they saw it clear: the foamy front dark with dirt and footed with blue flame.

Then the electricity-loaded piston of salt water struck.

Sally Harris and Jake Lesher nibbled scrambled eggs and caviar from a silver platter set over a blue flame and a crystal bowl set in ice.

'Gee, we're high up,' Sally said, gazing out across the penthouse patio. 'All I can see is the Empire State, RCA, the Chrysler, the Sixty Wall Tower . . . and is that bitty point the Waldorf Astoria?'

'Forty storeys before we switched to Hasseltine's private elevator,' Jake told her as he spooned caviar on to a toasted split bagel. 'I counted.'

Sally took her coffee up to the tubular chrome balustrade and peered over with a reckless swoop. 'Whee, people look like gumdrops,' she called back to him. 'They're running – I don't know why. Jake, once I asked you what those little hydrants are for that they have sticking out of buildings – I thought they were for putting out fires in cars, remember, or holding back mobs of rioting garment workers.'

133

'Naw, they're for washing down the sidewalks in the morning,' Jake instructed her, pouring himself a cup of coffee from the tall slim pot with the red light at its base.

She nodded. 'I thought so – they're using them now.'

'Naw, they do it at four a.m. Now it's eight.' His eyes grew distant. It felt to him as if the money-thought he'd had in Times Square were at last coming back.

'Well, maybe, but it looks awfully wet.' She studied a while longer. Then, 'Jake?'

'What now? Sal, I'm trying to think.'

'You're right. The water's not coming out of those little hydrants. It's coming out of the subways.'

Jake jumped up and came down with a heel-slam that jolted him painfully. The floor had jumped, too. The building roared and lurched – and lurched again. He flailed the air with his arms and grabbed the chrome balustrade where Sally was rocking and squealing above the roar. Blocks down, her coffee cup and large flakes of stone made pin-point flat splashes.

The lurching and roaring faded. Sally leaned over and pointed straight below at a black ribbon coming out of their building near the base.

'Look!' she yelled. 'Smoke! Oh Jake, isn't it exciting?' she demanded as he dragged her back. 'We ought to make a play out of it!'

In the chaos of the moment, Jake still was able to realize that this was the money-idea for which he had been groping.

Behind them the tell-tale red light at the base of the coffee pot went out, and the orange glow of the toaster faded.

The saucer students had outrun three more sloshing earthquake waves that were more spume than water – calf-deep fakes – and had actually reached dry sand and halted there, most of them winded, the Ramrod and Ida half dragging his other woman between them, when the really big combers started chasing them all.

Up ahead, the rounded foothills of the Santa Monica mountains loomed dark and heavy against a sky that had begun to grey with the dawn. Nearer, but already quite far, the bobbing light of the truck continued to recede. Hixon had taken the most direct course away from the sea, a course midway between the great hump of Vandenberg and the crumbled lower palisades that had buried the cars, and the others had followed the truck. This had been wise – any other course would have had them running slantwise to the waves across even lower beach; the trouble was that even the midway course was nothing but sand and flat sandy ground for a long distance – a dry river wash.

Behind them the Wanderer touched the ocean's rim. The curving moon-lozenge was crossing its front again. The planet itself was showing once more its yin-yang face, though seemingly tilted over – Doc, gasping, thought, *Why, this is where we came in. The thing's completed one rotation – it's got a six-hour day.* Then something black and square and lace-sided reared up and blocked off the Wanderer from him.

It was the platform where they'd held their saucer symposium, upended by the second of the big combers.

Six Hours

Then he heard the roar.

The others had started to run again and he pounded after them, tiny needles teasing his heart.

Then ... well, it was as if in one terrible, instantaneous swoop the Wanderer had leaped a quarter of a million miles out of the heavens and poised itself just above them, shutting off all of the sky except a circular grey horizon-border.

It was enough to stop them in their tracks, despite the pale, wreckage-fisted horrors roaring at them up the beach.

Hunter was the first to get distances and dimensions right, and he thought, *Why, it's simply (my God, simply!) a flying saucer forty feet across, antigravitically poised a dozen feet above us and painted with a violet-gold ying-yang.* Then he started running again.

The first and least of the big combers plastered them with spume and surged around them knee-high. Although most of their minds and senses were still glued to the thing above them, their bodies responded to the material assault. They grabbed at each other for support; hands clutched slippery hands or wet waists or soggy coats. Wanda went under, and Wojtowicz ducked for her.

Margo's nails dug into Paul's neck and she screamed in his ear: 'Miaow! Get Miaow!' and she jabbed her other hand beyond him. He glimpsed a tiny cat tail and ears disappearing in the dirty spume and he crazily dove after them, clutching ahead. So Paul missed what happened next.

A pink port five feet across flashed open in the saucer's centre, and there swung out of it, hanging just above their heads by two clawed limbs and a pointed prehensile tail, a green-and violet furred –

'Devil!' Ida screamed. '*She* said there'd be devils!'

'Tiger!' yelled Harry McHeath. Doc heard and his mind threw out, as uncontrollably as a pair of honest dice, the thought: *My God, the second Buck Rogers Sunday page! The Tiger Men of Mars!*

'Empress!' the Ramrod cried, his cold knees buckling, and in his nostrils, framed by the sea's mucky stink, the breath of a heavenly perfume. . . .

Big, black-centred violet eyes scanned them all very rapidly, yet with an impression of leisurely spectator disdain.

The second huge comber wasn't thirty yards away, the platform riding it like a surfboard, scattered chairs bobbing all around, and behind it the half-exploded beach house coming on, too.

A green paw shot out, pointed a taper-snouted grey pistol seaward, and fanned it back and forth.

There was no flash or glow or sign, but the great wave sank, shrivelled, dissolved. The platform slipped back over it and to the side. The broken beach house veered towards Vandenberg. All spume shot away, vanished. Confused loomings and shrinkings. The water was hardly thigh-deep and it lacked the punch of the first comber when it struck them at last.

The grey pistol kept on fanning back and forth over their heads.

A great gust of wind whipped past them from the land. Doc, caught off balance, started to fall. Rama Joan heaved back on him.

Paul's head and shoulders emerged from the foam. He was clutching a rat-wet Miaow to his shoulder.

The wind kept blowing.

The being hanging from the rim of the pink port seemed to lengthen out, almost impossibly, becoming a violet-barred green curve stretching towards Paul.

The grey pistol dropped, and Margo caught it.

Violet-grey claws dug into Paul's shoulder, and he and Miaow were swept up, by more than any mere human muscular force, into the pink port. Margo and Doc and Rama Joan, clinging together for support, saw that much very clearly.

The green and violet being whipped back into the saucer after Paul and the cat.

Then, without visible transition, the saucer was hundreds of yards overhead, no bigger than the moon, the port a big, pale dot.

Margo shoved the grey pistol inside her jacket.

The wind from the land faded.

The dot winked out, and the saucer vanished.

Then they were all struggling hand in hand up the beach, through knee-deep water sucking back seawards.

Bagong Bung, steering the *Machan Lumpur* out of the tide-swollen inlet south of Do-San after a successful though unpleasantly delayed delivery of a cargo of assorted contraband, saw the Wanderer rising out of the cloud-edged Gulf of Tonkin in the young night just as – almost half a planet away – the saucer students, escaped from the tsunami, were watching the last sliver of it sink into the Pacific. To Bagong Bung the yin-yang was a familiar Chinese symbol which he liked to think of as the Two Whales, but the deformed moon – at which he swiftly directed his brass spyglass – was now, to him, like a huge bag of faintly yellowed diamonds.

So to Bagong Bung, the Wanderer rising where the moon should have risen alone was not so much a staggering intrusion as a promise of good luck, a supernatural encouragement. Diamonds made him think of the lost treasure ships hidden under the shallow seas around him. He instantly and irrevocably decided that when tomorrow dawned, and with it the low tide came, he would spare time for at least one dive at the new location he'd guessed for the wreck of the *Sumatra Queen*!

'Come up, Cobber-Hume,' he called through the rusty speaking tube to his Australian engineer. 'Great good fortune for us. No, I must not tell you. Come up, then you'll see. Oh, you'll see!'

Chapter 19

Paul Hagbolt was plunged into a breathable sea of warmth, sweet spicy odours, and gay pastel colours dominated by pink – though here and there were bright green swatches.

For a few moments he hadn't been at all certain that he'd been snatched inside a vehicle. It seemed more like nearly instantaneous translation to another plane of existence, another spot in the universe – a jungly, bedroomy spot.

He'd hardly seen the saucer. Most of the time it was hovering, he'd been floundering and choking in the gritty salt water clutching Miaow. When he'd been whisked up, his first thought had been that he and Miaow had been spun aloft by the next comber and were riding its top.

Then had come three fleeting yet shockingly vivid flashes: first, a huge, tapering, greenish-purplish cat face; second, two staring eyes with incredible five-petalled irises around the black five-spiked stars of the pupils; third, a long, slim, hand-sized paw with narrow indigo pads and four cruel curving claws of translucent, violet-grey horn – he had the impression that they'd just been buried in the scruff of his coat, and maybe his neck, too, hastening him.

The next instant he was floating with a slow twist in the warm, sugary-flowery, green-flecked, pink sea.

A dark hole in that sea swung into view, and through it he saw Margo thigh-deep in dirty, foamed water holding something grey-gleaming and staring up at him, and beside her Doc, spume-patched, and Rama Joan, sand-streaked, with red-gold hair clinging wet and twisty. Then they were shrinking with incredible swiftness, as if a wrong-ended telescope had been interposed. Nevertheless, it was then that Paul began to believe that he was in the saucer he'd disjointedly seen – the saucer that now must be soaring faster than any mortar shell, though with no sensation of acceleration. Then the hole closed upon jumbly pinkness – in fact, yes, to strange pink flowers.

A word jumped up in his mind: *antigravity*. If this vehicle carried its own null-gravity field – possibly null-inertia too – that could explain the absence of any felt G-forces, and also his floating, dripping wet, surrounded by floating round drops of this wetness, in breathable perfumy air in a round, flattened room lined with live flowers.

Claws stung his left hand like a dozen wasps: Miaow was terrified by the strange jolts, and insulted by sea water, and she held on to him overtightly. In his sudden agony Paul flung off the soaking cat, and she shot twisting through the air and vanished with a puff of yellow-pink petals into a flower-bank.

The next instant he was grabbed from behind and slammed flat on his back against a hard, satin-smooth surface that had somehow been somewhere in the omni-surrounding flowers. The thing that terrified him most was that the limb that snaked around his neck – a sleek, spring-strong, green-furred limb, barred with violet – had two elbows.

With a whirling speed that did not allow his seeing it clearly, the green and violet tiger-thing worked at his outflung wrists and ankles. Paws with claws of violet-grey pinched without stabbing; once he felt the grip of something more like a snake. Then the thing kicked off from his side and dived into the flowerbank after Miaow. A long green violet-ringed tail, smoothly furred and tapering, vanished in a larger explosion of petals.

139

He tried to push himself up from the surface under him and discovered he could budge only his head. Though still in null gravity, he was somehow gyved tautly to that same surface – as was next brought home to him most graphically when he looked straight up and saw not ten feet above him (or below, or out to the side – he didn't know how to feel about it in null gravity) a spread-eagled, wet-sand-specked, pale, wildly staring reflection of himself, backed by a dozen dimming reflections of reflections of the same ridiculous, poignant picture.

The inner shape and décor of the saucer began to come clear to him. More than half the flowers he'd seen had been reflections. Ceiling and floor were round, flat mirrors facing each other, about nine feet apart and twenty feet in diameter. He was spread-eagled near the centre of one of them. The rim between the mirrors was luxuriant with exotic, thick-petalled flowers, large and small – pale yellow, pale blue, violet, magenta, but mostly pink and pinkish red. Seemingly live flowers, for there were leaves shaped like sickles and swords and spears, and there were glimpses of twisting branches – probably their hydroponic or whatever underpinnings filled much of the saucer's tapered outside rim.

But the triangularly cross-sectioned doughnut of the rim couldn't be entirely filled with vegetation, for bowered in it beyond his fettered feet he now made out a silvery grey control panel – at any rate some sort of flat surface with smooth silvery excrescences and geometrical shapes limned on it. Straining his head around, he could see similar panels beyond each of his spread and outstretched arms, the three panels being situated relative to each other at the apices of an equilateral triangle inscribed in the saucer, but each of them half hidden by the embowering flowers – very much as crassly functional objects such as heater and sink and phone and hi-fi might be masked in the small apartment of a modish and aesthetically-minded woman.

The whole was bathed in bright, warm, beachy light coming from . . . he couldn't see where. An invisible indoor sun – most eerie.

Eerier still and infinitely closer to home was the feeling that next came to him: that his mind was being invaded and his memories and knowledge riffled through like so many decks of cards. He tritely recalled how a drowning man is supposed to relive his life in a few seconds, and he wondered if it applied when you drowned in flowers – or were crucified by a tiger preparatory to being torn apart and devoured.

The sensations in his mind flashed so fast he could see and hear only blurrs. They were his own private mental possessions, yet he was unable to note them as they flashed and faded – an ultimate humiliation! A few images he was able to catch towards the end of this mental 'customs search' showed an odd preoccupation with zoos and ballets.

He looked around but could catch no glimpse of the tiger-thing or of Miaow. The invisible sun radiated on. The flower-banks were deathly still, exuding their perfumes.

Donald Merriam was midway in his third passage through the Wanderer's shadow. To his right was the strange planet's green-spotted night side, which still made him think of a spider's underbelly. Ahead lay the sheaf of stars, and to his left the black, ever-lengthening ellipsoid of the moon with the cobwebby black threads looping up from its nose against the thickly glittering background. He was beginning to feel tired and cold, and he'd quit working the radio.

A dim, yellowish point appeared against the Wanderer's face, ahead, near the star-sheaf. It rapidly became a yellowish dash, horizontal to him, then a double dash with a little black stretch in the middle like the popular new fluorescent auto headlights, then two yellowish spindles that grew in size.

Only then did Don realize that this wasn't some sort of surface appearance on the Wanderer, but a material something – or two things – headed straight at the Baba Yaga. He flinched and blinked his eyes, and the next instant, without any gradual deceleration that he could note, the two yellow spindles had come to a dead stop to either side of the Baba Yaga and so close that the frame of the spacescreen chopped off the outer dagger-end of each spindle.

They looked to him now like two saucer-shaped spacecraft between thirty and fifty feet across and three or four yards thick. At least, he rather hoped they were spacecraft – and not, well, animals.

His estimate of their shape was confirmed when, without any visible flash of vernier jets, they tilted towards him and became two yellow circles, one with a violet triangle inscribed in it, the other with a violet *V*, the legs of which stretched from centre to rim.

Then he felt his spacesuited body pushed gently backward as the Baba Yaga was drawn forward between its escorts – that was how he began to think of them – until only the forward edges of their rims showed in the spacescreen. They held position very precisely thereafter, as if they had locked on to his little moon-ship – and somehow on to his body too, a very strange sensation.

The next thing he noticed was that the pale green spots were crawling down the Wanderer's black rotundity as if they were so many phosphorescent sow-bugs!

Then he saw that the sheaf of stars was widening as the black ellipsoid of the moon dropped away.

From all indications the Baba Yaga was being drawn upward by its escorts at about one hundred miles a second. Yet he had not felt an atom of the G-forces that ought to have been crushing him against his ship's wall – or smashing him through it!

At no time in the past few hours, not even during his passage through the moon, had Don thought, *This must be an hallucination*. He thought it now. Acceleration and the price you paid for it in fuel and G-strains were the core of his professional knowledge. What was happening to his body and to the Baba Yaga now was not merely a monstrous intrusion of the unknown, it flatly contradicted everything he knew about spaceflight and its iron limitations. From five miles a second, Wanderer-relative, to one hundred at right angles to the first course, yet without feeling it, without even the hint of the firing of some main jet hotter than a blue star – that was not merely weird, it was impossible!

Yet the green spots continued to scuttle out of sight below and the star-sheaf to widen above, and suddenly the Baba Yaga burst into sunlight above the Wanderer. Reflected glare

142

stabbed at his eyes from the left-hand side of the spacescreen frame and the yellow rim of his port escort. He squeezed his eyelids together, fumbled for the polarizing goggles, got them on, then opened his eyes and looked.

The Baba Yaga, locked to its escorts, was still mounting up around the Wanderer at a fantastic velocity. The spacescreen swung a little to the right and, looking over the top of the planet, Don could see Earth, mostly Pacific Ocean now, and the glaring white sun which could sting his eyes even through the goggles.

The planetary surface below him was night side, then a crescent of the day side, mostly yellow but with the far edge violet.

Looping over and around him against star-speckled space were the white threads that came from the moon's nose. Two of them were thicker now – not threads, cords.

Ahead they converged and curved down towards the Wanderer's north pole. There, close together but still separate, they seemed simply to join the planet's velvet surface, some on the day side, some on the north side, a dozen or so of them in all. They looked now like weird, leafless vines sprouting from the top of the Wanderer. The Baba Yaga and its escorts were cannoning across the same spot.

Then, just as it seemed that in the next second they must flash past the thickening stalks or crash into them, Don's strongest convictions about spaceflight were once again battered as the Baba Yaga and its escorts lost most of their velocity in a tranquil instant and simultaneously headed straight down towards the black-and-yellow rooting place of the stalks.

Either his escorts had the inertia-less drive at which everyone but science-fiction writers scoffed, and were carrying the Baba Yaga in their null-G field, or he was hallucinating, or –

He turned to the control panel and tried for a radar fix on the surface below. Rather to his surprise he got an instant echo.

They were three hundred and twenty miles above the surface and closing with it at ten miles a second.

Automatically, he chorded the verniers to reverse the Baba Yaga's altitude so as to be able to brake with what little main-jet fuel he had left.

The vernier jets didn't budge the Baba Yaga. Its space-screen continued to face the planet below. And only now did he notice that they were plummeting down closely parallel to the day side of one of the threads that had become cords, then stalks. It looked enormous here, maybe a mile thick, its pale expanse filling a quarter of the spacescreen.

But in fantastic perspective, like some exaggerated Frank Lloyd Wright pillar, thick towards the roof, thin towards the floor, it narrowed almost to a point where it met the planet's night side very close to the daylight line.

And looking at the pillar's surface this close by, he could see that it wasn't all smooth, but smooth stuff filled with jagged chunks – surely the mixture of moon rock and moon dust he'd guessed was being sucked up from the whirlpool-pits in the moon's nose.

The chunks moved slowly downward past him, like a train moving just a little faster along a parallel railway track.

But that meant the whole pillar was hurtling downward at the same speed as the Baba Yaga – ten miles a second. Why wasn't it exploding in a tremendous rock-spatter where it hit the Wanderer?

Suddenly the rocks in the pillar began to flash downward past him, then the whole pillar was blurred smooth – as if the train on the next track had become an express.

Either the pillar had speeded up, or –

He radar-checked again. The altitude of the Baba Yaga and its escorts had shrunk to thirty miles, but now they were closing at only a mile a second.

His second guess had hit it: they'd slowed up.

But they weren't slowing any more than that, the radar showed. He used the last twenty seconds in scanning the surface below for detail. There wasn't any – no lights on the night side, nothing but lemon velvet plain on the day side. The plunging rock-dust pillar kept its massive width beside them.

Don was running out of seconds as they plunged into the Wanderer's shadow. He whipped off his goggles. The leading rims of his escorts showed up with the same lemon phosphorescence they'd shown behind the planet. For an instant he thought he saw them dully reflected in the black surface below. He nerved himself for the crash, and extinction.

Then all at once the black surface wasn't there, and, as if the Baba Yaga and its escorts had burst hurtlessly through the ceiling of a gigantic lamplit room, he was staring down at another surface far below.

It had to be far below, because the down-rushing pillar of moon rock, still bulking vast to the side, narrowed almost to a point where it touched it and was changed by this fantastic foreshortening from a pillar to a moon-rock triangle.

One inference seemed clear. All the surface of the Wanderer he'd seen up to this moment – the surface that had reflected sunlight and radar so truly – the surface that had been yellow and violet on the day side, black with phosphorescent green spots on the night side – was nothing more than a film, a film so thin and insubstantial that a frail spaceship like the Baba Yaga could burst through it at a mile a second without suffering the least shock or damage, a film roofing and concealing all the artificial daylight and true life of the Wanderer, a film stretched out everywhere about twenty miles above the true surface of the planet – if what he was gazing down at now was true surface and not some fresh illusion.

It was true surface if complexity and every appearance of solidity were criteria. Below him, filling the spacescreen, stretched a vast, softly-lighted plain gleaming with lakes, or at least with smooth turquoise patches of some sort, a plain dotted with dusky, deep-twinkling circular pits a mile or more across, a plain that was otherwise crowded with all sorts of huge objects of every colour and solidly geometric shape imaginable – cones, cubes, cylinders, coils, hemispheres, ziggurats, multilobed rondures – not one object of which Don recognized except as an abstraction.

Giant buildings, machines, vehicles, pure artistic forms? They might have been any or all of those.

Several comparisons flashed through his mind. The Japanese art of rock arrangement on a gigantic scale. Science-fiction book covers of the sort that show an endless floor covered with abstract sculptures looking half alive.

Then his thoughts went dipping far back into the mixed

memories and pseudomemories of very early childhood, and he remembered being taken to visit his grandmother in Minneapolis, and the sour, dry smell of her great-ceilinged living room, and being lifted to look at – not to touch – the doors of a whatnot covered with what he had later assumed must have been cowrie shells, Chinese coins, paperweights, polished rock specimens, flowers in plastic – chaste knick-knacks of many sorts, which had been utterly strange and meaningless though most fascinating to the baby Don Merriam.

Now he was a baby again.

Here and there between him and the plain, though not directly below, floated irregularly shaped, small dark clouds, each holding, as if it were a nest for rainbow eggs, a clutch of great glowing globes which shot upward light of all hues.

These clouds began themselves to shoot up past him, reminding him that the Baba Yaga, its speed hardly diminished, was nearing the grandly crowded surface below. Similarly, the visible section of the plain was swiftly shrinking and the beautiful, unidentifiable shapes growing rapidly larger. But he felt no fear – hitting the film had exhausted all that.

The Baba Yaga and its escorts were aimed at a point midway between two of the large pits, which lay so close together that at first they seemed to touch tangentially. Into one of these pits the rock pillar plunged. The other showed the dusky twilight that seemed characteristic of all the open pits.

At last the margin between the pits acquired a width, became a silvery ribbon. One of the escorts seemed to settle into the hurtling rock pillar, it flew so close to it.

The next instant, without the faintest shock or jar and with all the impossible feel of dream flying, the Baba Yaga came to a dead stop no more than a dozen feet above a dull silver pavement – so close to it, in fact, that Don could see designs etched on its surface: a whirlingly complex arabesque with bands of hieroglyphics.

Still weightless, he hovered above the spacescreen and goggled down through it, feeling like a fish looking through a window in the floor of its aquarium.

Then, as if a couple of verniers had been fired or a giant

hand had grasped it, the Baba Yaga began to upend. Don grabbed at the pilot's seat to steady himself.

The motion stopped half-way around, when the ship's main jet would be pointing at the pavement below. Gradually then a gravity field took hold of him and the ship. He heard three faint thumps and simultaneously felt three gentle jolts as the three legs of his ship footed themselves. He clutched the seat tighter as his weight grew until, so far as he could judge after a month on the moon, it was as much or almost as much as it had been on Earth. Then his weight stopped growing.

But he noted these things with a lower fraction of his mind only, for his main attention was absorbed by the view the spacescreen now gave him of the Wanderer's sky – the underside of the film through which he had broken some forty seconds ago.

Between him and it, the small dark clouds – darker now since he could no longer see the gleaming eggs they nested – sailed steadily past, much as small clouds move across the deserts of the American Southwest before a steady west wind, withholding their rain. At no time did they obscure more than an eighth of the sky. Nor did the down-rushing rock pillar, now tapering up to a point high as the sky itself, its triangle reversed, obscure more than another eighth.

That sky was neither pale violet nor yellow, nor dead black anywhere, nor did it show any stars. It was instead a slow swirling of all dark colours, a dusky rainbow storm sky sweeping along in ever-changing hues and curving patterns. It had the harmony and grandeur and menace of a perpetual colour-symphony, yet it seemed natural, promising endless vital variations. Whether its light came mostly from itself, or from that thrown upward by the now-concealed globes on the clouds, or from some other indirect source, Don could not tell. It resembled somewhat the marbling of a film of oil on water, and somewhat Van Gogh's wild painting, 'The Starry Night', and even more the deep, glinting hues that flow churningly past the mind's eye in the dark.

Just as he was thinking that last thought, which seemed to put him on the inside of some vast mind, he heard a tiny grating sound which chilled his blood. He looked down quickly enough to see the last of the dogs on the hatch move aside by itself and the hatch lift without visible agency, showing him the empty ladder moving down out of its housing to the empty silver pavement below.

Then a voice, strangely sweet and cajoling, called to him in only slightly slurred English: 'Come! Unsuit yourself and come down!'

Australia, Indonesia, the Philippines, Japan, and the eastern parts of China and Siberia had now swung into Earth's night side. The Wanderer, often first seen as the yin-yang or the mandala, set religious and mystical strings vibrating in millions of minds. And East Asian voices were added to the American ones warning the cluster of sceptical old continents to the west – the world's cultural heartland – of what they would see at nightfall.

Chapter 20

Paul Hagbolt had grown very tired of his bondage and peculiarly bored with his spread-eagled reflection, and the invisible sun had dried his front completely, when he spotted two cryptic cat faces peering at him from a stretch of flowerbank by the control panel beyond his feet. The one was Miaow's, the other was large as his own. They came floating forward from the gloom, and their bodies after their faces with a sinuous grace that hardly quivered a single pink petal or green spear, until they were barely emerged from the flowers – whereupon without further glance at him they settled themselves in the air facing each other, so that he saw them in profile.

The tiger-being held out Miaow facing her, cradling the little grey cat on one spread paw and slim green secondary forearm – Paul realized that the second elbow which had terrified him was simply the normal feline wrist above the elongated palm bones that make a secondary forearm above the paw.

Miaow's fur was now fluffy, dry, and she lolled on her back, fantastically at ease, grey tail draped over violet-barred wrist, staring gravely into the great, violet-petalled eyes of her captor – or rather, her new friend, to judge from appearances.

They looked remarkably like mother and tiny child.

Paul's feelings about the tiger-being, his very picture of her, underwent rapid changes as he watched her in repose – this time he thought of her from the first as 'she', an assumption bastioned by the apparent absence of external sex organs, except for two modest, indigo-ruddy nipples high in the green fur of her chest.

For a feline, she was short-bodied, long-legged, long-armed – in build more like a cheetah than any other terrestrial cat, though considerably larger; human size. The general proportions, too, were more human than feline – he guessed that in gravity she would be at least as much biped as quadruped.

The fur of her throat, chest, underbelly, and the insides of her arms and legs was green, the rest, green barred with violet.

Her head was prick-eared as any cat's, but with a higher and broader forehead, seeming to increase the triangularity of the whole face, which was nevertheless completely feline, even to indigo button-nose and pale whisker hairs. Here the fur was violet except for a green mask across the eyes.

Despite the secondary forearms above them, the slim paws looked quite like hands now – three-fingered hands with an opposed thumb. The claws were invisible, presumably retracted and sheathed.

The violet-barred green tail swung gracefully over a half-bent hind leg.

The total effect, he realized suddenly – even the tail! – was now very close to that of a slim, tall woman dressed in a skin-tight fur costume for some fantastic cat-ballet. He felt a disturbing pang as he had that thought.

And just at that moment the tiger-being began to speak in English – clipped and exotically slurred, yet English nevertheless – not directing her speech towards him but to Miaow.

It was all so 'impossible' that Paul listened as if in a dream.

'Come, little one,' the tiger-being said, poutingly parting only the two central inches of her mulberry lips. 'We friends now. No need be shy.'

149

Miaow continued to stare at her gravely, contentedly.

'You me same folk,' the tiger-being continued winningly. 'You easeful now, I feel. So speak. Ask question.'

A pause, with Paul feeling on the verge of understanding the fantastic cross-purposes that had begun to operate. Then the tiger-being said: 'You shy one! You want front names? I know yours. Mine? – Tigerishka! Name I invent especially for you. You think me terrible tiger, also beautiful toes dancer. Toe dancers call selves, "-enska, -skaya, -ishka." Tigerishka!'

Then Paul understood. It was the super-error of a super-being. Tigerishka had been reading his thoughts to the point of learning his language in seconds, but all the while attributing those thoughts to her fellow-feline Miaow.

At the same time he realized what the disturbing pang had been: plain male desire for a thrillingly attractive she-being.

Tigerishka must have caught that thought, too, for she waved an indigo-padded finger at Miaow in playful reproof and said: 'You have naughty feelings about me, little one. Really, you are not big enough – and we both girls! Come now, speak . . . Paul . . .'

At that moment the presumably horrible truth must have occurred to her, for she slowly turned her head to stare at the real Paul, simultaneously toeing the edge of the floor below her. The next second she had sprung across the cabin and was poised above him, dagger-claws spread, mulberry lips writhed back from inch-and-a-half needle canines in her upper jaw. She still held Miaow, who seemed not greatly startled by the sudden activity.

Beyond her green slope-shoulder were stacked reflections of her back and of Paul's own face grimacing madly.

'You – ape!' Tigerishka snarled. She thrust her great-jawed head down so that he winced his eyes three-quarters shut. Then, spacing out the words as one might to a barely literate peasant, she said: 'You treat – little one – like beast – like *pet*?' The horrified contempt in the last word was glacial-volcanic.

All Paul could do in his frantic terror was snatch at something Margo was always saying, and gibber: 'No! No! Cats are people!'

Don Merriam had stood on the rim of Earth's Grand Canyon. He had also looked over the edge of the Leibnitz Cleft near the south pole of the moon. But never – except when he had driven the Baba Yaga through Luna – certainly never from a solid footing, had he peered into anything remotely as deep as the open, mile-wide circular pit that yawned only two dozen paces across the silver pavement from where the Baba Yaga stood with its ladder thrust down between its three legs.

How far did the pit go down? Five miles? Twenty-five? Five hundred? It seemed to maintain its one-mile width indefinitely. The equivalent in emptiness of what the plunging pillar of moon rock was in solidity, it narrowed somewhere far below to a tiny, hazy round that was little more than a point – and that narrowing was only the consequence of the laws of perspective and the limitations of his visual powers.

He toyed with the notion that the shaft went straight through the centre of the planet to the other side, so that if he leaped off the edge now he would never hit bottom, but only fall four thousand miles or so – a weary fall, that, taking twenty hours at least, if terminal velocities in this planet's atmosphere were like those on Earth, almost time enough to die of thirst – and then, finally, perhaps after a few reverberations of reversed and re-reversed fall, come to rest in the air at the planet's centre and slowly swim to the side of the shaft, just as he'd swum through the air of the Baba Yaga's cabin in free fall.

Of course the air pressure down there, four thousand miles down, would be more than enough to crush him – perhaps enough to drive oxygen monatomic! – but *they* would surely have ways of dealing with that, ways of making the air exactly as thin or as thick as they wanted it at every depth.

Already he was doing a great deal of thinking in terms of *their* powers – powers which increased each time he turned his eyes, each time he thought, though he had yet to see a single one of *them*.

The false memory of his childhood came again, of the pit he'd found that went through the earth behind his family's farm. So now he stared down the shaft hunting for a star, or rather for a hint of the captive antipodean day under its section of vaulted sky-film eight thousand miles down there. But even as he hunted he knew it was a visual impossibility, and in any case it was made quite infeasible by the multitude of lights glowing, flashing, and twinkling from the sides of the shaft at every floor.

For the strangest and most unnatural thing about the shaft was simply that it *was* unnatural, not something occurring in or driven through solid rock – in fact, there was no sign of rock anywhere – but floor after floor, tiered endlessly downward, of artificial structure and habitable inner volume. The floors began after a blank hundred feet or so at the top and were never afterwards interrupted.

He could count hundreds of those floors, he was sure, before they began to merge and run together, again due solely to the limitations of his vision. Yet judging by the ones towards the top, they were very tall, spacious floors, suggesting a life of perhaps more than human grandeur and scope, despite the, to him, claustrophobic feel of such a downward infinity of rooms and corridors.

The only comparisons for it that he could dredge from his memory – and they were most inadequate comparisons – were the inner courts, tiered with balconies, of certain large department stores and office buildings, or perhaps a skylight shaft shooting down through the stacks of some vast unmicro-filmed library.

Far below now he thought he could see small airships winging across the shaft, and perhaps up and down it, like lazy beetles, and some of those seemed to twinkle too, like the phosphorescent beetles of the tropics.

In his desire to peer deeper into the pit, he leaned out farther over it, gripping tightly with his bare hands the upper of two satin-smooth silver rails that fenced it. Even that simple feature of his surroundings was unnatural and indicative of *their* powers, for the rails had no supports. They were a pair of mile-wide, thin silver hoops hung two and a little more than three feet above the pit's margin. Or, if there were invisible uprights, he had not yet touched or kicked into them. He could see only a couple of hundred yards of the hoops in either direction; beyond that they vanished like telegraph wires. However, he assumed they went all the way around.

But with so many signs of *them* down below, and evidences of their workmanship everywhere, their science and technology, so near magic, where were *they*? Why had he been left alone so long?

He turned his back on the pit and peered all around him uneasily, but nowhere on the silver pavement nor about the smooth, windowless, geometric structures rising from it could he see a living figure, or any figure he judged might be living – humanoid, animal, or otherwise.

The two violet-and-yellow, bulge-centred saucers still hung enigmatically a dozen feet above the pavement, just as when he'd last turned his back on them, and the Baba Yaga stood midway between them, exactly as he'd left it. This was what had happened so far: when the voice had called to him in its faintly slurred, oddly thrilling English, he had unsuited obediently, almost eagerly, and quickly climbed down out of the Baba Yaga, but there had been no one there. After waiting for minutes at the foot of the ladder, he had walked over to the pit and been enthralled.

Now he began to wonder if the voice mightn't have been pure illusion. It was unreasonable to think of an alien being able to speak English without any preliminary parleying. Or was it? *Their* powers . . .

He took a deep breath. At least the air seemed real enough.

The silence was profound, except that when he held still and relaxed and closed his eyes and let out his breath softly, he thought he could hear the faintest, muted, deep-throated rumbling. The blood of this strange planet, coursing? Or only his own blood? Or the rumbling might come from the pillar of moon rock hurtling into the other pit, no farther beyond the Baba Yaga and the invisibly suspended saucers than he was standing in front of them.

The grey pillar, occupying a full third of his horizon but tapering swiftly almost to a point at the top of the sky, looked at first glance like a solid mountain, except that he knew it was plunging steadily downward at a speed great enough to make its component particles and fragments individually invisible – presumably the same ten miles a second at which he'd

153

judged it to be moving above the sky-film that roofed the atmosphere.

As he watched the pillar, he began to see slow changes in its contours – bulgings and channellings that formed slowly and held their shape for many seconds and then shifted into other smooth forms. It reminded him of the grotesque bulgings and groovings that a stream from a faucet will hold – sometimes so persistently that the shape seems to be one of solid crystal rather than rushing water.

But how could the thing be moving at such a supersonic velocity – two seconds from the sky to the floor! – through the palpable air – the air he knew had to be there because he was breathing it – without creating a fierce and tumultuous dust storm of eddies in that air, without a roar like that of a dozen first-stage rockets or a score of Niagaras?

They must, somehow, perhaps using an unheard-of field, have created a wall-less vacuum channel, just as surely as they must have created – now he came to think of it – similar wall-less tubular vacua for the Baba Yaga and its escorts to travel through after they burst the sky-film . . . and, even before that, through the thin plasma and micrometeorites of space.

He continued to stare up the weirdly foreshortened grey pillar. How long could this monstrous transfer go on? How long would the moon last, even as an ellipsoid of pale gravel spreading into a ring, at this rate of depletion? How long would there be any moon-stuff left outside the Wanderer?

From the sector of his brain schooled in engineering and solid geometry sprang almost at once the first-approximation answer, that it would take eight thousand days for one such rock stream, moving ten miles a second, to transport the moon's entire substance. He had seen only a dozen of the rock streams.

But *they* might speed up the streams, and there might be another set at the Wanderer's south pole, and others being brought into existence. Looking aside from the pillar, he now did see three more in the distance : they looked like great grey waterspouts twisting up towards the sky.

The sky was now all dark blues and greens and browns, slowly swirling in a great edge-blended river, austere and menacing. He looked down towards the paler structures ringing the empty silver pavement except where the pits were; he let his gaze travel around the pillar-broken circle of those smoothly monstrous, multiform, pastel-shaded solidities, and it seemed to him that some of the more distant ones had changed position and shape – *and in some cases crept closer* – since he'd last studied them.

The idea of great buildings – or whatever they were – moving about when there were no other signs of life disturbed him greatly and he turned back to the silver-railed pit behind him to scan its topmost levels, almost desperately, for indications of some smaller-scale activity. He tried to look at the top floors immediately below him, or close to either side, but the silver lip on which he was standing overlapped the pit itself for several yards like a roof and cut off his view. So he peered across at the topmost windows and balconies, and after a while he began to think he could see small figures moving in them, but at a mile or even a half mile it wasn't easy to be sure of that, and anyway his eyes were beginning to swim and prickle. He was wondering whether he dared return to the cabin for the binoculars – when a voice, sweet-toned yet commanding, spoke from behind him.

'Come!'

Don turned around very slowly. Standing a little taller than himself, not twenty feet away, with the erect grace and pride of a matador, was a lean, silky, red-splotched black biped of shape midway between feline and anthropoid. It looked like a high-foreheaded cheetah a little bigger than a mountain lion and standing as a man stands, or like a slim, black-furred, red-pied tiger wearing a black turban and a narrow red mask – the turban being the unfeline frontal and temporal bulge. Its tail rose like a red spear behind its back. Its ears were pointed. Its serene eyes were large, with something flowerlike about the pupils.

Hardly shifting its close-set, narrow feet, yet with movements like those of a dancer, it extended a four-fingered arm in a gesture of invitation, and opened the thin lips in the black lower mask, showing the needle-tips of white fangs, and softly repeated: 'Come.'

Slowly, as if in a dream, Don moved towards the being.

When he had come close, it nodded, and then the section of pavement on which they were both standing – a circular silver section about eight feet across – began very slowly to sink into the body of the Wanderer. The being moved its extended arm until it rested lightly across Don's shoulders. Don thought of Faust and Mephistopheles descending to Hell. Faust had wanted all knowledge. With his magic mirrors Mephistopheles had given Faust a glimpse of everything. But what magic device can give understanding?

They had sunk barely knee-deep in the pavement when there was a flash in the sky. Suddenly beyond the Baba Yaga there hung a third saucer, and a ship so like the Baba Yaga that Don's throat tightened, and he thought of Dufresne. But then he saw the small difference in structure and the red Soviet star on it.

His view of it was cut off by the silver curve of the pavement as the platform continued to descend.

Chapter 21

While a very few human beings made thrilling and terrifying direct contact with the Wanderer and its denizens, and while a number more studied it with the magnifying and mensurating eyes of science, most of mankind knew the new-come planet only by its naked-eye visage and by the destruction it did. The first instalment of destruction was volcanic and diastrophic. The tides, or tidal strains, set up in Earth's solid crust delivered their effects more swiftly than those in the ocean layer.

Within six hours after the Wanderer's appearance, there had been major activity all along the great earthquake belts circumscribing the Pacific Ocean and stretching along the northern shore of the Mediterranean into the heart of Asia. Land was riven; cities were shaken and shattered. Volcanoes glowed, spouted, and gushed redly. A few exploded. Shocks originated as far apart as Alaska and the Antarctic, many of them occurring undersea. Great tsunami ranged across the oceans, monstrous long swells turning to giant, watery fists on reaching the shallows. Hundreds of thousands died.

Nevertheless there were many areas, even near the sea, where all this wrecking and reaving was only a rumour or a newspaper headline, or perhaps a voice on the radio during those hours of grace before the Wanderer peered over the horizon and poisoned the radio sky.

Richard Hillary had dozed through much of Berks, with no memory of Reading at all, and was only now beginning slowly to wake as the bus first crossed the Thames a little beyond Maidenhead. He told himself it wasn't so much last night's walking that had tired him – he was a great walker – as Dai Davies' literary ranting.

Now it was about noon and the bus was approaching the tideway of the Thames and the dark, smoky loom of London. Richard drew up the shade at last and began a melancholy but not unpleasant rumination about the curses of industrialism, overpopulation, and overconstruction.

'You've been missing it, mate,' said a short man in a bowler hat, who had taken the seat beside him.

On Richard's polite though tepid inquiry, he gladly summarized. During the last quarter of a day there had been a considerable number of earthquakes throughout the world – apparently a seismologist had counted squiggles on a drum and decreed: 'Utterly unprecedented!' – and as a result earthquake waves were a possibility even along British shores: small craft warnings had been posted and a few low coastal areas were being evacuated. Several scientists, presumably sensation-mongering, had issued statements about 'giant tides' in prospect, but such exaggerations had been sternly repudiated by responsible authorities. People with proofreader minds joyously pointed out that to confuse tsunami with tides was an ancient popular error.

At least the earthquake hullabaloo had knocked the giant American saucer out of the news. Though, to balance that gain, Russia was making bomb-rattling protestations about a mysterious assault, successfully beaten off, on her precious lunar base.

Not for the first time Richard reflected that this age's vaunted 'communications industry' had chiefly provided people and nations with the means of frightening to death and simultaneously boring to extinction themselves and each other.

He did not inform his seatmate of this insight, but instead turned to the window as the bus slowed for Brentford, surveying that town with his novelist's eyes, and was rewarded almost at once by a human phenomenon describable as 'a scurry of plumbers': he counted three small cars with the insignia of that trade and five men with toolbags or big wrenches, hurrying places. He smiled, thinking how overbuilding invariably brings its digestive troubles.

The bus stopped, not far from the market and the confluence of the canalized Brent with the Thames. Two women climbed in, the one saying loudly to the other: 'Yes, I just rang up Mother at Kew and she's dreadfully upset. She says the lawn is afloat.'

It happened quite suddenly then: an up-pooling of brown water from the drains in the street, and a runnelling of equally dirty water from the entries of several buildings.

The event struck Richard with peculiar horror because, at a level almost below conscious thought, he saw it as sick, overfed houses discharging, quite independently of the human beings involved with them, the product of their sickness. Architectural diarrhoea. He wasn't thinking at all of how the first sign of a flood is often the backing up of the sewers.

And then there was a scamper of people, and at their heels a curb-to-curb rush of cleaner water, perhaps six inches deep, down the street, washing away the dirty.

It pretty well had to be coming from the Thames. The tidy Thames, Spenser's 'Sweete Themmes'.

The second and larger instalment of destruction was delivered by the Wanderer through the seas covering almost three-quarters of Earth's surface. This watery film may be cosmically trivial, but it has always been a sort of infinity, of distance and of depth and of power, to the dwellers of Earth. And it has always had its gods: Dagon, Nun, Nodens, Ran, Rigi, Neptune, Poseidon. And the music of the seas is the tides.

The harp of the seas, which Diana the moon goddess strums with rapt solemnity, is strung with bands of salt water miles thick, hundreds of miles wide, thousands of miles long.

Across the great reaches of the Pacific and Indian Oceans stretch the bass strings: from the Philippines to Chile, from Alaska to Colombia, Antarctica to California, Arabia to Australia, Basutoland to Tasmania. Here the deeper notes are sounded, some vibrations lasting a full day.

The Atlantic provides the middle voice, *cantabile*. Here the tempo is quicker and more regular, and the half-day the measure: the familiar, semi-daily tides of Western history. Major vibrating bands link Newfoundland to Brazil, Greenland to Spain, South Africa to the Atlantic.

Where the strings cross they may damp each other out, as at the tidal nodes near Norway and the Windward Islands and at Tahiti, where the sun alone controls the little tides – fardistant Apollo plucking feebler than Diana, forever bringing highs at noon and midnight, lows at sunset and dawn.

The treble of the ocean harp is provided by tidal echoes and re-echoes in bays, estuaries, straits, and seas half landlocked. These shortest strings are often loudest and fiercest, as a violin will dominate a bass viol: the high-mounting tides of Fundy and the Severn Estuary, of Northern France and the Strait of Magellan, of the Arabian and Irish Seas.

Touched by the soft fingers of the moon, the water bands vibrate gently – a foot or two up and down, five feet, ten, rarely twenty, most rarely more.

But now the harp of the seas had been torn from Diana's and Apollo's hands and was being twanged by fingers eighty times stronger. During the first day after the Wanderer's appearance the tides rose and fell five to fifteen times higher and lower than normally and, during the second day, ten to twenty-five, the water's response swiftly building to the Wanderer's wild harping. Tides of six feet became sixty; tides of thirty, three hundred – and more.

The giant tides generally followed the old patterns – a different harpist, but the same harp. Tahiti was only one of the many areas on Earth – not all of them far inland – unruffled by

159

the presence of the Wanderer, hardly aware of it except as a showy astronomic spectacle.

The coasts contain the seas with walls which the tides themselves help bite out. In few places are the seas faced with long sweeps of flat land where the tide each day can take miles-long strides landward and back: the Netherlands and Northern Germany, a few other beaches and salt marshes, Northwest Africa.

But there are many flat coasts only a few feet or a few dozen feet above the ocean. There the multiplied tides raised by the Wanderer moved ten, twenty, fifty, and more miles inland. With great heads of water behind them and with narrowing valleys ahead, some moved swiftly and destructively, fronted and topped by wreckage, filled with sand and soil, footed by clanking stones and crashing rocks. At other spots the invasion of the tide was silent as death.

At points of sharp tides and sharp but not very high coastal walls – Fundy, the Bristol Channel, the estuaries of the Seine and the Thames and the Fuchun – spill-overs occurred: great mushrooms of water welling out over the land in all directions.

Shallow continental shelves were swept by the drain of low tides, their sands cascaded into ocean abysses. Deep-sunk reefs and islands appeared; others were covered as deeply. Shallow seas, and gulfs like the Persian, were drained once or twice daily. Straits were grooved deeper. Sea-water poured across low isthmi. Counties and countries of fertile fields were salt-poisoned. Herds and flocks were washed away. Homes and towns were scoured flat. Great ports were drowned.

Despite the fog of catastrophe and the suddenness of the astronomic strike, there were prodigies of rescue performed: a thousand Dunkirks, a hundred thousand brave improvisations. Disaster-focused organizations such as coast guards and the Red Cross functioned meritoriously; and some of the preparations for atomic and other catastrophe paid off.

Yet millions died.

Some saw disaster coming and were able to take flight and did. Others, even in areas most affected, did not.

Dai Davies strode across the mucky, littered bottom-sands of the Severn Estuary through the dissipating light fog with the furious energy and concentration of a drunkard at the peak of his alcoholic powers. His clothes and hands were smeared where he'd twice slipped and fallen, only to scramble up and pace on with hardly a check. From time to time he glanced back and corrected his course when he saw his footsteps veering. And from time to time he swigged measuredly from a flat bottle without breaking his stride.

The Somerset shore had faded long since, except for the vaguest loom through the remaining mist of maritime industrial structures upriver towards Avonmouth. Long since there had died away the insincere cheers and uncaring admonitions 'Come back, you daft Welshman, you'll drown!' – of the pub-mates he'd met this morning.

He chanted sporadically: 'Five miles to Wales across the sands, from noon to two while the ebb tide stands,' occasionally varying it with such curses as 'Effing loveless Somersets! – I'll shame 'em!' and 'Damned moon-grabbing Yanks!' and such snatches of his half-composed *Farewell to Mona* as, 'Frore Mona in your meteor-skiff . . . Girlglowing, old as Fomalhaut . . . Trailing white fingers in my pools . . . Drawing my waters to and fro. . . .'

There was a faint roaring ahead. A helicopter ghosted by, going downriver, but the roaring remained. Dai crossed a particularly slimy dip in which his shoes sank out of sight and had to be jerked plopping out. He decided it must be the Severn Channel and that he was now mounting on to the great sandy stretch of bottom known as the Welsh Grounds.

But the roaring grew louder; the going got easier because the sands were sloping down again; a last mist-veil faded; and suddenly his way was blocked by a rapid, turbid river more than a hundred yards wide, humping into foam-crested ridges and eating greedily at the sandy banks to either side.

He stopped in stupefaction. It had simply never occurred to him that, no matter how low the tide went, the Severn was a river and would keep flowing. And now he knew he couldn't have come a quarter of the way across the Channel.

Upstream he could see an angry white humping and jetting where – to be sure! – the Avon came crashing into the bigger river.

Far downstream loomed the canted stern of a steamer aground. The 'copter hovered over it. There were faint hootings.

He leaped back as a long stretch of bank caved in almost at his feet. Nevertheless he bravely stripped off his coat, since swimming seemed in order, stopping midway to get out the bottle. Through the near water a splintered black beam with laths nailed across it went slashing downstream like a great, hook-bladed knife. He put the bottle to his lips. It was empty.

He shivered and shook. Suddenly he saw himself as an ant with the ambitions of a Napoleon. Fear closed in.

He looked behind him. His footprints had smoothed to barely distinguishable hollows and bumps. And there was a glisten of water all over the sands that hadn't been there before. The tide had turned.

He threw away the bottle and began to run back along his footprints before they faded altogether. His feet sank in deeper than they had in coming.

Jake Lesher thumbed a light switch back and forth, although he'd had proof enough that the electricity was gone. He studied the elevator in the dimness of the living room. The cage had dropped six inches in the last quake and now tilted a little. Its aluminium looked rippled in the shadows. He thought he saw black threads curling out of it, and he retreated from them into the murky sunshine of the patio.

'There's more smoke coming out now, and I can see some flames,' Sally Harris called to him from where she was craning over the balustrade. 'The flames are coming up the building, and people are watching them from the windows across, but the water's coming up faster – I think. It's a race. Gee, Jake, this is a flood like in the Bible, and Hugo's penthouse is our Noah's ark. That's the idea we'll build our play around. We'll use the fire, too.'

He grabbed and shook her. 'This is all for real, you little moron! We're the ones that'll be fried.'

'But Jake,' she protested, 'you always got to have a real situation to make a play. I read that somewhere.'

All over Earth the senses and minds of very many people were locked against the change in the tides. Those inland were inclined to doubt or minimize what they could not see with their own eyes, and many of them had never seen an ocean. Men at sea, beyond sight of land, cannot perceive the tidal bulge beneath them – they can hardly perceive the vastly shorter earthquake waves – and so they could not note if that tidal bulge in which their ship moved were a few feet or a few dozen feet higher than it should be, or the tidal hollow, correspondingly lower.

The insurgents who had seized the *Prince Charles* had so much to do what with running the internal business of the great atomic liner, dealing with passengers, and heading off attempts on the part of the crew to turn the tables, that they found it necessary to elect four of themselves captain, with equal powers. It was hours before this revolutionary board of directors got the ship's course shaped towards Cape St Roque, for Rio, where their leaders were supposed to have overthrown the government last night – something which could not be confirmed because of the choking-off of radio communication. The imprisoned Captain Sithwise's urgent plea that they atomsteam for the tidal node by the Windward Isles was laughed at as an obvious ruse to bring them nearer ships of the British Navy.

Wolf Loner watched the great cloudbank close down around the *Endurance* until the dory was almost running through fog. In that tiny, ship-centred cosmos of water and blurry whiteness, the old fancies occurred to him that all the rest of the world might have vanished except for this one spot, or that there might be an atomic war now, with cities vanishing like coals that pop in a fire, or that a plague of virulent, artificially cultured germs might be sweeping all the continents and he be the only man alive when he stepped ashore in Boston. He smiled unanxiously. 'Brace yourself against your atoms,' he said.

But many minds were locked to facts that came pounding at the door. In the Tidal Institute at Hamburg, Fritz Scher explained away to his own satisfaction, and almost to that of Hans Opfel, every shockingly divergent tidal reading that came in. Either there was a precedent for the new reading – such a tide had occurred at the same spot forty or four hundred years ago – or the waters were being bulked by a storm the purblind weather men had missed; or someone of known carelessness had misread instruments; or someone of known instability had gone crazy; or someone of known Communist sympathies had lied.

'Just you wait,' Fritz smilingly told Hans Opfel when the latter indicated the growing pile of reports of the Wanderer and of the moon's destruction. 'Just you wait. When night comes, the jolly old moon will be up there all by himself – and laughing down at you!' He leaned lightly against the smooth case of the tide-predicting machine and patted it affectionately, almost hugged it. '*You* know what fools they are, don't you?' he murmured infatuatedly.

Other minds accepted the situation.

Barbara Katz swabbed up some last fragments of egg and sausage with a section of buttermilk pancake soaking in one hundred per cent maple syrup, pushed her coffee cup across the big kitchen table to Hester, and sighed her appreciation and gratitude. Outside the birds were warbling in the sunlight. The big old pendulum wall-clock said eight-thirty in Roman numerals. A big calendar showing a view of the Everglades hung below the clock.

Hester smiled broadly at Barbara as she poured out more of the wonderfully strong coffee, and said: 'Seems more natural and wholesome-like, now old KKK got himself a real fancy girl instead of that doll.'

Helen, the younger coloured woman, giggled and then looked away in mischief and embarrassment, but Barbara took it in her stride.

'I believe those are called Barbie dolls,' she remarked. 'Well, my name happens to be Barbara, too – Barbara Katz.'

Hester laughed heartily at that, and Helen smothered more giggles.

'Why do you call him old KKK?' Barbara asked.

'Middle name Kelsey,' Hester explained. 'Knolls Kelsey Kettering III. You Katz the fourth K.' And she started laughing again.

There was a long, soft creaking. 'Shut the screen door, Benjy,' Hester said sharply out of her laughter, but the tall Negro didn't move. He stood half-way through the door in his white shirt and his silver-grey trousers which had stripes of dark grey tape running down the seams. There was a big tuft of cotton in the top of the screen – a modern white fetish against flies.

'There's the most monstrous low tide ever,' he informed them earnestly. 'People walking straight out like they could get to Grand Bahama without wetting the ankle. Picking up fresh fish by the basket, some of them!'

Barbara sat straight up, set down her coffee cup and snapped her fingers.

'Other folk TV ain't working either – *or* radio,' Benjy added, looking at her, as did Hester and Helen.

'Do you know when low tide is, exactly?' Barbara asked intently.

'Seven-thirty, about,' Benjy answered without hesitation. 'Hour ago. It have it all on the backs of those calendar sheets.'

'Tear off the top one,' she told him. 'What kind of a car does Mr K have?'

'Only the two Rolls,' he told her. 'Limousine and sedan.'

'Get the sedan ready for a long trip,' she told him sharply. 'All the extra gas she can carry – take it from the limousine! We'll need blankets, too, and all Mister K's medicines and lots of food and more of this coffee in thermos jugs . . . and a couple of those table-water bottles in the corner!'

They stared at her fascinatedly. Her excitement was contagious, but they were puzzled. 'Why for, child?' Hester demanded. Helen started to giggle again.

Barbara looked at them impressively, then said: 'Because there's a high tide coming! As high as this one's low – and higher!'

'That because of the – Wanderer?' Benjy asked, handing her the sheet she'd asked for.

She nodded decisively as she studied its back. She said: 'Mr K has a smaller telescope. Where would that be?'

'Telescope?' Hester asked with grinning incredulity. She said: 'Now, why for – oh, sho, astronomy what you and Mr K have in common. Now, I expect he put that one – the one he spy on the gals with – back in the gun room.'

'Gun room?' Barbara asked, her eyes brightening. 'What about ready cash?'

'It'd be in one of the wall safes,' Hester said, frowning at Barbara just a little.

Chapter 22

The saucer students were at last beginning to feel alive again after their ducking and their exhausting race with the waves. The men had built a driftwood fire beside the empty highway near the low concrete bridge at the head of the wash, and everyone was drying out around it, which necessitated considerable comradely trading around of clothes and of the unwetted blankets and stray articles of dress from the truck.

Rama Joan cut down the trousers of her salt-streaked evening clothes to Bermuda shorts, ruthlessly chopped off the tails and half the arms of the coat, replaced the ruined dicky and white tie with the green scarf of her turban, and gathered her red-gold hair in a pony tail. Ann and Doc admired her.

Everybody looked pretty battered. Margo noticed that Ross Hunter appeared trimmer than the other men, then realized it was because, while most of them were getting slightly stubbly cheeks and chins, he simply still had the beard that had made him Beardy.

As the sky blued and brightened, their spirits rose and it became just a bit hard to think that all of last night had actually happened, and that a violet and gold planet was at this moment terrorizing Japan, Australia, and the other islands of the half-planet-spanning Pacific Ocean.

But they could see a monster slide blocking the road not two hundred yards north, while Doc pointed out the wreckage of the beach house and the platform lodged against the gleaming fence of Vandenberg Two, little more than a mile away.

'Still,' he said, 'humanity's scepticism about its own experiences grows like mushrooms. How about another affidavit for us all to sign, Doddsy?'

'I'm keeping a journal of events in waterproof ink,' the Little Man retorted briskly. 'It's open to inspection at any time.' He took his notebook and slowly riffled the pages to emphasize that point. 'If anyone's memory of events differs from mine, I'll be happy to make a note of that – providing he'll initial the divergent recollection.'

Wojtowicz, staring down over the Little Man's shoulder, said: 'Hey, Doddsy, some of those pictures you got of the Wanderer don't look right to me.'

'I smoothed out the details and made them quite diagrammatic,' the Little Man admitted. 'However, I did draw them . . . from the life. But if you want to make some memory pictures of the new planet – and initial them! – you're welcome to put them in the book.'

'Not me, I'm no artist,' Wojtowicz excused himself grinningly.

'You'll be able to check up tonight, Wojtowicz,' Doc said.

'Jeeze, don't remind me!' the other said, clapping his hand to his eyes and doing a little comedy stagger.

Only the Ramrod remained miserable, sitting apart on the wide bridge-rail and staring hungrily out towards the sea's rim where the Wanderer had set.

'She chose *him*,' he muttered wonderingly. 'I believed, yet I was passed over. *He* was drawn into the saucer.'

'Never mind, Charlie,' said Wanda, laying her plump hand on his thin shoulder. 'Maybe it wasn't the Empress but only her handmaiden, and she got the orders mixed.'

'You know, that was truly weird, that saucer swooping down on us,' Wojtowicz said to the others. 'Just one thing about it – are you sure you saw Paul pulled up into it? I don't like to say this, but he could have been sucked out to sea, like almost happened to several of us.'

Doc, Rama Joan, and Hunter averred they'd seen it with their own eyes. 'I think she was more interested in the cat than Paul,' Rama Joan added.

'Why so?' the Little Man asked. 'And why "she"?'

Rama Joan shrugged. 'Hard to say, Mr Dodd. Except she

167

looked like a cat herself, and I didn't notice any external sex organs.'

'Neither did I,' Doc confirmed, 'though I won't say I was peering for them at the time with lewd avidity.'

'Do you think the saucer actually had an inertialess drive – like E. E. Smith's bergenholms or something?' Harry McHeath asked Doc.

'Have to, I'd think, the way it was bumping around. In a situation like this, science fiction is our only guide. On the other hand –'

Margo took advantage of everyone being engrossed in the conversation to fade back between the bushes in the direction the other women had taken earlier on their bathroom trips. She climbed over a small ridge beside the wash and came out on a boulder-strewn, wide earth ledge about twenty feet above the beach.

She looked around her. She couldn't see anyone anywhere. She took out from under her leather jacket the grey pistol that had fallen from the saucer. It was the first chance she'd had to inspect it closely. Keeping it concealed while she'd dried her clothes had been an irksome problem.

It was unburnished grey – aluminium or magnesium, by its light weight – and smoothly streamlined. There was no apparent hole in the tapering muzzle for anything material to come out. In front of the trigger-bump was an oval button. The grip seemed shaped for two fingers and a thumb. In the left side of the grip, away from her palm as she held it in her right hand, was a narrow vertical strip that shone violet five-eighths of its length up, rather like a recessed thermometer.

She gripped the gun experimentally. Just beyond the end of the muzzle she noted a boulder two feet wide sitting on the rim of the ledge. Her heart began to pound. She pointed the gun at the boulder and tapped the trigger. Nothing happened. She pressed it a little harder, then a little harder than that, and suddenly – there was no recoil, but suddenly the boulder was shooting away, and a three-foot bite of ledge with it, to fall almost soundlessly into the sand a hundred feet off, though some of the sand there whooshed up and flew on farther. A breeze blew briefly from behind her. A little gravel rattled down the slope.

She took a gasping breath and a big swallow. Then she grinned. The violet column didn't look much shorter, if any. She put the gun back inside her jacket, belting the latter a notch tighter. A thoughtful frown replaced her grin.

She climbed back over the top of the ridge, and there on the other side was Hunter, his whiskers showing copper hairs among the brown in the sun's rays just topping the hills.

'Professor Hunter!' she said. 'I didn't think you were that sort of man.'

'What sort?' he asked her, perhaps smiling, but the beard made that hard to tell.

'Why, to follow a girl when she's on private business.'

He simply looked at her, and she smoothed her blonde hair. 'Aren't you used to the frank interest of men? Sexual or otherwise,' he asked blandly. Then, 'Fact is, I thought I heard a little landslide.'

'A rock did roll down to the beach,' she said, stepping past him, 'but the noise couldn't have carried far.'

'It carried to me,' he said, starting down the ridge beside her. 'Why don't you take that jacket off? It's getting hot.'

'I could think of subtler approaches,' she told him a bit acidly.

'So could I,' he assured her.

'I guess you could,' she agreed after a moment. Then stopping at the foot of the ridge: 'Ross, name a leading scientist, physicist especially, Nobel Prize calibre, who's got real wisdom for humanity? . . . Moral integrity, but vision and compassion, too.'

'That's quite a question,' he said. 'Well, there's Drummond, there's Stendhal – though he's hardly a physicist – and Rosenzweig . . . and of course there's Morton Opperly.'

'That's the name I wanted you to say,' she told him.

Dai Davies pounded on the frame of the diamond-paned door of the tiny pub near Portishead. His knees knocked together; his face was greenish pale; his hair, straight, plastered-down black locks; his clothes, soaking – and he would have been covered with mud from his falls except that it had been scoured off by the swim he'd had to make of the last hundred yards of his retreat back across the Bristol Channel.

And he was at the very end of his ebbing, drunken strength – if it had taken another dozen flailing overarm strokes and convulsive kicks, he'd never have made it to shore, he knew, out of the wild, foamy flood tide surging up-Severn. He needed alcohol, ethanol, spirits of wine! – as a bleeding man in shock needs a transfusion.

Yet for some reason the filthy Somersets had locked the door and hidden themselves – doubtless simply to thwart him, out of pure, mean, Welsh-hating, poet-despising cruelty, for these were open hours. By suffering Christ, he'd have the law on them for locking the place! He pressed his face to the lead-netted small panes to spy them out in their cowardly holes, but the shadowy taproom was empty, the lights were all out.

He reeled back, beating his arms across his chest for warmth, and hoarsely screeched up and down the road: 'Where are you all? Come out! Come out, somebody!' But not a soul showed himself, not a single house door opened, not even one loveless white she-face peered out a window. He was all alone.

He went trembling back to the pub door, grabbed the frame with both hands to steady himself, managed to lift a cramped leg, and kicked a short, convulsive kick with his heel. Three panes cracked and fell inside. He got his leg down, then he crouched against the door and thrust his arm through to the shoulder and reached around, found the lock, and worked it. The door opened, and he stumbled inside, retrieving his arm from the glass-jagged leaden web, then took four steps towards the bar, and stood wavering in the middle of the room, almost fainting.

And then as he swayed there gasping, and his eyes got used to the dimness, a wonderful change came over him and filled him brimful. Suddenly it was the finest thing in the world that he should be all alone at this moment; it was the fulfilment of an old, old dream.

He did not mind the faint roar behind him or glance once over his shoulder through the broken door at the Bristol Channel filling in dirty, low, foam-edged, flotsam-studded steps. He had eyes only for the amber and greenish, charmingly labelled bottles ranged on the shelves behind the bar. They were like treasured books to him, founts of all wisdom, friends of the lonely, a lovely library to be for ever sampled and savoured and of which he could never tire.

And as he approached them with loving deliberation, smiling a wide smile, he began softly and liltingly to read their titles from their spines:

'*Old Smuggler* . . . by Richard Blackmore. *Teachers*, by C. P. Snow. *The Black and the White*, by Stendhal. *White Horse*, by G. K. Chesterton . . .'

General Spike Stevens sloshed through cold salt water past the elevator shaft from which the water was welling more strongly every moment, making the metal door groan. A flashlamp strapped to his chest shone on the thigh-deep water and on a wall papered with historic battle scenes. Three more flashlamps came up behind him '. . . like we were a bunch of damn musical comedy burglars,' Colonel Griswold had put it.

The General felt around the wall, dug his fingers through the paper, and jerked open – the paper tearing – a light, two-foot-square door, revealing a shallow recess with nothing but a big black lever-handle in it.

He faced the others. 'Understand,' he said rapidly, 'I only know the entrance to the escape shaft. I don't know where it comes out any more than you do, because I'm not supposed to know where we are – and I don't. We'll hope it leads up into some sort of tower, because we know we're about two hundred feet below ground and that somehow there's some salt water up there. Understand? O.K., I'm going to open it.'

He turned and dragged down on the lever. Colonel Mabel Wallingford was standing just behind him, Colonel Griswold and Captain Kidley a few feet back.

The lever budged a quarter inch and stuck. He dragged down on it with both hands until he was only knee-deep in the water. Colonel Mab reached up and put her hands beside his and chinned herself.

Griswold called: 'Wait! If it's jammed, it means –'

The lever dropped eight inches. Three feet away, wallpaper

tore along a right angle as a door two feet wide and five feet high opened, and a black bolster of water came out and bowled over Captain Kidley and Colonel Griswold – Colonel Mab saw the latter's lamp pushed deeper and deeper.

The solid water kept coming, a great thick ridge of it. It grabbed at the feet of Colonel Mab and the General. They clung to the lever.

Chapter 23

Margo and Clarence Dodd were leaning their elbows on the upper rail of the concrete bridge, looking at the hills and speculating about the ceiling of diluted smoke that was moving up from the south and turning the sun red, giving its light an ominous brassy cast. She'd come here chiefly to get away from Ross Hunter.

'It could be only brush fires in the canyons and mountains,' the Little Man said. 'But I'm afraid it's more than that, Miss Gelhorn. You live in Los Angeles?'

'I rent a cottage in Santa Monica. Same thing.'

'Any family there?'

'No, just myself.'

'That's good, at least. I'm afraid, unless we get rain –'

'Look,' she said, glancing down. 'There's water in the wash now! Doesn't that mean there's rain inland?'

But just then, with a triumphant tooting of horns, Hixon's truck came rolling back from a reconnoitre down the coast, followed by a short, blocky yellow school bus. The two vehicles stopped on the bridge. Wojtowicz climbed down from the bus. He was carrying one of the army rifles. Doc came after him, but stopped on the step-down platform, which made a convenient rostrum.

'I am pleased to announce that I've found us transportation,' he called out loudly and jovially. 'I insisted on looking into Monica Mountainway, and there, in a little vale not one hundred yards off the highway, I discovered this charming bus waiting to begin its morning chore, which today will be carrying us! It's all gassed up and plentifully stocked with peanut butter and jelly sandwiches and irradiated, fluoridated milk. Prepare for departure in five minutes, everyone!' He stepped down and came swinging around the yellow hood. 'Doddsy, that's not rainwater in that wash there, that's salt tide – just look over the other side of the bridge and you'll see it stretching out in one gleaming sheet to China. Times like this, things creep up on people. You've got the other gun, Doddsy – you ride with the Hixons. Ida will be with you to nurse Ray Hanks. I'll command the bus.'

'Mr Brecht,' Margo said. 'Are you planning to take us over Monica Mountainway to the Valley?'

'Part way at any rate. To the two-thousand-foot heights, if I can. After that . . .' He shrugged.

'Mr Brecht,' she went on, 'Vandenberg Three is just the other end of the Mountainway. On the slopes, in fact. Morton Opperly's there, in charge of the pure science end of the Moon Project. I think we should try to contact him.'

'Say, that's not a bad idea,' Doc told her. 'He ought to be showing more sense than the V-2 brass, and he might welcome some sane recruits. It's a sound idea that we cluster around the top scientists in this para-reality situation. However, God knows if we'll ever get to V-3, or if Opperly will still be there if we do,' he added, shrugging again.

'Never mind that,' Margo said. 'All I ask is that if there's a chance to contact him, you help me. I've a special reason which is extremely important but which I can't explain now.'

Doc looked at her shrewdly, then grinned. 'Sure thing,' he promised, as Hunter and some of the others closed in on him with other questions and suggestions.

Margo boarded the bus at once and took the seat behind the driver. He was a scowly old man with a jaw so shallow she wondered if he had teeth.

'It's very good of you to help us out this way,' she remarked.

'You're telling me?' he retorted, looking around at her incredulously and flashing some yellowed, stumpy incisors and scattered, black, amalgam-roofed molars. '*He* told me,' he went on, jerking a thumb at Doc just outside the door, 'about this five-hundred-and-sixty-foot tide that would drown me if I didn't get up in the hills fast. He made it mighty vivid. And then he told me I needn't strain myself making up my mind whether to take you folks too, because he had a guy with a gun. Good o' me? I just had no choice. Besides,' he added, 'there was a big slide blocking off my regular route south. Might as well throw in with you crazy folks.'

Margo laughed self-consciously. 'You'll get used to us,' she said. At that moment the Ramrod came shouldering into the bus, calling back to Doc: 'Very well, Wanda and I will ride in this conveyance, but I categorically refuse to drink milk with fallout rays and rat poison in it!'

The driver looked at Margo. 'Maybe,' he said sourly.

The rest came crowding aboard. Hunter had sat down beside Margo while the driver was talking to her. She ostentatiously made extra room, but he didn't look at her. Doc stood in the door and counted noses. 'All here,' he announced. He leaned out and shouted to the truck, 'O.K., off we go! Reverse course and follow in line astern!'

The school bus turned around on the bridge, and the truck behind it. Margo noticed that the water in the wash was now a yard higher. A tiny roller came up it, foaming along the sides. The beach on to which she'd shot the boulder was under water, too. Last night the road here had been over half a mile from the surf.

Doc settled down in the strategic spot he'd reserved for himself, opposite Hunter and behind the door. He sprawled a leg over the extra seat beside him.

'On to Monica Mountainway,' he told the driver. 'Keep her at an easy thirty and watch for rocks. We've hardly four miles to go along the highway – ample time to dodge Mrs Pacific as she fattens up. Remember, everybody, the Pacific Coast tides are the mixed kind. Fortunately for us, this morning's the *low* high. McHeath,' he called over his shoulder, 'you're our liaison officer. Keep an eye on the truck. Rest of you, don't crowd the seaside. I want this bus balanced when we start uphill. We're well ahead of the tide – there's no danger.'

'Unless we get some more –' Margo began, but checked herself. She'd been going to say 'earthquake waves' or 'tsunami'.

174

Hunter flashed her a smile. 'That's right; don't say it,' he whispered to her. Then, in a not much louder voice, across to Doc: 'Where did you pick up that five-sixty figure, Rudy?'

'Eightly time the L.A. tidal range of seven feet,' Doc replied. 'Much too big, I devoutly hope, but we have to make some kind of estimate. Oh, a life on the ocean wave, a home on the rolling deep, da-da-da-da-da-da-*da* . . .'

Margo winced at the raucous voice 'singing for morale' – how well was certainly an open question – and wished it were Paul's. Then she clasped her hands together and studied the back of the driver's seat. It looked recently scrubbed, but she could make out, 'Ozzie is a stinker', 'Jo-Ann wears falsies', and 'Pop has 13 teeth'.

Despite Doc's reassurances, there was considerable excited watching of the creeping waters and scanning of the misty horizon, and a mounting feeling of tension as the bus chugged south. Margo felt the tension slacken the moment they turned up the sharply mounting, two-lane black ribbon of the mountainway – and then, almost immediately, gather again as people scanned the road ahead for slides or bucklings. There instantly sprang out of Margo's own memory Mrs Hixon's vivid phrase: 'Those mountains have stirred like stew.' But the first stretch, at least, straight up a low-domed hill, looked clear and smooth.

'Truck turning inland after us, Mr Brecht,' came a soldierly voice from the rear.

'Thank you, McHeath,' Doc called back. Then, to Hunter and Margo with grinning enthusiasm, and loudly enough for all to hear, 'I'm banking on Monica Mountainway. There hasn't been much about it in the general press, but actually it's a revolutionary advance in roadbuilding.'

'Hey, Doc,' Wojtowicz called, 'if this road's clear to the Valley, there'd be traffic coming through.'

'You're sharp this morning, Wojtowicz,' Doc agreed, 'but we only need the mountainway clear the first three miles – that'll put us over six hundred feet up. We don't have to worry about the other twenty-two miles. In fact, it's probably better for us if it's blocked somewhere beyond that.'

'I get you, Doc: we'd be fighting fifty million cars.'

'The sky looks blacker ahead, Mommy,' Ann piped up. She

and Rama Joan were in the seat behind Doc. 'A big smoke plume.'

'We're between water and fire,' the Ramrod announced, some of the dreamy note coming back into his voice. 'But be of good cheer; Ispan will return.'

'I'm only too afraid it will,' Hunter said to Margo, *sotto voce.* Then, in the same tone, his glance dropping to her zippered-up leather bosom, 'Would you care to show me the thing the cat-woman dropped from the saucer? I saw you catch it, you know, and I think you tested it this morning. Work?'

When she didn't answer him, he said: 'Keep it to yourself if it makes you feel more secure. I heard the questions you asked Doc and I heartily approve. Otherwise I'd take it away from you right now.'

She still didn't look at him. He might have combed his beard, but she could smell his musky sweat.

The bus topped the first hill, took a slow, dipping curve, and started up a steeper one. Still no falls or crumblings came into view.

Doc said loudly: 'Monica Mountainway is laid almost along the ridge tops and built of an asphaltoid that's full of long molecular cables. Result: it's strong in tension and almost impervious to falls. I learned that poking into engineering journals. Ha! Always trust a diversified genius, I say!'

'Diversified loudmouth,' someone behind them muttered.

Doc looked around with a hard grin, squinting suspiciously at Rama Joan. 'We have already gained some three hundred feet in altitude,' he announced.

The bus turned and ran along the second hilltop, giving them a last glimpse of the Coast Highway. It was covered with water. Waves were breaking against the brush-grown slopes.

Dai Davies, as negligently casual about it all as some poetic son of Poseidon in his father's study, watched the broad grey Bristol Channel glinting steely here and there in the mist-filtered silver light of the setting sun as the water inched and footed up the briary slope to the other side of the road fronting the pub.

The last time he'd looked, there'd been two freighters and a liner battling down-channel against the flood. Now they were gone, leaving only a scattering of wreckage and distant small craft not worth his squinting at.

He'd turned on the wireless a while back and listened to the taut-throated reports of the monster tides; and chittering insistences that they were caused by the great muster of earthquakes that had tramped Terra's crust the last half-day; and cries for boats and buses and trains to do this, that, and the impossible; and grim, hysterical, complex commands to all England, it seemed to Dai, to go somewhere else, preferably to the top of Mount Snowdon.

He'd decided it must have been earlier instalments of these frantic warnings that had put all the cowardly Somersets to flight – locking their liquor up miserly behind them! – and then he'd gone Disney for a while and jigged about and sung loudly: 'Who's afraid of the big bad tide? Certainly not Dai!'

But then the lights had gone out with a greenish-white flaring and the wireless with them, and he'd hunted up candles for cheer and affixed seven of them with their own whitehot wax artistically atilt along the bar.

Now he turned back towards them, and they were all guttering beautifully, the flames swaying like seven silver-gold maidens, their radiance glittering softly back from all the beautiful green-and-amber, neatly labelled books beyond.

Let me see, he thought as he moved slowly past the maiden flames, *it's many a day since I've looked into Old Bushmills by Thomas Hardy, but I'm mightily tempted by some of the cantos of Vat 69, by Ezra Pound. Which should it be now? Or perhaps – yes! – for a foreign fillip, Kirchwasser by Heinrich Heine!*

General Spike Stevens and Colonel Mab lay side by side a foot or so under the concrete ceiling on the cot-size top of a big steel cabinet. She'd lost her flashlamp, but he still had his strapped to his chest. It shone on a still surface of black water six inches below the top of the cabinet.

They lay very still themselves. Their heads roared from the pressure of the air, which was warm due to the same compression.

There was nothing to look at along the wall-top or on the ceiling, except the grille of a ventilator beyond Colonel Mab's head.

The General said – and his voice was weirdly gruff yet distant – 'I don't understand why with this pressure the air doesn't puff up through here' – he pointed towards the ventilator – 'and then, finis. Must be a block – maybe some anti-fallout valve got triggered.'

Colonel Mab shook her head. She was lying on her back, looking up over her eyebrows. 'It isn't easy to see at first,' she said softly, 'but the ventilator shaft is full of water. It bulges down just a little in the squares in the ventilator, like tiny black pillows or big black fingertips. The water pressure from above and below balance – for the moment, at any rate, and so long as the surfaces in the grille aren't disturbed.'

'You're seeing things,' the General told her. 'That's bad hydro-statics. The head of pressure on the water below us is bound to be greater. It'd still push the air out.'

'Maybe the elevator shaft hasn't filled entirely yet,' Colonel Mab answered with a little shrug. 'But I'm not seeing things.'

She reached up and poked a finger through the nearest hole in the ventilator, then snatched it quickly away as a stream of water as thick as a cigar spurted straight down and rattled loudly into the still water below, with the effect of an elephant relieving itself of fluid.

The General grabbed her by the shoulder. 'You goddamn stupid bitch,' he snarled. Then he looked her in the face and he slid his fingers inside her collar, and took hold of it to tear it down. 'Yes,' he said harshly, nodding once. 'Whether you like it or not.'

He hesitated, then said apologetically but very stubbornly, 'There's nowhere else to escape to, is there, except into each other.'

She grinned with her teeth at him. 'Let's do this right, you big brass bastard,' she told him. Her eyes narrowed. 'We're finished,' she said thoughtfully, hitting each syllable as if she stepped on stones, 'but if we could work so that we hit the climax just as we drowned . . . We'll have to wait till the water's over us – *It mustn't be too soon . . .*'

'My Christ, you've got it, Mab!' the General said loudly, grinning down at her like a blocky death's-head.

She frowned. 'Not all of it,' she said, just loudly enough for him to hear her over the sizzling water-spurts – there were three of them now. 'There's something else. But it's enough to start on, and I'll think of the other thing after a while.'

She unbuttoned her soaking coat and shirt and unhooked her brassière. The flashlamp strapped to his chest shone on her breasts. He entered her, and they got to work.

'Take it slow now, you old bastard,' she told him.

When he clutched her to him, the flashlamp made a reddish square in her chest that shone out faintly through her breasts.

When the water was an inch from the top of the cabinet they paused for a while.

'Like rats in a trap,' she said to him fondly.

'You got quite a tail, Mrs Rat,' he said to her. 'I always thought you were a Lesbian.'

'I am,' she told him, 'but that's not all I am.'

He said, 'About that black tiger we thought we saw –'

'We saw it,' she said. Then her face broke into a smile. 'Strangling is a very quiet death,' she said. She dabbled her hand in the water, as if she were on her back in a canoe – and, for a moment, she was. 'That's from *The Duchess of Malfi*, General. Duke Ferdinand. Nice, don't you think?' When he frowned speculatively, she said, still smiling tranquilly: 'I've read in more than one place that a hanged man always has a climax – and strangling's like hanging. I don't know if it's true of women, but it could be, and my sex always has to take the chances. At least it ought to help the water a little, and if we could make the three things come together . . . Enjoy killing a woman, General? I'm a Lesbian, General, and I've slept with girls you never got. Remember the little redhead in Statistics who used to twitch her left eye when you barked at her?'

Just then the water came rilling over the cabinet top, and the ventilator tore loose, and a great inorganic sobbing began as, alternately, a log of water shot down the hole and a log of air escaped up it, rhythmically. The cabinet shook.

The General and Colonel Mab got to work again.

'I won't squeeze so hard right away, you goddamn girl-defiling bitch,' he shouted in her ear. 'I'll remember you're the woman.'

'You think so?' she shouted back, and her long-fingered, strong-fingered strangler's hands came up between his arms and closed around his neck.

Chapter 24

Paul Hagbolt's joints and muscles had begun to ache from his starfished posture, despite the easement of null gravity. He thought some modest complaints about it, to no effect. After getting over his first terror of Tigerishka, he'd spoken his complaints and started to ask many questions, too. But she had said: 'Monkey chatter,' and run a dry velvet paw across his lips, and a paralysis had gripped his throat and his face below the nose – somehow an invisible gag had been applied.

At least his aches took his mind off his humiliations. He was naked now. After discovering that the primitive mind in the saucer was Paul's and not Miaow's, Tigerishka had riffled through his thoughts again with contemptuous speed. Then she had stripped off his wet clothes with even greater dispatch, momentarily freeing an invisible gyve from ankle or wrist to facilitate the process. Next she had subjected him to an unfeeling anatomical inspection, as coldly as if he were a cadaver. Finally – capping indignity! – she had affixed to his crotch a couple of sanitary arrangements.

Tubes snaked from them to the same silver-grey panel into which, through a briefly dilating door, she'd thrown his wet clothes. Paul named it the Waste Panel.

In the warmth of the cabin it was more comfortable being naked, though comfort did not cancel humiliation.

After attending to the obviously distasteful Paul-chore, Tigerishka had gone about her own activities. First she had groomed herself and Miaow, using not only a long, pointed, pale violet tongue more like a frog's than a cat's, but also two silver combs which she wielded equally well with all of her four paws and also her prehensile tail. As she rhythmically combed, she softly wailed discordant, eerie music, somehow producing three voices simultaneously. The captured hair from her combing went into the waste panel.

Then, with sublime or simply horrid feline indifference to the world in agony below them – if, as Paul wondered, the saucer were still hovering over Southern California or even Earth – she had fed Miaow. From the second of the three panels – Paul named it the Food Panel – she had produced a fat, dark red worm which Paul uneasily felt was synthetic rather than natural. It wriggled just enough to vastly interest Miaow, who played with it for some time in free fall while Tigerishka watched, before slowly chewing it up with signs of great satisfaction.

Then Tigerishka had gone to the third panel, which after a bit Paul was calling the Control Panel, and busied herself with what he assumed to be her regular work, which seemed to be that of observer.

The first time the mirror he faced turned to transparency, Paul was distinctly glad of the sanitary arrangements.

About half a mile below him churned and spouted an angry grey sea from which a solitary, rocky island poked and in which a large long tanker wallowed, green water flowing over its bow.

The transparency of the facing wall was perfect. He felt he was about to drop through a large ring of flowers towards the maelstrom. Then the mirror was there again.

The same thing happened half a dozen times in quite rapid succession, observation heights varying sharply. He hung cringe-stomached over sea, coast, and farmland. Once he thought he recognized the north end of the San Fernando Valley with a section of the Santa Monica mountains, but he couldn't be sure.

There was no mistaking the next view, though. They were at least five miles up, but there was nothing below them almost to the edges of the thirty-foot window but city – sunlit city, bordered by sea on one side, mountains on two, and just stretching out on the fourth.

The city was smeared across with six parallel brush strokes that began, mostly near the sea, in bright vermilion but quickly changed to the brownish black of heavy smoke spreading over the mountains inland.

It was Los Angeles burning. This time the saucer hung low enough for Paul to identify the main fire-spots: Santa Ana, Long Beach, Torrance, Inglewood, the Los Angeles Civic Centre, and Santa Monica, the last blaze licking along the southern slopes of the Santa Monica mountains through Beverly Hills and Hollywood.

Margo's tiny house in Santa Monica and his own apartment were gone, it looked like.

They were too high for him to more than fancy the ant-scurry of cars, the clustering of the rectangular red beetles of fire trucks.

The seacoast to the south looked wrong. In places the Pacific came too far inland.

He started to strangle and realized he'd been trying to scream to Tigerishka, against the invisible gag, to do something about it.

She never gave him a look, but turned from the control panel to crouch on the invisible floor, staring towards the south-west and the sea.

Two miles below them a thick grey cloudbank with a dark skirt was moving in swiftly over the changed coast. The dark skirt touched the Long Beach fire, turning its smoke white – rain! Heavy rain!

Paul looked over towards the other blazes lying in the path of the cloudbank and saw the silver-and-vermilion of two military jets face on to him. Smoke puffed from their wings and he could see the four rockets on collision course with the saucer, swelling as they came.

Then it was as if Los Angeles had been jerked down twenty miles. The scene expanded thirtyfold. He saw more smoke-strokes, tiny from this altitude, down the coast and up towards Bakersfield. Then the wall winked on again – not a mirror this time, but pool-table green, presumably just for a change.

Tigerishka reached a long paw into the shrubbery and re-trieved Miaow. She cuddled the little cat to her and, turning half away from Paul, said loudly: 'There, we save his monkey-town for him. Call big saucer over the sea. Make rain. Small thanks. Help monkey, monkey shoot.'

Miaow squirmed as if she'd rather get back to flower-climbing, but Tigerishka licked her face with her dagger-tongue, and the little cat writhed luxuriously.

'We don't like him, do we?' Tigerishka went on with a sideways eye-flicker towards Paul, in a voice that was half-way between purr and cruel laughter. 'Monkeys! Cowardly, chattering, swarming – no individuality, no flair!'

Paul wanted to strangle her, his hands locked in the sleek green fur of her neck. Yes, he wanted to lock his hands around her neck and –

Tigerishka hugged Miaow closer and whispered loudly: 'We think he smells. Makes smells with his mind, too.'

Paul remembered disconsolately how he'd thought Margo bullied him. But that was before he met Tigerishka.

Don Merriam sat on the edge of a bed that was like one large, resilient cushion in a small room with restfully dim walls.

At his knees was a low table on which stood a transparent cup and a jug full of water, and also a transparent plate piled with small, white, rough-surfaced, spongy cubes. He had drunk thirstily of the former, but only nibbled experimentally at one of the latter, although they smelled and tasted quite like bread.

The only other features of the room were a lidded toilet seat and a corner area about three feet square where a soothing patter of rain was falling steadily without splashing or running over into the rest of the room. He had not yet stepped into this shower although he had stripped to his underwear.

The temperature and humidity and illumination level of the room suited themselves so to him that the room was almost like an extension of his body.

Before a wall-hued door, sliding sideways, had shut out his host or captor, the walking red-and-black tiger had said to him: 'Drink. Eat. Relieve and refresh yourself. Rest.'

Those had been his only words since he had summoned Don. During the brief passage downward on the platform elevator and then the short walk along a narrow corridor, the being had been silent.

Don was relieved that the being had left him, yet irked with himself for the awe and timidity that had kept him from asking questions; now he almost wanted the being to come back.

183

That was only one of the many contradictory paired feelings maintaining themselves in him: weariness-uneasiness, safety-alienage, the urge to let his thoughts go and the urge to hold them in, the urge to face his situation and the urge to escape in illusion.

It was easy to think of this spot as a small hospital room. Or, as a small stateroom in a great ocean liner. Well, what was a planet but a sort of ship, moving through space? At least, this planet, with its endless decks ...

Tiredness took hold; the lights dimmed; he sprawled full length on the bed, but at the same time his mind became ripplingly active, began to *babble* – though in a quite orderly sort of way.

The effect, which was rather like that of sodium pentothal, was almost pleasant. At least, it neutralized his restless anxiety.

It occurred to him that *they* were getting at his mind, examining it, but he didn't care.

It was engrossing to watch his thoughts, his knowledge, and his remembered experiences arrange themselves in ranks and then parade, as if past some central reviewing stand.

Eventually these mental items began to move too swiftly for him to follow them, but even that was all right, because the blur they made was a warm, tender, enfolding, somnolent darkness.

Chapter 25

The freaks of the monster tides were innumerable, as the Wanderer-humped waters washed around the world.

Currents in straits like Dover, Florida, Malacca and Juan de Fuca became too strong for steamers to breast. Small boats were gulped down like chips in a millrace.

High bridges built to hang firm against winds had their resistance tested to rushing water. They became barriers to ships, which piled up against and broke them.

Moored steamers lifted their docks, or broke free and lodged in the downtown streets of ports, shouldering in the walls of skyscrapers.

Lightships were torn from their great chains, or dragged down by them. Lighthouses were inundated. The Eddystone Light gleamed on for hours in the deeps after it went under.

The permafrost of the Siberian and Alaskan coasts was ripped from below and melted by salt water. In America and Russia atomic-armed rockets drowned in their silos. (One inland newspaper suggested atomic bombs be used to blow the water back.) High-tension lines were shorted out and re-appeared six hours later draped with wreckage.

The tiny tides of the Mediterranean became big enough to create disasters of the same magnitude that low-lying oceanic ports regularly suffer from hurricanes combined with a high lunar tide.

The Mississippi's fresh water was spread thin over the salt tide pushing up from the Gulf across its delta to cover the streets of New Orleans.

The Araiza brothers and Don Guillermo Walker encountered a similar phenomenon on the San Juan. Late in the afternoon the river reversed its current, spread into the jungle to either side, and began to taste brackish. Wreckage appeared, floating upstream. They cursed in wonder – the Latins with a certain reverence, the Yankee theatrically, drawing a bit on *King Lear* – and headed the launch back for Lake Nicaragua.

The population of great ports found refuge on inland hills or – less securely – in the upper floors of tall buildings, where dreadful little wars were fought for living space. Airlifts rescued a random scattering. Heroic and merely stubborn or incredulous people stuck to posts of duty. One of these was Fritz Scher, who stayed on all night at the Tidal Institute. Hans Opfel, braving the shallowly flooded Hamburg streets, went out for supper, promising to return with a Bratwurst on rye and two bottles of beer, but he never came back – overpowered by floodwaters or his own sense of self-preservation.

So Fritz had no one at whom to direct his mocking laughter when the tide went down during the evening hours. And later, around midnight, he had only the tide-predicting machine with whom to share his rationalizations as to why the tide had gone down so far, according to the very few reports that were still trickling in. But that rather pleased him, as his devout

185

affection for the long, sleek machine was becoming physical. He moved his desk beside her, so he could touch her constantly. From time to time he went to a window and looked out briefly, but there was heavy cloud cover, so his disbelief in the Wanderer was not put to the crucial test.

Many of those fleeing the tides ran into other troubles that made them forget the menace of the waters. At noon, Pacific Standard Time, the school bus and the truck carrying the saucer students were racing against fire. Ahead, walls of flame were swiftly climbing the saddle-backed ridge along which Monica Mountainway crossed the central spine of the Santa Monica mountains.

Barbara Katz watched the tiny bow wave from the left front wheel of the Rolls Royce sedan angle across the road and lose itself in the tall green swords of the saw grass, as Benjy stubbornly kept their speed down to a maddeningly monotonous thirty. As captain of the car, at least in her own estimation, she ought to be sitting up in front, but Barbara felt it was more vital that she keep in direct contact with her millionaire, so she sat behind Benjy with old KKK beside her and Hester beyond him, which put Helen up in front with Benjy and a pile of suitcases.

The sun had just begun to look into the front of the car from high in the sky as they travelled due west through the Everglades. The windows were all closed tight on Barbara's side and it was hot. She knew that Lake Okeechobee ought to be somewhere off to the right and north, but all she could see was the endless green expanse of saw grass, broken here and there by clumps of dark, mortuary-looking cypress, and the narrow, mirror-like corridor of water ahead covering the string-straight, level road to a depth of never less than one inch or more than four – so far.

'You sure right about that high tide, Miss Barbara,' Benjy called back softly and cheerily. 'She come way in. Never hear tell she come so far.'

'Hush, Benjy,' Hester warned. 'Mister K still sleeping.'

Barbara wished she were as confident about her own wisdom as Benjy sounded about it. She checked the two of old KKK's wrist-watches strapped to her left wrist – two-ten, they averaged – and the time for today's second high tide at Palm Beach on the back of the calendar sheet – 1.45 p.m. But wouldn't a high tide moving inland be later than on the coast? That was the way it was with rivers, she seemed to recall. She didn't know nearly enough, she told herself.

An open car moving at almost twice their speed roared past them, deluging the Rolls with water. It forged swiftly ahead, beating up a storm in the water-mirror. There were four men in it.

'Another of them speeders,' Hester growled.

'Wowee! Sure lucky we Sanforized,' Benjy crowed. 'I Sanforize this bus with lots of high-yellow grease,' he explained. Helen giggled.

The encounter roused old KKK, who looked at Barbara with red-rimmed, wrinkle-edged little eyes that seemed to her to be almost awake for the first time today. He'd gone through the preparations and actual departure in a kind of stupor that had alarmed Barbara but not Hester. 'He just not had his sleep out, he be all right,' Hester had told her.

Now he said briskly: 'Phone the airfield, Miss Katz. We want two tickets to Denver by the next plane out. Triple premiums to the reservation clerks, the pilot, and the air line. Denver's a mile high, out of reach of any tides, and I have friends there.'

She looked at him frightenedly, then simply indicated their surroundings.

'Oh yes, I begin to remember now,' he said heavily, after a moment. 'But why didn't you think of the air, Miss Katz?' he complained, looking at the black shoulder bag of the Black Ball Jetline on her lap.

'I borrowed this from a friend. I hitchhiked down from the Bronx. I don't fly much,' she confessed miserably, feeling still more miserable inside. Here she'd been going to rescue her millionaire so brilliantly and – dazzled by a Rolls Royce sedan – had missed the obvious way to do it, maybe doomed them all. Dear God, why hadn't she thought like a millionaire!

A corner of her mind outside the misery area was asking whether old KKK had made a slip in mentioning just two

187

tickets. Surely he'd meant five – why, he talked to Hester and Helen and Benjy like they were children.

'We did at least bring some money with us?' he asked her dryly.

'Oh yes, Mr Kettering, we took everything from the wall safes,' she assured him, drawing a little comfort from the thickness of the sheaves of bills she could feel through the fabric of her shoulder bag.

The Rolls was slowing down. The last car to pass them was off in the saw grass, its hood half submerged, and the four men who'd been in it were standing shoetop-deep, blocking the roads and waving.

The sight galvanized her. 'Don't slow down!' she cried, grabbing the back of Benjy's seat. 'Drive straight through!'

Benjy slowed a little more.

'Do as Miss Katz says, Benjamin,' old KKK ordered him, with a harshness that set him coughing on the next word, which was, 'Faster!'

Barbara could see Benjy's head drawn down into his shoulders and imagined his eyes wincing half shut as he stepped on the gas.

The four men waited until they were two car lengths away, then jumped aside, yelling angrily. It hadn't been a very good bluff.

She looked back and saw one of them grappling with another, who'd pulled out a gun.

Maybe I did the wrong thing, she thought.

Like hell!

Dai Davies was sitting on top of the bar, watching his candle-girls rill out their last white tears, their maiden-milk, and topple their black wicks in their wax-pools and drown. Gwen and Lucy were gone and at this moment Gwyneth. It was a double loss, for he needed their simple warmth and light: the sun had set, and a clear but intense darkness was settling on the great grey watery mead that was all he could see through the diamond-paned windows and door. He'd hoped for a twinkle of lights from far Wales, but it hadn't come.

The Severn tide had entered the pub some time ago and was now so high he'd tucked his feet up. Two brooms, a mop,

188

a pail, a cigar box, and seven sticks of firewood floated around, circling slowly. He'd fleetingly thought of leaving at one point, and had tucked two pints in his side pockets against that eventuality, but he'd recalled that this was the highest bit of ground for a space around, and the candles had been warm and dear, and now he'd taken on more alcohol, he knew, than would allow sprightly perambulation for a bit.

In any case it was the best sport of all to play King Canute atop a crocodile's coffin. Two inches more and the tide would stand and turn, he suddenly decided – and loudly ordered the water to do so.

After all, one o'clock, or a bit after that, had been low tide, and so now must be high or near – if this mad salt flooding obeyed any of the old rules at all.

He deeply sniffed at the open fifth in his hand – an American import, *Kentucky Tavern* by Erskine Caldwell – and watched Eliza shiver and fade and unexpectedly flame up blue and bright.

The lead-webbed windows pressed in at a new surge of the tide. Water gushed through the hole he'd kicked in the door. Then he distinctly felt the bar under him shift a little – in fact, the whole building moved. He took a sour hot swig of the bottle and cried laughingly: 'For once it's the pub that staggers, not Dai!' Then a great seriousness gripped him, and he knew at last exactly what was happening and he cried with a wild pride: 'Die, Davies! Die! Deserve your name. But die dashingly. Die with a whisky bottle in your hand, wafting your love to come again to Cardiff. But . . .' And then, for once wholly conquering his carping jealousy of Dylan Thomas – 'Do not go gentle into the good night. Rage, rage, against the dying of the light.'

And at that very moment, just as Eliza winked out, and the last pearly light seemed to die all over the grey Severn plain, there came a loud knocking at the door, a heavy, slow, authoritative triple knock.

Supernatural fear took hold of him and gave him strength to move against the whisky, to drop down into the icy water and slosh through it thigh-deep and pull the door open. There, just outside, pressed against the doorframe by the tide, he saw by the dying light of Mary and Jane and Leonie a long, dark, empty skiff.

He sloshed his way back to the bar, the water steadying if impeding him, and gathered three fresh bottles in the crook of his left arm, and on his way back grabbed up the two floating brooms.

The skiff was waiting. He tossed in the brooms, put in the bottles carefully, and then laid his upper body across the boat and grasped the opposite gunwale. He almost blacked out then, but the water was cold on his crotch and he jumped up clumsily and wriggled and pulled until he was in, face down on the wet wood. Then he did black out. His last kick caught the doorframe and sent the skiff moving out and away.

Richard Hillary trudged through the dying twilight ten yards to the side of a road noisy with cars. The cars were moving slowly, almost bumper to bumper, in three lanes abreast so that there was no room at all for traffic in the opposite direction. No use to try for a lift, the cars were all packed with people – and if an empty place should turn up, it would immediately be taken by someone with more obvious claim to it or simply someone nearer the road. Besides, he was walking almost as fast as the cars were moving, rather faster than the majority of pedestrians.

Cars and folk on foot and he were all somewhere beyond Uxbridge, moving northwest. It had been a relief when the glaring sun had gone down, though every sign of time passing momentarily speeded up the walkers and pushed the vehicles closer together.

Never had Richard experienced such a revolutionary disaster, neither in his life nor in the flow of events around him – not even in the bombing raids remembered from childhood – and all in six hours. First the bus turning north out of the little street flood at Brentford . . . the driver mum to passengers' protests except for a reiterated 'Traffic Authority orders!' . . . wireless reports of the larger flood in the heart of London, of the American flying saucer seen in New Zealand and Australia and called a planet . . . the wireless choked by static just as someone began to recite a list of 'civilian directives' . . . people

190

frantically wondering how to get in touch with families, and he feeling both wounded and relieved that in his own case there was no one who mattered very much. Then the bus stopping at West Middlesex Hospital, with the information that it had been commandeered to move patients . . . more unsuccessful protests . . . advice to move northwest by foot, 'away from the water' . . . the refusal to believe . . . wandering briefly around the grounds of a new brick university . . . cars and white-faced refugees in greater and greater numbers from the east . . . the helicopter scattering paper thriftily . . . a fresh-inked sheet that read only: 'WESTERN MIDDLESEX MOVE TO CHILTERN HILLS. HIGH WATER EXPECTED TWO HOURS AFTER MIDNIGHT.' Finally, joining a northwest trek that grew and grew – becoming part of a dazed and trudging mob.

Richard judged he had been walking about two hours. He was tired; his chin was tucked against his chest, his gaze fixed on his muddy boots. There had been clear signs of recent flooding in a low stretch just overpassed: turbid pools and grass plastered flat. He had no idea of exactly where he was, except that he was well past Uxbridge and had crossed the Colne and the Grand Junction Canal, and that he could see hills far ahead.

The twilight was strangely bright. He almost walked into a clump of people who had halted and were staring back over his head. He turned around to see what they were looking at and there, riding low in the eastern sky, he saw at last the agent of their disaster, looking at least as big as the moon might look in dreams. It was mostly yellow, but with a wide purple bar running down its middle and from the ends of the bar two sharply curving purple arms going out to make a great *D*. He thought, *D for danger, D for disaster, D for destruction.* The thing might be a planet, but it didn't look beautiful – it looked like a garish insignia of the sort you might see in a bomb factory.

He found himself thinking of how safe the Earth had swung in all its loneliness for millions of years, like a house to which no stranger ever comes, and of how precarious its isolation had really always been. People get eccentric and selfish and habit-ridden when they're left long alone, it occurred to him.

191

But why, he asked himself angrily, *when there finally is a murderous intrusion from the ends of the universe, should it look like nothing but a cheap screaming advertisement on a circular hoarding?*

Then a flickering afterthought: *D for Dai.* He remembered that the tides at Avonmouth have a vertical range of forty feet at full moon, and he wondered fleetingly how his friend was faring.

Dai Davies came to consciousness dreadfully cold and biting wood. He managed to get his elbows on the wood – rocking it as he did, and realizing it was the midthwart of the skiff – and to lift his face up off the wood and prop it on his hands. Over the gunwales he saw only the dark plain of the swollen Bristol Channel with a few tiny distant lights that might be Monmouth or Glamorgan or Somerset, or the lights of boats, except it was hard to tell them from the scattering of the dim stars.

He felt the cold cylinder of a bottle against his chest. He twisted off the cap and got down a mouthful of Scotch. It didn't warm him at all, but it seemed to sting him a little more alive. The bottle slipped from his hand and gurgled out on the strakes. His mind wasn't working yet. All that would come into it was the thought that a lot of Wales must be under him, including the Severn Experimental Tidal Power Station. The first part of that thought recalled scraps of Dylan Thomas' poetry which he mumbled disjointedly: 'Only the drowned deep bells of sheep and churches . . . dark shoals every holy field . . . Under the stars of Wales, Cry, Multitudes of arks! (*Skiff-ark. Noah solo.*) Across the water liddled lands . . . Ahoy, old sea-legged fox . . . Dai Mouse! (*Die!*) . . . the flood flowers now.'

At regular intervals the skiff lurched. Dai laboriously worked his mind around to the thought that the low little waves might be the dying undulations of Atlantic combers rolling up-channel against the turned tide. But what was it that was speckling their tiny crests with burgundy and beer, with blood and gold?

Then the lurching swung the skiff around and he saw, risen in the east, the purple bulk of the Wanderer with a golden dragon curling on it. Floating before the dragon was a triangular golden shield. Swinging into view around this foreign globe was a curved, fat white granular spindle, like the gleaming cocoon of some great white moth. Memories filtering up of the crazy Yankee news reports, and perhaps the thought-chain of moth, Luna moth, Luna told him that the spindle was the same moon to whom he and Dick Hillary had bid good night fifteen hours ago.

Speechless and still, he soaked in the sight for as long as he could bear. Then as the cold set him shivering convulsively and as the skiff swung away from the sight, moving faster now, and as the lurchings became stronger, he found the nearly empty bottle and took a careful swig from it. Then he wriggled himself up until he was sitting on the mid-thwart, found the two brooms and set them in the oarlocks and began to row.

Sober, or only vigorously drunk after resting, he just might have been able to pull out of his predicament, although the tide had begun to ebb fast and he was nearer Severn Channel than the Somerset shore. But he only rowed enough with his brooms to keep the skiff heading seaward and west, so he could watch the heavenly prodigy. And as he watched, he muttered and crooned: 'Mona, dear moon-bach . . . got yourself a new man, I see . . . a fierce emperor come to burn the world with water . . . you're raped and broken, Mona mine, but more beautiful than ever, spinning a new shape out of your tragedy . . . is it a white ring you would be? . . . I'm your poet still, Luna's poet, lonely . . . I'm a Loner, a new Loner, Welsh Loner, not Wolf, going to row to America this night just to watch you . . . while the Lutine bell tolls unceasingly at Lloyds for the ships and cities drowned until the tide stills that, too, and there is only a faint clangour going around the world deep under the seas. . . .'

The rollers grew higher, foaming golden and wine. A quarter mile beyond the bow, had he ever turned to look ahead, a nasty cross-chop was developing, the net of jewel-flecked waves spurting high at the knots.

Bagong Bung, tiny beside his big Australian engineer, watched the rust-holed, weed-festooned stack rise by visible stages from the sparkling water fifty yards beyond the bow of the *Machan*

Lumpur as the Wanderer set over Vietnam and the sun rose over Hainan.

A lively current strained at the lacy stack and foamed through its holes and tugged at the *Machan Lumpur*, too, so that the tiny steamer had to keep her screw turning just to hold her position, as the Gulf of Tonkin went on emptying into the South China Sea.

A low sonorous sound came from the south, like a very distant jet boom. The two men on the *Machan Lumpur* barely noted it. They had no way of knowing it brought news of the explosion of the volcanic islet of Krakatoa in the Sunda Strait, two and a half hours ago.

And now the colourfully-encrusted bridge of the wreck came into sight, and the current began to slacken. As the full length of the sunken ship became apparent, Bangong Bung knew to a certainty it was the *Sumatra Queen*.

Then the little Malay dropped to his knees and bowed west to the Wanderer, and coincidentally to Mecca, and said, softly: *'Terima kasi, bagus kuning dan ungu!'* Having thanked the yellow and purple miracle-bringer, he rose briskly to his feet and with a playful, lordly wave of his hand cried out gaily: 'We will tie up to our treasure ship, oh Cobber-Hume, *baik sobat*, and board her like kings! At last, my good friend, is the *Machan Lumpur* truly the Tiger of the Mud!'

Sally Harris leaned in the dusk on the balustrade of the penthouse patio and sighed.

To the west the last flames of sunset mingled with those of the oil that had gushed from flood-broken tanks and was now floating and burning on the salt water flooding Jersey City. To the east the Wanderer was rising in its dinosaur face.

'What's the matter, Sal?' Jake called to her from where he was sipping brandy and chopping away at various cheeses. 'Don't tell me our fire's started again.'

'Nope, it looks pretty much out. The water's half-way up and still coming.'

'Is that what's bothering you?'

'I don't know, Jake,' she called back listlessly. 'I been watching churches going under. I never knew there was so many.

Saint Pat's and Epiphany and Christ and Saint Bartholomew's and Grace and Actors' Temple and Saint Mary the Virgin, and Calvary, where they started AA, and All Souls and Saint Mark's in the Bouwerie and B'nai Jeshurun and The Little Church around the Corner and –'

'Hey, you can't see all those from there,' Jake protested. 'You can't see half of them.'

'No, but I can see them in my mind.'

'Well, get your mind out of the dumps, then!' he ordered. 'Hey look, Sal, our planet's got King Kong on him and he's rising over the Empire State Building. How's that for a crazy gag? Maybe I can work it into the play.'

'I bet you can!' she said, the excitement coming back into her voice. 'Hey, have you finished my Noah's Ark song?'

'Not yet. Jesus, Sal, I got to relax after the fire.'

'You've relaxed half a fifth. Get your mind to work.'

Chapter 26

Doc shouted: 'All out, everybody, for a stretch, and to answer Nature's calls,' forcing a rudely jolly note into his hoarseness. 'Wojtowicz, it looks like we've finally found the roadblock you deduced.'

The saucer students eagerly yet complainingly piled out into the cool, damp, high air. From almost behind them shone a strange greenish light from the setting sun – the party's scientific consensus was that it was due to volcanic ash already crowding the stratosphere, though the Ramrod had ideas about planetary auras.

It was very clear they'd been through a lot in the day just ending and that the effects of last night's lost sleep were showing up with a vengeance.

The yellow paint of the school bus and the white enamel of the panel truck behind it both showed flaring black streaks where they'd barely outraced brush fires. There was a heavy bandage around Clarence Dodd's right hand, which the Little

Man had badly burned holding up a tarpaulin to shield Ray Hanks, Ida and himself from the swooping, sweeping flames.

Hunter cursed as he almost fell out of the bus, stumbling over two spades carelessly left in the aisle after a wearisome two-hour stretch of digging sand and gravel to level a buckled stretch of Monica Mountainway enough for the two cars to get through. He shoved them under the seats with another curse.

Several of the wayfarers looked quite damp, and the black flame marks on bus and truck were runnelled by the mighty rain which had come marching across the Santa Monica mountains in steel-grey waves out of the west, ten minutes after they had won their race with the fire. Its great dark curtain-clouds still obscured the east, though the west was clearing spottily.

They were almost twenty miles into the mountains and topping the next to the last ridge before the descent to the Valley, Vandenberg Three, and inland Route 101 leading north from Los Angeles towards Santa Barbara and San Francisco.

There were wet patches on the borrowed raincoat Doc had thrown over his shoulders, with the barest suggestion of a military cape, as he led the others forward, Rama Joan and Margo just behind him.

At this point the Mountainway traversed a half natural, half blasted step in a great slope of solid rock, which from a boulder-crowned summit ridge fifty yards up on their right ran down at an angle of thirty degrees and then, after the step holding the road, continued down at a slightly greater angle for a dozen yards or so and then plunged away precipitously, nothing visible beyond it but the side of another small mountain a half mile off.

The awesome grey rock-slope was patched with lichen, pale green, orange, smoky blue and black, and was scored and gouged with smooth-edged trenches and potholes, some of them holding boulders ranging up to panel-truck size.

One of the biggest of the latter lay squarely across the road, indenting it deeply. A lichen-free area just above showed the spot from which it had been dislodged, presumably by one of the quakes.

'Wow, I'll say we've found the roadblock, Doc,' Wojtowicz called from behind. 'She's a bitch!'

Drawn up sideways just in front of the boulder was a top-down, four-passenger Corvette. Lipstick-red, freshly washed by the rain, it added a saucy touch to the sombre landscape. But there was no one in sight, and Doc's cheery 'Hello there!' was answered only by echoes.

Ida came hurrying up behind Doc, saying: 'Mr Brecht, Ray Hanks isn't going to be able to take any more travelling today. We've propped his shoulders up a bit – it eases him, he says – but he's in continual pain and has a two-degree fever.'

Doc rounded the red hood, then all of a sudden stopped dead and reared up and back as if invisible grapples had lifted him eight inches by the shoulders. He turned on those behind him a face that looked greener than the sunlight and swept out an arm, saying, 'Stay where you are. Don't anybody come any closer.' He whipped off his raincoat and drew it across something lying just beyond the car.

With a thin, wavery moan Ida quietly collapsed on the asphaltoid.

Then Doc turned to them again, leaning on the car for support and brushing a trembling hand across his forehead, and said in jerky rushes, with difficulty, as if he were fighting down an impulse to retch: 'It's a young woman. She didn't die naturally. She'd been stripped and tortured. Remember, way back, the Black Dahlia case? It's like that.'

Margo was half doubled over with nausea herself. She had just glimpsed, before the pale raincoat covered it, the blood-less mask of a face with cheeks slashed so that the mouth seemed to stretch from ear to ear.

Rama Joan, pressing Ann's head to her waist, but her body on tiptoe as she peered ahead, called: 'There are two sedans on the other side of the rock. I don't see anyone in them.'

The Little Man moved forward behind her.

'Where's your gun, Doddsy?' Doc demanded of him.

'Why, I can't handle it with this hand,' the other retorted. 'It's all I can do to jot down notes in my journal. I left it in the truck.'

'I got mine, Doc,' Wojtowicz called. He stumbled as he hurried forward through the press, but caught himself by driving the gun's butt against the asphaltoid. As he recovered balance he was holding it for a moment by the muzzle, like a pilgrim's staff.

At the same moment a voice from close by called out very sharply the trite words: 'Don't move. We've got you all covered. Don't move a finger, anybody, or you'll be shot.'

A man had stepped out from behind a boulder just above the road, and two more men from another just below it. These two levelled rifles at Wojtowicz, the other slowly wagged back and forth, only an inch or so either way, the muzzles of two revolvers. The head of each of the men was entirely covered with a bright red silk mask with large eyeholes. The man above the road had a jauntily collegiate black felt hat pulled down over the top of his, and he was slim and nattily dressed, but for all that he gave the impression of wiry, jigging age rather than of real youth.

Now he came stepping down, rather quickly and very sure-footedly. His eyes twitched as ceaselessly across the knot of travellers as did the muzzles of his two revolvers.

'That was a happy guess about the Black Dahlia,' he said rapidly but very clearly, enunciating every word with a finicky precision. 'She was the masterpiece of my youth. This time everything will go much more pleasantly – and a chance of survival for each of you – if the man with the gun will just let go of it *now*.' Wojtowicz's hand unclasped, and the gun teetered oddly for a second before starting to fall. 'And if all the men will separate themselves from the women, moving back and a little downhill, so –'

Rock chips spattered from a point on the road-blocking boulder five feet to the side of the black-hatted, red-masked man. Almost simultaneously there was a *zing-spat-zing*, and immediately the crack of a rifle behind them. Ray Hanks had managed to get off a shot from his cot in the truck.

Wojtowicz snatched up his fallen gun and shot from the hip at the two masked men with rifles. Almost at once they both fired, and Wojtowicz fell.

By that time Margo had the grey pistol out of her jacket and was pointing it at Black Hat and squeezing the trigger. He slammed flat back against the boulder with a crunch, his hands thrown out like a man crucified, and his revolvers shot out of his hands to either side. The boulder rocked, just a fraction.

Someone was screaming fiercely, exultantly.

Wojtowicz shot from the ground, the men with the rifles fired again, then Margo had turned the pistol on them, and they went sailing backward, cartwheeling and somersaulting, one of them clipping a boulder, their rifles whirling along separately, until they were a dozen yards beyond the cliff's edge and had dropped out of sight.

Black Hat fell slowly forward from the boulder, revealing a red stain where his head had rested against it. Margo ran towards him, pointing the pistol at him, and simply swept him across the downward slope and off the cliff after his henchmen, three small boulders with him.

Doc, nearest to Margo's line of fire, waltzed around with arm outstretched, as if doing a dance, took three long steps down the slope, and managed to check himself with his feet against a rock ridge three inches high.

Hunter ran to Margo, grabbed the grey pistol with one hand and pulled her finger off the trigger with the other, shouting: 'It's only me!' in her face.

Only then did she stop screaming her killer's scream to gasp to him a fiendishly grinning, 'Uh-huh.'

The Ramrod ran forward towards Ida.

Harry McHeath knelt by Wojtowicz, who was saying: 'Wow, oh wow!' Then 'Hell, kid, I was planning on dropping after the first shot, anyhow. They just creased my shoulder – I think. Better we look.'

Doc came loping up to Margo and Hunter, demanding: 'My God, what *is* that gun? I got an arm in the beam edge, and it was like I was throwing the hammer and forgot to let go of it.'

Margo said rapidly to Hunter: 'You don't have to worry about it being out of power. It's still half-charged – see, the violet line, right there.'

Doc said: 'Let me –' and then suddenly snapped erect and quickly stared around him. 'McHeath,' he shouted, 'bring me Wojtowicz's gun! Rama Joan, look after Wojtowicz. Hixon, get Hank's gun – if that hero cares to give it up. Ross, give

Margo back her pistol. She knows how to use it. Margo, you and I are going to reconnoitre this area until we're sure there's no more vermin. Get on my left hand and shoot anything with a gun that isn't one of us, but watch how you swing that beam.'

Margo, who had gone very pale, started to grin again and placed herself by Doc as directed, assuming a wary half-crouch. Wanda, coming up to help the Ramrod revive Ida, took one look at Margo and shrank away from her.

The Little Man said thoughtfully: 'I really think it was the Black Dahlia killer, but now we'll probably never know what he looked like. Why, we might even have recognized him.'

Wojtowicz, wincing as Rama Joan ripped his bloody shirt off his shoulder with her teeth, snarled up at Doddsy: 'Oh, nuts!'

Rama Joan pushed blood off her lips with her tongue and said quietly: 'Fetch your first-aid kit, Mr Dodd.'

Doc took the gun McHeath offered him, threw a fresh cartridge into the chamber and started up the slope, saying to Margo: 'Come on, while there's still light. We've got to secure our camp site.'

Barbara Katz suppressed a wince as the big policeman shoved his head and flashlight through the back window on her side of the sedan and demanded loudly but unexpectedly: 'You niggers steal this car?'

She began to talk rapidly, in the role of secretary-companion to Knolls Kelsey Kettering III, meanwhile sliding her hand back and forth on the window frame to draw the policeman's attention to the hundred-dollar bill in it, but he only went on shining his flashlight in their faces.

When it stabbed at KKK Barbara realized with a shock that the wrinkle-meshed face did look rather like that of an old darkie. And he had turned almost stuporous again – the heat had been too much for him. But then the little pale blue eyes opened and a cracked but arrogant voice commanded: 'Stop shining that thing in my face, you blue-coated idiot!'

This seemed to satisfy the policeman, for he switched off his flash, and Barbara felt the bill drawn smoothly from under her fingers. He took his head out of the window and said good-humouredly: 'O.K., I guess you can go on now. But tell me one thing, what do *you* folks think you're running away from? Most say high tides, but there's no hurricane. A couple cars talked about something coming from Cuba. You're all running like rabbits. It doesn't make sense.'

Barbara stuck her head out of the window. 'It *is* the tides,' she insisted. 'The new planet is making them.' She looked back east down the road they'd just travelled to where the Wanderer was rising all purple with a yellow monster-shape on it. The glittering spindle of the deformed moon, one end of the spindle foreshortened by the curve of its orbit, might be a sack the monster was carrying.

'Oh, that,' the policeman said, his big face grinning. 'That's something way off in the heavens. It doesn't matter. I'm talking about things on Earth.'

'But that's *the moon* breaking up around it,' she argued.

'Wrong shape for the moon,' he pointed out to her patiently. 'The moon's somewhere else.'

'But the new planet *is* making high tides,' she pleaded with him. 'The first tide wasn't so bad, but they'll get higher. Florida's not more than three hundred feet high anywhere. They may wash straight over it.'

He spread his hands, as if to invoke the testimony of the balmy night fragrant with orange blossoms, and chuckled tolerantly.

Barbara said: 'I'm trying to warn you. That planet's a doom-sign.' He continued to chuckle.

She felt herself seethe with sudden anger. 'Well, if nothing that matters is happening,' she demanded, 'why are you stopping all cars?'

The grin vanished. 'We're keeping order in Citrus Centre,' he said harshly, moving towards the next car in line. 'Tell your boy to drive on before I change my mind. Your boss ought to know better than to let his nigger girl talk for him. You college-educated niggers are the worst. They try to teach you science, but you get it all mixed up with your crazy African superstitions.'

They drove north in silence while the Wanderer slowly climbed, and the moon-spindle crawled across it, and the monster changed to a big purple *D*.

Knolls Kelsey Kettering III began to breathe gaspingly. Hester said: 'We got to find him a bed. He got to stretch out.'

Benjy slowed to read a sign. 'You are leaving Glades and entering Highlands County.' Suddenly he laughed whoopingly. 'That *high lands* sure sound good!'

But would they be high enough? Barbara wondered.

Richard Hillary woke shivering and aching. He'd pushed aside in his sleep the straw covering him. And through the straw under him, crushed flatly, had mounted the chill of the ground – the chill of the Chiltern Hills, his mind, half sleep-locked, alliterated it. Overhead the strange planet glared, revolved back to its dismal *D* again. He recalled some of the other faces it had shown – equally ugly faces, looking more like signs or a psychologist's toys than natural formations – one a bloat-centred *X*; another, a big yellow bull's-eye in a purple target. Still, it seemed to bulk out more like a true globe now, less like a circular flat signboard. And there was a beauty akin to that of Brancusi's 'Bird in Space' in its curving white half-ring. Could that last conceivably be the moon, as a fellow-trudger had assured him? Surely not. Yet the moon had travelled the sky all last night and where else was the moon now?

He sat up quietly, hugging himself for warmth, rebuttoning his coat collar and turning up the inadequate flap. The straw stack from which he'd taken his bedding was all gone now, and where he'd had at most a dozen comrades when he'd laid down some two hours ago, there were now scores of low straw mounds, each covering one or more sleepers. How quietly they had come – hushing each other, perhaps, as they scooped up and hugged their straw; late arrivers at a sleeping hostel. He envied those huddled in pairs their shared warmth, and he remembered very wistfully the Young Girl of Devizes who had seemed at the time so stupid and coarse. He remembered her sausage-and-mash, too.

He looked towards the farmhouse where he'd bought a

small bowl of soup last night and paid for his straw. Its lights were still on, but the windows were irregularly obscured. He realized with mild amazement that this was because of the people outside crowded together against its walls like bees for warmth. Surely many of the late-comers must have gone hungry; the ready food would be gone like the straw. Or perhaps the farmer's wife would be baking? He sniffed, but got only a briny smell. Had she opened a barrel of salt beef? But now his mind was wandering foolishly, he told himself.

Despite the crowd of new sleepers, there seemed to be no more people coming. And the road beyond the gate, which had been loud with traffic when he'd gone to sleep, was quiet and empty.

He stood up and looked east. The valley through which he'd just trudged was now full of dark silvery mist, fingers of it stretching around the hill on which he was now, pushing up each grassy gully.

The mist had a remarkably flat top, gleaming like gunmetal.

He saw two lights, red and green, moving across it mysteriously, close together.

He realized that they were the lights of a boat and that the mist was solid, still water. The stand of the high tide.

Chapter 27

Doc and Margo scouted the rock slope to its crest and the road for two hundred yards beyond the boulder-block without finding any signs of human life, though they did disturb four lizards and a hawk. The valley ahead between the last two mountain ridges was all blackened. It held only wet ashes of its manzanitas and yuccas, and charred skeletons of its scrub oaks. Presumably it had been fiercely burned out a few hours before – which helped explain why no more people had come this way.

Clarence Dodd and Harry McHeath voluntarily joined in the reconnoitre, speeding it up. The latter made his way to the downslope precipice edge and reported that it fell away sheer for five hundred feet to a rocky knob and a steep, rock-studded, brush-grown slope.

Neither of Black Hat's revolvers turned up – either they'd carried over the cliff or been lost in the pitted and creviced rocks.

The two sedans beyond the boulder still had their ignition keys, which Doc pocketed. Doddsy jotted down the names on the steering-column registration papers, using his flashlight to eke out the fading green daylight, and he speculated as to whether one of them was that of the Black Dahlia sadist. Presumably Black Hat and his acolytes had come in the sedans, the lone girl, from the other direction in the red Corvette – a purely chance meeting at the roadblock – and then, probably before the rains, while flames were still roaring to the east, making an appropriately hellish backdrop . . . it didn't do to think about it.

Meanwhile, Ross Hunter and the Hixons corded up the murdered girl's body in Doc's borrowed raincoat and the smallest of the truck's tarpaulins. The olive-drab bundle was lugged a hundred feet up the rock slope and eased into a coffin-size cave young McHeath had spotted. Pinned to the tarpaulin was a brief account in Doddsy's waterproof ink of the circumstances of her death and, with a question mark, the woman's name and address, found on the Corvette's registration papers. The Ramrod spoke a brief, unfamiliar service, signing himself with a cross that ended in a finger-traced Isis-loop in front of his forehead.

Then everyone began to feel a bit better, though as horror and excitement died it also became obvious that everyone was tired half to death and this must be their bivouac. Preparations were made for sleep, most of them bedding down in the school bus, the two injured men certainly, since it was already chilly, and would get a lot chillier before dawn. Hixon was bothered about more boulders on the slope above rolling down in case of a quake, but Doc pointed out that they'd stayed in place through a couple of dillies, and that anyway the Wanderer's gravity had probably triggered off during the first few hours after its emergence most of the quakes it was going to.

Doc decided two persons would sit guard through the night,

well blanket-wrapped in a low-ramparted natural scoop in the rocks two-thirds of the way up the slope and almost directly above the boulder block. They would be armed with one of the rifles and Margo's grey pistol. Doddsy and McHeath would take it to midnight, Ross Hunter and Margo, twelve to two-thirty, himself and Rama Joan, two-thirty to dawn. Hixon would have the other rifle and nap in the driver's seat in the bus. The women on guard duty would sleep in the truck cab with Ann. Wanda commented on the co-educational sentry arrangements, and Doc snapped out a peppery answer.

The primus stove was fired with charcoal. Water was heated on it for the powdered coffee. They made supper of that and the milk and peanut butter and jelly sandwiches from the bus.

Margo thought she wouldn't be able to stomach such sweet, gooey child's fodder, but found herself ravenous after the first bite and disposed of three, along with a pint of *café au lait*. She felt lightheadedly drunk, her mind from time to time happily jumping with visions of the red-hooded sadists being swept by her pistol to their deaths, and she said what she felt to everyone she met.

Catching the Ramrod behind the bus, she asked him point-blank: 'Mr Fulby, is it true you're married to both Ida and Wanda?'

He, quite unoffended, nodded his narrow, grizzled head and replied: 'Yes indeed, in our eyes they are both my wives, and I their breadwinner. It's been an enriching relationship, on the whole. I originally married Wanda for the body's glory – she was a Baby Wampas star – and Ida for the spirit's exaltation. Of course, things are a bit different now. . . .'

The scowly old bus driver heard most of that speech and turned away with a snort.

'Jealous, Pop?' Margo asked him with a friendly sort of maliciousness.

Tigerishka finished feeding Miaow for a third time and glanced at Paul. Then, with what he surmised was a deliberately human and mocking shrug of those lovely violet-barred green shoulders that had more play and stretch in them than any tennis star's

205

or Hindu dancer's, she returned to the food panel, then swam over to him with a small kit in one paw and two narrow tubes trailing behind her. She hovered by him, eyeing him up and down, as if momentarily uncertain whether to force-feed him down the throat, or through a vein, or perhaps rectally.

His throat now ached with thirst, matching his general muscle ache, and he had begun to feel very lightheaded, though more likely from experience-fatigue than hunger. What he was mostly conscious of was unhappy irritation at the change in Tigerishka. While Miaow fed, the large cat had been dancing – a wonderfully swift, rhythmic pirouetting and somersaulting and cartwheeling between ceiling and floor of the saucer, pushing off from each in turn. Simultaneously, strange music had filled the saucer, and its mysterious sunlight had pulsed in time.

Tigerishka, Paul realized now, was a toe-dancer by anatomy, her feet being all toe – digitigrade, not plantigrade – and her heel the leg-joint above them, corresponding to the lower elbow in her forearm.

The dance had enthralled him completely, taking his mind off all his pains and anxieties.

Now the lovely ballerina had become again the impersonally sadistic nurse – a hateful transformation.

So in spite of his thirst he sadly shook his head and tried to press his numb, thick-feeling lips together tight. Then he pushed up his eyebrows and solemnly lifted his face towards hers in the only expression of appeal his mind could devise – though he was very conscious of how exquisitely like a gagged and pinioned monkey begging for freedom he must be making himself look.

She grinned at him without parting her long lips – another mocking imitation of a human sign, he felt sure, and continued to contemplate him.

It was night again, he knew, and he had been in the saucer a full twelve hours, for the last observation had been another unmistakable one – of San Francisco sinking into evening, but showing the black stains and smokings of fires put out by rains, and also a crowding of ships in the Golden Gate. Then the saucer had tilted, and he had seen the Wanderer rising in the east in its mandala-face with an asymmetric glittering ring around it that a few seconds of frantic thought convinced him was most likely the crushed moon.

Tigerishka reached out and brushed his right wrist with the back of a green paw, then sat back again. He realized with rather incredulous wonder that his right arm was free. He worked the fingers, bent and unbent the elbow with less pain than he'd anticipated, then started to lift his fingers to his lips, but stopped them midway.

If he simply touched his lips, she might interpret it as meaning he wished to be tube-fed that way.

He brought his fingers to his forehead, then in one smooth movement dropped them to his lips and out towards her pointed ears. Inspiration continuing, he dropped them towards her muzzle, then swept them back to his own ear.

'Yes, want talk,' she interpreted. 'Monkey cat have great gossip, eh?' She slowly shook her green-masked face from side to side. 'No! Be all chatter-questions – one, ten, five thousands! I know apes.'

His expectations crumbled. At the same time it was occurring to him, with curious certainty, that she could have said that in grammatically perfect English, but deliberately chose not to – very much as a brilliant European quite capable of speaking any language flawlessly will hang on to his accent and his first, makeshift constructions to emphasize his exotic individuality, and also as a subtle criticism of the arbitrary English pronunciations and of its swarms of silly little auxiliary words.

'Still,' Tigerishka temporized, 'are things I will tell.' Then, at court-stenographer speed, and a little singsong, as if it were very boring to her: 'I come superior galactic culture. Read minds, throw thoughts, sail hyperspace, live forever if want, blow up suns – all that sort stuff. Look like animal – resume ancestral shapes. Make brains small but really huge – (psycho-physiosubmicrominiaturization! We *stay* superior.) You not believe? So listen. Plants eat inorganic: they superior! Animals eat plants: *they* superior. Cats eat fresh meat: we *most* superior! Monkeys try eat anything: a mess!'

Then without pause: 'Wanderer sail hyperspace. Yes, star photos, I know. Need fuel – *much* matter for converters. Your moon good woodpile. Smash, pulverize, dredge. We fuel up, then go. No need you monkeys get hot and bothered.'

After she broke off, Paul continued to seethe for all of five seconds, utterly enraged at her heartless over-simplifications. Then it occurred to him that there was nothing whatever he could do about it. He took a deep, slow breath and calmed his features, hoping they were growing less red. Then he held his hand tightly over his mouth and suddenly threw it out, as if to say: 'Away with the gag.'

It also occurred to him that there was really no point to this gesture game, since she must know his thoughts, but immediately on the heels of that came the realization that the point simply was that it *was* a game. Cats like games; they like to play with helpless victims; and here Tigerishka seemed no exception.

She confirmed this by smiling as she slowly shook her head – smiling and wrinkling her upper lips so that her five-bristle moustaches made little circles.

He took another tack. He repeated the 'Away with the gag' gesture, but immediately followed it by bringing his hand to his mouth as if holding a glass, and tipping it as if drinking. Finally he laid his forefinger across the centre of his lips.

Tigerishka's star-shaped pupils narrowed to points as she stared at his eyes. 'I let you drink mouth, you no talk? No say single word?'

Paul nodded solemnly.

She took from her kit a limp white flask of what looked like half-pint capacity and held it against his lips: 'I squeeze gently, you suck,' she said, and brushed the back of her other forepaw across his cheek and chin. Sensation flashed back into them and at the same time a cool seeping was solacing his dry and aching throat. After a bit the taste came: milk. Milk with a faint musky tone. He wondered if it were feline or synthetic, humanly assimilable or not, but decided he must trust Tigerishka's judgement.

When the first edge of his thirst was quenched, he reached up his hand to take over the job of squeezing. She neither rebuffed this gesture nor immediately relinquished her hold on the flask, so for a few moments he felt, through the edges of his

208

fingers and hand, the velvet of her pads and the resilient silk of her fur and, through the latter, the hard curve of a sheathed claw. Then she withdrew her paw, saying only: 'Gently, remember.'

When the flask was crushed flat, he handed it back to her, unintentionally adding: 'Thank you' – but before the words could come out, her pads had lightly slapped his lips and the gag was back again.

He wondered dully if the gag was a matter of pure suggestion or some impalpable film, or some instantaneous electrophoretic tissue-impregnation – *cat*aphoresis, doctors actually called it! – or whatnot else – but a thought-jumbling lethargy was swiftly stealing over his body and mind. Fatigue or drugs? That too was too hard to think about.

Drowsily he realized that the saucer's invisible indoor sun had faded to twilight. Through sleep-mist he felt the freeing brush of Tigerishka's fur against his left wrist and ankle, so that only his right ankle still fettered him.

He folded himself into a uterine position and drifted towards deeper sleep.

The last thing he was aware of was Tigerishka's neutral, ' 'Night, monkey.'

Chapter 28

The Wanderer showed Earth its yin-yang face for a fifth time. For a full day now it had hung in Terra's night sky. For the meteorologists at the South Pole International Observation Station, deep in the unbroken night of the Southern Hemisphere's winter, the Wanderer had made a full circuit of the sunless sky, keeping always the same distance above the icy horizon, and now hung once more where it had first appeared above the Queen Maud Range and Marie Byrd Land. Great green auroras sprang from the snows and glowed around it.

The strange planet mightily restimulated some supernatural beliefs and many sorts of mania.

In India, which had thus far escaped the severer earthquakes and suffered minimal tidal damage, it was worshipped by large congregations in night-long rites. Some identified it as the invisible planet Ketu, at last disgorged by the serpent. Brahmins quietly contemplated it and hinted it might mark the dawn of a new kalpa.

In South Africa it became the standard of revolt for a bloody and successful uprising against the Boers.

In Protestant countries the Book of Revelation was searched through in thousands of Bibles never before read or even opened.

In Rome the new Pope, who was a Jesuit-trained astronomer, combated superstitious interpretations of events, while the *paparazzi* found films and lenses for their cameras which would enable them to snap movie stars and other notorious notables gesturing at the Wanderer or backgrounded by it – as Ostia fought flood, and the new Mediterranean tides pushed up the Tiber.

In Egypt a felinoid being landing from a saucer was identified as the benign goddess Bast by an expatriate British theosophist, and the cult of cat-worship got off to a new beginning. According to the theosophist, the Wanderer itself was Bast's destructive twin: Sekhet, the Eye of Ra.

There was an odd echo of this development in Paris, where two felinoids, repeating Tigerishka's mistake, loosed from the zoological gardens all the tigers, lions, leopards, and other large felines. Some of the beasts appeared in Left Bank cafés. A similar liberation occurred at the Tiergarten in Berlin, where the animals were threatened by flood waters.

Strange, strange to think that Don Merriam was sleeping snugly now in his little cabin aboard the Wanderer, just as Paul was sleeping as soundly aboard Tigerishka's saucer.

While the Wanderer caused numerous panics and outbursts of mania, its sudden appearance and the catastrophes attendant on it acted in other instances as a sort of shock therapy. There were literal outbursts of sanity in the violent wards of mental hospitals. Seeing the impossible made real, and even nurses and doctors terrified by it, satisfied some deep need in psychotics. And private neuroses and psychoses became trivial to their possessors in the face of a cosmic derangement.

On others the Wanderer bestowed a last-minute ability to look on the truth, if not to struggle against it. As Fritz Scher, now waist-deep in salt water, looked out of the window in the Tidal Institute at Hamburg towards dawn, the clouds lifted a little in the west like a curtain half drawn up, and from beneath them the Wanderer glared at him full in the face. Things at last came clear in his mind as a powerful new surge of water toppled him and carried him back from the window. As he clutched futilely at the sleek sides of the tide-predicting machine while the tide carried him along it, he used his last breaths to cry out over and over: 'Multiply everything by eighty!'

Barbara Katz felt the bed under her move a little on its casters, as the dark, third-floor hotel room rocked with the building holding it. She mastered the impulse to jump up and she pressed closer to old KKK, then reached her hand across to Helen on his other side. An hour ago the old man had shaken with a chill. This afternoon it had been the heat that had troubled him, but now with the icy waters of the Atlantic washing across Florida, it was the cold.

Benjy, standing at the window, his face ghostly in the Wanderer-light, reported: 'Water over first-floor windows and pressing us hard. Here come a summer house. Hear it bang us? Sort of crunchy.'

'Get in you cot, Benjy, and get some rest,' Hester called from the corner. 'If this place go, it go. Water no knock to come in, you cain't tell it. "Stay out!"'

'I ain't got your calm, Hes,' he told her. 'I should've stayed with the car, make sure they leave it on top the mound. Water be pretty close to it by now, though.'

'They'd better not have moved it!' Barbara called softly but feelingfully over her shoulder. 'That parking place was part of the five thousand we're paying for this room.'

From the other side of old KKK Helen called with just a ghost of her giggle: 'I wonder those skinflints remember to bring the cash box upstairs. Else she be washed away sho!'

'Quiet,' Hester called. 'Benjy, get in you cot.'

'Where's the attraction?' he asked pensively from the window. 'Helen got to sleep with the Old Man, help keep him warm. And that pancake makeup and powder Miss Barbara put on my face itch it.'

'Quit bellyachin', darkie,' Hester told him. 'Helen and I get by as nurses, but you need a little lightening. Don't make you pass, but it justify you. Show you trying to please. With that and a thousand-dollar bill, you get anywhere.'

Benjy said, the pale light in his eyes now as he lifted them: 'Old Wanderer got the monster on him once again. He spin fast.'

The room rocked. Timbers creaked. Benjy announced: 'Water up another hand's width. Seem to me the angles is shifting.'

Helen raised up: 'You think we should --' she began in a tight, breathy voice.

'Quiet!' Hester commanded heavily. 'Everybody *got* to be quiet now, and lie down. We enjoyin' five thousand dollars. Benjy, you tell me when that water up to you neck – and not before! *Good night.*'

In the dark Barbara thought of the Sebring race course a mile off, and all those fine-tuned motors in their pits under the salt sea, the oil washed away. Or had they been smart and roared north to safety in a red-blue-green-yellow-silver pack? She pictured outboards racing the Sebring course. She pictured the drowned rockets a hundred miles beyond at Cape Kennedy.

Old KKK groaned faintly and mumbled something. Barbara stroked his papery, furrowed cheek, but he kept on muttering. His fingers, which he kept close to his chest as one praying, were working a little. She reached down the bed and found the fashion doll in its black lace underwear and laid it in them. He quieted. She smiled.

The room rocked.

Sally Harris had put on a pearl-encrusted evening sheath from the very interesting wardrobe in the bedroom adjoining Mr Hasseltine's. Jake Lesher had draped his frame in a dark blue serge suit that was a little long for him everywhere, making it zooty looking. They sat at the grand piano, which was topped by flat wine glasses and two champagne bottles.

The room was lit by twenty-three candles – all Sally had been able to find – and two flashlights. Dark drapes hid the windows and even the stalled elevator, and especially the French doors to the patio.

Silence was seeping in through the dark drapes, freezing the candle flames, pressing on their throats and hearts. But then Jake's fingers came down on the keyboard and drove the silence back with the rippling burst of an introduction. Sally stood up, weaving a little, and sang loudly and quite clearly:

> Oh, I am the Girl in Noah's Ark
> And you are my old Storm King.
> Our love is not merely as big as the sun,
> Orion or Messier-31 –
> You launched me a private skyscraper, Hon!
> Our love is a very big thing.

As Jake played the vamp with his left hand, he reached over and handed Sally a sheet of paper.

'Try the second stanza,' he said.

She scanned it owlishly. 'Gee, it's got some crazy words. And how do I sing ink-blots?'

'I found what you call crazy words in a fancy "list of outstanding celestial objects", in one of your intellectual boy friend's big books. We got to keep up the astronomical motif to go with the new planet.'

'Planet-shplanet. If it weren't for Hugo, you'd be in the drink. I wonder where Hugo is now? Okay, Jake, play it.' And she sang, with the sheet to her nose:

> Oh, I am the Girl in Noah's Ark
> And you are my old Storm King.
> Our love is not merely as big as the sun,
> Orion or Messier-31 –
> You launched me a private skyscraper, Hon!
> Our love is a very big thing.

Jake beamed at her. 'We got us a hit, baby! A real blazer!'

'That's very good,' Sally told him, thrusting a hand out for her glass, 'because the chances are we'll be putting it on in a very damp theatre.'

Richard Hillary felt a weird exhilaration as he tramped along springily beside a salt-reeking road leading west a distance south of Islip. Stranded on the mud-filmed, tide-combed grass within his view of the moment were two silvery fish and a small green lobster feebly crawling across a long sodden twist of black cloth that might well be a college gown. Looking south, he could see some of the grey towers of Oxford and clearly distinguish the brown tide-mark half-way up them. He held his breath, his hands moved upward, and his next step was almost turned to a leap as in imagination he frantically swam up through the waters of the North or Irish Sea that had been here some five or six hours ago.

He turned his leap back to a step with a snickering laugh, maintaining his exhilaration. Sometimes, of course, the weirdness of the contrasts constantly presented by the stranded flotsam got a bit too much, especially when they involved sodden human bodies, or even the bodies of horses and dogs. Here his rule, and apparently that of the people tramping with him, was, 'If they don't stir, look away from them quickly.' He'd had to invoke that rule several times in the past mile. Thus far, none of the sprawled wet forms had stirred.

Richard had been lucky in that he had got a lift almost all the way from the field where he'd slept on the far edge of the Chiltern Hills. He had set out at night, immediately after seeing the flooded east behind him, and had been picked up by a couple in a Bentley, come from Letchworth in the East Anglian Heights. They'd been nervously intent on picking up their son at Oxford. They hadn't seen much of the flood and were inclined to minimize it. They'd given him a sandwich. After a bit, a good many other cars had turned up, and the going had got slow, and when they had finally driven slippingly down after dawn on to the sodden Oxford plain into the midst of a muddy traffic tie-up, Richard had thanked them and left. The tie-up looked like a lasting one, and he couldn't bear the stunned, hurt, planless expressions on their faces.

One must have a plan, he told himself now, as he marched along quickly among a pack of fellow marchers, beside another double file of spattered cars slowly moving west. They crossed the Cherwell by a crowded bridge hardly two feet above a

214

foaming flood. He wondered how salt the water was, but he didn't stop to taste.

He wondered, too, whether last night's flooding here had come up from the Thames Estuary, or a hundred miles down from the Wash across the fenlands, roaring over the height of land between Daventry and Bicester, or even striking through gaps in the Cotswolds from the west coast, where the normal tides have a range of thirty feet. But such speculation wasn't bringing him any closer to a plan. The sun was getting hot on his back.

There was a low, heavy drumming, and the crowd around him pressed closer to the road as a small helicopter settled to a landing fifty yards away. The pilot, a young woman in muddied nurse's whites, sprang out and ran to the one live figure that hadn't run away from the noise and downdraught: another young woman sitting in the mud with a baby in her arms. She took the baby from her, dragged her to her feet, and hurriedly led her to the 'copter and put her aboard. Then, making no answer to the diverse shouted questions that now began to come from the crowd, she quickly climbed aboard herself and took off.

Richard shook his head self-angrily and strode on. Watching such things made him feel horribly lonely, and got him no nearer to a plan, either.

After a bit, though, he had one formulated. He would reach the Cotswolds before the next high tide, harbour upon them during it, cross the Severn plain by way of Tewkesbury to the Malvern Hills during the next low, and finally make his way by the same stepping-stone process to the Black Mountains of Wales, which should be proof against the highest tides that might come. His ebbing exhilaration returned a bit.

Of course it might be wisest to return to the Chilterns or seek the moderate heights just east of Islip, but he told himself one ought to leave room there for the hordes that must still be pressing west, somehow, from London. Besides, he hated the thought of stopping anywhere, even on a safe-seeming height, and waiting and thinking. That was intolerable – one must keep moving, keep moving. And one feels loyalty towards a course of action one has just hammered out.

He finally told his Cotswolds–Malvern Hills–Black Mountains plan to two older men beside whom he walked for a space. The first said it was utterly impractical, a mad fool's vapourings; the second said it would save half of England and should be communicated at once to responsible authorities (this man waved his cane wildly at a cruising helicopter).

Richard became disgusted with both of them, particularly the second, and tramped swiftly ahead, leaving them arguing loudly and angrily with each other. Suddenly all his exhilaration was gone, and he felt that both his plan and his reasonings were the purest rationalizations for an urge to rush west that had no more sense to it than the crowded scamper of the lemmings across Scandinavia to the Atlantic and death. Indeed, he asked himself, mightn't shock and disorientation, in himself and all those around him, have stripped away civilized thought-layers and laid bare some primeval brain-node that responded only to the same call that the lemmings hear?

He continued to hurry, however, moving closer to the road and watching for an empty place or clinging-spot on one of the faster-moving vehicles. After all, lemming or no, his silly plan was all he had, and he had just remembered the most cogent objection to it made by the first man: that it was a good twenty-five miles to the Cotswolds.

As the morning tide flooded up the Bristol Channel, up the Severn, bringing wrecked ships and shredded hayricks, and buoys burst from their anchors, and telegraph poles trailing wires below, and torn houses, and the dead, flooding higher than last night, Dai Davies returned with it, past Glamorgan and Monmouth, twisting and turning like T. S. Eliot's drowned Phoenician sailor, a fond Welshman poetic to the end, forty feet down.

Chapter 29

Margo and Hunter, each wrapped in a blanket, occupied the bowl-shaped lookout post, which McHeath and Doddsy had scooped and wiped dry of rainwater. Above them stars twinkled to the west amid scattered clouds, but the top and eastern half of the sky were still solidly masked. Below them a narrow cone of light shone on the locked sedans and along the road towards the Valley. Since Doddsy had several battery-changes for his big flashlight, Doc had the notion of setting it on top of the boulder-block. 'It'll help whoever's on guard to see anyone sneaking in from the Valley,' he'd said. 'They'll be apt to investigate the light, and if they're friendly they'll probably yoohoo. But don't shoot 'em just for being quiet. Cover 'em and order 'em to stand first. And don't wake the whole camp because we get a visitor. But wake me.'

Now Hunter and Margo were smoking, which flawed the perfection of Doc's ambush – but not too seriously, they'd decided. The little orange glow as Margo inhaled lighted her hollow-cheeked face and gold hair combed down heavy and flat after last night's salt-soaking.

'You look like a Valkyrie, Margo,' Hunter said softly in a deep voice.

She drew the grey pistol from under the blanket and held it high on her chest, so that it gleamed in the cigarette's brief glow. 'I feel like one,' she whispered happily. 'I didn't like it when the others had this gun, though it was interesting the things Doddsy noticed.'

During his and McHeath's sentry-go, the Little Man had examined the pistol with his small flashlight and an eight-power pocket magnifier, and had discovered a fine scale alongside the violet charge-gauge. 'It was made by beings with finer eyesight than ours,' he had deduced. He had also discovered something else Margo had never noticed: a tiny, recessed lever on top of the grip – the lever pointed its narrow end at the muzzleward extreme of a similarly fine, circular scale. No one had any firm guess about the function of this lever, and it was decided not to experiment with it.

'I wonder on how many planets it's killed,' Margo whispered now.

'Yes,' Hunter said, 'you look like a vestal Valkyrie guarding the sacred flame of the weapon.' He hitched a little closer to her. She smelled the musk of his sweat.

'Shh – did you hear something then?' she breathed very rapidly. They stubbed out their cigarettes and waited tensely, their eyes scanning. Hunter softly crawled to the ridge crest by a route he'd memorized earlier and checked all around from there, although the other side of the ridge fell away quite precipitously for thirty feet.

The bus-and-truck camp was quiet and there was no sign of alien movement, though the whispering wind made them think of the tomb in the cave five yards away. After a while they arranged themselves as they'd been, and lit up again.

'You know, Margo,' Hunter went on where he'd left off, 'I think killing those men brought you to life. It awakened you, maybe for the first time. A primal experience does that to a person.'

She nodded intently with an inward-directed smile. 'Everything's twice as real now,' she whispered. 'As if reality were built of solider stuff, and yet I could see and feel more around and into it, especially people's bodies. It's wonderful.'

'It's made you beautiful,' he said, laying his hand on the inside of her wrist. 'More beautiful. Beautiful Valkyrie vestal.'

'Why, Ross,' she whispered solemnly, 'anyone would think you're trying to make me.'

'I am,' he said, firming his hand a little on her wrist.

'You have a wife and two boys in Oregon,' she whispered, pulling away, but not quite hard enough to get free.

'They don't matter,' he said, 'though I'm steadily worried about them. But we're living from day to day now, from second to second. Any hour may be the last. Margo, let me kiss you.'

'I only met you yesterday, Ross. You're years older than I am. . . .'

'Ten, at the most,' he breathed harshly. 'Margo, the old rules

218

and shibboleths don't count. Like Rudy said, it's para-reality. . . .'

At that moment winds high above them tore the clouds, and they saw the Wanderer in its mandala face with the moon making a glittering half girdle around it. The wonder of that gold-notched violet sphere gripped them, but after a few seconds Ross Hunter put his other arm around Margo and pulled her towards him. She broke away and pointed overhead.

'I have a young man up there,' she said. 'He was stationed on that . . . that diamond jumble. But maybe he got away; maybe he's on the Wanderer now.'

'I know,' Hunter said, looking only at her face, which now in the Wanderer-light needed no cigarette glow to show it. 'I even read about your romance in a magazine. I thought you looked disgustingly snooty and smirking, like you needed to be grabbed by life and manhandled.'

'By you, you mean? And then there's Paul,' she went on rapidly, 'snatched up in a saucer and now God knows where. He's crazy about me, but all tied up inside. Maybe what's happening to him now will free him.'

'I don't care about either of them,' Hunter said, getting up on his knees beside her and holding her by the shoulders. 'I have no ethical qualms about taking advantage of the immediate difficulties of younger men crazy about you. You're beautiful, and whoever gets you first wins. Besides, I know you better than they do. I know the awakened gold-haired Valkyrie, and I'm crazier than they are. Nothing counts now but you and me. Oh, Margo –'

'No!' she said sharply, suddenly standing up from her blanket and wiping his hands down off her arms. 'I'm glad you're crazy about me, but I don't need you, I don't need the you-and-me. Just living by myself in the new reality is quite enough; it's all the excitement I want; it's using all of me. Understand?'

After a couple of hard breaths he admitted: 'O.K., I guess I have to.' Then: 'We'd better have a careful scan around with all this new light. You take the western half. Let your eyes get used to it.'

After a minute or so of that, back to back, he began to talk quietly without looking around. 'Granting that you're all absorbed with yourself now, I doubt if you were really ever in love. Paul you bullied and exploited – that was obvious. I imagine you managed . . . who was it? – oh yes, Don – by flattering his manliness.'

'Interesting,' Margo murmured.

'No, I don't think either of those two young men amount to much as rivals,' Hunter went on. 'Morton Opperly's a greater danger, because he's a father figure: a sinisterly beautiful magician who – I bet you dream about this! – is some day going to carry our young Valkyrie away to his grim castle in the Land of Higher Mathematics. Incest with Einsteinian overtones.'

'Very interesting,' she commented. 'There seems to be a very faint general glow to the east. Maybe it's the highway.'

Five minutes more and Hunter burst out, most spontaneously-seeming, with: 'Christ, it's cold. It'd help if we bundled together, the old Puritan style –'

'Nuh-uh, soldier,' she interposed. 'Lovemaking and guard duty don't mix.'

'*Au contraire*, they combine beautifully. You become vibrantly alive, aware of everything.'

'Nuh-uh, Ross, I said.'

'I wasn't trying a new approach,' he protested, 'just being practical. I'm freezing.'

'Then wrap your blanket around you, tight,' she suggested. 'I don't need any heater.' She smiled straight at him. 'Right this minute I'm hot as fire from my neck down to my toes. *And* vibrantly alive. All by myself.'

'You *are* a bitch,' he said thoughtfully.

'Yes, I am,' she agreed with a happy smirk. 'And right now I'm going on a little scout, first down the road fifty yards beyond the sedans. I'll carry the rifle. You stay here with the big gun and . . . cover me.'

'Bitch,' he repeated bitterly as she stole crosswise down the slope.

A cloud was shrouding the Wanderer when they waked Doc for sentry change. He groaned guardedly a couple of times as he unkinked stiff joints, then grew more chipper.

'Have to renew the flash batteries,' he noted. 'Got 'em here in

220

my pocket. Should have turned one of the sedans around and used its headlights. Can't do it now, though – it'd wake people.'

By the time Margo had taken over Rama Joan's bed in the truck, the Wanderer was out again, showing the Jaws. Ann was awake. Ever since the afternoon's horror, the little girl who 'loved everything' had been very thoughtful. Now Margo wondered uneasily what she was thinking when those wide eyes looked at her, a screaming killer.

But, 'Why does Mommy have to go away?' was all Ann asked, rather fretfully.

Margo explained about guard duty.

'I think Mommy likes being with Mr Brecht,' Ann commented dolefully.

'Look at the Wanderer, dear,' Margo suggested. 'See, the moon's growing into a ring. She's broken her cocoon and is spreading her wings.'

'Yes, it's lovely, isn't it?' Ann said, a dreamy note at last coming into her voice. 'Purple forests and golden seas . . . Hello, Ragnarok. . . .'

In the bus Mrs Hixon leaned forward from the seat behind the driver's and whispered in Mr Hixon's ear: 'Bill, what if these people find out we're not really married?'

He whispered back: 'Babe, I don't think it'd matter to them a bit.'

Mrs Hixon sighed. 'Still, it's a kind of distinction being the only normal married couple in the bunch.'

Paul woke up as alone in black space as a hobo angel, it seemed to him – so high above Earth that the stars glittered more thickly above the scythe-curve of the black horizon than he'd ever seen them, even in the desert. Yet he felt so snug and refreshed, and the transition from sleep to waking had been so gradual, that he experienced no fear at all. Besides that, there was an invisible warm glassy surface he could touch. It shut off all the harshness of space from him, and his right foot was guyed to it reassuringly. He gave himself up to the great sight.

He was poised in the night at least one hundred miles above Arizona, he decided, and looking west, for he could see all of Southern California and the northwest corner of Mexico, including the neck of the peninsula of Baja California, and beyond them the Pacific. No mistaking that pattern.

He could see the lights of San Diego – at least some city-like glow, about where San Diego should be – and he realized he was voicelessly thanking God for that, very tritely, but sincerely.

There were no clouds. The Wanderer was hanging in the west it its bull's-head face, girdled by the shattered moon. Its violet and golden light sparkled in a wide wake across the Pacific straight towards him, and also spangled the northern end of the Gulf of California, so that all coasts were sharply defined.

The land areas reflected only a diffuse yellowish glow, like multiplied moonlight but far duller than the glittering sea.

But then he saw, with a feeling of dim but growing horror, that the Gulf of California extended at least a hundred miles too far northwest in a glittering tongue that narrowed at first but then widened. No mistaking that one departure from pattern, either.

Either because of the earthquakes or the high tides or both, the salt waters of the Gulf had burst through and filled the land below sea level in and around the Imperial Valley and the drying Salton Sea, and stretched on towards Palm Springs. He remembered that one of the towns there, a pretty big one, had been called Brawley, and another, Volcano –

Space turned to a pink wall in front of his nose, and a neutral voice called: ''Morning, monkey.'

Blinking, Paul slowly hunched around, easing his right foot in its invisible fetter. Tigerishka was floating bent by the control panel, as if she were sitting in an invisible swing. Miaow clung to her lap and was industriously grooming the larger cat's green knees with her tiny pink tongue.

Paul swallowed and then lifted his fingers wonderingly to his lips. The gag was gone.

Tigerishka smiled at him. 'You sleep seven hours,' she volunteered. 'Feel better?'

Paul cleared his throat, but then only shut his lips and looked at her. He did not smile back.

'Oho, we learn a little wisdom, eh?' Tigerishka purred. 'Monkey not jabber, we get along better. O.K. talk now, though.'

222

Paul kept his lips shut.

'Don't be sulky, Paul,' Tigerishka directed. 'I know you civilized by your lights, but I tie you, gag you, call you monkey to teach you little lesson: how you not so important in scheme of things, how others can treat you like you treat potentially superior animal Miaow here. Also I do it to give you birth-experience any psychologist know you badly need.'

Paul looked at her a bit longer, then slowly shook his head.

'What you mean?' Tigerishka demanded sharply. 'What you think my reason?'

Enunciating each syllable as sharply and carefully as if he were teaching a speech class, Paul said: 'You tell me you have a mind vastly superior to my own, and in many ways I must agree with you, yet for at least twenty minutes yesterday you confused my thoughts with those of that charming but speech-less and cultureless little animal on your lap. So you took out on me your irritation at having made such a very stupid mistake.'

'That's a lie, I never did!' Tigerishka retorted instantly in unslurred English quite as good as his own. She stiffened, her claws came out, and Miaow stopped grooming her. Then she caught herself and leaned back luxuriously, relaxed and chuckling. A delicious shrug rippled her violet-barred shoul-ders. 'You right there,' she admitted. 'That a little part my reason. Few cosmic cat strains, me let hopes run away. You notice. Monkey sly.'

'Just the same, you made the error, and it was a gross one,' he told her quietly. 'How could you expect an animal tiny as Miaow to have a reasoning brain?'

'Me think it miniaturized,' she answered quickly. 'Could have told it wasn't if I'd checked by clairvoyance, but I de-pending on telepathy.' She petted Miaow. 'Any more monkey-quibbles?'

Paul waited a bit again, then said: 'You claim to belong to a super-civilized galactic culture, yet you exhibit a fantastic xenophobia. I should think a true galactic citizen would have to be able to get along with intelligent beings of all strains: sea dwellers, grazers, arachnoids and coleopteroids possibly, winged beings, wolves and other carnivores like yourself, yes, and simians, too.'

Tigerishka seemed to start just a little as he said, 'wolves and other carnivores', but she recovered nicely with a sweet, 'Monkey much the worst strain of those, Paul.' She added huskily: 'Also cosmos not so pretty-pretty lovey-lovey you think.' She had begun to stroke Miaow rhythmically, kneading the small cat's shoulderblades.

'I am inclined to agree,' Paul commented. 'You pretend to near omniscience and to a great consideration for life – at least you boasted of saving two anthropoid cities from fire – yet when you crushed our moon for fuel, you ignored the presence on it of a number of human beings, including my best friend.'

'Too bad, Paul,' Tigerishka sympathized coolly. 'But they on airless planet, they have ships. Get away.'

'Yes, at least we can hope that Don and the others escaped,' Paul agreed with equal coolness, 'but I don't believe that you even knew they were there! I don't believe that when you emerged from hyperspace you had any idea that this planet was inhabited by intelligent beings. Or if you did, you didn't care.'

Tigerishka still seemed quite relaxed, but she was stroking Miaow in a faster rhythm, as a nervous woman might puff harder on her cigarette. 'You a little right there too, Paul,' she conceded. 'Things bad in hyperspace: storms, et cetera. Our need fuel acute. We feel beat when we come out, truly. Also last galactic survey show no intelligent life here, only promising feline strain.' And she twitched her nose at him as she interrupted the stroking to pat Miaow twice.

Ignoring this humorous sally, Paul continued: 'Here is another sidelight on your unfeeling and blundering haste: when you rescued Miaow from the earthquake waves – and myself too, mistakenly assuming I was a cat's beast of burden – you left a score of precious human beings, including my girl friend, to sink or swim.'

'That damn lie, Paul!' Tigerishka retorted. 'I quiet waves for them, they get out safe. I even lose momentum pistol.'

'Another super-feline blunder?' Paul shot back at her. 'Well, at least it was on the side of generosity, so we'll pass over it. But –'

Paul broke off, momentarily overcome by a sudden awareness of the ridiculousness of the situation. Here he was, naked and foot-fettered, trailing the tubes of a sanitary arrangement, playing district attorney to the most fantastic 'Madame X' ever to float on the witness chair.

The most fantastically lovely, too, he added uneasily in his thoughts.

Or was all this, he wondered, only the age-old racial business of the monkey teasing the leopard?

But then he remembered Brawley and Volcano.

'So you got girl friend now, hey, Paul?' Tigerishka put in wickedly. 'That really true? Margo know? And you so fair – that fair to Don?'

He waved these mean diversions aside with a certain dignity. Hot feeling came into his voice as he said: 'But the most crushing indictment of your boasted high culture and great sensitivity is the way human beings are dying beneath this saucer at this very moment because of the Wanderer's distortion of our gravity field – all because you needed fuel and wouldn't take a little extra time to find a proper source – such as the moons of Jupiter or Saturn. I'll grant you put out some fires, but only after hundreds, more likely thousands, died in the blazes and in the quakes that began the blazes. And now whole cities are being wiped out by the floods you've caused. If this goes on –'

'Shut up, monkey!' Tigerishka snarled, her claws out, her hind paws touching back towards the control panel. Miaow sprang away from her. 'Look, Paul,' she continued, seeming to contain herself with difficulty. 'I never boast you I humanitarian, monkey-tarian, cosmo-tarian! Cats have cruel culture some ways. Other cultures cruel, too! Death part of life. Some always suffer. Our refuelling just normal course of things. It just –'

She broke off, frowning at the finger Paul was pointing at her. His face was glowing, for he had just seen what he believed to be the tremendous significance of Tigerishka's apparently honest attempt to defend herself and her people.

225

'I do not believe you,' he said ringingly. 'Tigerishka, I think that your blundering haste and that of your people, your lack of proper scouting and preparation, and most of all your crude, belated efforts to repair some of the damage you've done, all go to show that *you were rushed into action by something of which you are deeply afraid.*'

With a high-pitched snarl Tigerishka launched herself at him, drove him against the wall with one forepaw around his throat and the other poised like a four-tined rake a foot above his face.

'That is a damnable lie, Paul Hagbolt!' she said in flawless English. 'I demand that you take it back at once!'

He got his breath. Then he shook his head.

'No,' he said, smiling at her, though there were bright tears dripping from his eyes. 'You're scared to death.'

Don Guillermo Walker slapped mosquitoes and stared at the flooded housetops of San Carlos red in the dawn as the launch beat its way back into Lake Nicaragua. During the night the current in the San Juan River had once more reversed itself, opposing the launch strongly, and now it was clear this was because the lake itself had risen a dozen feet or more – though why that happened was harder to say.

The sky presented a mystery, too. To the east it was clear, the sun already shooting his rays hotly, but to the west a thick white cloud-wall rose from the strip of land between the lake and the Pacific and extended as far north and south as one could see.

Although night before last he had witnessed the great outburst of volcanism, it did not occur to Don Guillermo that here, as along many other stretches, the Pacific Ocean was bordered now by a steam curtain, where seawater was flowing into volcanic cracks.

He asked why the launch was heading north, and the Araiza brothers informed him they were going up-lake to their home in Granada. Something sharp and clipped in their voices kept him from disputing this decision.

It did not deter him, however, from launching a little later into an account – not the first one he'd given them, either –

226

of how, over a hundred years ago, his great-great-grandfather had landed in Nicaragua with only fifty-eight bold Yankee followers, and soon had successfully stormed Granada itself.

Bagong Bung watched the sun that was rising for Don Guillermo sink into the Gulf of Tonkin, now swollen as big as it had been shrunken small twelve hours ago, so that it seemed to engulf North Vietnam. He thought of his strongbox in the cabin and how it now held a small bag of golden guineas and condors and morocotas and two larger bags of silver coins – the modest loot of the *Sumatra Queen*. He touched the yellow silk handkerchief bound so piratically around his head, and he looked roguishly around at Cobber-Hume and said:

'Yo-ho-ho, eh, *baik sobat?*'

'And a bottle of rum,' the big Australian affirmed. 'And a pipe of the poppy for you, since that's not against your religion.'

Bagong Bung grinned, but then his face grew grave and he said softly and intently: *'Pagi dan ayer surut!'*

Morning and the low tide! Truly, he could hardly bear to contemplate the waiting for them. He had long ago decided what wreck he would try for then: the near-legendary Spanish treasure ship Lobo de Oro. The Tiger of the Mud would try conclusions with the Wolf of Gold!

Barbara Katz's first reaction to the double-barrelled shotgun muzzle poked through the driver's window near Benjy's hunched shoulders was that here was just one more weary bit of the weird flotsam and scour they'd been driving and skidding over, past, through, and around for the first three hours of daylight. Sandy soil – lots of that; leaves and fronds and matted sedge; uprooted bushes and small trees; ruined cars and farm machinery; dead animals and – Don't stop! – people; wire – that could be devilish, especially the barbed stuff; they'd had to lay boards across one dragged and levelled fence to get the Rolls over without puncturing the tyres; sodden flowers plastered here and there, including a remarkable number of scarlet poinsettias; houses and barns, both fragmentary and almost intact – they'd had to find a looping sideroad to get around one monstrous cluster of those. Everything steaming in the heat, as if a swiftly dissipating fog were coming out of the ground. Of course there had been live people, too, though not so very many of those, and they either acting stunned and helpless or else going very much about their business, such as shoring up houses on high ground, hoisting planks into big trees, or going places in cars or on horses. Once a small airplane had passed overhead, its motor sounding loud and self-important.

Barbara's second reaction to the shotgun muzzle was that here was the nasty emergency she'd been expecting all along, and thank God she had the short-barrelled .38 revolver in her right hand under her thigh next to old KKK, and if she had to, she hoped she could whip it up and start shooting through the window – though if that just got Benjy and Hester blown to bits in the front seat it wasn't going to do any good, even though the motor of the Rolls was idling softly. If they had a few seconds' start –

Her third reaction to the shotgun muzzle was to see the fresh rust on it and wonder if its cartridges were wet, in which case she might hold the balance of power and needn't actually fire, only threaten – but that was guessing.

The voice from behind the shotgun had a buzz in it that was lazy yet menacing, rather like the horsefly going back and forth against the inside of the sedan's rear window.

'This is an inspection point. We're collecting toll. What were you doing –'

'We were only changing a tyre,' Barbara answered sharply.

'– back in Trilby?' the buzzing voice finished.

So that, she thought, was the name of the miserable smashed village through whose crookedly choked main street they'd zigzagged twenty minutes ago. They should have called it Svengali!

Aloud she said hurriedly, 'We were just coming through from Palm Beach. We can pay the toll,' but as she fumbled with her left hand at the black bag on her lap, two thick-corded sun-reddened arms came through the window and took the bag and one horny hand shifted to her chin and tilted her face up, and for a second she glared into a thin, unshaven, fish-eyed face and fought down the impulse to put a bullet in it or bite the

228

hand, and then the arms went away with the bag, and the voice behind them said: 'Hey, the old geezer must be one of them Palm Beach millionaires. Lots of paper money here.'

Barbara said, 'He's very sick. He's in a coma. We're trying to get him to –'

'One of them Yankee millionaires,' the buzzing voice cut her off, 'who come down here and lord it and pay nigras white man's wages and then run like chickens when the Lord tests us. We'll take the money for the Jubilee Fund and we'll take the two nigra gals – they'll make the hill a little more comfortable. Get out, you two, quick! – or I'll blow a hole in your high-yellow chauffeur.'

And he rested the muzzle of his gun against Benjy's side.

This is it, Barbara thought, but as she started to bring up the revolver she felt old KKK's clawlike fingers grip her hand on the gun with startling strength, holding it down. He cleared his throat hawkingly and next he was speaking in a voice louder than she'd ever heard from him, a voice that rasped imperiously.

'Did I hear some goddam turkey-necked cracker questioning the colour of my son Benjy? I thought by your words you were Southrons out there, not mud-eating gophers!'

There was a murmuring outside, angry but uncertain. The gun pulled away from Benjy. Then old KKK, his features creasing like an old vulture's as he stared at the men in overalls, intoned portentously, 'When will the Black Night end?'

Slowly, almost as though it were drawn out of him against his will, the one with the buzzing voice replied, 'With the dawn of the White Jubilee.'

'Hallelujah!' old KKK responded. 'Convey to the Grand Chanticleer of Dade City the greetings of the Grand Chanticleer of Dade County. Benjamin, it would pleasure me if you drove on!'

They were moving forward – a foot – five – fifteen – then they were going faster, and Hester was saying, 'Don't hit that stump, Benjy!' and the Rolls veered abruptly and veered again, and then they were going faster still, and Benjy was laughing his whooping laugh, only this time it was pretty hysterical, and finally he was wheezing, 'Old KKK sho live up to his name!' He glanced back. ''Scuse me . . . Dad!'

Hester said, 'He cain't hear you, Benjy. He pass out again. It take all his stren'th.'

Helen stared back wide-eyed. 'I never suspect he Kluxer.'

Hester said: 'You must be grateful, girl.'

Chapter 30

Doc took charge of the business of striking the rock-slope camp, as greenish dawn shifted through chartreuse to lemon yellow. He operated with a high-handed mysteriousness that would have been even more irritating if it hadn't been for his sardonically-tinged high spirits. In particular, he refused to discuss the question of their next objective or the problem of the boulder-block until they were organized for departure.

He scaled down by one-third the breakfast ration Ida and McHeath presented for approval, prescribed penicillin for the flushed and fretful Ray Hanks on the latter's recollection that he wasn't allergic to it, and answered with a curt headshake Hixon's suggestion that they make this a permanent camp and send out foraging parties.

The two sedans were searched. In the glove compartment of the first there was turned up a loaded .32 revolver and on its back seat a black hat. Doc appropriated both objects for himself, clapping the hat on his bald dome with a grinningly callous, 'It fits.'

Wojtowicz, resting his left hand on his belt to ease his bandaged shoulder, protested: 'Don't wear that, Doc, it'd be bad luck,' while the Ramrod said sombrely: 'I wouldn't want my head contaminated by particles from a sadistic murderer's aura.'

'And I don't want mine worse sunburned than it is,' Doc laughed back at him. 'Murderer's dandruff I can stand.'

The first sedan coughed and purred at once when Doc turned the ignition key and touched the gas to test it, but the second's battery seemed to be dead. Doc refused to let Wojtowicz study around under the hood, but as soon as it had been drained of gas and oil, he let off the emergency, cut its wheel sharp, and ordered the others to help him push it off the road down the rock slope.

It went over the edge with a fine scrape and bound, and five seconds later its crash drifted up, shortly followed by three buzzards.

Doc snapped his fingers and muttered: 'Certainly didn't mean to disturb their breakfast, if it's what I think it was.'

Mrs Hixon heard him and made a sick face.

Next Doc tested the red Corvette, cutting it back and forth dashingly, tyres on the road's edge. 'Sweet job,' he commented as he stepped out. 'This is for me.'

As breakfast was finishing he quietly gathered Hunter, Rama Joan, Margo, and Clarence Dodd and drew them off with him back of the truck.

'Well, what is it?' he demanded of them. 'Do we keep on for the Valley or cut back to Mulholland and try for Cornell or Malibu Heights? Got to keep this outfit moving or it'll lose heart.'

'If we decide on the Valley, how do we get around the boulder?' the Little Man asked.

'Table that one, Doddsy,' Doc told him. 'First things first.'

Hunter said, 'A few of us could take the sedan and scout the Valley.'

Doc shook his head decisively. 'Nope, we can't afford to split up this outfit. It's too small.'

'I know some artists in Malibu,' Rama Joan began tentatively.

'And I know some on Cape Cod,' Doc shot at her with a grin and a wink. 'They're probably swimming for Plymouth Rock.'

'But I was going to say,' Rama Joan went on with an answering grimace, 'I vote for the Valley.'

'Anyone know the Valley's elevation?' the Little Man asked. 'It could be flooding from around the mountains.'

'We'll find out,' Doc answered with a shrug.

'It's got to be the Valley,' Margo put in. 'Vandenberg Three's at the foot of the Mountainway. And I think you all know that I want to give the inertia gun to Morton Opperly.'

Doc looked at their faces. 'The Valley it is, then,' he pronounced. 'I do think, though,' he remarked to Margo, 'that momentum pistol might be a better name for it.'

'But the boulder –' the Little Man began.

Doc showed him a palm. 'Come on,' he said to them all and headed past the truck and bus for the boulder.

As they went by, Bill Hixon asked with a jokingness that was three-quarters antagonism: 'Well, doctor, has your executive committee decided on our further tasks for today?'

'We're keeping on for the Valley,' Doc said sharply, 'where we will resupply ourselves and contact responsible Moon Project scientists. Any objections?'

Without waiting for any even slightly delayed answers, he took a stand on the slope just above the boulder and motioned Margo to come up.

'I saw the boulder rock,' he explained, 'when you slammed that gunman against it. Give it three seconds of down-trigger from here and I bet she rolls. Spread out of the way, everybody!'

Margo took the momentum pistol from her jacket, then suddenly turned and gave it to Hunter.

'You do it,' she told him, delighted to realize that she no longer needed the big gun to give her a feeling of security and excitement – that, in very fact, she herself was now the big gun she could rely on and experiment with. She also noted with satisfaction the sour hungry look in Hunter's dark-circled eyes.

He crouched and firmed the gun in both hands. He'd been told it had absolutely no recoil, but his body refused to believe that. All his muscles tightened. From the corner of his eyes he saw Doc wave. He pressed the button.

Whatever field or force the pistol generated, its effect was cumulative, as if the boulder had to soak it up. At first the great rounded rock didn't move at all – long enough for Hixon to say: 'Look, it isn't –'

Then the side nearest Hunter began to lift, slowly at first, then faster. McHeath cried: 'It's moving!'

It overbalanced. Hunter snatched his finger off the button. The boulder came down on the rock slope with a tremendous clank, then crashed over and over, seeming at first to move just a little faster than a rolling boulder should.

The whole rock slope shook. Some of the people clutched at those nearest them.

A final crash carried the monster over the edge, from which it took a wide shallow bite of stone.

The Little Man said loudly, pulling out his notebook: 'That is the most amazing demonstration of impossible physics that I have ever –'

A great sullen thud drowned his voice. The rock slope vibrated again as the boulder hit below.

Hunter looked at the scale on the pistol and said, 'Still a good third of the charge left.'

Doc studied the spot where the boulder had rested. There was a smooth two-foot dip in the asphaltoid, deepest on the downslope side where the black stuff was squeezed out in a lip that smoothly joined the rock. Abruptly Doc nodded approvingly.

'I'm not so sure,' Hunter said, coming down the slope. 'A skid sideways –'

But Doc was already striding back towards the red Corvette.

Two of the three buzzards – presumably they were the same – came winging up from the depths, heading away from the road. But there they ran into a big, two-rotor military 'copter which had come droning from the direction of the Valley during the excitement. The birds veered off from it and headed back.

Hixon was for signalling the 'copter with his gun, but Doc said: 'No, we'll take care of ourselves. Anyhow, they can see us, and if that boulder didn't fetch 'em, nothing would.'

The 'copter sped off seaward.

Doc climbed in the red Corvette, yelled: 'Clear the road!' and drove it across the dip with only a small sideways lurch, just as the two buzzards winged rapidly across the road, hardly fifty feet up, and disappeared over the ridge.

Doc stopped the Corvette just beyond the sedan. 'Clear everyone out of the bus and bring her across!' he shouted back. Then to Hunter, Margo, and Rama Joan, who'd come after him: 'I'll lead off in the Corvette. Then the order'll be: sedan, bus, truck. You come with me, Joan, but Ann had better ride in the bus. You drive the sedan, Ross. Better get her turned around now. Margo, you keep the momentum pistol and ride with him. You're our heavy artillery, if we get into trouble, but wait

233

for orders from me. Doddsy, we ought to have a rear-guard rifle in the back of the truck, but your hand's still bad.'

'Harry McHeath knows how to use the gun,' the Little Man said, 'and he's responsible.'

Doc nodded. 'Go tell him he's promoted,' he said. 'Hixon can keep the other rifle.'

The driver, Pop, came up to demur at taking the bus across the dip. 'Back tyres are old,' he explained. 'Worn slick. She'll be apt to take a sideways slip when she drops into that hole. . . .'

Doc was already striding back. He climbed aboard the bus and brought her across without a great deal more sideways lurch than the Corvette.

Hixon brought the truck over. Ray Hanks was carried across then in his cot and, at his feverish insistence, loaded once more into the back of the truck, rather than the bus. He was joined there by Ida and young McHeath, stern-faced with his rifle.

As the bus loaded up, Doc said to Clarence Dodd: 'You command her – and ride herd on Pop.'

Walking ahead to the Corvette, he found Ann sitting in the middle of the front seat beside her mother. He planted his fists on his hips, then grinned and shrugged and climbed behind the wheel. 'Hi, sweetheart,' he said, tousling her hair. She shrank away from him towards her mother, just a little.

Doc started the motor, then stood up and faced back.

'Listen to this!' he shouted towards sedan, bus, and truck. 'Follow at twenty-yard intervals! I'll be taking it easy. *Three* horn blasts from me means *slow! Four* means *stop! Five* – from one of you – means you're in *trouble*. Got that?

'O.K.! We roll!'

The people of Earth responded to the Wanderer catastrophes as necessity constrained them, or did not constrain them.

A skeletal new New York of refugees and tents and emergency hospitals and airlift terminals grew in Putnam and Dutchess Counties and across the river in the southern reaches of the Catskills.

In Chicago a few people walked down to Lake Michigan to marvel mildly at the four-foot tide, and to tell each other they'd never known there'd always been a three-inch one. They briefly lifted their eyes to watch a string of light planes flying east from Meigs Field to join in some airlift. Behind them traffic roared along the Outer Drive unheedingly, about as heavy as any other day.

In Siberia tidal waters invading an atomic bomb plant contributed to a great fizzle-explosion which scattered deadly fallout on trudging refugees.

From foundering Pacific atolls long canoes took off on enforced voyages of discovery, echoing those of their paddlers' adventurous forefathers.

Wolf Loner sailed confidently on towards Boston by dead reckoning. He wondered placidly why twice last night the moonlight had glowed very brightly through the clouds with a faint violet tinge.

The *Prince Charles* hugged the Brazilian coast as it atomsteamed south. The four insurgent captains commanding it ignored the warnings of Captain Sithwise to swing wide around the mouth of the Amazon.

Paul Hagbolt surveyed northern Europe from five hundred miles up. It was sunlit and clear, except that a wide white cloudbank was creeping across the Atlantic towards Ireland.

Immediately below him was the North Sea, about as big as the page of an atlas when you study it, and dull grey except where the sun made an irritating highlight in the Dover Strait corner.

The British Isles, the southern half of Scandinavia, and North Germany and the Lowlands made three more atlas pages placed to the left, the right, and below.

Scotland and Norway looked about as they should, but the pendant of southern Sweden was laced by the encroaching grey of the Baltic.

Below a skeletal Denmark, a wide scimitar of water, the cutting edge of the blade faced south, lay across the Netherlands and northern Germany. Paul thought, *Oh well, this isn't the first time Holland's been flooded.*

England now: it was grey-laced, too, and something had taken a big bite out of the east coast. The Thames? The . . .

Humber? Paul felt guiltily that his mind ought to be able to pop out the correct answer at once, but geography had never been his strong point. *Why didn't Tigerishka look into his unconscious mind and tell him?* he asked himself pettishly, glancing to where she was serenely grooming herself with a silver comb and her dagger tongue.

Paul's accusations and her fierce reactions to them had ended in pure anticlimax. She had lowered her threatening claws, turned her back on him, and spent the next hour at the control panel, sometimes manipulating the silver excrescences but mostly sitting still. Then she had begun a new series of manoeuvres and observations.

Midway she had broken off to release him, without comment, from his last ankle fetter and the sanitary connexions. Then she had explained to him tersely and impersonally, but in monkey-English again, the basic rules for manipulating one's body in null gravity and for using the waste and food panels. Finally she had gone back to her business, leaving Paul with the feeling of being an interloper in a very fancy office. He had hurriedly eaten a meal of tiny protein cookies, swallowing them down in plain water, almost like so many pills. They still sat heavy in his stomach.

The observations had been frantically exciting at first, then had swiftly grown wearisome.

He tried to think of Margo around the world in Southern California and of Don the other side of the earth on the crushed moon – or escaped from it in a moon ship – but his imagination was tired out.

He pulled his attention back to the observations with an effort – away from the troublingly delightful sight of Tigerishka titivating herself and back to the live atlas outspread below the saucer's transparent floor with its scattered invisible handholds through two of which he now had a toe and finger hooked.

Let's see, that bite in England might be something they called the Wash, which was connected with something they called the Fenlands. . . . He sighed.

'You feeling bad 'bout your planet, Paul?' Tigerishka called over to him. 'Peoples suffering and all?'

He shrugged and shook his head. 'It's too big,' he said. 'I've lost my feelings.'

'Like see things closer?' she asked, pushing off and drifting slowly towards him.

'What would be the use?' he asked.

'Then you feeling bad 'bout something smaller, Paul, something nearer you,' she told him. 'Girl? You worry 'bout her?'

He grimaced. 'I don't know. Margo's not my girl, really.'

'Then you feeling bad 'bout nearest thing of all: you-self,' Tigerishka informed him, checking her drift beside him. She laid a velvet paw on his bare shoulder. 'Poor Paul,' she purred. 'All mixed up. Poor, poor Paul.'

He angrily twisted his shoulder away from the thrilling touch, flipping air towards her with a short sweep of his hands to keep a few inches back. 'Don't treat me like a pet that's out of sorts,' he demanded angrily. 'Don't treat me like a sick monkey. Treat me like a man!'

She grinned at him, her whiskers laying back across her violet cheeks, the black pupils of her eyes shrinking to pinpoints, and she pointed a violet-grey foreclaw at his heart and said: 'Bang!'

After a moment he chuckled miserably and admitted, 'All right, Tigerishka, I guess I have to be some sort of lower animal to you, but in that case look into my mind and tell me what's wrong with me. Why *am* I so mixed up?'

The pupils of her eyes expanded to stars – black spidery stars in a violet sky.

'Why, Paul,' she said gravely, 'ever since you forced me to treat you as an intelligent being – primitive but intelligent, bearing a little living universe inside – it has no longer been a simple thing for me to go deep into your mind. It's more a matter of having to ask your permission now. But I have gathered some notions about you, and if you want I will tell them to you.'

He nodded. 'Go on.'

'Paul,' she said, 'you resent being treated like a pet, yet that is how you treat the people around you. You stand back and watch their antics with tolerant understanding and you nurse and guard and cajole the ones you love: Margo, Don, your

237

mother, several others. You call this friendship, but it's nurse-maiding and devouring. A decent cat wouldn't do it to her own kittens.

'You stand back and watch yourself more than is healthy. You live too much in the self watching you and in the third self watching the second, and so on. Look!' She switched the windows to mirror. Her foreclaw placed itself between his right eye and his own stacked reflections and somehow ticked off the edges of the first six of them exactly.

'See?' she said. 'Each watching the one in front. I know – all intelligent animals are self-observing. But you live too much in the reflections, Paul. Best to live mostly in front of the mirror and just a little in the watchers. That way courage comes. Don't live in Watcher Number Six!

'Also, you think other people same as your watchers. You cringe from them, then criticize. But they not. They got watchers too, watching just them.

'Also, love yourself more, or you can't like anybody.

' 'Nother thing 'bout you,' she finished, drooping wholly back into monkey-talk, 'fight-reflexes pretty poor. Likewise dance. Likewise sex. Not 'nough practice. That's all.'

'I know you're right,' Paul said haltingly in a small, tight voice. 'I try to change, but –'

' 'Nough thinking 'bout self! Look! See one our big saucers save one your towns.'

Ceiling and floor were transparent again. They were descending at a rapid slant towards a dark branchwork merged with a pale checkerboard mesh, from the centre of which brown rings were expanding outward towards a circular brown rim that merged into bluish grey. High above the centre of the circles hung a golden and violet saucer which he judged had to be huge from the cloud-arm between them.

The mesh grew larger – it was streets. And the squares were blocks of buildings.

The brown rings were humpings of silt-laden water being driven out of the city.

He recognized, from remembered pictures, the great buildings of Elektrosila and the Institute of Energetics, the blue-green of the Kirov Theatre, the Square of the Decembrists. The branchwork must be the streams of the Neva delta, and the city itself, Leningrad.

'See? We save your beloved cities,' Tigerishka said complacently. 'Momentum engine of big saucer move only water. Very smart machine.'

Suddenly the saucer dipped so close he saw the cobblestones, a mud-buried gutter, and the sprawled, silt-drifted, water-greyed bodies of a woman and a little girl. Then a low brown wave surged over them, a grey arm and a grey, bearded face lifelessly flinging out of the dirty foam.

'Save?' Paul demanded incredulously. 'Yes, after killing your millions – and if the rescue isn't worse than the disaster! Tigerishka, how could you bring yourself to wreck our world just to get fuel a little faster? What frightened you into it?'

She hissed: 'Stay off that subject, Paul!'

Richard Hillary limped along swiftly – a dimensionless point in the atlas-page England Paul had been viewing, but a living, breathing, frightened man for all that. He was sweating profusely; the sun beat in his face. He was panting and at every other step he winced.

The pedestrian equivalent of a fast car on a big highway, Richard had outdistanced the pack behind but yet had not caught up with the pack ahead, if there was one. The last sign-post he had seen had pointed, quite appropriately, he was certain, to 'Lower Slaughter'.

Squinting ahead, he could see that after some hundred yards the road began leisurely to wind up a high, forest-capped hill.

But, looking behind, his sun-dazzled eyes could see only a crazy scattering of sheets and serpents of water.

The fattest serpent was the road he was travelling, and now it suddenly began to fill where he was, brimming over from the ditch to the left. Hardly an inch, yet it unnerved him.

To the right was a forbiddingly fenced field of young barley, a bit higher than the road and mounting directly towards the hilltop. He climbed the fence, unmindful of the tearing of the barbed wire, and set on again through the swishing green. With a startling sudden beat of wings, a crow emerged just ahead and took off, cawing with hoarse disapproval. Although Richard's legs were cramping now, he increased his pace.

He heard a rumble of low, distant thunder. Only this was the sort of thunder that doesn't die away muttering, but gets louder, louder, louder. Richard didn't think he could do it, but he began to run, run at his top speed uphill. There was a rush of rabbits from behind him. At one point he could see a dozen white bounding forms.

From the sides of his eyes he began to glimpse brown-frothy, whirling, pursuing walls. The thunder became that of a dozen express trains. At one moment there was yellow foam around his feet, at another it looked as though a swinging, dust-raising surge would cut him off.

Yet he did make it to the hilltop, and the waters didn't get quite that far, and the thundering began slowly to fade.

As he swayed there panting, his lower chest feeling as if it had been kicked, there stepped out of the trees just ahead a straight-backed, small, elderly man with a shotgun.

'Stand, sir!' this apparition cried, directing the weapon at Richard. 'Or I'll fire.'

The apparition was dressed in brown gaiters, grey knicker-bockers, and a lilac pullover. His narrow, wrinkled, watery-eyed face was set in lines of grimmest disapproval.

Richard stood, if only because he was so utterly and pain-fully winded. The thundering died away completely as the turbid water levelled a little way down the hill.

'Speak up!' the apparition cried. 'What lets you think you have the right to trample my barley? *And how did you let in all that water?*'

Finally getting some of his breath, Richard shaped his lips in a grave smile and said: 'It wasn't deliberate on my part, believe me.'

Sally Harris, the midmorning sun glowing from the solid gold threads in her bikini, peered down over the balustrade and called back a running commentary.

Jake Lesher sat by a cup of black coffee flaming almost invisibly with Irish whisky and puffed a long greenish cigar.

Occasionally he frowned. A notebook stood open at two blank pages beside the coffee cup.

Sally called, 'The water's ten storeys higher than last time. The roofs are packed with people and there's two or three at every window I can see. Some are standing on the ledges. We're lucky our skyscraper had a fire and the elevator's stuck. Somebody's shaking his fist – why me, what have I done to you? Somebody else just took a high dive – ouch, bellywhopper! The current's fierce – it's pushing a police launch backwards. You there, quit pointin' your cane at me! There's mothers and kids and –'

There was a zing and a crack and the tubular chrome rang along its length. Sally flipped her hands off it as if she'd been stung and turned around.

'Somebody just shot at me!' she announced indignantly.

'Move back, baby,' Jake instructed her. 'People are always jealous of the guy at the top. Or the gal.'

Chapter 31

The saucer students heard four rapid horn-beeps which came winging back through air heavy with the sour, acrid fumes of burnt-over land – and reeking more than ever since a hot, damp wind had set in from the southeast. Overhead the sun was hot but there was a big black cloudbank to the south.

Hunter brought the sedan to a stop behind the Corvette, which had just topped a rise, the road passing between two natural rock gateposts some fifteen feet high.

Doc was standing in the seat, studying the terrain ahead. He looked just a little like a pirate, with the brim of his black hat pulled down in back but turned up sharply in front. He reached out his right hand, and Rama Joan put the field glasses into it. He resumed his scanning, using the seven-power instrument. Rama Joan and Ann stood up, too.

Hunter stopped the sedan's motor, set the brake, and as the school bus drew up behind them third in line, he and Margo got out and hurried forward until they could see too.

In front of them a slope stretched downward for a quarter of a mile in gentle undulations to a broad-ditched flat, then rose again, though not so high.

The slope was black to the left, dusty greenish-brown to the right. Monica Mountainway went down it in swinging curves, crossing and recrossing the demarcation line between the burned and the unburned.

Towards the bottom, almost on the demarcation line, it passed three white buildings surrounded by a wide gravelled space and a high, wire-mesh fence. Then the road joined the broad-ditched flat which led off in either direction, almost level but gently curving, until the hills hid it each way.

Down the centre of the flat, following its contours, stretched what looked for a long moment exactly like a miles-long, flattish, scaly serpent thirty yards wide. The individual scales, which ran in glitter-bordered rows eight or nine across, were mostly blue, brown, cream and black, though here and there was a green or red one. Judging by its glittering sides, the serpent had a silver belly.

Wojtowicz, coming up behind them, said, 'Cripes, we're there. That's it. Wow!'

The scaly serpent was inland Route 101, jammed with cars bumper to bumper. The glitter-border was the freeway's wire-mesh fence.

Doc said hoarsely, 'I want to talk to Doddsy and McHeath.'

Rama Joan said, 'Ann, you can get them.' The little girl climbed past her mother and hopped out.

As soon as Hunter's and Margo's eyes stopped swinging and started to linger, details began to destroy the serpent illusion. At many spots cars had been driven wide on the shoulder, up against the fence. Some of these had their hoods up and dabs of white at their sides – Hunter realized these last must be towels, shirts, scarves, and large handkerchiefs: pitifully obedient 'askings for assistance' set up before the jam got impossible.

At several points the serpent scales were twisted and whorled: accidents never cleaned up and attempts of whole groups of cars to turn and go back the way they'd come, either by crossing the median strip or by using the shoulder.

At three places the wire-mesh fence bulged acutely outwards, each bulge filled with cars nose-on: these must have been trying to ram their way out. One of these attempts had been limitedly successful: the fence was down, but the way out beyond it blocked by a mess of cars ditch-overturned and crushed together, two half-climbed on to the others' backs.

Here and there a few cars still moved in senseless-seeming, backward and forward jerks of a few feet each way. Stale exhaust-stench mixed with the burnt reek coming on the moist southeast wind.

Hunter thought of what it must have looked like at night in the last stages of general movement: five thousand cars in sight from here, ten thousand headlights swinging and blinking, ten thousand bumpers to clash and snag and rip, a few police speeding up and down trying to keep open lanes that relent-lessly shortened and narrowed, five thousand motors, belching exhaust pipes, horns. . . . And about a hundred thousand more cars between here and L.A.

He heard the Ramrod saying, 'It is the valley of dry bones. Lord of the Saucers, succour them.' From the car beside him Rama Joan said softly: 'Even an evildoer sees happiness so long as his evil deed does not ripen; but when his evil deed ripens . . .'

The biggest and worst car-crush of all was where Monica Mountainway entered 101 just beyond the three white build-ings: a hundred or so cars slewed every which way, several overset, others ditch-jammed sideways, and the nearest three dozen burnt black – it occurred to Hunter that he was very possibly looking at the source of the brush fire.

Only after he and Margo had studied the cars for quite a while (or for an interminable, incredulous, eye-darting moment) did they begin to see the people. It was as if some universal law forced vision to descend by size-stages.

People! – three or four to each car, at least. Many of them still sitting in them, by God. Others standing or walking be-tween them, a few standing or sitting on fabric-or-cushion-spread car roofs. Off to the left, beyond the burnt swathe, many people had climbed the fence and set up blanket-and-beach-towel-shaded bivouacs, yet few if any of them seemed to have

243

gone far from the freeway that penned their vehicles; perhaps they figured the jam would be cleaned up somehow in a few hours or a day. And there wasn't much walking around – they were sticking to the shade.

It was a stale old joke, Hunter recalled, that Angelenos, using cars even to visit the people across the street, had forgotten how to walk – one of those jokes that are little more than the unretouched truth.

Just to the left of the Monica Mountainway outlet and car-crush, a clutch of black and white police cars was drawn up on a cleared stretch of shoulder, in a semicircle reminiscent of a wagon-train camp. This 'laager' guarded a car-wide break in the fence, looking as if it had been done with heavy wire-clippers. A half-dozen police were inside it, and right now one of them took off on a motor-cycle through the break, immediately turning and gunning along north on the flat outside the fence. A few people came out of their bivouacs and seemed to hail him, but he kept on, and they stood there as his dust-wake broadened and billowed around them.

To the right, where the big black cloudbank was growing rapidly higher, there were fewer bivouacs but more people in the open – slim people moving around fast, mostly, waving and leaping, gathering in clumps, dispersing, regathering. And it seemed to be from this direction that there was coming, quite tinny and faint, the squawk and squeal and drumbeat of jazz.

Between the two groups of people behaving so differently, there was a hundred-yard stretch, including the Mountain-way outlet, that had no people at all in it, even sitting in the cars – except for ten or so stretched here and there on the ground. Hunter wondered for a moment why they chose to rest in the baking sun, before it occurred to him they were dead.

He was fringe-aware of his comrades from the school bus and the truck gathered around the Corvette, too. Now he heard more footsteps coming and the Little Man saying, 'Look at the cloudbank. I don't know that I've ever heard of a wet south-east wind like this in Southern Cal,' and McHeath replying, 'Maybe the ocean's broke through and filled the Salton Sea and other low spots, Mr Dodd. And with – gee! – maybe a hundred miles of tidewater, there'd be lots of evaporation.' Hunter continued to scan the overpowering scene ahead.

Three of the slim, active ones came into the no-man's land along the shoulder, moving in a cavorting, dancing run. One of them, by his gestures, might be carrying and swigging from a bottle. They'd come sixty yards when there was a crackle of gunfire from the police-car camp. One of the three fell – hard to tell at this distance whether he lay quiet or writhed. The other vaulted over the nearest line of stalled cars and hid.

Hunter put his arm around Margo tight. 'My God, Doc, what goes on?' he demanded.

'Yeah, for crissakes, Doc, tell us what you can see through the glasses,' Wojtowicz put in. 'It looks like war.'

'It is,' Doc reported crisply. 'Now listen to what I say, everybody that wants to,' he went on loudly, continuing to scan through the glasses, 'because I'm not going to tell it twice and there'll be no time for anybody else to sight-see with these. It's a war, or a big skirmish, anyhow, between a lot of young people and the older people – or I should say the police helped by a few older people, but most of the rest of those neutral or at any rate useless. Big kids versus police protecting families. It's the Day of the Children.

'Those slim ones are teenagers, mostly. They're drinking – I can see a liquor truck bust open and kids handing out bottles. They got a live jazz band going in a cleared space. There are fights – knife and fist. A gang with sledges is smashing car windows and beating in car bodies for no sane reason.'

Doc censored from his account the acts of stark lovemaking he noted inside the cars – for shade rather than privacy, it seemed – the two girls dancing naked near the jazz band, the wanton beatings-up and terrorizings, and – in the other direction – the group draining a car radiator and eagerly drinking the . . . well, he hoped there weren't too many additives in the water.

'But not all their violence is against cars or each other,' he went on. 'There's a bunch of them sneaking up right now between the empty cars towards the police camp. A few of them have guns, the rest bottles.

'I think the police have set up a little ambush on their side.

At any rate I can see two or three of them crouched behind cars in the middle of the jam.

'But before the battle starts, we're going to be out of here, heading back for Mulholland,' he went on in a louder voice, handing the glasses to Rama Joan and turning to face his crowd. 'Doddsy! McHeath! Have Pop and Hixon turn their cars – there's room to do it – and . . .'

'You mean you're asking us to turn tail and run?' Hixon himself demanded loudly from where he was standing, rifle in hand, just beyond the Ramrod. 'When there's decent folks down there about to be swamped? When we could turn the tables easy with that gravity gun? Look, I been a cop myself. We got to help them.'

'No!' Doc rasped back at him. 'We've got to protect ourselves and get the momentum pistol to some responsible science group – and while it's still got power in it. How much charge is there left in the thing, Margo?'

'About one-third,' she told him, checking the violet line.

'See?' Doc continued to Hixon, 'the thing has only four or five big shots left in it, at most. There are miles of those maniacs down there on 101. If we mix in, we'll only turn a little battle into a big one. What's down there is dreadful, I'll admit, but it's something that's going on all over the world right now and we can't afford to lose ourselves in it – one bucket of water tossed on a burning city! No, we back-track! Go back and turn your truck around, Hixon –'

'Wait a minute, Doc!' This time it was Margo who interrupted, in a ringing voice. She moved in front of the Corvette.

'That's Vandenberg Three down there,' she said, pointing with the momentum pistol at the three white buildings. 'Morton Opperly may still be there. We've got to check.'

'Not one chance in fifty!' Doc barked at her. 'Not in five hundred. He'll have been 'copted out – maybe by the one we saw this morning. No!'

'I've seen people moving inside,' Margo lied. 'You agreed the idea is to get him this pistol. We've got to check.'

Doc shook his head. 'No! Too crazy a chance to take for next to nothing.'

Margo grinned at him. 'But I've got the pistol,' she said,

holding it against her chest, 'and I'm going to take it down there if I have to walk.'

'That's telling him!' Hixon cheered excitedly.

'All right, Miss Strongheart, then listen to me,' Doc said, bending forward towards her. 'You go down there with that pistol, walking or in a car, and some crazy sniper picks you off, or you get jumped from three sides at once, and Opperly doesn't get the weapon – these maniacs do. It's got to stay here.

'But I'll make you a proposition, Miss Gelhorn. You go down there without the weapon – I'll give you my revolver – and bring Opperly back, or just find he's there, and we'll make the deal with him. How about it?'

Margo looked at Hunter. 'You drive me?' He nodded and jumped for the sedan. She came around the side of the Corvette and held the momentum pistol towards Doc. 'Trade.' He gave her his revolver and took it. Hunter started the sedan and drove it alongside the red car.

Hixon came forward. 'Hey, I'm going too.'

'You want him?' Doc asked. Margo nodded. He asked Hixon: 'You promise just to help them find Opperly?'

Hixon nodded, muttering, 'Whoever *he* is.'

Doc said: 'Okay then, but you're the last one we can spare. No more volunteers!' He barked the last almost into the face of McHeath, coming up eagerly. 'Gimme your rifle,' he told the boy. 'You climb up those rocks back there' – he pointed to the easier gatepost – 'and watch for us being outflanked . . . by anybody, including police!'

Hixon piled into the back of the sedan, Margo got in beside Hunter, Doc vaulted down and leaned an elbow on her window. 'Hold on a second,' he said, scanning the jammed highway again just as action broke out there.

A dozen figures popped up from behind and between cars near the police camp. They threw things. Guns cracked and two or three of them fell. Things hit the police cars. Flames exploded.

'Molotov cocktails,' Hixon whispered, gnawing his lip.

Doc said: 'Now's a good time – they all got other things to think of.' He shoved his head in the window.

'I just got one thing to say to you,' he growled at the three of them. 'Bring yourselves back, you bastards!'

Barbara Katz sat in the topmost spread of the big, pale rung-like, right-angling branches of a gigantic dead magnolia tree, the westering sun hot on her back, and watched east under the blue sky for the Atlantic to come mounding back from Daytona Beach and Lake George over the neck of Florida. From time to time she tried to study the figures on the darkly-creased, sweat-stained tidal chart on the back of the calendar page Benjy had torn off for her yesterday morning, although she knew it could hardly apply closely any more, if at all. But there had been a high tide last night at three a.m. and so there should be another around the middle of this afternoon.

In the next spread of the branches down old KKK was tied to his seat with blanket strips around the big trunk, which shielded him some from the sun. Hester sat beside him, supporting his slumping head and easing his position as best she could. Near by Helen and Benjy had their spots. Benjy had the rope he'd used to draw up the old man and some other things.

In their soiled and torn pale grey uniforms the three Negroes looked like bedraggled and ungainly brown-crested silver birds as they perched there high in the huge, nearly leafless tree.

The tree rose from a slight mound half covered by the exposed section of its own thick grey roots, on which the mud-spattered Rolls was now parked.

South of the mound stretched a tiny graveyard, its wooden headboards sand-drifted and some pushed down and all sedge-draped by the scour of the last high tide. At the foot of the graveyard was a small wooden church that had once been painted white. It was shifted a dozen feet off its foundation bricks and strained and twisted at the corners, though not broken apart. The brown mark of the tide went up about eight feet on it, almost to the flaking but newer-painted black letters over the door, which read CHURCH OF JESUS SAVER.

Barbara squeezed her eyes shut several times rapidly. It looked to her as if several patches of the blue sky had come down on to the flat, brown-green land to the east, a little like the watery reflections one sees far ahead on a level concrete road on a burning hot day. The blue patches grew and merged. No longer conscious of blinking, Barbara watched with an intensity approaching that of trance. Second linked to second and minute to minute seamlessly, as if the hooves of time had halted, or as if something in her stood still so that she could no longer hear their pounding.

Nor – so attentive was she to the strange phenomenon of the sky overflooding the land – did she much hear the physical roar coming louder and louder from the east, or the awed, excited calling back and forth of the three great grey featherless fowl beneath her, or even much feel the tree shake and strain as the waters came surging around it, or hear Helen's scream.

But it did seem to her that the whole earth was tipping and sliding up into the sky as that blue came reaching dizzyingly underneath, and she leaned farther and farther backwards and would have fallen, except that now a body came pressing up against her side and a strong arm came around her back, bracing her.

'You hold on, Miss Barbara,' Benjy was shouting in her ear. 'You watch so hard you fall.'

She looked around the watery plain. Florida was gone. The Church of Jesus Saver was floating off upside down with its eight short legs crookedly in the air.

She looked down again. The magnolia, its height halved, was a lonely midsea refuge. She thought of the Rolls Royce and giggled.

'I don't know about that, Miss Barbara,' Benjy said, diviningly. 'I hoist out the battery and 'stributor and some more parts. Grease others heavy – might help. Plug up gas tank tight at both ends, same for oil. Tide go down, she *might* run again, though I be surprise.'

The tree swayed with the surge and then swayed back. Helen squawked. Hester clutched at her. Benjy laughed crowingly. He said to Barbara: 'But I still got hopes – some.'

Chapter 32

Ross Hunter, driving conservatively fast, swung the sedan around the last curve. Now the road lay straight along the high mesh fence of Vandenberg Three.

Margo hit his shoulder and pointed at a small open door in the first corner of the fence.

Hunter didn't slow down. 'No good,' he grunted. 'I'll try for a gate that can take the car.'

'Hurry it up,' Hixon urged from the back seat.

The landscape turned suddenly spectral. The big cloud-bank had cut off the sun. There was thunder. Through the thunder, guns cracked ahead. A police car came out of the flaming laager through the opening clipped in the freeway fence, plunged down a little slope, and headed in their direction, bumping and jouncing around the edge of the burned car-crush at the mouth of Monica Mountainway. A second police car come out, hind end foremost but backing fast, and followed the first.

Hunter slowed. There was a big gate with an empty guard booth. The gate was open. He swung through it as a third police car, this one front end first, escaped from the laager.

Hunter gunned the sedan across the dusty grey gravel towards a wide black door in the biggest of the three white buildings.

Beyond them Margo saw teenagers climbing the far fence and crowding in through a little door in it.

Hunter pulled up. Hixon and Margo piled out. There were three concrete steps, a narrow porch, then the black double door with a tag of white on it.

Hixon and Margo ran up the steps. She tried the door. It was locked. Hixon pounded on it with the butt of his rifle and yelled: 'Open up!'

Hunter started to turn the sedan around.

The first police car came screeching through the gate and headed towards them. Through the clouds of dust the first raised, the second police car followed, still backing.

Hixon ran to the nearest window and smashed with his rifle butt through it, then chopped away at the big fangs of glass left.

With a squeal of brakes, a surge of springs, and a ten-foot skid, the first police car drew up beside the sedan. Two officers jumped out, their faces soot-smeared, their eyes wild. One waved a Tommy gun.

'Drop your guns, all of you!' he yelled.

The other covered Hunter. 'Get out of that car!'

Hixon, holding his rifle muzzle away from the police, yelled: 'Hey, we're on your side!'

The officer let off a couple of shots that holed the stucco over Hixon's head. He dropped the rifle.

Margo was holding the revolver behind her.

Hunter climbed out of the car and came up the steps, hands held shoulder high.

The backing police car drew up behind the first. More officers piled out of it. The third police car drew up outside the gate.

Something dropped through the sedan window and bounced on the seat. Something else smashed against the windshield of the first police car, and hissing flames jetted out in a blue-yellow burst.

The police fired around the side of the building from which the Molotov cocktails had come. Two or three unseen guns returned their fire.

Margo was looking at the white tag on the black door. She ripped it down and crumpled it up.

The driver of the first police car lunged out of it, face arm-shielded from the flames. There were flames inside the sedan, too.

Hunter, keeping his hands raised, came up to Margo and Hixon.

The Molotov cocktail that had fallen unbroken into the sedan exploded. Big, blue-yellow flame-jets flared from the four windows.

Hunter said: 'Let's run for it. The little gate we saw first.'

They did. The police didn't shoot at them. The officers were already piling back into their second car. Thunder rumbled again, much louder.

Margo and Hunter and Hixon ran past the last white building just as a bunch of teenagers came around it on the other side. Margo felt the gust of their crazy high spirits like an electric wind, and for a moment she was on their side. Then gravel jumped ahead of Hunter, there was a crack, and she realized one of the kids was shooting. They were waving bottles and knives and one of them had a handgun. It was still more than fifty yards to the little gate.

The teenagers came at them whooping and screaming. A girl threw a bottle.

As she ran, Margo shot at them three times with the revolver and didn't hit anyone. Making the third shot, she tripped and sprawled on the gravel. The thrown bottle hit beside her and broke. She threw up her hands to shield her face from the flames, but there was only the smell of whisky.

Hunter yanked her up and they ran on. Ahead, Hixon was pointing at something and yelling.

The teenagers no longer came straight at them, but a dozen or so raced ahead towards the little door, cutting them off.

Margo and Hunter saw what Hixon was pointing at: a bright red car with a black hat at the wheel coming fast down Monica Mountainway, tyres screeching at the turns.

The teenagers had them blocked off from the door but they still ran towards it.

The Corvette lurched to a stop in front of the door. Rama Joan stood up beside the driver and pointed a grey-tipped hand at the teenagers. Dust and gravel blew up in their wild faces, they went staggering, lurching, sprawling backwards as if struck by a gale; the fence sagged inward.

Doc stood up beside her and yelled towards Margo and the two men: 'Come on! Make it fast!'

They ran through the gate and piled into the tiny back of the Corvette. Doc cut the wheels sharp and turned it.

They saw the second police car, escaped from Vandenberg Three, bouncing back around the burned car-crush.

But the third police car was coming straight at them up Monica Mountainway along the fence.

Rama Joan pointed the momentum pistol at it.

Hixon cried: 'Don't do it. They're police.'

The police car seemed to brake to a stop, except that its occupants were not thrown forward but back. The whole car started to skid back. Rama Joan quit pointing the pistol.

The Corvette roared uphill. Hunter protested: 'Not so fast, Doc.'

Doc retorted: 'This is nothing. Didn't you see me coming down?' But he did slow a bit.

Hixon chortled: 'I'll say we did! You sure swung it, Captain!'

Behind them the car Rama Joan had stopped had turned back, and both police vehicles were headed north along the flat outside the freeway fence. The flames of the abandoned laager waved and twisted higher. The fire had spread to other cars.

Hunter snorted and said: 'That was the last useless, heroic nonsense I'll ever go in for.' He scowled at Margo.

Thunder roared. A big drop or two of rain spattered.

Margo fished a small ball of paper from her bosom and un-crumpled it. 'Useless?' she grinned at Hunter, holding the paper forward between Doc and Rama Joan, but so Hunter could see it, too.

The big-scrawled message was: 'Van Bruster, Comstock, rest of you! We're being lifted out to Vandenberg Two. Join us by Monica Mountainway. Luck!'

It was signed: 'Opperly.'

A big raindrop hit the paper. The rain was black.

Don Guillermo Walker and the Araiza brothers were half-way up Lake Nicaragua. The launch would soon head around the island of Ometepe. From the island's two volcanoes rose thick black smoke plumes that glared red towards the base even in the bright sunlight.

The sunlight came through a wide break in the curtain of steam to the west. The break should have showed the towns of La Virgin and Rivas on the Isthmus of Rivas between Lake Nicaragua and the Pacific, but instead there was only water stretching endlessly.

The Araizas had supplied the information that the normal

tides along the Pacific coast by Brito and San Juan del Sur across the isthmus were about fifteen feet.

The inference was incredible, yet inescapable. The Wanderer-multiplied tides were flowing over the isthmus, joining the Pacific to Lake Nicaragua. That was why the lake had gone up and why its waters now tasted of salt. Where once the white and sky-blue coaches of Cornelius Vanderbilt's Accessory Transit Company had carried the gold-dreaming Forty-niners and their baggage from ocean to ocean, from Virgin Bay to San Juan del Sur, there now stretched the blue waters of the Peaceful Sea. The Nicaraguan Canal, of which so many men had dreamed, had become a twice-daily reality.

A red glare appeared half-way up the thickly vegetated cone of Madera. Almost immediately pale smoke puffed from around it. Then the red glare began to lengthen downward, the smoke following. Red-hot lava must have broken through a crack and be flowing towards the lake.

The launch kept on. Don Guillermo wondered that the waters around them were so calm. He did not think particularly of the stupendous pressure they must be exerting on this whole stretch of coast, nor did he see anything ominous in the absence of the steam curtain, though if he had thought about it he would have guessed that steam was still generating far below.

There was no definable stimulus, but suddenly the three men looked at each other.

Don Guillermo slapped a mosquito on his neck.

A thick button of water swelled up like a grey pimple from the placid surface in the direction of the inundated Isthmus of Rivas and without a sound grew in three seconds to a mushroom of water a half mile high and a mile wide.

Something that turned the surface of the water from bright to dull was travelling from the mushroom to the launch.

The three men stared unbelievingly.

The blast wave from the explosion broke their eardrums and knocked them down in the launch.

Don Guillermo glimpsed the great vertical hillside of steam-driven water an instant before it engulfed him and his comrades in the launch. It seemed to be everywhere thickly

254

covered with a water-vegetation of lacy, dull grey fronds. He thought, *The blasted heath. There to meet with Macbeth. I come, Graymalkin.*

The Isthmus of Rivas vanished, too. The Nicaraguan Canal became a permanent reality.

Chapter 33

Don Merriam had eaten and slept once more in his tiny cabin aboard the Wanderer, when he woke with a feeling of great inner clarity. He gazed tranquilly at the neutral-coloured ceiling as it lightened.

He did not feel the bed under him and was barely aware of his body – the little nerve messages of touch and tension were at a minimum. Insofar as he could tell at all, he was stretched on his back with his arms straight and relaxed at his sides.

Suddenly he was filled with a boundless curiosity about the great ship on which he was an involuntary passenger. His whole being was suffused with the yearning to know, or if that were impossible, at least to see. This feeling was most intense, yet he felt no impulse to work it out in grimacings and gestures and muscular strainings.

Without warning, the ceiling swiftly descended towards him.

He tried to throw himself off the bed, but the only result was that he turned over, very smoothly, and saw by the bottom of the wall and the pattering shower area that he was about six feet above them.

The ceiling had not moved. He was floating in the air, first on his back, now on his face, two feet below the ceiling.

His chin was tipped forward and his head bent back, though without any sensation of strain, so that his vision was directed straight ahead, like the point of a spear. He couldn't look down at any part of the bed beneath him, although he tried to, because he wanted to know whether he would see his body lying there – whether a real body or a body in a dream.

Nor could he bring his hands in front of his face to look at them. Either he was unable to feel and move his arms, or else he had none.

He couldn't tell whether he had a real body up here, or even a dream body, or whether he was only a levitating viewpoint with an imagined body behind it.

One bit of evidence for the last: he couldn't seem to see in the periphery of his vision the dim edges of nose and brow and cheek that one normally sees and ignores. But perhaps that was only because his vision was directed so fiercely forward.

All at once he began to move swiftly in that direction, straight towards the wall. He flinched his eyes shut – he could do that, at least, or somehow momentarily turn off his vision – and when he opened them, although there had been no blow, not the least sensation of resistance, he was flying rapidly along a silver corridor etched with arabesques and hieroglyphs. It opened almost at once into one of the great pits or wells, and with a sudden rush of exultation he plunged down.

In this way there began for Don Merriam an experience that might be pure vivid dream, or a dream induced in him by his captor-hosts, or a clairvoyant extrasensory experience presented to him in the form of a flying dream, or even – and this was how it felt – that his body had been made perfectly permeable to all walls and airs and other barriers by an alien physics and chemistry, and immune to gravity and all other ordinary forces, and whirled and swooped about, half involuntarily yet guided to a degree by its mind's raging curiosities, on a wonderful nightmare journey.

Or perhaps, it occured to him, this was all taking place in a single instant, outside time.

Don Merriam could not tell which of these, or some yet unimagined other, was the basis of his experience. He could only flit and plummet and *see*.

At first his movements were limited to empty corridors and shafts. Or if there were beings or perambulating machines or small ships in them, they were blurred to invisibility by the speed of his passage. The rule was that for a few instants he would travel almost as fast as light, it seemed, aware only of the general shape and attitude of the passageway he was traversing; then he would float rather slowly for a brief space, able to glimpse all that was immediately around him; then he would dart off again, in part involuntarily, in part because an imperious urge to see something else would take hold. This process went on interminably, yet without weariness or boredom, as though time were unlimitedly telescoped.

Gradually the three-dimensional picture firmed in his mind of the Wanderer, artificial throughout, globe within globe of floors – fifty thousand of them at least – everywhere veined with corridors, like a vast silvery sponge. Many of the great wells did go all the way through the planet, intersecting at its centre in an immense empty globe that had a dark sky of its own glittering with random lights like stars between the mile-wide holes of the pits with their darkness and their softly glimmering lights.

But although his imagination surged delightedly with its increasing grip on the structure of the Wanderer, one feature of the planet oppressed and then began to frighten him, more by its implications than by its simple nature: the thirty-yard-thick skin of dark metal that was its silver-filmed roof – the ground on which the Baba Yaga and the Soviet moon-ship had landed – and the mile-wide rounds of equally thick metal set to swing across the mouths of the pits, sealing up the planet like a fortress.

Re-enforcing this particular ominousness were sets of great coils circling some of the planet-piercing pits, as if the pits might sometimes serve as monstrous linear accelerators.

Recoiling inward from the forbidding armour plating, Don found himself again in the very centre of the star-speckled, central immensity. It might be only twenty miles across, but now it seemed a universe, and the great holes in its starry sky doorways to other universes, and he felt that there were invisible beings around him, impalpable thinking mists that lived in the cold intergalactic depths of space, and this engendered in him a sudden fear sharper than had the planet's defensive skin.

It was perhaps this sharper fear that launched his winging vision on its second exploration of the Wanderer. He no longer stuck to corridors, but flashed without flinching through wall after wall, aware of the thickest of them only as a fleeting blink in his seeing as he sped through room after room. And now when he paused, it was always near living beings. These living beings were not of one sort, but many.

Although felinoids or cat-people like his conductor formed a large minority of the Wanderer's crew, especially near the planet's surface, there were beings that seemed an end product of almost every line of terrestrial evolution, and un-earthly lines, too: great-headed horses with organs of manipulation nesting in their hooves; giant, tranquil-eyed spiders pulsing at their joints with a strongly pumped arterial blood-flow; serpents with large and small grasping tentacles; glintingly scaled and gorgeously crested humanoid lizards; beings shaped and moving like thick wheels with a counter-rotating central brain and sensorium; land-dwelling squid that stood proudly on three or six tentacles; and beings seemingly inspired by such creatures of myth as the basilisk and the harpy. These last Don found deep in the planet, winging about in a room like a gigantic aviary. This room, so big that it occupied many floors – an interior world – was grown over with slim, multibracing trees with tiny leaves, and lighted by a dozen great floating lamps like suns.

Some of the turquoise lakes he had glimpsed from the Baba Yaga were as deep as they were wide, and in them dwelt great-eyed and presumably vast-brained whales with arms like cables fingered at the ends with filaments. And beside the whales swam other seemingly intelligent, mobile-visaged sea beings.

Don wanted to stop and study all of these beings, observe their actions in detail, but always the urge to see some yet more mysterious or wonderful life form was greater, with the result that his pauses were hardly longer than when he had been hurtling along the empty avenues. In no case did the beings he observed appear to be aware of his presence.

None of the life forms seemed to keep racial privacy: there had been a few cat-people engaged in apparently amicable converse with the smaller harpies in their aviary-world, and there had been giant spiders arm-oaring in translucent diving suits through one of the deep lakes of the whales.

It began to seem incredible to him that the variety and numbers of the beings he was spying on could be held by an

Earth-size planet, but then it occurred to him that with her decks the Wanderer had about 15,000 times the surface area of Earth.

Despite their numbers and variety, most of the beings he watched so briefly appeared to be urgently busy. Even the motionless ones seemed to be rapt in work – crucial cogitations. There was an omnipresent sense of crisis.

Occasionally, as if by a failure of flight pattern, or perhaps for relief, Don would pause in a room without living occupants; great tanks filling up with moon rock; halls of silent glowing machinery and pipes coursing with fluids of many colours; rooms of strange vegetation sunlit by lamps – only these might be intelligent plants; rooms of smoothly geometric structures that seemed on the verge of life, like those on the Wanderer's surface; spherical rooms filled with pure, raw, fiery sun-stuff, although it neither burned nor blinded him.

Occasionally he saw physical work being done by artificial-seeming protoplasmic beings like giant amoebas whose manipulatory columns and sense organs varied with the task being performed. Elsewhere there laboured metal robots counterfeiting spiders, wheel-beings, and many other life forms – though some of these robots seemed truly alive, as did certain large structures like gigantic electronic brains. Their transparent walls showed dark jellies glinting with tangled silvery lines finer than hairs, as if they grew nerves and thought-cells as needed.

The greater the variety of intelligent life Don saw, the more he became sensitive to its presence. Now, when he paused in the star-specked central globe, it seemed to swim with faint violet mist-beings of ever-changing shape and multi-armed: cold creatures of the darkness beyond the stars. And once when he soared briefly to the upper deck, he glimpsed one of the great coloured abstract forms split like an egg and spill out a horde of beings.

Yet the more sensitive he became to the presence of intelligent life, the more he was racked by the conviction that there were all around him invisible forms of it beyond his sensing – as if the Wanderer had more ghosts aboard than all her crew members.

He paused in a profoundly still room of many balconies and almost an infinitude of cases of tiny drawers, like the card catalogue room of a library. Filament-like tracks led from the drawers to viewing instruments suggesting great microscopes, and it seemed to Don that there was travel along the multiplicity of cobwebs, and he had the thought that here servile microbes and viruses were sorting and ordering for inspection molecules on which were etched the total knowledge of races and the histories of worlds. All Earth's thought and culture, he told himself, would easily fit into just one of the tiny drawers. It was almost as if he brushed here the universal, all-encompassing viewpoint of eternity which is sometimes called God.

From that room he flashed into a busier one crowded with command tables, maps, charts, screens, and tanks for three-dimensional viewing. On and in the latter were ever-changing scenes of catastrophe: landscapes and cities riven by earthquake, seared by fire, inundated by great waves and silent rises of water. He peered excitedly for a while, then it came to him with horror that this was his own planet Earth suffering tidal mutilation in the grip of the Wanderer's mass – the Wanderer, which could turn gravity on and off as suited its purposes.

He wanted to stay and watch, or thought he did, but instead he was irresistibly hurried off through several walls into a chamber that was one great dark viewing tank with alien faces all around it, some with two eyes, some with three and some with eight. In the tank hung models of Earth and the Wanderer and a looping, swelling quarter-ring that was the remnants of Luna. Here and there, mostly clustering close to the two planets, were points of violet and yellow light which he guessed were spaceships.

The larger globes were the right distance apart – some thirty times their diameter – and Don could not tell whether they were replicas or three-dimensional projections. The illusion was so good that he felt he was drifting in space, with the weird alien faces replacing the constellations.

Then without warning other planets, green, grey, gold, some as strangely figured as the Wanderer, began to appear by ones and twos. Bright bolts of light that travelled with a curious slowness shot between them – radiation moving 186,000 miles a second, but slowed down to scale. There were miniscule explosions. Light-point spaceships moved in warring fleets. Then all the planets but Earth began to move about swiftly as if manoeuvring in a battle.

But he never saw the outcome of the engagement, for the forces moving him through the Wanderer began to work on him with greater urgency, as if he were nearing the end of his trip. For the first time he felt a pang of weariness.

The next three rooms he was hurried through were all viewing tanks with backgrounds velvet black except for the alien faces of the viewers. The first showed a swirled lens of bright points, and clusters of light – a galaxy, certainly, probably the Milky Way.

The second room held a great swarm of tiny, soft, spherical and disc-shaped puffs of light spaced rather more than their own diameters apart. There was something strange about the space in this tank – it seemed to curve back upon itself mysteriously, so that as he moved about everything changed more than it ought. Just before he was whirled on, Don guessed he was seeing the entire cosmos of star-islands: the totality, the universe.

His imagination began to wander sleepily, independently of his viewing. Phrases drifted through his mind: *This artificial planet . . . the umbilicus of the cosmos . . . the central brain . . . the eternal eye . . . the book of the past . . . the womb and zygote of the future . . . transcendent as God, yet not God. . . .*

He returned to himself, or to his winging viewpoint, with a start, to realize that he was gazing into a great black viewing tank in which the cosmos he had just seen – it was recognizable by its mysteriously twisted shape – was only one small, pale puff of light floating alone. Then ghostlier light-puffs of other shapes and hues began to appear and vanish, some swiftly as a firefly's flash, some lingering a while. Don wondered dreamily if these were other universes known to the beings of the Wanderer. Or perhaps only universes guessed at . . . sought . . . there was something hypothetical about their ghostliness and their swift vanishing . . . and stars and galaxies and universes are truly such unreal things, no more than the dim points of light that swim before one's eyes before one sleeps. . . .

Then the one bright cosmos began to dip and dart about like a leaf in a whirlwind, and he worried dreamily why that should be, since surely the universe is firm-based . . . and then the ghost cosmoses began to swirl too, hypothetically. . . .

The last room Don traversed shocked him briefly awake as no other sight might have, and there seemed to be a moral to it, though his weary mind was unable to put it into words. It was a huge, worldlike room, similar to that of the harpies, with a furnace-red sky arching above a veldt dotted with rocks and tree clumps. Small hoofed animals more delicate than deer and armed with a single slim horn grazed fastidiously. Birds with ruby and topaz and emerald plumage and with elaborate combs and wattles flew low, frequently settling into the tall grass and the tree clumps as if in search of seeds and fruit.

Suddenly three birds whirred up at once from the grass, and the nearest group of unicorns held tremblingly still, sniffing the air and peering about fearfully, then took off with great bounds. Simultaneously there sprang from behind a rock a grey-barred tan felinoid otherwise resembling Don's conductor. He raced after the unicorns, his long legs flashing, hurled himself on the last, brought it crashing down from mid-bound, grasped it by chest and chin, and dipped his jaws towards its throat.

A topaz bird winged past the nearest tree-clump and from it there sprang a green-furred felinoid, female by her smaller size and slightly different contours. She leaped with the soaring grace and almost incredible elevation of a ballet dancer executing a *grand jeté*. Her long arm flashed and barely brushed the bird, but three long talons deeply pricked its breast. Grasping it by the comb with her other hand, she carried it to her lips and bit expertly into its ruffling neck.

There was a redness on her dull olive lips and on the one long white fang showing as she looked across the yellow feathers straight at Don with her large and flowerlike, jade-irised eyes. It may have been coincidence, but he felt that she saw him. And as she sucked the blood, with the blood-red sky behind her, she smiled.

Then a swooning tiredness came, and things grew dim and neutral-hued, and Don realized he was floating once more in his tiny cabin. He tried to look down at the bed, but was again unable to. The next instant he was lying on it. He felt its soothing touch from toe to head as all vision faded and his sense of rocketing, swooping movement gyrated down to darkness and to rest.

Chapter 34

Doc tootled the horn four times and stopped the Corvette just short of the rock slope where they'd camped last night. Hixon was back driving his truck now. In the Corvette, Ann was riding between Doc and her mother, while Margo and Hunter sat behind them.

All these five had been chattering in high spirits, despite or more likely because of their faces being blackly smeared and their clothes damp and dirty from the weird warm black rain, which had just now stopped and which they'd decided might well be from volcanic ash blowing up from Mexico and points south.

'Or sea-muck uncovered by low tides and whirlwinded up,' Doc had second-guessed. 'It tastes a touch salty.'

The sky was wild masses of dark low clouds trapping bright silver light.

'All out,' Doc ordered gaily. 'Ross, run ahead and check for water in the dip. I want to take her across before I get goosy.'

Hunter obeyed. Margo went with him.

The truck pulled up behind the Corvette, and behind the truck the school bus, its yellow streaked more blackly than ever.

Doc shouted to Hixon in the truck: 'Tell your passengers to get out before we take the vehicles across, just like this morning. McHeath! – pass the word back to Doddsy, and tell him to shoo his folks out of the bus fast. We don't want to waste any more time here than we have to. Then post yourself by the bus and watch the road behind us.'

Ann snuggled up against Doc. She said excitedly: 'Let me stay in the car with you. I'm not scared of us slipping off.'

'That'd be great, sweetheart, but your Ma would say I was tempting Kali,' Doc said, ducking his head and rubbing his smeary cheek against hers. Rama Joan smiled fondly at him as she pulled her daughter out giggling.

'No water in the dip,' Hunter called back. At that moment his legs went out from under him and he sat down. 'But it's damn slippery,' he qualified as he scrambled to his feet, Margo grinning at him unfeelingly. 'This film of wet ash is treacherous.'

Rama Joan's smile faded. From beside the Corvette she whispered urgently to Doc, 'Can't we fill the dip with stones and earth, or at least clean it off?'

He leaned towards her and answered in a low, fast voice: 'Look, darling, those murdering drunken kids are bound to get some cars on this road soon and come whooping for the beach. A lot of them have been doing it all their lives. Second nature to them. We really haven't a minute to lose.'

He sat back, honked the horn once and roared the motor. 'Here I come!' he warned.

He drove fast and the Corvette jounced through the dip with no sideslip at all. He parked it well ahead, then came jog-trotting back to where Rama Joan, Margo, and Hunter were standing above the dip. Ann was back by the bus, chattering to McHeath and admiring his rifle.

'That was a rousing anticlimax,' Doc said. 'I guess I'm getting chicken in my old age.' Hunter and Margo laughed. Rama Joan smiled uncertainly.

Ida called thinly from beside the truck: 'Mr Brecht! Ray Hanks doesn't want to be lifted out again.'

Doc looked around at the others, shrugged, said: 'It'll save time,' and yelled: 'O.K., let him chance it! Bring it over, Hixon!'

The truck got off to a fast start, too. Only as it jounced by them safely did they see that Mrs Hixon was in back, braced over Hanks and holding on to the side across the cot.

The school-bus passengers came trudging across: the Ramrod, Wanda – and Ida with them – but not Wojtowicz, who'd stopped by McHeath and Ann; finally Clarence Dodd and Pop arguing together, the latter protesting.

Doc pulled his doubly black hat down on his forehead and headed towards them briskly. 'I know, I know!' he said as Pop opened his ill-toothed mouth at him. 'The back tyres are slicker than ever . . . and so forth. Leave it to Hotrod Rudy.'

'One cylinder's missing, too,' Pop called after him, but Doc just kept on going towards the bus.

Clarence Dodd took note of Margo's and the others' blackened faces. 'That shower would have delighted Charles Fort,' he said, smiling. 'You look as if you were all getting ready for an Indian funeral.'

Margo thought for the first time since last night of the tortured girl in her tomb up the slope.

Rama Joan suddenly started back towards the school bus after Doc. Ann waved to her from beside him. 'Hi, Mommy!' Rama Joan stopped and waved back uncertainly.

Ann giggled, and McHeath and Wojtowicz laughed at something Doc said as he climbed aboard the bus. The motor coughed into life and it came on, gathering speed but then hesitating.

Pop muttered: 'She sometimes balks shifting into second.'

The bus entered the dip very slowly. Its front wheels hesitated coming out, and then its rear end began to slide swiftly sideways. Doc gunned the motor. The back tyres wailed against the black-slimed stone. Doc cut the wheels and braked. The bus slid backward down the slope.

McHeath shoved his rifle into Wojtowicz's hands and ran down across the rock towards the bus, his feet hitting pot-holes and tiny ridges.

The bus hesitated, then paused on the verge of the five-hundred-foot drop with one front wheel against a small rock in a pothole. They could all see Doc pulling himself out of the backward-tilted seat, bracing himself on the slanted floor, and grabbing for the lever that opened the front door.

Hunter suddenly grabbed Margo by the shoulder, thrust his hand in her jacket, and pulled out the momentum pistol.

McHeath was almost to the bus and near the verge himself. Wojtowicz wondered what the kid thought he could do: maybe, he guessed, brace himself and offer a hand to steady Doc when he jumped down on to the slippery slope.

Doc got the door open and his head out of it. Then the little rock popped out of the pothole and the back wheels of the bus slid over the edge, the floor slanting still more against Doc's escape effort, and the underbody grated harshly on the rock lip as it slowly slid over.

Hunter squeezed the tiny recessed lever on top of the grip of the grey pistol between his finger and thumb and twisted it around so that the arrow pointed not towards the muzzle but away from it.

Doc had his upper body out of the door when the bus overbalanced, setting him back on his heels in the door. As the bus swung out and down with him in it, he looked at his friends up the slope and took off the black hat and waved it.

Hunter pointed the momentum pistol at him and pressed the button.

Doc's face dropped out of sight and his upstretched hand too, but the black hat came sailing back over the lip, and a chill breeze with it.

McHeath threw himself down on the verge, gripping a rock ridge with foot, knee, elbow, and hand, and peered over.

The slope vibrated faintly underfoot and the big crash came hollowly.

The chill breeze quickened. The black hat sailed straight at Hunter and hung itself on the muzzle of the momentum pistol. A small boulder started to roll uphill after it. Hunter flipped his finger off the button and bowed his head. The small boulder reversed course and rolled down the slope, clinking.

McHeath called hoarsely, his voice cracking half-way through: 'He's gone. He was thrown out. I saw him hit. Then the bus rolled over him.'

Hunter said: 'Just one second sooner ...'

Clarence Dodd said to him: 'You switched the arrow one hundred and eighty degrees, and it reversed the momentum?' And when Hunter nodded heavily, the Little Man commented: 'Well, that's logical.'

Hunter snatched the black hat off the muzzle and swung it

up as if to throw it down and stamp on it. Then he just looked at it in his hand.

There was a faint hollow crack as the small boulder hit five hundred feet below and the sound came up.

On the sunbeaten mesa in Arizona, as if it were a Parsi Tower of Silence, vultures tore away the last shreds of the flesh of Asa Holcomb's face, laying wholly bare the beautiful grinning red bone.

Paul Hagbolt rested lightly against the warm, smooth, trusty window that half spanned Tigerishka's saucer. He gazed down at Earth's northern ice-cap breaking up, the white crust of frozen water lifted and collapsed by the great tides that had been moving in and out through the Greenland Sea, Baffin Bay, and the Bering Strait. Almost the whole Arctic zone was out of shadow, as Earth's summering northern hemisphere tilted towards the sun.

The interior of the saucer was dark, but some light was reflected into it by the snow-freighted ice, which twinkled with highlights wherever ice-tables tilted to reflect the sun directly – stars in a white sky.

Tigerishka was stretched out against the window, too, a few feet from Paul. She was caressing Miaow, but now the little cat drew away from the velvet-padded, three-fingered hand and bent her hind legs against the violet-barred, green-furred shoulder, and sprang off across Paul into the flowerbank beyond him – presumably to re-explore it by the mysterious ice-sent twilight. Miaow had adapted quickly to free fall and delighted in worming her way through the plants along the thick vines, her tiny face cat-smiling out between the leaves and flowers from time to time.

Tigerishka made a quick, soft singing sound that was rather like a sigh. It occurred to Paul that she might have brought them here to escape the reproachful thought of people dying as they looked down at Earth. He almost started to tell her that there was, or yesterday had been, a Russian weather station at the North Pole, but decided she could read that in his thoughts if she wanted to.

Without warning the saucer began to mount very swiftly. First the ice cap, then the whole Earth, shrank rapidly.

Paul repressed his reactions. Excited emoting was not admired feline behaviour and he already knew that Tigerishka could work the control panel without touching or even looking at it.

Stars came out everywhere. As Terra continued to shrink, the Wanderer came sliding into view. It too had a polar cap of sorts, a lopsided yellow one against the violet background, but with a yellow neck going down from it – the neck of the dinosaur. From here the yellow shape was like a battle axe.

They were mounting at right angles to the sunlight: none came directly into the saucer. The two planets below began to show half phases, the Wanderer with the crescent of moon fragments out to its sunward side.

It grew dark in the saucer as the ice light faded. When the planets finally stopped shrinking, they were two small, almost indistinguishable half moons, not very far apart, against the starfields, largely unfamiliar to Paul, which one sees from the southern hemisphere.

With no great amazement he realized that the saucer had mounted several million miles in less than a minute – something not too far below the speed of light.

The effect was as if he and Tigerishka, walking through a city, had retreated into a big unlit park and were now seeing the lights of the city across several acres of dark lawn and trees. After a bit, it did begin to feel very lonely.

Tigerishka said quietly: 'You feel like God? The Earth your footstool?'

Paul said: 'I don't know. Could I change the past? If someone were dead, could I bring him to life?'

Tigerishka did not answer, though it seemed to Paul in the darkness that she slowly shook her head.

There was a time of silence. Then Tigerishka made again the short melodic sound that was a little like a sigh. Then, softly: 'Paul?'

'Yes?' he said quietly.

She said, softer still, but rapidly: 'We *are* wicked. We hurt your planet terribly. We *are* afraid.'

She went on, this time not quite so like a little girl confessing naughtiness: 'Your lost generation, your Hungarian refugees, your anarchists, your Satanists, your beats, your fallen angels, your parole-jumpers, your juvenile delinquents – we're like those. Running, running, running. Every step, pounding the hollow planetary pavement under the cold streetlights of the stars: a billion light-years.'

He knew she was picking the words, concepts, and images out of his mind, yet his mind did not feel it at all.

She continued: 'The Wanderer is our getaway car, our escape wagon – a very hip and handsome Dunkirk ship! Fifty thousand decks for fun and games! Skies to suit every taste – sunsets to order! Hot and cold running gravity in every state-room – pro or anti, take your pick! The Star of the Rejected. Satan's Ark!'

And now it was the voice of a rather bigger girl, covering guilt with bravado and with lurid images chosen with a deliberate facetiousness.

She went on: 'Oh, what a stylish Planet of the Damned! We paint our air on top for privacy. That shocked them in the solar slum we swung in. Those drab conformists thought we must have naughty things to hide behind our two-toned glamour. Well, we did!'

'The Painted Planet,' Paul murmured, trying to match her mood – and use at least one image before she did.

She flashed back: 'Like your Desert, yes. And your wild painted women, no? Violet and yellow, like a desert dawn. We even paint the Wanderer's boats to match – launches bigger than liners, dinghies like this. Oh, we're the top of the mode, we are, we passengers on Satan's Ark, we devil host, we angels going bump!'

She grinned swiftly at him, wrinkling her muzzle, but then she looked out again at the stars and down again at the two half moons, and her voice grew a little graver, though not entirely grave.

'The Wanderer sails the true void: hyperspace. You want a rugged roadway, a cruel sea, a storm that makes a hurricane seem a breeze; a nova-front, a match-flash? Try the void! Formless as chaos, hostile to all life. No light, no atoms, even,

269

no energy we superbeasts can tap – as yet! It is like quicksand you must tunnel through, or like a killing desert, waterless, which you must cross to reach a star with palms. A black, malignant seething that's to space as the unconscious is to consciousness. Alleys to which the streetlight never gets, mouthless and twisted, full of dirty death – or dark, cold, oily water under docks, roiled by great waves. The Sargasso of the Starships! The Graveyard of Lost Planets! Oh, a most charming sea for Satan's Ark, giving his angels nausea and nightmares – the flaming, freezing, formless Sea of Hell!

'This whole star-marqueed universe of ours – the cosmos you think rock-based, firm as God – rides in the endless hyperspatial storm just as a paper scrap might ride the whirlwind's gust. And . . . the Wanderer sails only in the fist of wind that holds the scrap. We're timid sailors; we always hug the coast.'

Paul stared out at the randomly scattered, lonely stars and wondered why he had always so easily accepted that they represented order.

'The power of a billion fission piles,' Tigerishka went on, 'are what you need to burst into the void – and still more power, fantastic subtlest skill, and luck, too, to burst out. The Wanderer eats moons for breakfast and asteroids for snacks! Or rather, they are eaten by the void the Wanderer sails through, that gobbler of neutrinos – food tossed to hyperspatial wolves to buy our way.

'It takes no time to travel hyperspace, except the launching and the landfall times,' Tigerishka continued, 'but oh, the wit it takes to spy your port, the waits before you burst back to the world! – like threading an unknown coast in thickest fog. In hyperspace there are signs of our space here – shadows of suns, of planets and of moons, of dust and gases and of emptiness – but they are far more difficult to read than radar in a sky chockful of foil, than unknown, drip-worn, lime-brushed hieroglyphs within a cavern half as old as time.

'We ended this last trip battered and strained, starving for mass and sunlight. Our insulation from raw hyperspace had shrunk to zero; we almost lost our sky and atmosphere; no one could venture on our upper deck except the inorganic giants which dwell there – the crystal minds which are like coloured hills.

'At that we made two false exits in your system, each gobbling up some cubic leagues of fuel we could not spare, but each time had to cancel because the signs weren't right or else the vectors wrong, the exit spots not near enough your sun or to a moon that wholly suited us.'

Paul interposed automatically: 'Only two false exits? There were four photos of twisting starfields.'

'Four photos, but only two false exits – one near Pluto, one near Venus,' she asserted sharply. 'Don't interrupt me, Paul. We finally managed our exit near your moon, the eclipse line-up making a perfect shadow. We surfaced from the sea of hyperspace. But we were almost powerless by then. Why, if we'd had to do battle we could barely have thrown the Wanderer into null gravity for manoeuvring.'

'Tigerishka!' Paul protested. 'You mean you could have nullified the Wanderer's gravity field, so that it wouldn't have caused quakes and huge tides on Earth – and you didn't?'

'I'm not the Wanderer's captain!' she snarled at him. 'Besides, we had to have full gravity to catch and crush your moon, don't you see? Full gravity augmented by local churn-fields and torque-volumes. And even in the worst emergencies we must maintain a general fuel reserve for battle – that's obvious, surely!'

Paul said, 'But Tigerishka, compared to the Wanderer's, the world's space forces and atomic weapons are a joke. What conceivable battle –'

'Paul, I told you once we were *afraid*.' There was a dark violet flash from her petalled irises as she turned her head away from him. 'The Wanderer's not the only far-ranging planet in the universe.'

Chapter 35

Hunter stopped for one last look down the slope before walking ahead past the truck to the Corvette and taking his place behind the wheel. Rama Joan and Margo stood beside him. All the rest were already aboard: Ann and Wanda in the Corvette, the Hixons and Ida in the cab of the truck, the remaining five men crowded in the back of the truck with Ray Hanks. Hunter didn't like the arrangement, but nothing felt right since Doc's death: everything was cold and hard and clumsy and uncomfortable, like his own insides.

He hadn't wanted to take command, he'd tried to wish it on Doddsy, but Hixon had just looked at him steadily and said: 'I think Doc would have picked you,' and that had settled it.

He hated making final decisions, like turning down Hixon's suggestion they use the momentum pistol to move some boulders to block the road; he'd answered that one by pointing out there was a bare one-eighth charge left in the gun, if the violet scale meant what they thought it did. Or ruling whether they should take Mulholland or backtrack all the way to Vandenberg Two; he'd tabled that one until they came to that particular crossroad – and then had to suffer the private criticism of Margo, who'd taken it for granted they'd continue their pursuit of Morton Opperly, especially now that they had his note saying he was going to Vandenberg Two. Margo told Hunter he should have smothered dissension by making this clear to everyone from the start.

Hardly a word had been spoken about Doc, though that only underlined the gloom. Hunter had quietly asked Wojtowicz what last thing Doc had said that they'd laughed at, and Wojtowicz had replied: 'I was just asking him again to take the hat off, that it was bad luck, and he said to me, "Wojtowicz, when you're as bald as I am and aren't allowed to hide it any more, you'll know that's worse luck!"'

The Ramrod had overheard and said, shaking his head sadly: 'I warned him about that hat, too,' and then added something that sounded like, 'The sin of pride'.

Wojtowicz had called the Ramrod on that, and Doddsy had tried to smooth things out by saying: 'I'm sure Charles Fulby was referring to *hubris* – the sort of high optimism some of the great Greek heroes had that made the gods jealous, so that they destroyed them.'

Wojtowicz had flared back: 'Greeks or not, I don't care, nobody's going to say anything against Doc!'

Now Hunter looked down at that same black hat, which he'd been carrying crumpled up all this time, and he thought of Doc down there with the three murderers, all the same meat to the buzzards.

'God,' he muttered bitterly, 'we're not leaving him as much of a monument as he did Doddsy's big stupid mutt.'

He thought of sticking the hat up somewhere, but that was all wrong. He smoothed out the brim and, when a lull came in the breeze, skimmed it down the slope. For a moment he thought it was going to land on the rim, and how horribly inept that would make him out, but it sailed over and out of sight.

Rama Joan gripped his upper arm tight and Margo's on the other side. Her face and reddish hair were still blackly streaked, her limp, dirty, chopped-off evening clothes a tramp clown's costume.

'God knows it's not any monument,' she said in a low voice, huskily, 'but Doc laid me here last night.'

Hunter's eyes filled up. He said chokily: 'The fornicating old buzzard!'

Off in the distance, very faintly, he heard the whine of a motor. It seemed to come from the direction of the freeway.

'Do you hear that, Mr Hunter?' young McHeath called, crouching in the back end of the truck, his rifle ready. Hunter remembered Doc saying how 'those murdering drunken kids' would be coming.

The three of them ran for the Corvette. As Hunter piled behind the wheel, Margo in back, Rama Joan in front, on the other side of Ann, he thought, *Doc would have walked. Or would he? At least, he'd have said something.*

He started the motor, then faced around, holding up his right arm.

273

'If cars come up behind us, you pass me,' he shouted to Hixon. 'That way we'll be able to use the momentum pistol. If they start pointing guns, fire on 'em! O.K., everybody, here we go!'

It wasn't good, he thought as he shifted into gear, *but it will have to do.*

Richard Hillary made the acquaintance of Vera Carlisle at a moment when the girl was sitting in the mud in Tewkesbury and crying quietly.

Sitting in the mud was getting to be quite the way to meet people, Richard reflected, and truth to tell it was at least a great deal better than finding them lying face down in it.

She was crouched so mouselike in the little side street and crying so quietly that he might well have missed her had not the night been still so light two hours after sunset. She was carrying nothing but a small transistor wireless, which she hugged like a baby.

During the past thirty-six hours Richard had witnessed several rescues and reunions and numerous befriendments, and now he realized that he wanted very much to befriend someone himself. He was acutely anxious that no one but he should hear this girl's soft sobs, or come upon them before her sobs had been stilled and at least the first gestures of comradeship made.

As he approached her he had the thought of how chilly it was getting and the memory of how warmly the couples had seemed to be sleeping last night under the straw, and also the thought of how this was the end of the world, or at least a very good imitation; yet at the same time it seemed to him that those thoughts did not fully describe his present motives.

He offered her fresh bread he had saved from a thrifty scatter of little loaves dropped near Cleeve from a helicopter, but it turned out that Vera's chief discomfort was that she was thirsty. Getting water in the new tidal areas was no simple matter, with all the reservoirs and wells and springs salt-drowned. Some pipes held fresh water, but that was chancy.

He remembered a pub being looted two squares back, and as they went towards it past the water-marked, half-timbered

274

houses and a hotel named the Royal Hop Pole, he discovered another of her griefs: she had lost a heel and in any case her tight, pointed slippers weren't the best for walking.

There was quite a line of looters at the pub. *Oh, we law-abiding Britons*, Richard thought, *we queue up even for looting*. He remembered a shoe store just beyond it and broke into it determinedly – which was quite easy, since the tide had done that before him – and managed to find in the wet, reeking drawers a pair of tennis shoes for Vera and some heavy socks for both of them. All the articles were sopping, of course, but that was of no consequence.

By that time the queue was shorter, and soon he and Vera had received a bottle of beer apiece and one small flask of rum between them, under the fierce watchful eye of a brawny man who might even have been the actual proprietor, though he did not say so.

Outside, a fat man was pointing down the street and saying: 'Ah, there's the bastid now!'

It was the Wanderer, rising in its bloated-*X* face and ringed almost symmetrically by the white shards of the moon.

Vera glanced at it for a moment, then pressed her lips together and looked away. Richard felt a surge of approval at her reaction. She held her elbow out towards him just a little. He took it firmly and escorted her down the street in the way he'd originally been going, setting an easy pace at first as they drank their beer and munched some bread. He told her nothing about his Malvern Hills plan. Time enough for that when they'd crossed the roaring Severn by Telford's old iron bridge – if it hadn't been torn away.

Vera turned on her transistor wireless, and they listened all the way around the dial to a sound like bacon frying. Richard wanted to tell her to throw it away, but instead he asked her how her new shoes fitted, and she smiled at him and said: 'They're heavenly.'

Only an hour ago Richard had been tramping lonely in the midst of a mob, and thinking of all the millions or scores of millions of new dead there must be all over the world, and wondering if it really mattered at all.

He had thought, *Does the world need so many people?*

Take the crowd around me now – winnowed by the flood, yet most of them still stupid stereotypes the world could well do without. How many people does it take to sustain a reasonably rich culture? Aren't more than than a waste? And aren't millions of stereotypes an overly high price to pay for a few exceptions? Isn't there something utterly gross about the concept of an endlessly, planlessly multiplied humanity, perhaps eventually swarming like rats to the stars? Did having so many people ever matter, except to the people? The world needs and deserves this winnowing!

But now his thought was that if just one more person had been taken, that person might have been Vera. In theory there were tens of thousands of Veras, he supposed, but only one where this Richard Hillary could have found her. He gripped her arm a little more snugly.

Chapter 36

Paul Hagbolt stared down into the bottomless dark as if the circular window on which he rested were the top of a great aquarium, the stars and the tiny semicircles of Earth and Wanderer a mysterious marine luminescence, or as if the round were that of a glass slide under a microscope, and the stars, diamond infusoria.

There was a faint rustling and then a little cry – Miaow crawling weightless through the flowers and calling some discovery to Tigerishka.

From beside Paul, the larger cat said: 'Because mankind is young, you think the universe is, too. But it is old, old, old. Tomorrow and tomorrow . . . petty pace . . . last syllable of time . . . tale told by an idiot . . . yes!

'You think that space is empty, but it's full. Your own solar system is one of the few primeval spots, like a small, weed-grown lot overlooked by builders in the heart of a vast and ancient city that has overgrown all the countryside.

'In the galaxy where the Wanderer grew in orbit, the planets are so thick around each sun they shroud its light and make

276

a slum of space, a teeming city of a galaxy. It is the boast of our engineers, "Wherever a sunbeam escapes, we place a planet." Or they moor a field, to turn the sunlight back.

'Tens of thousands of planets around each sun, troubling each other with ten thousand tides, so that tidal harmonizing is half our civil engineering. Planets following each other so closely in the same orbit that they make elliptical necklaces, each pearl a world. You know those filigree nests of balls your Chinese carve of ivory, so that you peer and peer to find the centre, and end with the feeling that there's a little of infinity locked in there? That's how solar systems look, most places.

'You haven't yet heard this news, simply because of the snaily slowness with which light travels. If you could wait a billion years, you'd see the galaxies grow dim, not by the death of stars, but by the masking and miserly hoarding of their light by the stars' owners.

'All but a tiny remainder of the star-shrouding planets are artificial. Billions of trillions of dead suns and cold moons and planetary gas giants have been mined to get the matter to make them – your Egyptian pyramids multiplied by infinity. Throughout the universe, natural planets are as rare as young thoughts.

'Your own galaxy of the Milky Way is no exception. Planet-choked suns chiefly make the great central cloud which puzzles your astronomers.

'A pond can fill with infusoria almost as quickly as a ditch-water puddle. A continent can fill with rabbits almost as swiftly as a single field. And intelligent life can spread to the ends of the universe – those ends which are everywhere – as swiftly as it grows to maturity on a single planet.

'The planets of a trillion suns can fill with spaceship-builders as quickly as those of one. Ten million trillion galaxies can become infected with the itch of thought – that great pandemic! – as readily as one.

'Intelligent life spreads faster than the plague. And science grows more uncontrollably than cancer. On every undisturbed natural planet, life crawls and flutters for billions of years, then overnight comes the blossoming, the swift explosion across the great black distances of seeds that grow like weeds wherever they fall, and then the explosion of *their* seeds on, on, to the incurving ends of the universe.

'There is the drama of meeting other life forms – shocks, moments of poignant wonder. And then, much too soon, comes the ennui.

'The ditch-water puddle, where yesterday a few amoebas swam, is thick with writhing life – and the pond, too. The algae gleam like jewels. Then soon the pool grows clouded.' She pointed a claw towards the thick stars. 'Those diamonds you see out there are lies. The suns that sent that bright light now are masked.'

Tigerishka turned her tapering muzzle from the star-spangled window and spoke to Paul directly.

'The universe is full, Paul. Intelligent life is everywhere, its planets darkening the stars, its engineers recklessly spending the power of the suns to make mind's environment – burning matter to energy everywhere to make more form, more structure, more mind. The Word – to call mind that – goes forth, and soon there is nothing but the Word. The universe with all its great reaches and magnificent privacies becomes a slum, begins to die of too much mind – though *they* can never see that – just as a shallow sunlit bay can die of too much life.

'Immortality is achieved, breaking down the individual mind's limits futureward. Your world, Paul, is one of the few islands of death left in the sea of life everlasting.

'With hyperspatial travel and psionic communication, the ends of the universe are closer together than the planets of your solar system. The far-flung galaxies are more centralized than the countries of your world, than even your country's fifty-one states. And the affairs of the cosmos are ordered by a democratic rulership more benign and more terrible than that of any imagined god.

'It may be that your own primitive visions of heaven – and especially your ambiguous attitude towards it: that heaven is both a great wonder and a great bore – are merely valid intuitions of that government.

'Security and safety are its watchwords. It is conservative, ruled by the old, who are everywhere a great majority since the achievement of immortality. It is painstaking, patient, just, merciful – but only to the weak! – and infinitely stubborn. Its records alone, etched on molecules, occupy the artificial planets of two star clusters. Its chief aim is simply to remember and treasure – but only as a memory! – everything that has ever happened.

'Any minimally intelligent, respectable, safe race of beings can confidently expect from it support for their life-ways. It is always against the expenditure of energy for any purpose except conservation and security: it opposes the exploration of hyperspace, or even its use, except for the transport of its police. Its greatest fear is of something that might seriously injure or altogether disrupt the universe, for now that – bar hyperspace – it is no longer possible to think of safety in infinity and the unexplored, a great cosmic death-dread has arisen.

'Yet since even immortals must reproduce, if only at a minimal rate, to keep up the illusion that they are still truly alive, the government must continually find space for new beings. They'll be coming for your space soon, Paul. There's been a change in the policy towards the remaining wild worlds. Heretofore they were looked on as preserves of novelty, to be shielded until they grew to galactic stature. But now their living surface is needed, and their matter, and the energy of their suns. They are to be integrated into the cosmic superculture. Carefully, thoughtfully, and with kindness – but it will happen to you and probably within the next two hundred of your years. And it will not be a slow process – once it begins, all the wild worlds will be occupied and integrated within decades.

'To reduce its policies to a single statement, the aim of the cosmic government is to conserve intelligence until the cosmos dies. There was a time when this meant "for ever", but now we see it means until mind is maximized, until all matter that can be is shaped to the service and sustaining of intelligence, until entropy is reversed to the greatest degree possible within the limits of this universe.

'*They* look on this as the millennium. *We* look on it as death.

'*My* people are the Wild Ones – the younger races, races like my own which grew from solitary killers, which have lived closer to death and valued style more than security, freedom more than safety; races with a passionate sadistic tinge; or coldly scientific, valuing knowledge almost more than life.

'We rate growth above immortality, adventure higher than safety. Great risks and dangers do not trouble us.

'We want to travel more substantially in *time*. Not just observe, but change the past, make it a fuller one, revitalize the countless dead, live in a dozen – a hundred! – presents and not one, go back to the beginning and rebuild.

'We will explore the future time-wise, too, not just to reassure ourselves that there's a comfortable hearth-fire dying there – Intelligence in its last bed and moribund. We'd grow another cosmos to live on in!

'We want to range through *mind* more thoroughly – that crumpled rainbow plane inside our skulls. Although telepathy and psi are commonplace, we still don't know if there are other worlds upon the other side of the collective inward darkness – and how to visit them, an undared dream.

'We'd change all that: explore the realms of the spirit like strange continents, sail them like space, discover if all our minds rest like tiny rainbow seashells on the shores of the same black, storm-beaten, unconscious sea. Maybe that way there lie untrodden worlds. Also, we want machines that make thoughts real – another little job no one has done.

'But mostly we would open *hyperspace* – not use it just for rapid coastal trips, navigating only its surge-troubled fringes and keeping always in sight, however dimly, the shores and headlands of our own particular cosmos . . . but boldly sail beyond the universal shelf into the deep unknown with its vaster storms. That is a task for galaxies, not for planets – one or a hundred – though we will take our chances if we must.

'We think that countless cosmoses besides our own ride in the whirlwind void of hyperspace – a billion trillion scraps in the tornado, a billion trillion snowflakes in the storm. These won't be cosmoses like ours, we think, but built of different basic particles – or never particles at all, but ever-changing continuities. Worlds of solidity or holes in that. Worlds without light. Worlds in which light may move as slow as spoken words or swift as thought. Worlds in which bits of matter grow on thought as here mind seems to grow on molecules.

'Worlds with no wall between mind and mind, and worlds that are more prison-celled than ours. Worlds where thought is real and every beast's a god. A fluid universe – its planets bubbles – and worlds that branch in time like mighty vines.

'Worlds in which space is crossed with spiderwebs instead of flecked with stars – cosmos of vines or roads. A cosmos with solids but no gravity, worlds of dimensions more and less than ours, worlds different in every basic law – chromatic scales of cosmoses, spectra of creation.

'Or if we find no worlds in hyperspace, then build them there! – create the monster particle that births a cosmos, bursting from this cosmos as from a chrysalis, no matter if this cosmos be destroyed.

'So much for our larger aims. Our smaller ones: a screen for all we do. Privacy for our planet and our thoughts. Weapons as we may need them. Free research, as secret as we want it. No inspection! The right to take our planet where we will, even if there's no orbit waiting us which we have paid the rent on. To live between the stars if we so choose, out in the chilly, sunless wilderness, burning the prairie grass of hydrogen – or in the oceanic spatial deeps that lie between the island galaxies. The right always to travel hyperspace, now reserved for government and police. The right to take a chance, the right to suffer. The right to be unwise, the right to die.

'These aims are hateful to the government, which values every frightened mouse and falling sparrow as equal to a tiger burning bright. The government wants a police station winking blue by every sun, a cop pounding a beat around each planet, squad cars roaming the interstellar dark – fuzz everywhere, blurring the diamond-pristine, lucent stars.

'Millennia ago the government began to nibble at our freedoms – we Wild Ones, we Recalcitrants, we Untamed.

We banded on one planet of our own, won some prestige and powers, kept up our screens, lived our own lives, seemed to be gaining ground – only to find we'd made ourselves a single easy target for the police.

'A century ago we all were put on trial. Soon it was clear the case would go against us: no privacy, no secret research, no hyperspatial travelling, no chance to solve the universe's problems or our own.

'Surrender then – or die? We cut and ran.

'Since then it's been a never-ending chase. The Hounds of Heaven always on our track: planet pursued by planets untiring. No spot in all the cosmos safe for us. No outback far enough in all the galaxies, except the hyperspatial storm we have not mastered – reality's hurricane.

'Think of the sea as being hyperspace, its surface as the universe we know, its ships as planets, we, a submarine.

'We surface near some solitary sun not yet built up with artificial orbs. Then *they* appear, and we must dive again. Sometimes we stay too long, must fight a battle before we vanish in the void's cruel dark. We've blown up three suns just for diversions! Those novas are in distant galaxies. We may have killed a planet; can't be sure.

'Sometimes our cold pursuers make a truce and plead with us a while, and make us offers before they aim their killing bombs and rays – hoping we'll see the arc light of their reason that glares always above the cosmic prison yard.

'Twice we risked all to find another cosmos – cut loose in hyperspace and sailed off blind. But by some twist of hyperspatial gusts we were brought back to this same universe – enchanted thorn-forest around a castle, or tunnel ending by some trick of space inside the same jailyard that it was dug from.

'We are the Vanderdecken Planet of the Cosmos, making our knight's tour round the universe – but always comes the untiring pursuit along the crooked curves of hyperspace.

'We try to keep our standards, but we slacken. We didn't need to hurt your planet, Paul! – or so I think, I really can't be sure – I'm but a servant on the Wanderer. But though I can't be sure, I'll say this now: I hope before we harm one creature more, we plunge for ever into the dark storm. They say the third time you drown – May that be so!'

Her voice changed and she cried out sharply: 'Oh, Paul, we're charging around with all these beautiful dreams and yet all we can do is hurt people. Should you wonder that we're falling in love with death?'

Tigerishka broke off. After a bit, her voice neutral yet tight, as if she had drawn into herself, she said: 'There, I've told the monkey everything now. The monkey may feel superior to the cat, if he wishes.'

Very quietly, Paul drew and let out a deep breath. His heart was thudding. At another time he might question Tigerishka's story and his understanding of it, but now it simply stood there as she had told it, as if the stars beneath him were an emblazoning of it – a diamond script spelling only what she had said.

This fantastic eyrie was so like the viewpoint of dream, so like what is lightly called 'the mind's eye', that Paul could hardly say whether he were living only in his fancy or in the whole great starry cosmos; for once, imagination and reality were seamlessly mated.

Pushing his shoulders from the great warm window with less effort than a sigh, he looked sideways and down at the fantastic figure beside him, seeming in silhouette more than ever like a slim woman costumed for a cat ballet. Her hind legs were sprawled out, her forepaws folded together to cushion her chin, so that her head was up and he saw in black outline the snub nose, the height of her forehead, and the spearpoints of her ears. Her tail arched off beyond her, where its tip twitched in a slow rhythm against the stars. She looked like a slim black sphinx.

'Tigerishka,' he said softly, 'there was once a long-haired monkey who lived hungry and died young. His name was Franz Schubert. He wrote hundreds of monkey songs – pongo ballads and ape laments. One of them was to words written by an altogether forgotten monkey called Schmidt von Lübeck. That monkey song strikes me now as if it had been written for you and your people. At least, it's named for your planet – *Der Wanderer* . . . The Wanderer. I'll sing it for you. . . .'

He began, '*Ich komme von Gebirge her* . . .

'No,' he said, breaking off, 'let me put it in my own language and change some of the pictures just a little, to fit better, without changing any of the key lines or the feeling.'

The words and phrases he wanted came effortlessly.

He heard a soft rustling wail, all exactly pitched, in more voices than one, and he realized that Tigerishka was lifting the piano accompaniment from his mind and reproducing it with a lonelier beat than even the piano gets.

After the sixth bar, he came in:

> I come here from the stars alone,
> The way is twisted, the deeps moan.
> I wander on, am seldom gay,
> And keep on asking, 'What's the way?'
> All space is dark, the suns are cold,
> The flowers are pale and life is old.
> Talk that's not noise is getting rare –
> I am a stranger everywhere.
> Where are you, world that's all my own? –
> Longed for and sought, but never known;
> The cosmos that's as green as hope,
> One fiercely flowered starward slope;
> The world where all my friends can walk,
> My dead stand up, nor white as chalk,
> The universe that talks my talk –
> Where are you?
> I wander on, am seldom gay,
> And keep on asking, 'What's the way?'
> A ghostly answer comes from space:
> 'There where you are not – there's your place.'

When the last line was sung, and Tigerishka had hummed the accompaniment out to its end, she sighed and said softly: 'That's us, all right. He must have had a little cat in him, that Schubert monkey – and that Schmidt monkey, too. You've got a little cat in you, Paul. . . .'

He looked for a moment at the slim, star-edged figure beside him and then he reached out a hand that was star-edged, too, and laid it on her shoulder. He sensed no tightening, no anger, under the faintly warm, dry, short soft fur. After a moment, although it was nothing he'd consciously planned –

284

perhaps the fur was giving cues to his fingers – he began to scratch gently the curving margin between shoulder and neck, exactly as he might have done to Miaow.

For a while she did not move, although he thought he felt muscles relaxing under the fur. Then there was the faint murmur of a barely-breathed purr – just a flutter of sound – and she leaned her head against his hand so that her ear brushed his wrist. He shifted his kneading towards the back of her neck and she raised her head, rolling it from side to side with a deeper fluttering purr. Then she rolled her body away from him a quarter turn, and for a moment he thought it was to tell him to stop, but quickly discovered it was only that she wanted to be scratched under the chin. And then he felt a silky finger press against the back of his neck and draw smoothly down his body and he realized it was the tip of her tail caressing him.

'Tigerishka?' he murmured.

'Yes, Paul. . . .' she answered faintly. With a tiny dragging of elbow and knee against the warm transparency he drifted against her, and his arms met around her slim, brushy back and, while the tail-tip continued to caress, he felt her velvet pads resting lightly against his spine with only the ghosts of claws at their tips. He heard Miaow mewing plaintively. 'She jealous. . . .' Tigerishka breathed with the faintest chuckle as her cheek brushed against his, and he felt her harsh narrow tongue lightly touch his ear and begin to scrub against the back of his neck.

Up to this moment he had done everything quite gravely, as if his every gesture were part of a ritual that he must get just right and never be excited, but now safely welded to this fantastic feline Venus in Furs the excitement did come, and the images began to flood up into his mind, and he let go altogether, though strangely without losing control. For the images came with a queer orderliness as when his mind had first been riffled through by Tigerishka, but now they came slowly enough so that he could see them all clearly, through and through. They were pictures of men, women, and beasts. They were pictures of erotic love, rape, torture, and death – but he realized that even the deaths and the tortures were only

to underline the intensity of the contacts, the exquisite viola-
tion of all bodily taboos, the completeness of the togetherness;
they were the inward décor for the actions of two bodies.
These pictures alternated regularly with mind-filling symbols
like elaborate jewels and patterned enamellings, or meaningful
shapes in a richly bright kaleidoscope. After a long while the
symbols began to dominate the pictures; they began to throb
like great drums, to shiver and resound like great cymbals;
there was a feeling of the universe around, of darting out
towards it in all directions, of outspreading to totality in one
great series of building and diminishing surges that went
plunging through the stars to velvet darkness.

After a space he came slowly floating up out of the infinite
softness of that bottomless black bed, and there were the
stars again, and Tigerishka lifted up a little above him so that
very faintly, by starlight, he saw the violet of her petalled
irises and the bronzy green of her cheeks and her mulberry
lips parted, careless that she showed her whitely-glinting
fangs, and she recited:

> Poor little ape, you're sick again tonight.
> Has the shrill, fretful chatter fevered you?
> Was it a dream-lion gave you such a fright?
> And did the serpent Fear glide from the slough?
> You cough, you moan, I hear your small teeth grate.
> What are those words you mutter as you toss?
> War, torture, guilt, revenge, crime, murder, hate?
> I'll stroke your brow, poor little ape – you're cross.
> Far wiser beasts under far older stars
> Have had your sickness, seen their hopes denied,
> Sought God, fought Fate, pounded against the bars,
> And like you, little ape, they some day died.
> The bough swings in the wind, the night is deep.
> Look at the stars, poor little ape, and sleep.

'Tigerishka,' Paul wondered with a sleepy puzzlement, 'I
started to write that sonnet years ago, but I could get only
three lines. Did you –'

'No,' she said softly, 'you finished it by yourself. I found
it, lying there in the dark behind your eyes, tossed in a
corner. Rest now, Paul. Rest. . . .'

Chapter 37

When the saucer students reached the crossroads, the problem of which route to take was solved for Hunter by circumstances. The entry to Mulholland was blocked by three sleekly expensive though much-muddied cars of the fashionable dragon design. Their occupants had got out and were clustered together, probably to argue about which direction to take on Monica Mountainway. Though somewhat muddied like their cars, they looked to be sleekly expensive people – probably Malibu folk.

So, to take Mulholland would take time, and Hunter felt that his little two-vehicle cavalcade had none of that to spare, for the pursuit from the Valley and inland 101, after hanging back for some while in an ominous chorus of revvings and honkings, was at last catching up.

Monica Mountainway ran straight here for three-quarters of a mile through the blackly burned-over central heights of the Santa Monica mountains. The Corvette and the truck had hardly covered half of the straight when two sports cars, packed to the sides, came around the last turn abreast, and more behind them. Hunter slowed the Corvette a little and waved the truck on. Hixon remembered instructions and roared past him. Hunter got a flash of the men's grim faces in the back: Fulby, Pop, Doddsy, and Wojtowicz – and McHeath crouching with the one rifle they had left.

The women in the car with Hunter were tensely silent. Ann beside him hugged tight to her mother.

Then he got another flash of faces, this time those of the Malibu folk standing by their expensive cars and looking surprised and rather pained, as if to say, 'What bad manners to rush past us without so much as a wave – and in these catastrophic times when togetherness is mandatory!'

Hunter didn't exactly wish them evil, but he did hope they'd divert and delay a bit the crazy pursuit from the Valley. When he heard brakes behind him and then a shot, he drew back his lips in a grimace that was half satisfaction, half guilt.

287

Hixon's truck was disappearing around the first of a series of hairpin turns leading upward, which Hunter remembered from yesterday's trip. He scowled and squinted ahead, the sinking greenish-white sun in his eyes, and he began to hunt for a certain configuration of road also remembered from yesterday.

He found it at the second of the sharp turns: a clutch of big boulders on the inside of the U-curve. He slammed to a stop just beyond it and jumped out.

'The momentum pistol!' he demanded of Margo, got it, and scrambled up the steep, acidly odorous, blackly burned slope until he was behind the boulders. He pointed the gun at them and fired. For the first two seconds he was afraid they weren't going to move and the last charge be wasted for nothing, but then they turned over, grating together loudly, went thumping down the slope, and thudded ponderously into the asphaltoid.

He dashed forward after them and peered down through the mounting dust to see if an adjustment shot would be needed, but they blocked the road perfectly.

From above came a faint cheer and looking up he saw the truck moving along a stretch two hairpin turns farther on. He ran back to the car. Before he tossed the grey pistol back to Margo, he quickly checked the scale on the grip and saw there was at least a bit of violet still showing. As he drove off he heard brakes squeal again behind them, and angry shouting.

Ann said, 'Those people won't be able to use this road now, will they?'

'Nobody will be able to use it, dear,' Rama Joan told her.

'Or so we hope,' Margo put in a bit sardonically from the back seat. 'Was it a good job, Ross?'

'A real bank-to-bank choke-up,' he told her curtly. 'Two of the rocks it'll take a derrick to move.'

Ann persisted: 'I meant the nice people we passed standing beside their cars.'

'They had their own road, the one they came on,' Hunter lashed out harshly. 'They had their chance to turn around and use it to get away. If they didn't, well, they were damned rich-bitch fools!'

Ann moved away from him, closer to her mother. He lashed at himself inwardly for taking out his feelings on a child. Doc hadn't been that way.

'Professor Hunter did absolutely right, Ann,' Wanda put in with a smug positiveness from the other back seat. 'A man always has to think first of the women with him and their safety.'

Rama Joan said softly to Ann: 'The gods always had problems about how to use their magic weapons, dear. It's all in the myths.'

Hunter, his smarting eyes fixed on the snakelike road, wanted to tell them both to shut up, but he managed not to.

It was a good twenty minutes before they caught up with the truck. Hixon had stopped just short of another side road.

'It says, "To Vandenberg",' he called down, pointing ahead to a sign, as the Corvette drew up beside him. 'I figure it leads more direct to Vandenberg through the hills. Since I guess we're going there, to find this Opperly and all, I think we ought to take it. Save us those miles along the coast highway.'

Hunter stood up in the seat. The side road looked all right, the first short stretch of it, asphaltoid like the one they were on. He thought for a couple of seconds.

In the pause, a profound sound, soft as a sigh, passed overhead travelling from the southeast. None of the saucer students had the dictionary that would translate it into the vanishing three and a half hours ago of the Isthmus of Rivas, Don Guillermo Walker, and José and Miguel Araiza.

Hunter shook his head and said loudly: 'No, we'll keep on Monica Mountainway. We were over it yesterday and we *know* it's O.K. – no falls or anything. A new road's an unknown quantity.'

'Yeah?' Hixon commented. 'I see you finally took my advice about using the gravity gun to block off those nuts.'

'Yes, I did,' was all Hunter could think of to say, and he didn't say it pleasantly.

'Then there's the tide, as Doddsy's reminded me,' Hixon went on. 'Along the Coast Highway we've got to worry about that.'

'If we get there before sunset it'll be O.K. Low tide's at five p.m.,' Hunter told him. 'That is, if the tides are sticking anywhere near their old rhythm, which they were doing yesterday.'

'Yeah – if,' Hixon said.

'*Anywhere* we reach the coast we'll have the tides to contend with,' Hunter retorted. His nerves were snapping. 'Come on, let's get going,' he ordered. 'I'll take the lead from here.'

He sat down and drove off along Monica Mountainway. After a bit Margo said reassuringly: 'Hixon's following you.'

'He'd damn well better!' Hunter told her.

For forty hours the Wanderer had been raising higher and higher tides, not only in Earth's crust and seas, but also in her atmosphere – a tide four times greater than the daily heat-tide caused by the sun warming the air. Also, the volcanoes and evaporation from the greatly widened tidal zone had been making their unprecedented contributions to tomorrow's weather. Vortexes were forming in the disturbed air. Storms were brewing. In the Caribbean, up across the Celebes, Sulu, and South China Seas, and in a dozen other critical areas, the wind was rising as it had never risen on Earth before.

The *Prince Charles* was boldly atom-steaming southeast by the port of Cayenne. Darkly silhouetted against the wild sunset, Cape d'Orange told the great ship it was passing the mouth of the Oyapock River and nearing that of the Amazon. Captain Sithwise sent messages to the four insurgent captains imploring them to head out into the South Atlantic, away from all land. The messages were sneered at.

In one of the areas yet unruffled by the Wanderer winds, Wolf Loner scanned through the greying overcast for Race Point, or Cape Ann, or even for the one-four-three I L-O-V-E Y-O-U wink of the Minot's Ledge Light, or the sober six-second double flash of the Graves Light in Boston's Outer Harbour. He knew he should be nearing the end of his voyage, but he had noticed some garbage and odd wreckage floating past the *Endurance* and he hadn't calculated he was *that* close to Boston. However, there was nothing to do but keep watch and sail on.

Barbara Katz took the small telescope and climbed on top of the stalled Rolls to scan around over the low tops of the mangrove forest stretching out to either side of the narrow, tide-littered road. There was only the yellow afterglow of the sunset left to see by, reflected from the clouds rapidly moving in on a chilly southeast wind. The weather had changed completely in the last twenty minutes.

Hester stuck her head out of the back and whispered up loudly: 'Stop pounding around up there, Miss Barbara. You 'sturb what little power of life Mr K got left.'

Helen was squatting to hand tools to Benjy under the back of the car, where he was trying to free the inside of the left wheel from a great length of heavy wire that it had somehow picked up and wound tightly around itself, coil on coil, and which had only been noticed when the wheel jammed.

Benjy crawfished out and squatted down beside Helen, and after he'd breathed hard and rested his head in his hands a bit, he shook it and said: 'I don't know if I can free it. I ain't got proper clippers, and that wire on there just solid like. Must be wrap around two hundred times.'

To Barbara, scanning around from the roof and trying to shift her feet as little as possible as she braced herself against the wind, the wonder was that Benjy had been able to get the car going at all after its drowning, and that they had actually managed to drive a whole skidding, spitting, backfiring hour north before this new trouble had come.

Hester leaned out to say harshly: 'You *better* free it, Benjy. This the lowest-lookin' region we been yet, and these twisty little trees ain't no good for roosting.'

'Hes, I don't think I can. Not in less than two-three hours, anyway.'

'Hey!' Barbara called down to them, her voice excited. 'Down the road – not more than a mile – I can see – sticking out of the treetops – a white triangle! I think we're saved!'

'Now what good is a white triangle to us, child?' Hester demanded.

'Benjy,' Barbara called, 'do you think you could figure out a stretcher for Mr K – or carry him for a mile?'

'Well,' he called back, 'I done just about everything else.'

Bagong Bung crouched calf-deep in fish-stinking bottom-muck and shovelled into it frantically with a short-handled infantry spade. Every now and then he'd drop the spade to scrabble in the mud for something muck-coated and small which he'd thrust without inspection into a cloth bag and go on shovelling.

There were jellyfish weals on his legs, and his left hand was puffy where a shell had stung it, but he paid no attention to these hurts though he would occasionally spare a moment to drive his spade viciously through some sinister-looking worm, or knock aside a green crab that came crawling too close.

He was doing his spading almost in the centre of a sharp-ended lozenge seventy feet long and twenty wide, intermittently outlined by black, rotted wood crusted with shells and coral. It mightn't be the *Lobo de Oro*, but it certainly looked like the remains of some old ship.

Fifty feet away Cobber-Hume stood bent over on a hatch cover from the *Machan Lumpur* furiously working a bicycle pump. The pump was attached to a bright orange life raft that was hardly a quarter inflated. Two small orange cylinders tossed aside were of the gas that should have inflated the raft effortlessly, but hadn't.

Another fifty feet beyond him the *Machan Lumpur* lay flat on her side, showing all of her pitifully rusted, weed-draped bottom.

The new-risen sun intermittently cast grotesquely tall shadows of the two men and the little steamer across the tide-drained floor of the Gulf of Tonkin and illumined the Wanderer setting in the west in her bull's-head face, which Bagong Bung called *besar sapi* – 'big cow'.

Ragged clouds were scudding north with a wild swiftness, driven by a wind that moaned around the toppled Tiger of the Mud. A sudden gust took Cobber-Hume by surprise, and he staggered and slipped about on his none too stable pumping platform.

Bagong Bung paused with elbows on knees and panted for breath. Then '*Lekas, lekas!*' he cried reprovingly at himself and began to shovel again. His spade brought up a sea-eaten angle of wrought iron which might have been the corner of a chest and that set him working still faster.

Cobber-Hume shouted earnestly: 'You better quit mucking for loot, *sobat*, and get some tucker and fresh water *lekas* out of the "Lumpy" or give me a hand with this ruddy pumping. When the tide comes she'll be a bloody bitch, and this wind'll bring her faster, and then all the golden wolves in the world won't help us – or even a platinum dingo!'

But all Bagong Bung would answer was, '*Lekas, lekas!*'

The little Malay shovelled and scrabbled, the big Australian pumped, the clouds sped thicker between Earth and the new-risen sun, the wind whistled.

Barbara Katz shouted over the wind: 'There it is!'

The same lightning flash that showed the upper mangrove branches lashing against the dark speeding clouds also revealed the white triangle of the prow of a sailboat sticking out at least fifteen feet overhead from between two of the close-crowding trees.

Barbara shifted the heavy thermos jug to her left hand and the big flashlight to her right and switched it on as she walked towards the trees under the prow. It showed the deep keel jammed between the lower branches of three of the mangroves.

Benjy laid down old KKK in his blanket on the road.

Hester and Helen set down their bags and knelt anxiously beside the old man.

Benjy came up behind Barbara. He was panting. 'Shine her – on the hull,' he managed to say.

They pushed their way through the undergrowth, shining the flashlight upward on one side of the keel, then on the other. Barbara made out the boat's name: *Albatross*.

'Don't seem to be no holes in her,' Benjy said after a bit, speaking close to Barbara's ear. 'Reckon her mast must be broke off short, though, or you'd have seen it. I think she float with the tide. Maybe she jam too tight, but I don't think so. I can climb up by the branches, and then I got this to help you all up.' He touched the rope slung in loops around his chest.

The wind died a little and he cupped his hands around his mouth and shouted up: 'Hello! Anybody aboard?'

The lull in the wind held for two seconds more, then as it

rose again, Benjy said: 'Seem to me I hear a wailing then, different from the wind.'

'So did I,' Barbara replied, her teeth chattering – mostly from the cold, she told herself. She flashed her light straight overhead. 'Oh, my God!'

Poking out over the side of the boat in the middle of the flashlight beam was a tiny white furious face with mouth open wide.

'It's a little kid!' Benjy cried.

'Be ready to catch him, Benjy,' Barbara cried.

'It's a baby!' Helen yelled, coming up behind them. She waved her hand at the little wailing face. 'You stay up there now, baby! Don't you drop. We a-coming!'

Sally Harris and Jake Lesher cringed from the downdraught of the big rotors which whipped their clothes and made them squint their eyes, and which wildly blew about the charcoal-starter flame they'd fired in the barbecue bowl as an SOS beacon.

It was dark but clear, and the golden and purple beams of the Wanderer rising in its dinosaur face twinkled from black wavelets almost level with the penthouse patio floor and occasionally foaming over it, but the wind from the rotors drove the foam back.

The big helicopter masked the grey sky overhead and its rotors cut darkened circles in it.

A white rope-ladder came snaking down towards them and with it a big voice that called: 'I got room for only one more!'

Jake snagged the ladder with one hand and lunged for Sally with the other, but the flames were between them, and as she started past she knocked the barbecue bowl over ahead of her, and the hot fuel hissed against the water and went up in a great blinding sheet, driving her back. An instant later all flame was gone, but now the ladder was tugging Jake away. He turned and grabbed the lowest rung with both hands and pulled himself clear. His feet skimmed the patio floor. The next moment he dropped off and tumbled in a heap against the balustrade, the wavelets foaming around him.

The helicopter dipped violently. The wavelets cringed from its rotors, which almost touched them. The ladder fell away from the helicopter and floated on the wavelets like the skeleton of a giant centipede. The 'copter lifted and beat off north without another word.

Jake scrambled to his feet and watched its small lights grow tinier.

Sally came behind him. 'Why'd you let go, Jake?'

'I was afraid I'd crack my shins against the railing,' he told her self-disgustedly. 'I couldn't help it.'

She clung to him.

Chapter 38

As Hunter steered the Corvette slowly down the next to the last hill to the Coast Highway, the emerald sun setting on the watery horizon was still bright enough to show what looked like at least a mile of new beach stretching out beyond the old one to the edge of a calm sea. He grinned around at the others, his nerves untouched by the eeriness of their green-lit faces. He had a childish impulse to shout to Hixon in the truck just behind: 'What'd I tell you? Dead low or near it! – I hit it on the nose!'

'Look, Mommy,' Ann said, 'a vine growing across the road.'

It couldn't be that, Hunter knew, but it was some sort of vegetable debris, perhaps a branch torn down and blown there by yesterday's rainstorm. There was the faintest popping sound as the tyres rolled across it. The car skidded a little, and he straightened it and decreased speed. He did this quite automatically since like the others his attention was preoccupied by the degree to which the sea had receded. A mile now seemed a gross underestimate. He was at first amazed, then fascinated, finally plain awestruck.

Going downhill made the sun set faster. The green light grew gloomy. Although the ocean was so far away, its reek was strong and fishy. There was no wind, and save for the chug of the two motors there was a general hush. No cars were passing along the Coast Highway, he remarked to himself – and only then realized that the stupid part of his mind had still been expecting them.

They started down the last hill. Again the car skidded a fraction, and this time Hunter shifted into low as he straightened.

'I don't remember that ruined house,' Rama Joan said thoughtfully.

'And I don't remember the old boat out in the field,' Margo chimed in from behind her.

There was a sudden squawking. 'Look at those white birds pecking on the hillside,' Wanda observed shrilly. 'Why, I do believe they're gulls.'

'Here comes another vine,' Ann informed them. 'No, two. Oh, and a fish.'

At that word a horror gripped Hunter and the scene around him turned nightmarish, though for the moment he didn't quite know why – there was something dreadfully obvious his mind refused to see. Hixon was honking behind him. Did the fool want to pass? One – two – three – four. Four honks meant something, but he couldn't remember what, because now he realized that the horror was the illusion that they were travelling under the sea – the silence, the gloomy green light, the black road changing by imperceptible degrees to a feather-smooth slope of silty slime, the fishy reek ('. . . and a fish'), the seaweed bladders popping as they drifted across the two 'vines'. . . .

Four means stop, Doc had said. Instantly, but very gingerly, Hunter put on the brakes. At first the car hardly slowed at all. Then gradually it came to a halt, slewing around in spite of all his steering – came to a stop because its tyres were pushing up ridges of silt from a smooth coating an inch or more thick on the road.

He looked back along the road, simply because the car was now facing almost backwards, and he saw the truck, green in the last of the sunlight, stopped, unslewed, fifty feet or so behind. His hands were shaking on the wheel, and his heart was pounding.

It was Rama Joan who put the dreadfully obvious into words. She said, rather casually: 'We must have passed the highwater mark a quarter of a mile back.'

That was what was jolting his muscles and drumming his heart, Hunter realized – and as he realized it, his body began to quiet – simply the thought of the salt water that had been everywhere here and dozens of feet overhead, only six hours ago, leaving behind its sea-life and its sea-earth and its wreckage, the salt water that would be here again six hours from now – the thought of the tides of a few feet now sinking at low beneath the continental shelves and rushing back at high over the foothills of mountains.

The women were taking it with an incomprehensible calm, he thought. It would have seemed more natural if they'd been screaming.

Hixon and Doddsy and Wojtowicz and McHeath were coming down to them from the truck. They were walking oddly – stiff-legged and with elbows out. But, of course – the mud-coated road would be very slippery.

Hixon and Doddsy stopped beside him, while the others walked on. The Little Man said, looking out to sea: 'It's . . .' and then words evidently failed him.

The last sliver of green sun went under, but the whole sky stayed green – pale as a transparent wave to the west, dark as a forest to the east.

There was a rhythmic throbbing. Hunter realized that the engine of the Corvette was still turning over. He twisted the ignition key.

Only then did he realize that everyone else must be as stunned as he was.

A couple of minutes later they were all pulling out of their shock. Most of them had got out of the cars and were standing gingerly in the muck.

Wojtowicz and McHeath came trudging back uphill. The latter's pants were covered with mud and his shoes were big blobs of it. 'You can't take a car that way, Mr Hunter,' he said cheerfully: 'It gets feet deep on the highway.'

Wojtowicz nodded emphatically. 'The kid went further than I did,' he averred. 'Just look at him.'

'And all deposited in only three tides,' the Little Man said, shaking his head. 'Amazing.'

Hunter said bitterly: 'There's nothing else for it – we're going to have to go back and take that other road with the sign saying it led to Vandenberg.' He looked at Hixon. 'You were right.'

Hixon nodded. He surveyed the Corvette's mired wheels. 'I guess I can pull you out of this,' he said. 'I got a towline, and where I'm stopped the mud's a lot thinner and almost dry. I should have good enough traction. And I got chains if I need 'em.'

'I don't want to be a bird of ill omen,' the Little Man said, 'but when we go back there's the danger of running into those young goons from the Valley.'

Hixon shrugged. 'That's one of the chances we got to take. There's no other road. We'll hope Ross's roadblock held 'em and they headed for Malibu. I'll get the towline.'

Margo said to Hunter, 'It's only four miles to Vandenberg. Couldn't we walk it? Even with the mud it shouldn't take more than a few hours.'

Hunter said to her in a harsh whisper: 'Use your head. In less than a few hours the coast road will be under water. Even this spot'll be fifty or more feet deep.'

'Oh, I'm getting stupid,' Margo sighed wearily. 'I wish . . .' She didn't say what.

He inquired, rather bitterly: 'Isn't living by yourself in the new reality so much fun any more?'

She looked up at him. 'No, Ross,' she said, 'it's not.'

The Little Man interrupted: 'And when it comes to walking, we've got to remember we've got Ray Hanks to carry. I don't like his condition, Ross. I've given him all the barbiturates I think I should. He fell asleep as soon as the truck stopped, but he'll probably wake when it starts again. He's in a lot of pain.'

Just then Pop came limping up. 'Mr Hunter,' he said, 'I can't stand riding the back of that truck anymore. I'm all bent up.'

Hunter was about to give him a hot answer when Ida said:

'You can have my place in the cab. You men don't know how to care for Mr Hanks, and it's my job anyway.'

Hixon tossed down the end of the towline. 'Hitch it on your front end,' he directed Hunter. 'Think you can?'

'I'll do it,' said Wojtowicz, grabbing hold of it first.

'I imagine the Corvette's getting low on gas,' the Little Man said to Hunter.

'It is, Mr Dodd,' Ann called from beside her mother. 'I was watching the needle and it said empty.'

'I'll get one of the reserve cans,' the Little Man said.

Hunter nodded. He felt simultaneously furious and impotent. Everyone was taking charge for him. Doc would have found something humorous to say at this point, but he wasn't Doc. He looked at Margo, who was looking at the distant sea, and he felt a sullen hunger.

Sally Harris and Jake Lesher, blanket-wrapped, hooked their elbows for extra safety over the low ridge of the penthouse roof. Two feet below the eaves, the wavelets glittered richly with the beams from the Wanderer's needle-eye face, which Jake alternately called the Clutching Hand – for the coiled Serpent – and Pie in the Sky – for the Broken Egg.

'And we thought we could make a play of this,' Sally said softly.

'Yeah,' Jake echoed. 'We thought we could – a supercolossal spectacle. But we were still thinking indoors.'

Sally looked around at the black waters over Manhattan and at the few low, lonesome towers poking up from it here and there.

'Imagine, some of them still got lights,' she commented.

'Gas engines in their attics,' Jake explained. 'Or maybe batteries.'

'What's that one way down there?' Sally wondered. 'The Singer Building or Irving Trust?'

'What's the difference?'

'But I want to be able to remember exactly . . . or anyway, know exactly, if I'm not going to be able to remember.'

'Forget it, Sal. Look, I brought a flask of Napoleon. How about a snort?'

'You're sweet,' she said, touching his cold hand lightly with her own, no warmer. And then she sang very softly, as if not to disturb the mounting wavelets:

> Oh, I am the girl on Noah's Raft
> And you are my Castaway King.
> Our love is not as big as a wink
> Or one single hair from a silver mink –
> But you stayed with me and you found me a drink;
> Our love is a very big thing.

Richard Hillary and Vera Carlisle lay a distance apart on green hay taken from a small stack they'd found high in the Malvern Hills. Richard thought restlessly, *Last night straw, tonight hay. Straw, seedless and dry, for death. Hay, sour and sweet, for life.*

The Wanderer glared down on them from the west, again in its bloated-*X* face. The planet was becoming as dreadfully familiar as the face of a clock. Some three quarters of an hour ago, Vera had said: 'Look, it's half past *D*.'

It wasn't chilly. There was an almost warmish breeze from the southwest – eerie, unnatural, agitating.

One might well think that watching the bore of the Severn rush up its valley, like some white thunder-wall released by the tearing of an eighth seal in the Book of Revelation, would utterly outweary the senses. But, as Richard was now discovering, the senses do not work that way. Experiencing the almost unimaginable only makes them more acid-bittenly alive.

Or perhaps it was simply that they were both too tired, too aching with fatigue poisons, to sleep.

Vera had earlier told him her story. A London business-machine typist, she had been rescued from the roof of an office building during the second high, and had come all the way to the valley of the Severn in a small motorboat, which had navigated the standing highs as Richard had tramped and cadged rides across the muddy lows, only to be wrecked in the edge of the bore near Deerhurst, she alone of the boat's company surviving, as far as she knew.

A little while ago Richard had asked her to tell her story in more detail, but she had protested that she was much too tired. She had listened to the static on her transistor wireless for a while, and Richard had said: 'Throw that away.' She hadn't, but she'd turned it off. Now she was saying softly: 'Oh, I shall never sleep, never. My mind's revving and revving. . . .'

Richard rolled over and put his arm lightly around her waist, his face above hers, then hesitated.

'Go on,' she said, looking up at him with an oddly bitter smile. 'Or do you have sleeping pills?'

Richard thought for a moment, then said rather formally: 'Even if I did have them, I should much prefer you.'

She giggled. 'You're so stiff,' she said.

He pulled her to him and kissed her. Her body was tense and unyielding.

'Vera,' he said. Then hugging her determinedly, 'For a pet name I shall call you Veronal.'

She giggled again, more at him than appreciatively, he thought, but her body relaxed. Suddenly her fingers clutched at his back. 'Go on, try me,' she whispered throatily in his ear. 'I'm strong, strong sleeping medicine.'

Barbara Katz had first been depressed by the lowness and narrowness of the one little cabin of the *Albatross*, but now she was glad of those dimensions because it meant there was always a surface close at hand to brace herself against when the boat rocked or pitched farther than she'd been expecting it to. And the slightly-arched roof being so low somehow made it seem more secure whenever a solid wave-top banged down on it deafeningly.

The cabin was pitch dark except when lightning blazed in whitely through the four tiny portholes, or when Barbara used her flashlight.

Old KKK lay blanket-tied to one of the little bunks with Hester sitting braced at his head and holding the unknown baby. Helen stretched out in the other bunk, moaning and retching with seasickness, while Barbara was scrunched in at the foot of that bunk like Hester across from her. Every once in a while Barbara felt through a trap in the planking of the floor for water. So far she hadn't felt any to amount to much.

The *Albatross* had almost foundered before the west-rushing tide lifted it out of the grip of the mangroves. Then it had almost been keeled over by a taller tree. After that it had been rather fun, until the storm waves had got so high and wild that everyone except Benjy had been forced below.

After a long silence – that is, a long space of listening to nothing but the baby crying and the timbers straining and the waves and the wind hitting the boat – Barbara asked: 'How's Mister K, Hester?'

'He die a little while back, Miss Barbara,' the other replied. 'Hush now, baby, you had your canned milk.'

Barbara digested the information. After a while she said: 'Hester, maybe we should wrap him in something and put him up front – there's just enough room – and you should lie down in that bunk.'

'No, Miss Barbara,' Hester replied positively. 'We don't want to chance his hip get bust again or anything. He in good shape now, except he dead, and if he lie soft he stay that way. Then we got evidence we took the best care of him we could.'

Helen started up, crying: 'Oh Lord, there's a deader in the cabin! I got to get out!'

'Lie down, you crazy nigger!' Hester commanded. 'Miss Barbara, you hold her!'

There was no need. A fresh attack of seasickness stretched Helen out again.

A little later the motions of the *Albatross* became less violent. Solid water no longer thumped the roof of the cabin.

'I'm going to take some coffee up to Benjy,' Barbara said.

'No, you not, Miss Barbara.'

'Yes, I am,' Barbara told Hester.

When she'd cautiously slid aside the little hatch at the back of the cabin and stuck her head out, the first thing she saw was Benjy kneeling spread-legged behind the little wheel. The clouds had broken overhead, and through the narrow rift the Wanderer shone down in its bull's-head face.

She crawled out. Wind tore at her from the bow, but it wasn't too bad, so she slid the hatch shut and crawled back to Benjy.

He swigged coffee from the small thermos she'd brought and thanked her with a nod.

She peered around over the low coaming of the cockpit. The Wanderer, vanishing behind the clouds again, showed nothing by its last light but waves that looked very high indeed.

'I thought it was getting calmer,' she shouted to Benjy over the wind.

He pointed towards the bow. 'I find a mattress,' he shouted back, 'and tie one end of a rope to it and the other to the front end of this boat and throw her over. It hold the boat so she head into the wind and the waves steady-like.'

Barbara remembered the name for that: a sea anchor.

'Where do you think we are, Benjy?' she shouted.

His laughter whooped over the wind. 'I don't know if we in the Atlantic or the Gulf or what, Miss Barbara, but we still on top!'

Sally Harris and Jake Lesher climbed down from the penthouse roof. Despite the activity, they were shaking with cold. Beyond the balustrade the wavelets were sinking at a rate almost visible.

Sally looked into the living room by the light of the Wanderer in its jaws face, which she called Rin-Tin-Tin.

'It's a mess,' she told Jake. 'The furniture's tumbled every which way. The piano's got its legs in the air. The black rug's got waves in it, and all those soaked black drapes make the place look like a storm-tossed mortuary. Come on, let's hunt for driftwood or candles or something to make a fire. I'm freezing.'

Chapter 39

The Wanderer put on its yin-yang mask for a ninth time. For two full days it had tormented Earth with fire and floods and shakings and now with storms. Bagong Bung dropped his spade, snatched up his muddy sack, and dove for the orange life raft as it rushed by on a foam-crested step of water. Cobber-Hume grabbed at him. The four insurgent captains of the

Prince Charles, terrified by the hurricane winds that struck through the inky night from the east like ten thousand invisible planes buzzing them and by the tall regiments of waves marching under the winds like black grenadiers, steered the great atom-liner for safety into one of the mouths of the Amazon. Waves began to break over the *Albatross* again despite its sea anchor, but Barbara Katz wouldn't go below. A chill wind began to blow in gusts across Mr Hasseltine's penthouse patio, rippling thin pools of water there, and Sally Harris and Jake Lesher retreated once again to the soaked living room. By the masthead light of the *Endurance* Wolf Loner saw two corpses float by among the ever-thickening flotsam.

The saucer students' Corvette and truck, headlights peering, cautiously nosed their way along the mountain road that had signs pointing, at intervals, to Vandenberg Two. Twice already most of the huddling passengers had had to unkink and climb out to shovel and heave away rock-and-gravel slides not big enough to warrant expending the last charge in the momentum pistol. At any moment another earth-fall might show up in the watchful headlight beams of the Corvette. Chains clinked rhythmically on the truck's rear wheels.

The east breeze coming over the mountains at their back was mostly tepid – fortunately for people all bone-weary and all exposed, except for the Hixons and Pop in the cab of the truck.

Save for that of the motors and wheels, the only sound was a faint, rhythmic, hissing roar from ahead.

The Wanderer had risen two hours after sunset and now rode above the same eastward mountains in the cloudless slate-grey sky, its warm winy and golden light creating the illusion that it was the source of the friendly breeze. It was no longer quite spherical, however, but slightly gibbous, like the moon two days after full. A narrow black crescent cut off the rim of the purple half of its yin-yang face as, mimicking the movements of the moon it had destroyed, it moved east around the earth, or rather, around a point between the two planets. Loosely girdling its equator like a filmy diamond-studded scarf, the trophy-ring of moon fragments glittered and gleamed.

The road now mounted gently to a wide saddle, the sides of which rose in smooth earthen slopes to flat, low rock crests. The Corvette reached the top of the saddle, pulled to the right, and stopped with four rapid horn-beeps, dousing its lights. The truck pulled up beside it to the left, and did the same.

Most of the party had at one time or another in their lives had the experience of looking down on a fog or a low cloud layer from a mountainside or an airplane, and seeing the hilltops lifting up through it, and marvelling at how flat and far it stretched – a veritable ocean of clouds. Now the same persons had for a second or two or three the illusion that they were witnessing the same sight again, by Wanderer-light.

This illusory, nocturnal cloud-ocean began scarcely fifty yards beyond and no more than a dozen yards below them and it stretched to the western horizon, closely following to either side the contours of the hills. There was only one island, low and flat, but so big it stretched out of sight past the dark hillsides to the north. Red and white lights shone sparsely from this island and the Wanderer-light revealed two clusters of low, pale-walled, pale-roofed buildings. And already in the first moments of watching, there was a faint drone and a tiny red and green pair of lights slanting down from the south, as a small airplane landed on the island. A strait a quarter of a mile wide separated the island from the mainland.

Then the illusion faded and one by one the saucer students realized that it was not cloud-ocean that stretched to the horizon but salt ocean, not mist-water but solid-water sea, its waves breaking rhythmically against the hillside and the descending road fifty yards ahead; that the island was Vandenberg Two; and that the strait between covered among other things the Pacific Coast Highway where it swung inland of the Space Force base, home of the Moon Project – of Morton Opperly and Major Buford Humphreys, of Paul Hagbolt and Donald Merriam, though those last two were elsewhere now.

At the wheel of the Corvette, Hunter felt on his left shoulder fingers that lay lightly at first, but then gripped strongly. He put his right hand on top of the hand there and turned his head and looked at Margo's face – the yellow hair drawn flat, the long lips, the hungry cheeks, the dark eyes – and she looked back, expressionless, at him.

Without lifting his hand from hers he called up to the truck: 'We'll camp here by the sea. When the tide goes down we'll enter Vandenberg.'

Don Merriam gazed up the elevator shaft at the circle of sky swirling symphonically with a red-black storm, as if the colours had been chosen to match the fur of his conductor standing silently beside him.

The circle grew slowly, then rapidly, then the elevator stopped, and its floor was once more seamlessly part of the etched silver pavement.

Nothing seemed to have changed. The pillar of hurtling moonrock still towered like a grey pinnacle four times the height of Everest. Beyond the empty pavement the great plastic structures crouched off into the distance like an army of abstract sculptures. The pit yawned with its unsupported silver railings.

Then Don saw that only one saucer – coloured with a violet-yellow yin-yang – hovered beside the Baba Yaga. That stained moon-ship gleamed as if newly burnished, and instead of the ladder there hung below the hatch a stubby man-wide metal tube that looked telescoped.

Beyond the Baba Yaga, the Russian moon-ship gleamed freshly, too, and a similar extensible-looking metal tube projected outside its hatch, which was located near the nose.

The felinoid lightly touched Don's shoulder and said in his caressingly slurred English: 'We are taking you to an Earth friend. Your ship is fuelled and serviced, and it goes with us, but you will ride in mine at first. There will be a transfer in space. Have no fear.'

Paul Hagbolt woke up with a start. Tigerishka was snarling at him: 'Wake up! Get dressed. We've got a visitor!'

The start carried him a yard away from the window against which he'd been resting, so for the moment all he could do was grope around impotently in null gravity while he tried to get the sleep out of his eyes and mind.

The inner sun had been switched on again, and the windows were solid pink once more, creating with the flowers the effect of a combination conservatory and boudoir.

Tigerishka was jerking some flappy objects out of a door in the waste panel. She proceeded to throw them at him.

'Get dressed, monkey!'

One of them got hooked on her claws and she ripped it loose in a fury and hurled it after the others.

Paul, or rather his body, intercepted the objects without difficulty, since they were well aimed. They were his clothes, nicely laundered and smelling freshly of cotton and other fabrics, though there were no creases in his pants. He fumbled at them, saying in a voice still squeaky with sleep: 'But, Tigerishka –'

'I'll help you, you stupid ape!'

She coasted to him quickly and, grabbing the shirt, started to ram his foot into the arm of it.

'What's happened, Tigerishka?' he demanded, not helping her. 'After last night –'

'Don't ever mention last night to me, monkey!' she snarled. The shirt ripped, and she tried to shove his foot into the next garment she grabbed, which happened to be his coat.

'But you're acting as if you were angry and ashamed about what happened,' he protested, still ignoring her attempts to dress him.

She stopped what she was doing and grabbed him by the shoulders as they floated there and glared her violet-irised eyes into his.

'Ashamed!' she repeated vibrantly. Then, very coldly: 'Paul, have you ever masturbated a lower animal?'

He just stared back at her stupidly, feeling his muscles tighten, especially around the neck.

'Don't act so shocked!' she commanded irritably. 'It happens all the time on your planet. One way or another, you do it to get seed from bulls and stallions for artificial insemination . . . and so on!'

He said quietly: 'You mean that what happened last night wasn't a real embrace?'

She hissed at that, just like a cat, then said harshly: 'A real

307

embrace would have shredded your flimsy anthropoid genitals! I was silly, I was bored, I felt sorry for you. That was all.'

For a moment Paul saw clearly how a superbeast would at its level have neuroses just like those of a talking anthropoid, how it would suffer from attacks of irrealism, do the wrong thing, get bored, fritter away time and feelings. For a moment he realized how lonely and confused he himself would have to be to pretend to love a cat as if it were a girl, to fantasize an erotic passion for Miaow. . . .

But just then Tigerishka slapped him with her pads and snarled: 'Don't dream, monkey. Get dressed!'

The fragile bridge of understanding which his intuition had been building crashed, though this was not instantly apparent on the surface, for he continued as quietly as before: 'You mean that was the whole experience, that was all that last night meant to you? Just being "nice" to a pet?'

She said firmly: 'Last night my feelings were fully ninety per cent pity for you and boredom with myself.'

'And the other ten per cent?' he persisted.

She dropped her great eyes from his. 'I don't know, Paul. I just don't know,' she said very tautly, grabbing his coat again. Then, 'Oh, get dressed yourself,' she hissed exasperatedly and pushed off for the control panel. 'But be quick about it. Our visitor's almost at the door.'

Paul ignored that. A hot maliciousness was flooding up into his cold misery. He slowly pulled his coat sleeve off his foot. He said evenly: 'It seems to me that last night began with me treating *you* like a pet, scratching you under the neck and stroking your fur, and you were lapping it up, you were responding just like –'

The pink floor jumped up and bumped him, jarred his spine. She called: 'I've switched on earth-normal gravity so you'll be able to get dressed! Oh, if you had any idea of what it means to be cooped up this way with a repulsive bald body and with an utterly inferior mind and to have to wear out one's throat with the nonsense of sound-making. . . .'

Now at last he did begin to attend to his clothes, though without haste, locating his shorts and his pants and laying them out for pulling on. But at the same time his maliciousness was searching for something – anything, it didn't matter what – to hurl back at her. Rather quickly he found it.

'Tigerishka,' he said slowly, feeling unaccustomedly heavy but quite comfortable as he sat on the pink velvet floor and pulled on his shorts and reached for his trousers, 'you boast that you never miss a mental trick. Certainly your mind works much faster than mine. Presumably you have eidetic memory for everything that happens around you – including what you spy on in my mind. Yet last night when I mentioned the four crucial stellar photographs I'd seen – photographs of a planet making a false exit from hyperspace, I realize now – you assured me there could have been only two twist-fields involved, the first near Pluto, the second near Venus.

'Well, whatever you think, there *were* two other twist-fields represented, two other false exits.' At this point he felt her entering his mind. Nevertheless he went on: 'They were the second and fourth in the series, and they involved Jupiter and Luna.'

Her answer rather surprised him. She said curtly: 'You're right. I'll have to check with the Wanderer at once. It could be . . . what we're afraid of.' She turned sharply to the control panel. She was standing on her hind legs now in the same gravity that gripped Paul. 'You, welcome our visitor!'

A port like a manhole opened in the centre of the pink floor and, facing away from Paul, a man in the uniform of the U.S. Space Force pushed up through it. He lurched his elbows heavily against the rim as the artificial-gravity field took hold of him, but evidently this didn't startle him particularly, for he quickly boosted the rest of his body into the saucer.

Paul, barely into his shirt, stood up quickly too, getting a glimpse of the interior of a wide, corrugated-looking metal tube as the port closed.

The newcomer, having stared at Tigerishka, looked around.

'Don!'

'Paul!'

'I thought you were lost with the moon. How –'

'And I thought you were – I don't know what. But how –'

They were both clumsily silent, waiting for the other to begin. Then Paul realized that Don was looking him up and down curiously. He hurriedly zipped his pants and buttoned his shirt.

Don looked at Tigerishka, looked at her for quite some time. Then he looked at the flowers and the other furnishings. Then his gaze came back to Paul and he raised his eyebrows and spread his hands helplessly and grinned with the air of one who means, 'I don't care if the solar system's falling apart and we're in an impossible gravity field in an impossible flying saucer in the midst of space – *This is as funny as a bedroom farce!*'

Paul realized he was blushing. He felt enraged at himself.

Tigerishka looked around at them from the control panel just long enough to say rapidly: 'Greetings, Donald Barnard Merriam! Please excuse the monkey, he's ashamed of his nakedness. But I suppose you're ashamed, too. Really, you should both try fur!'

Chapter 40

For the saucer students it was a quarter past dinosaur, as Ann would have said, except she was asleep. By that token the Wanderer was about an hour and fifteen minutes higher in the sky than it had been when the Corvette and the truck had first drawn up side by side on the saddle to look at the high tide. Now late supper had been eaten, scrapes and scratches gotten rock-moving had been cleaned and bandaged, and more than half the saucer students were asleep in and around the two vehicles, wrapped, despite the relative mildness of the night, in coats, blankets, and the edges of the big tarpaulin.

Three figures still cozied up around the primus stove where they'd boiled water for coffee: Pop, curled up on his side like a pillbug and fingering his bad teeth through his parchmenty cheeks as solemnly and sourly as if God were a dentist and Pop preparing to sue him for malpractice; the Ramrod, sitting cross-legged in the easiest variant of the lotus position – right ankle atop left knee, right knee atop left ankle – and staring up at the dinosaur rotating east on the Wanderer as if that now rather phallic-looking golden beast were the navel of the cosmos; and the Little Man, squatting on his hams and writing up the events and observations of the day in his notebook by Wanderer-light.

Hunter, holding Margo's hand in his, she walking beside him, stepped up to the Little Man and touched him on the shoulder and said quietly, 'Doddsy, Miss Gelhorn and I are going up to the crest across the road. If there's a serious emergency: five horn blasts.'

The Little Man looked up and nodded.

From beyond the primus, Pop glanced at the blanket Margo was carrying and then turned his eyes away and blew through his lips a small, ugly, contemptuous sound, half cynicism, half angry disapproval.

The Ramrod withdrew from his contemplation to look down at Pop. 'Shut up,' he said softly and calmly. Then he looked at Hunter and Margo, and above them at the Wanderer, and a smile came to his fanatical, abstracted face, and while his right forefinger traced tiny Isis-loops on his right knee he said, 'Ispan shower blessings on your love.'

The Little Man bent his head to his note-jotting. His lips were compressed, as if to hide a grin and perhaps suppress a chuckle.

Hunter and Margo crossed the road. Ann and her mother were lying blanket-wrapped just beyond the shadow of the truck and it seemed to Hunter that Rama Joan was smiling at them open-eyed, but as he came closer he saw that her eyes were closed. Just then he became aware, from the corner of his eye, of a tall dark figure standing back in the shadow of the truck. Even its face was dark, shadowed by a black hat with brim turned down.

A shiver mounted Hunter's spine, because he was certain it was Doc. He wanted Doc to speak and show his face, but the figure only raised its hands to its hat and pulled it further down and drew back farther into the shadow.

At that instant Hunter felt Margo's fingers tighten hard on his, and he looked directly into the shadow of the truck. There was no longer a figure there.

They walked on, saying nothing to each other about it.

311

Wild grass crunched faintly under their feet as they mounted the slope in the grey midnight noon of the Wanderer. They were strongly aware of the sea invading the hills – the high tide at its stand fifty yards away, its waves creaming the hillside – and of the Wanderer invading the sky, or rather invading Earth's space and bringing its own dark, pearly sky with it, and of strangeness invading the life of all mankind, of all Terra.

They stepped on to a low stone ledge and from that to another, and there before them was a flat-topped rectangular grey rock big as a giant's coffin. Margo spread the blanket on it and they kneeled on it facing each other. They stared at each other intently, unsmilingly, or if their lips smiled at all they smiled cruelly, devouringly. The hushes between the surges of the surf were filled with the rhythmic poundings of their blood, louder than the steady sigh-crash of the sea itself. The hills seemed to echo those poundings and almost to move yielding with them, and the sky to resound. Margo zipped down her jacket, laying the momentum pistol beside it, and lifted her hands to her throat and began to unbutton her blouse, but Hunter took that work away from her, and she ran the fingers of her right hand up into his beard and made a fist of it, trapping the wiry hairs, and dug her knuckles into his chin. Then time seemed to stop, or rather to lose its directional urgency of movement; it became a place in the open where one stood rather than a low, narrow corridor down which one was hurried. The sea and the rocks and the hills and the sky and the cool enfolding air and the wide rich planet overhead all came alive in their ways, becoming fixtures of the room that is the mind, or – truer – the mind reaching out to embrace them. The more Hunter and Margo became aware of each other's bodies and each other, the more, not the less, intensely they became aware of everything around them, the largest and the least, even the tiny violet dash, scarcely an eighth of an inch long, in the scale on the grip of the momentum pistol – and aware of things unseen as well as things seen, the dead as well as the living. Their bodies and the heavens were one, the engorged sun wooed the dark moon-crescent and was at last received by it. The driving, punishing surf was in them, and the sea with all its swell and storm and certainty of calm. Time stretched out, passing with silent tread, for once not humming a death-spell but seamlessly joining death with life. Overhead the golden lingam beast swinging east through the dark purple became the back of the golden serpent coiled round the broken egg in the next hour-face of the Wanderer – the female serpent contending with and constricting about and finally crushing the male seed-bringer – while around about the great intruding planet the moon-fragments glittered and danced like the million sperm dance supplicatingly, vyingly, fiercely, about the ovum.

Don Merriam had given Paul Hagbolt a brief account of his experiences in space and aboard the Wanderer. It seemed to confirm the background of much that Tigerishka had told Paul and it revived in him something of the mood that she had induced in him by her story, though he was still shaken and hurt by the subsequent change in her feelings. Now he was telling Don what had happened to him and Margo on the night of the Wanderer's appearance – at the flying saucer symposium and by the gate of Vandenberg and in the earthquake waves – when Tigerishka interrupted sharply.

'Stop chattering, please! I have some questions for you.'

She was standing at the pinkly embowered control panel – had presumably been in silent contact with her superiors. Paul and Don were sitting on the pink floor, across which Miaow made periodic scampering sorties from the flower banks – evidently much intrigued or at least stimulated by the simulated terrestrial gravity.

'Have you two beings been well treated here and during your contacts with my people? Donald Merriam?'

He stared at her, thinking how much she resembled, except for the colouring of her fur, the felinoid he had seen catch a great topaz bird and drink its blood with the air of a ballerina nibbling at an after-theatre snack.

He said: 'After I escaped from the moon – wholly by my own efforts as far as I know – I was picked up by two of your ships, escorted to the Wanderer, kept in a comfortable room there for two days, apparently, then brought here. Nobody

313

talked to me much. I think my mind was turned inside out and inspected. In a dreamlike vision I was shown many things. That's about it.'

'Thank you. Now you, Paul Hagbolt, have you been well treated?'

'Well . . .' he began, smiling at her questioningly.

'A simple yes or no will do!' she snapped.

'Then – yes.'

'Thank you. Question two: Have you seen evidence of your Earth people being given aid in their tidal troubles?'

Paul said: 'There were those things you showed me over Los Angeles and San Francisco and Leningrad: fires put out by rain, tides being driven back by some sort of repulsion field.'

Don said: 'I think I saw television pictures of the same sort of thing in one huge room of the Wanderer during my vision or dream.'

'It was a true vision,' she assured him. 'Question –'

'Tigerishka,' Paul interrupted, 'does all this have something to do with the two star photographs that don't match the Wanderer's false exits from hyperspace? Are you people afraid the pursuit will catch up with you, and are you preparing a defence of your actions here?'

Don looked at him in surprise – Paul had as yet told him nothing of Tigerishka's story – but she said simply, 'Stop chattering, monkey – I mean, being. Yes, that is possible. But, question three: So far as you know, have your companions suffered by reason of the Wanderer?'

Don said harshly: 'My three companions at Moonbase were killed when Luna broke up.'

She nodded curtly and said: 'One of them may have survived – it's being checked. Paul Hagbolt?'

He said. 'I was just telling Don about that, Tigerishka. Margo and the saucer people were O.K. when I last saw them – I mean at least they were alive, though in the wash of some earthquake waves which you'd done something to make smaller. But that was two days ago.'

'They're still alive,' Tigerishka asserted. Her violet eyes twinkled and she shaped her lips in a thin, humanoid smile as she added: 'I've been keeping my eye on them – you mortals never realize how much the gods worry about you: all you see are the floods and the earthquakes. However I won't ask either of you to accept my word for that, I'll show you! Stand up, please, both of you. I am going to send you down to Earth to see for yourselves.'

'You mean in the Baba Yaga?' Don asked as they complied. 'As I'm sure you know, it's linked to this saucer now by a space tube and I was given the idea that I – I mean that we now, Paul and myself – would be able to use it to return to Earth. Which the Baba Yaga can manage, I think, if we are released above the atmosphere with no orbital speed to –'

'No, no, no,' she interrupted. '*Later* you'll do that – in an hour or two, say, and at your Vandenberg Two space field – which is just five hundred miles below us now, by the way – but *now* I send you there a much quicker way. Face the control panel! Stand close together!'

Don commented with a somewhat grim chuckle, 'It's as if you were going to take a snapshot of us.'

Tigerishka said, 'That's just about what I am going to do.'

The sunlight in the saucer began to dim. Miaow, as if scenting excitement, came scampering out of the flowers and rubbed around their ankles. On a sudden impulse Paul scooped up the little cat.

Margo and Hunter had dressed and folded the blanket and started down the hillside arm in arm, at one with each other and the cosmos in the afterglow of their lovemaking, when they heard a voice calling faintly: 'Margo! Margo!'

Below them at the foot of the slope lay the camp around the two cars. No one was stirring. The Wanderer-light streaming down from the serpent-egg face showed only wrapped, recumbent figures. The pool of shadow by the truck had grown smaller as the Wanderer mounted the sky, yet it was still there.

But the voice did not seem to come from the camp, but from the air.

They looked towards the sea and it had sunk ten yards or more, leaving a wide band of hillside darkly stained where the high tide had been. What water now lay between them and Vandenberg Two was more like a wide river, with islets showing in it here and there. Their gaze mounted from the point, and against the dark grey sky they saw two faintly luminous figures of men descending the air, erect yet with unmoving feet. The figures descended at a slant, floating swiftly and weightlessly, and vanished into the hillside midway between them and the camp.

Hunter and Margo held each other tight, their skin chilling and prickling, for both remembered the figure they had seen in the shadow of the truck, and both had the thought that one of the weightless figures was Doc – and the whole sight another, though bolder, ghostly manifestation, or a continuation of the first.

When nothing more happened they went a few steps farther down the hill, and then Margo looked down and gasped with horror and retreated a sudden two steps as if from a snake, dragging him back with her.

From the ground in front of them rose two heads of men, their figures earth-encumbered to the shoulders. The features of the heads were blurred, though one misty face seemed namelessly familiar to Hunter. Necks and shoulders identified one as a uniformed spaceman, one – the familiar one – as a civilian. The thought flashed through Hunter's mind of how much this was like Ulysses' encounter with the spirits of the dead in the Underworld, these two spirits summoned not by the hot shed blood of the bull, but by the pounding blood of his and Margo's lovemaking.

Then the two figures rose out of the ground, not by their own efforts, for they moved neither hand nor foot, but drawn up by a power outside them until their feet touched the surface of the ground, yet not quite as if they stood but rather floated there, facing Hunter and Margo six feet away. Then what was blurred came into focus and Margo gasped: 'Don! Paul!' although she clutched more tightly at Hunter as she did so, and as he, too, recognized the second figure.

The Paul-figure smiled and opened its lips, and a voice which synchronized perfectly with the lip movements yet did not come from the throat said: 'Hello, Margo and Professor . . . Excuse my poor memory. We're not ghosts. This is merely an advanced form of communication.'

In similar fashion the Don-figure said: 'Paul and I are talking to you from a small saucer out in space, between you and the Wanderer, but nearer the earth. It's wonderful to see you, Margo, dear.'

'That's right,' Paul chimed in. 'I mean about being in the saucer. It's the same one that picked me up. See –' He lifted something in his hands. 'Here's Miaow!'

The little cat rested quietly for a moment, then its lips writhed back, there was a synchronized spitting hiss and it vanished into the darkness in a whirl of its own little limbs.

The Paul-figure scowled and momentarily raised a hand to his lips and sucked at it, then explained: 'She got excited. It's all a little too weird for her.'

Margo let go of Hunter and put his arms away from her and stepped forward, reaching a hand towards Paul but raising the other to Don's cheek and lifting her face to kiss him.

The hand went through the cheek, however, and with a little nervous gasp – not so much of fear as of exasperation at her own nervousness – Margo retreated back to Hunter.

'We're only three-dimensional images,' Paul explained with a quirking smile. 'Touch doesn't transmit on this system. We're seeing *your* two images up here in the saucer, except they aren't always together *in* the saucer, especially when they were moving into focus. It's really pretty weird, if you'll excuse my saying so, Professor . . .'

'My name's Ross Hunter,' he said, at last managing to speak.

Don said to Margo: 'I'm sorry I'm too insubstantial to kiss, dear. I'll make up for that when I really see you. Incidentally, I've actually been on the Wanderer.'

'And I've been talking to one of their beings,' Paul put in. 'She's quite a person – you'd have to see her. She wants us to –'

Hunter interrupted, 'You've been on the Wanderer, you've talked with them – *Who are they? What are they doing? What do they want?*'

Paul said: 'We haven't time to try to answer any questions like that. As I was about to say, our . . . well, captress . . . wants

317

us to assure ourselves that you survived the tidal waves and that you're all safe. That's half the reason for this . . . call.'

'We're safe,' Margo said faintly, 'as far as anyone on Earth is.'

'Our whole party's survived so far,' Beardy amplified, 'except for Rudolf Brecht, who was killed in a mountain accident.'

'Brecht?' Paul questioned him doubtfully, frowning.

'You remember; we called him Doc,' Margo explained.

'Of course,' Paul said, 'and we called that funny old crackpot the Ramrod and Professor Hunter Beardy. Excuse me, Professor.'

'Of course,' Hunter said impatiently. 'What's the other reason for the call?'

Don said: 'To let you know that if everything works out right, we'll be landing at Vandenberg Two in a few hours, probably in my moon-ship.'

'At least Don will,' Paul added. 'We have to stay up here in space now. The Wanderer may be in danger, there's an emergency developing.'

'*The Wanderer*, in danger?' Margo repeated incredulously, almost sardonically. 'Emergency *developing*? What do you call what's been happening the last two days?'

Hunter said to Don: 'We're in sight of Vandenberg Two, as you know, and we're planning to go there as soon as we can.'

'We're trying to find Morton Opperly,' Margo put in automatically.

Don said to Hunter: 'That's good. If you bring them the news about me, it'll be easier for you to get in. Tell Oppie the Wanderer has linear accelerators eight thousand miles long and a cyclotron of that diameter. That should convince him of something! It'll help me if they're informed ahead of time about my intended landing.' He looked towards Margo. 'Then I'll be able to kiss you properly, dear.'

Margo looked back at him and said: 'And I'll kiss you, Don. But I want to you to know that things have changed. I've changed,' and she pressed more closely to Hunter to show what she meant.

Hunter frowned and pressed his lips against his teeth, but

318

then he tightened his arm around her and nodded and said curtly: 'That's right.'

Before Don could say anything, if he'd been going to, the ground suddenly turned bright red, faded, turned red again. The same thing was happening to the whole landscape: it was lightening redly, then darkening, then reddening again, as if from soundless red lightning flashes coming in a steady rhythm. Hunter and Margo looked up and instantly flinched their eyes away from the blinding red pinpoint flares winking on and off at the north and south poles of the Wanderer, rhythmically reddening its own polar caps as well as the Earth's whole sky. Never in their whole lives had they seen anything like such bright sources of monochromatic light.

'The emergency's arrived,' said the Paul-image, the red light striking weirdly through it, making it doubly unreal. 'We're going to have to cut this short.'

The Don-image said: 'The Wanderer is recalling its ships.'

Hunter said strongly: 'We'll tell them at Vandenberg. We'll see you there. Oppie: eight-thousand-mile linear accelerators and a cyclotron of that diameter. Good luck!'

But in that instant the two images were gone. They didn't fade or drift, just winked out.

Hunter and Margo looked down the red-lit hillside. Even the surf was red, the foaming of a lava sea. The camp was astir; there were small figures moving about, clustering, pointing.

But one was nearer. From behind a boulder not twenty feet away the Ramrod stared at them wonderingly, enviously, in his eyes an unappeasable hunger as the red light rhythmically bathed his face.

Chapter 41

Fifty million miles starward of Earth, spaceman Tigran Biryuzov could see the Red Recall plainly as he and his five comrades orbited Mars in the three ships of the First Soviet People's Expedition. For Tigran, Earth and the Wanderer were two bright planets about as far apart as adjoining stars in the

Pleiades. Even in airless space, their crescent shapes were not quite apparent to the Communist spaceman's unaided eye.

Radio communications from home had stopped with the Wanderer's appearance, and for two days the six men had been in a frenzy of wonder about what was going on in the next orbit sunward. The projected surface landing on Mars, scheduled for ten hours ago, had been postponed.

Their telescopes showed them the astronomic situation clearly enough – the capture and destruction of the moon, the weird surface patterns of the Wanderer – but that was all.

Not only was the Red Recall plainly visible to Tigran, but also its dark red visual echoes from the night side of Earth. He started to note down, '*Krasniya molniya* –' and then broke off to beat his cheeks with his knuckles in a fury of frustrated curiosity and to think, *Red lightning! Mother of Lenin! Blood of Marx! What next? What next?*

The saucer students had many questions to ask about the tantalizingly limited conversation with Paul and Don. When Hunter and Margo had finished answering them, the Red Recall had stopped flashing, and the swiftly-sinking tide had uncovered more of the road to Vandenberg, even a stretch of the Pacific Coast Highway.

Hixon summed it up, jerking a thumb at the Wanderer. 'So they got saucers, which we knew. And they got energy guns'll shoot rays that can chop up mountains and puncture planets probably. And they got three-D TV a lot better than ours, which makes sense. But they're supposed to be in danger, which doesn't! Why should *they* be in danger?'

Ann said brightly: 'Maybe there's another planet after them.'

'Anything but that, Annie, please,' Wojtowicz protested comically. 'One weird planet is all I can stand.'

At that moment the landscape brightened, and Clarence Dodd, who alone of them was looking east, made a single strangling, clucking noise, as if he'd tried to cry out and choked on the cry, and he hunched away from the east and at the same time pointed his hand in that direction above the mountains.

Hanging there, between the Wanderer and the serrated eastern horizon, was a gibbous shape half again as wide as the

Wanderer, all an unvarying, bright steely grey except for one glittering highlight midway between its round rim and its flatter rim.

Margo felt, *Now the sky's too heavy – it must fall.*

The Ramrod thought, *And a voice like a trumpet spoke and the Lamb opened another seal . . . and another . . . and another . . . and another. . . .*

Wojtowicz yelled softly: 'My God, Ann was right. It *is* another planet.'

'And it's bigger.' That was Mrs Hixon.

'But it's not round,' Hixon protested, almost angrily.

'Yes, it is,' Hunter contradicted, 'only it's partly in shadow, more than the Wanderer is. It's as much in shadow as the moon would be if it were there.'

'It's at least seven Wanderer-diameters down the sky from the Wanderer,' the Little Man pronounced, so quickly recovered from his original shock that he was already pulling out his notebook. 'That's fifteen degrees. An hour.' He uncapped his pen and studied his wrist-watch.

Rama Joan said: 'The highlight's the reflection of the sun. Its surface must be like a dull mirror.'

Ann said, 'I don't like the new planet, Mommy. The Wanderer's our friend, all golden and lovely, but this one's in armour.'

Rama Joan pressed her daughter's head against her waist, but kept her eyes on the new planet as she said ringingly: 'I think the gods are at war. The stranger devil has come to fight the devil we know.'

The Little Man, already jotting notes, said eagerly: 'Let's call it the Stranger – that's a good enough name.'

Young Harry McHeath thought, *Or you could call it Wolf – no, that might confuse it with the Jaws.*

Mrs Hixon snarled at them: 'Oh, for Christ's sake, spare us the poetry! A new planet means more tides, more quakes, more God knows what.'

Through it all Ray Hanks was calling querulously from the truck: 'What is it you're talking about? I can't see it from here. Somebody tell me. What is it?' Young Harry McHeath was thinking how glad he was to be here and alive, how wonderful it was to have been born to these sights, how miserable for those who missed them. So it was natural that Ray Hanks' cry came through to him. He vaulted up on the back of the truck, laid his hand on a mirror, and held it so that Hanks could see the reflection of the Stranger in it.

Wanda and Ida and the Ramrod had been standing together. Now Wanda simply sat down and moaned loudly: 'This is too much. I think I'm going to have another heart attack.'

But Ida pounded on the Ramrod's shoulder, demanding, 'What is it, Charlie? What's its real name? Explain it!'

The Ramrod stared at the Stranger with a tortured expression and finally said, in a voice that, though defeated-sounding, had a strange undertone of relief and of opening doors: 'I don't know, Ida. I just don't know. The universe is bigger than my mind.'

At that instant two bright lines sprang out from the sides of the Stranger and travelled to the Wanderer, in the tick of a wrist-watch, and passed it one in front and one behind, and then went on seemingly more slowly across the grey heavens as straight as if drawn with a ruler and a penful of luminous blue ink. But where the blue line passed in front of the Wanderer there was an eruption of white coruscations almost blindingly bright.

One of the lines came from the dark side of the Stranger, touching faintly the black crescent with blue, revealing its shape and the sphericity of the entire body.

'Jesus, it *is* war.' Again Wojtowicz was the quickest to respond vocally.

'Lasers,' said the Little Man. 'Beams of solid light. But so big – it's almost incredible.'

'And we're just seeing the sides,' Hunter put in awestruck, 'the leakage. Suppose you had to look one of those in the face. A million suns!'

'A hundred, anyway,' said the Little Man. 'If one of those beams should point even for a moment at Earth . . .'

Blue and steel touched off an intuition in Hixon's mind. 'I tell you what,' he said excitedly, 'the new planet's police! It's come to arrest the Wanderer for disturbing us.'

'Bill, you're nuts,' Mrs Hixon yelled across at him. 'Next you'll be saying angels.'

'I hope they fight! I hope they kill each other!' Pop yelled shrilly, his whole body trembling as he shook his clenched fists at them. 'I hope they burn each other's guts out!'

'I sure don't,' Wojtowicz told him, walking around in an odd little circle as he stared at the sky. 'What's to keep us from getting hit, then? You *like* having a battle fought across your back yard? You *like* being a sitting duck for stray shots?'

Hunter said rapidly: 'I don't think the near beam's hitting the Wanderer. I think it's hitting the moon-ring and disintegrating the fragments it touches.'

'That's right,' the Little Man said coolly. 'Those beams bracketing the Wanderer look more to me like a shot over the bows.'

Hixon heard that. 'Like I said, arrest,' he pointed out eagerly. 'You know – "Don't move or we'll shoot to kill!" '

The bright blue beams were extinguished at their source and died along their length as swiftly as they had first shot out. They left behind two yellow after images drawn on the grey sky, but moving with the eyes that saw. Yet the two original blue beams, though rapidly growing shorter and fainter, could still be seen crawling away beyond the Wanderer like straight blue worms into the grey infinity.

Hixon said: 'My God, I thought they'd never quit. They must have fired for two minutes.'

'Seventeen seconds,' the Little Man informed him, looking up from his wrist-watch. 'It's a proven fact that in a crisis time estimates vary wildly, and witnesses are apt to disagree on almost everything. That's something we've got to watch out for.'

'That's right, Doddsy, we got to keep our heads,' Wojtowicz agreed loudly, almost skipping around in his little circle now, his voice quite gay. 'They keep throwing surprises at us, and all we can do is keep taking them. Whee-yoo! It's like the front line – it's like sitting out a bombardment.'

As if the word 'bombardment' had pulled a trigger, there came a dull roaring from all around them and then a vibration, and then the road under their feet began to rock. The springs

323

of the Corvette and the truck whined and groaned. Ray Hanks whimpered with pain, and McHeath, still standing over him, had to grab at the truck's side to keep from being pitched out.

To a floating observer, everyone would have seemed to be joining Wojtowicz in his eerie circular dance and making it a staggering one. One of the women screamed, but Mrs Hixon cursed obscenely, and Ann cried: 'Mommy, the rocks are skipping!'

Margo heard that and looked up the slope where she and Hunter had been, and saw boulders descending it in fantastic bounds – among them, she thought, the giant's coffin on which they'd spread the blanket. Unslowed by the weird gust of guilt that went through her, she pulled the momentum pistol out of her jacket and thrust out with her other hand to steady herself against the Corvette, but there was no steadiness there, only a greater rocking. The boulders came on. Hunter saw what she was doing and sprang to her and shouted: 'Is the arrow pointing towards the muzzle?'

She shouted, 'Yes!' And as the boulders converged like bounding grey beasts, she pointed the momentum pistol into their midst and, herself fighting to keep on her feet, clamped down her finger on the trigger-button.

As the earthquake shocks themselves lessened and damped out, the boulders coincidentally slowed in their wild, smashing descent, seemed almost to change to great grey pillows, slowly rolled instead of bounding, rolled slower yet, and stopped moving beside the road, almost at Margo's feet, the giant's coffin lying where the edge of the truck's shadow had been.

Hunter pulled her finger off the button and looked at the scale on the grip. There was no more violet.

He looked down the quarter mile of mountain road to the Coast Highway and for a wonder it looked free of new slides and with the water all gone – though it was sloshing wildly in the farther distance. Just across the highway brightly gleamed the mesh fence that guarded the foot of Vandenberg, while across from the mouth of the mountain road loomed the big gate.

Overhead shone the Wanderer and the Stranger, the former trending into the three-spot – the half-hour stage between the

324

serpent-egg and the mandala – the latter as coldly serene as if its gravity had nothing whatever to do with the earthquake just triggered.

In the resounding silence Ida was moaning: 'Oh, my ankle.'

Wojtowicz asked in a snickering voice: 'What do we do now? What's next on the show?'

Mrs Hixon was snarling at him: 'There's nothing to do, you clown! It's the end!'

Hunter pushed Margo into the Corvette and got in himself, then stood up behind the wheel and honked the horn for attention. He said loudly: 'Get into the cars, everybody! Throw our stuff into the back of the truck if anybody wants to, but be quick about it. We're driving into Vandenberg.'

The Stranger gave many who saw it the feeling which Wanda and Mrs Hixon had voiced – 'This is too much. This is the end.' The more scientifically minded of these pessimists noted that the Stranger was near enough to the Wanderer – only about forty thousand miles away if it were the same distance from Earth – so that its gravity would largely augment rather than oppose the great tides the Wanderer had been raising.

But many others were naïvely delighted by the steely new planet and the exciting rays it shot. For a while, at least, the astronomical spectacle took their minds off their troubles, worries, and even life-or-death problems. In the stormlashed sea somewhere near Florida (horizontally or vertically), Barbara Katz cried out from the cockpit of the *Albatross* to the spirit of old KKK: *'Thrilling Wonder Stories!* Oh, but it's beautiful,' and Benjy shouted to her solemnly: 'Sure is a wonder, Miss Barbara.'

'Boy, this second act was a long time coming,' Jake Lesher complained to Sally Harris as they sat once more side by side on the patio, each damp-blanket-wrapped and warmed with a 'Hunter's Friend' and wearing patented hand-warmers for skiers that they'd found among Mr Hasseltine's things. 'If *our* play doesn't move faster, it'll die in Philadelphia.'

In an untoppled astronomical observatory in the Andes, the seventy-year-old French astronomer Pierre Rambouillet-Lacepède rubbed together his ivory-dark fingers with delight and snatched for pencil and paper. *At last, a really challenging instance of the Three Body Problem!*

Still others on the night side of Earth didn't see the Stranger at all because of clouds or other hindrances. Some of them had not even yet seen the Wanderer. Wolf Loner spied a faint yellow light through the overcast that had settled into fog. Sailing closer, he saw it was a kerosene lantern set a few feet above the water in a tall stone window with a round top. When the *Endurance* had come closer still, he saw the narrow wall of yellowish stone and the dark steeple rising about it, and he recognized the place because he had climbed to it more than once, but he could not believe his eyes. He swung the tiller and let go the mainsheet, and the *Endurance* gently bumped the narrow roof below the window. The sail flapped idly, there was no current in the water around the stone structure. He took up the mooring line and stepped out on the roof and through the window, carefully setting aside the lantern, and looked around. Then he could no longer doubt: he was in the belfry of the Old North Church. Standing across from him, backed against the wall as if she were trying to disappear into it, was a dark-haired, Italian-looking girl of perhaps twelve who stared at him, her teeth chattering. She did not respond to his questions, even when he phrased them in scraps of Italian and Spanish, except to shake her head, and that might only have been a kind of shivering. So after a time, still holding the mooring line, he went close to her, and although she shrank from him he took her up gently but firmly and carried her out the window, carefully replacing the lantern on the sill, and stepped with her into the *Endurance* and set her down half-way into the narrow cabin and put a blanket around her. He noticed the water was moving a little now in the direction from which the sailing dory had come. So with one thoughtful headshake downward, towards where Copps Burying Ground would be, he brought the *Endurance* about and, taking advantage of the outgoing tide, set sail out of Boston's North End for the open sea.

With unintended diabolic precision the four insurgent captains atom-steamed the *Prince Charles* into the Pororoca. This tidal bore of the Amazon is normally a mile-long waterfall five yards high, which travels upstream at fifteen miles an hour with a roar that can be heard ten miles away. Now it was a great seething slope half as high as the *Prince Charles* was long and carrying that great city of a ship – a smaller Manhattan Island – canted forward at an angle of twenty degrees, up the mightiest of rivers, now Wanderer-swollen and Stranger-swollen, too. All around, the hurricane roared with the Pororoca and its waves augmented the bore. To the east the storm completely masked the dawn. Ahead to the west was a wilderness of darkness and torn clouds. At this moment Captain Sithwise reached the bridge – a counter-coup having met no opposition whatever in the period of cataclysm – and he took the wheel and began to send orders to the atomic engine rooms. At first he guided the ship by the slant and gleam of the Pororoca, but then – since they hung to starboard brightly and firmly through the whirling cloud wraiths – he began to depend somewhat on the beacon globes of the Stranger above and the Wanderer below.

Paul and Don stared up at the blank Stranger and the moon-girdled Wanderer through the transparent ceiling of Tigerishka's saucer, poised five hundred miles above Vandenberg Two.

The artificial gravity field was still on, so they were sprawled on the floor of the saucer. This was transparent also. Through it they could see, by sunlight reflected from the two planets that had erupted from hyperspace, the dark expanse of Southern California, here and there invaded by the dim silver of the sea, and for the other half of the floor-picture the relatively bright expanse of the Pacific itself, though both sea and land were somewhat blurred by the layers of Earth's atmosphere.

There was one obstruction in this lower picture. From the now-invisible port in the centre of the transparent floor, the thick worm of the space tube stretched off to the side, where presumably the Baba Yaga hung out of view. The reflected light from the Stranger and the Wanderer, striking through the two rigid transparencies, gleamed on the ridged metal of the tube outside and in, showing the first two of the inner handholds by which a being in free fall could pull himself through the tube.

Both Paul and Don avoided looking down. The artificial gravity field, although Tigerishka had assured them it extended only inside the saucer, made the depths below distinctly uncomfortable.

They had the same view as did those approaching Vandenberg of the Stranger and the Wanderer, except that for Paul and Don the two planets were much brighter, and were backgrounded not by slate-grey sky but by the star-spangled black of space.

The sight was weird, arresting, even 'glorious', yet because of their knowledge of the underlying situation, however partial and fragmentary, Paul and Don felt chiefly an ever-mounting tension. There above them hung the Pursued and the Pursuer, Rebellion and Authority, Adventure and Restraint – hung in the stasis of an uncertain truce, while the two orbs watched and measured each other.

The bulge-sided yellow triangle in the purple needle-eye face of the Wanderer and the bright solar highlight in the vaster, gibbous, gunmetal round of the Stranger were two great eyes staring each other down.

The tension was deadly, shrivelling. It made Don and Paul, despite the support of each other's presence, want to shrink out of sight, want to sink down, down, down through the layers of Earth's atmosphere and rocky, maternal flesh to some lightless womb. Even the eagerness of any eye to watch such wonders hardly balanced in them with this urge.

Paul asked in an almost childish voice: 'Tigerishka, why haven't you gone back to the Wanderer? It's been a long while since the Red Recall flashed. All the other ships must have gone.'

From the embowering darkness by the control panel, where not a ray of Wanderer-light or Stranger-light touched her, Tigerishka replied: 'It's not time, yet.'

In nearly querulous tones, Don said: 'Hadn't Paul and I better get aboard the Baba Yaga? I can manage the braking drop through the atmosphere, since there's no orbital speed to kill, but it'll be tricky, and if we have to wait much longer –'

'Not time yet for that, either!' Tigerishka called. 'There is something I must demand of you first. You were saved from space and the waves. You owe a debt to the Wanderer.'

She leaned forward out of the dark so that her violet and

328

green muzzle and breast, vertically shadowed at eye and cheek and neck, showed in the planet's light.

'In the same way I sent you to Earth,' she began softly yet piercingly, 'I am now sending you to the Stranger to testify on behalf of the Wanderer. Stand in the centre side by side and face me.'

'You mean you want us to plead for you?' Paul asked as he and Don complied almost automatically. 'Say that your ships did everything possible to save humans and their homes? Remember, I've seen a lot of catastrophes that weren't averted, too – more than I've seen of rescues, in fact.'

'You will simply tell your stories – the truth as you know it,' Tigerishka said, throwing back her head so that her violet eyes gleamed. 'Grip hands now and don't move. I am blacking out the saucer entirely. The beams that scan you will be black. This will be a realer trip for you than the one to Earth. Your bodies won't leave the saucer, but they will seem to. Hold still!'

The stars darkened, the Earth went black, the twin violet sparks of Tigerishka's eyes winked out. Then it was as if a whirlwind ripped a great doorway in the dark, and Don and Paul were whirled across space almost swift as thought – one second, two – then they were standing hand-in-hand in the centre of a vast, seemingly limitless plain, flat as the salt desert by Great Salt Lake, only all glaringly silver grey and torrid with a heat they could not feel.

'I'd thought it would seem rounded,' Paul said, telling himself he still stood inside the saucer, but not believing it.

'The Pursuit Planet is bigger than Earth, remember,' Don replied, 'and you can't see Earth's curvature when you're on its surface.' He was recalling the moon's close horizon, but chiefly thinking how indistinguishable this experience was from his dream trip through the Wanderer, and wondering if it could have been managed the same way.

The heavens were a star-pricked hemisphere topped by the shaggy-margined glare of the sun. A few diameters from the sun Earth stood out darkly, edged by a bluish crescent. On the gunmetal horizon stood the Wanderer, half risen, five times as wide as Earth now, enormous, but the great yellow eye cut in two by the silver horizon line, so that it seemed to peer more fiercely, almost to narrow its lids.

'I thought we'd be projected inside,' Paul said, indicating the glaring metal ground at their feet.

'Looks like they stop even images for customs inspection,' Don replied.

Paul said: 'Well, if we're radio waves, they're carrying our consciousness, too.'

Don said: 'You forget – we're still in the saucer.'

'But then what instrument sees this out here and transmits the picture to the saucer?' Paul wanted to know. Don shook his head.

A white flash exploded from the metal plain between them and the violet-and-yellow hemisphere of the Wanderer. It vanished instantly, then there were two more flashes, farther off.

Paul thought, *The fight's begun.*

Don said: 'Meteorites! There's no atmosphere to stop them.'

At that instant they dropped down through the gunmetal ground into darkness. Only a black flash of that, however – barely an instant – and then they were hanging in the centre of a huge, dim, spherical room everywhere walled with great inward-peering eyes.

That was the first impression. The second was that the patterned lozenges were not actual eyes, but dark, circular portholes, widely ringed with different colours. Yet now there was the uneasy impression that eyes of all sorts were peering through those pupil-like ports.

Both Don and Paul had essentially identical memory flashes of being sent to the principal's office in grade school.

Don and Paul were not alone in the vast chamber. Hanging clumped with them there at the centre of the sphere were at least a hundred other human beings or their three-dimensional images – an incredible clot of humanity. There were people of all races, uniforms of African and Asiatic countries, two of the Russian Space Force, a glowingly brown Maori, a white-hooded Arab, a nearly naked coolie, a woman in furs, and many others of whom only patches could be seen because of the intervening figures.

A silver beam of light thin as a needle shot out from beside one of the black portholes and probed at the other side of the clot – the ports meanwhile twinkling as if with peering eyes – and suddenly someone began to speak rapidly though quite calmly from, it seemed, the point in the clot where the silver needle touched. At the sound of the voice Don felt an instant thrill, for he recognized it.

'My name is Gilbert Dufresne, Lieutenant, United States Space Force. Stationed on the moon, I left it in a one-man ship to scout the alien planet just as the moonquakes began. As far as I know, my three comrades died in the break-up.

'I began to orbit the moon east–west and soon sighted three huge, wheel-shaped spaceships. Tractor beams of some sort, as far as I can judge, took hold of me and my vessel then and drew us inside one of the ships. There I met a variety of alien beings. I was questioned, I think, by some form of mind-scanning, and my physical wants were attended to. Later I was taken to the bridge or control bulge of the ship, where I was permitted to observe its operations.

'It had dropped from the moon and was hovering over the City of London, which was flooded by a high tide. Beams or some sort of force-field from our ship drove the water back. I was asked to enter a small ship with three alien beings. This ship descended and hovered near the top of a building which I recognized as the British Museum. I entered an upper storey with one of the beings. There I saw him revive five men I was certain were dead. We re-entered the small ship and after several similar episodes we returned into the huge ship.

'From London we moved south to Portugal, where the city of Lisbon had been thrown down by a severe earthquake. There I saw . . .'

As Dufresne continued to speak, Paul (who had never met him, though he knew of him) began to have the feeling that, no matter how true the words might be, they were nevertheless pointless, useless – the merest chattering on the margin of great events that were relentlessly moving their own way. The peering ports seemed to leer cynically, or filmed with a cold, reptilian boredom. The grade school principal was listening to the painfully honest story without hearing it.

Apparently this feeling of Paul's was a valid intuition, for

331

without another shred of warning the whole scene vanished, and was instantly replaced by the small, brightly-lit interior of the familiar saucer, green of floor and ceiling now, and Tigerishka calling from the flower-banked, silvery control panel: 'It's no use. Our plea is rejected. Get in your ship and drop to your planet. Hurry! I'll cut loose from you as soon as you're in the Baba Yaga. Thanks for your help. Good-bye and good luck, Don Merriam. Good-bye, Paul Hagbolt.'

A circle of green floor lifted. Without a word Don lowered himself headfirst through the port and began to pull himself through the tube.

Paul looked at Tigerishka.

'Hurry,' she repeated.

Miaow came waltzing up warily. Paul stooped, and when the little cat glanced towards Tigerishka, grabbed it up with a sudden snatch. As he stepped towards the port he smoothed the ruffled grey fur. His hand slowed in the middle of the stroke and he turned around.

'I'm not going,' he said.

'You have to, Paul,' Tigerishka said. 'Earth's your home. Hurry.'

'I give up Earth and my race,' he replied. 'I want to stay with you.' Miaow squirmed in his hands, trying to get away, but he tightened his grip.

'Please go at once, Paul,' Tigerishka said, at last looking and moving towards him. Her eyes stared straight at his. 'There can never be any further relationship between us.'

'But I'm going to stay with you, do you hear?' His voice was suddenly so loud and angry that Miaow became panicky and clawed at his hands to get loose. He held her firmly and went on: 'Even as your pet, if it has to be that way. But I'm staying.'

Tigerishka stood face to face with him. 'Not even as my pet,' she said. 'There's not *quite* enough gap between our minds for that. Oh, get out, you fool!'

'Tigerishka,' he said harshly, staring into her violet eyes, 'ninety per cent of what you felt last night was pity and boredom. What was the other ten per cent?'

She glared at him as if in a frenzy of exasperation. Suddenly, moving with almost blinding speed, she snatched Miaow from

332

him and slapped him hard across the face. The three pale violet claws of that forepaw showed bright red the first half inch as they came away.

'That!' she snarled, her fangs bared.

He took a backward step, then another, then he was in the tube. The artificial gravity above squeezed him down into it in free fall. Looking up, he could see Tigerishka's snarling mask. Blood streamed from his cheek and hung in red globules against the ridged silver inside the tube. Then the green port closed.

Chapter 42

The saucer students entered Vandenberg Two without hindrance or fanfare and altogether unromantically – like workers on the graveyard shift arriving at their factory.

There was no one at the mesh fence that had so lately been many yards under salt water, no one at the big gate now sagging open – nothing at all of note, in fact, except six inches of stinking mud – so they just drove through, most of them out of the cars to lighten them, and they started up the ramp to the plateau.

Hunter drove the Corvette. Occupying all of the small back seat and overlapping it a bit, lay Wanda, breathing heavily. Not even Wojtowicz had been able to bully her out of this heart attack.

Mrs Hixon was driving the truck because Bill Hixon wanted to watch the sky, where the Wanderer in mandala face and the Stranger now bracketed the zenith – and because she didn't give a damn, as she said more than once. She was alone in the cab – Pop had wanted to stay, but she'd told him right out he smelled worse than the mud, and it was Bill's truck, and she wouldn't take it.

In the back of the truck were Ray Hanks and Ida, she nursing both his broken leg and her own swollen ankle. She didn't believe in sleeping pills and was feeding both herself and the feebly protesting Ray large quantities of aspirin.

'Chew them,' she told him. 'The bitterness takes your mind off things.'

The rest were walking. Three times already some of them had had to heave at the truck to get it through bad places, and twice the truck had had to nudge the Corvette out of spots in which its tyres just spun. Everybody was smeared with mud, their shoes globbed with it; and the truck tyres were so muddied that their chains didn't chink.

There was a blue surge in the almost shadowless, mixed planet-light bathing the muck landscape. Harry McHeath, by his youth better able than most of them to keep an eye on two things at once, called out: 'It's started again! They're both doing it!'

Four ruler-straight, string-narrow, bright blue beams stretched across the grey sky from the Stranger to the Wanderer. But now instead of shooting past her they converged. Yet they did not strike the Wanderer, but stopped short of her by just a hair of grey sky, and were thrown back in four faint, semi-circular, bluish-white fans.

'They must be hitting a field of some sort,' the Little Man guessed.

'Like the Lensmen battles!' McHeath chimed excitedly.

Similarly three violet beams shot from the Wanderer to the Stranger and were intercepted. Blue and violet beams stretched, criss-crossing, between the two planets, like a long, geometrically drawn cat's cradle.

'This is it!' Hixon yelled fiercely.

Wojtowicz was watching so singlemindedly that he walked off the ramp. From the corner of his eye, McHeath noted him drop out of sight and raced over.

'I'm O.K., kid, I just slipped down here a little ways – see, I can reach you,' Wojtowicz replied reassuringly to McHeath's anxious call. 'Only give me a hand up, will you, so I don't have to stop watching?'

Hixon called up to the truck: 'You should be out here seeing this, babe – it's amazing!'

From inside the cab Mrs Hixon shouted back: 'You watch the fireworks for me, Billy boy – I'm driving the truck!' And

334

she honked viciously at the Corvette, which seemed to be stopping.

But Hunter was only slowing a bit. He'd taken a couple of quick glances at the battling planets, and it still seemed to him more important to get this gang into the Space Force base while the excitement lasted and perhaps as it ran interference for them. He had to get that done and the juiceless momentum pistol delivered, too – he had come to share much of Margo's obsession on the latter point. While she, tramping along to the left of the hood, was obviously still of the same mind and mood.

So Hunter called out: 'Come on, everybody! Here we turn right. Don't walk off the end!' And he swung the car up on to the plateau.

There at last they found personnel – three soldiers who might well have been on guard duty, judging from the three weapons leaned against the wall of the tin hut behind them, but who were now crouching restlessly on their hams to stare up at the interplanetary battle. One of them was snapping his fingers.

As the truck swung up on to the plateau after the Corvette and both cars almost stopped, Margo quickly walked up behind the soldiers.

Overhead three more blue lines and two more violet ones added themselves to the laser barrage, complicating the cat's cradle.

Margo touched the nearest soldier on the shoulder, and when he didn't react, shook him by it. He turned a wild sweating face up at her.

'Where is Professor Morton Opperly?' she demanded. 'Where are the scientists?'

'Christ, I wouldn't know,' he told her. 'The longhairs are over there somewheres.' He waved vaguely towards the interior of the plateau. 'Don't bother me, lady!' He whirled back, his face on the sky again, and pounded one of his buddies on the shoulder.

'Tony!' he yelled. 'I got two more bills says Old Goldy beats the bejesus out of Cannonball!'

'You're faded!'

(Twenty-five hundred miles east, Jake Lesher clutched Sally

Harris and gasped: 'Oh, Sal, if I could have made book on this!')

Margo walked on. Mrs Hixon honked again. Hunter drove on slowly, following Margo. He called sharply to the figures close around the two cars: 'Keep moving, everybody. Watch and walk.'

Ahead floodlights went on against white walls, silhouetting knots and huddles of men, none of them moving, all of them staring at the sky.

Two more blue beams flashed on, not exactly from the Stranger, but from points a half diameter out from her – huge battleships of space, perhaps. One of the new beams needled through to the Wanderer. There was an incandescent gout at the edge of the north yellow notch of the mandala, and when the dazzling white light faded there was a long ragged black hole there in the Wanderer's golden and purple skin.

Ann's voice cut through, shrill with tragedy, 'Mommy, they're hurting the Wanderer! I hate it!'

Pop, stumbling along and shaking his fists once more, snarled gleefully: 'Fry 'em, oh, fry 'em! Keep it up! Kill yourselves!'

Suddenly the nine blue beams impinging just short of the Wanderer spread out, generating a pale blue hemispherical shroud half masking the Wanderer – a sort of mist-curtain through which the yellow and violet features of the planet showed dimly. The violet beams vanished.

'They're drowning them,' Hixon yelled. 'It's the kill!'

'No, I think the Wanderer's putting up a new kind of defensive screen,' the Little Man contradicted.

Five blinding points of white light sprang out on the steely surface of the Stranger.

'Missiles exploding!' McHeath guessed. 'The Wanderer's fighting back!'

The Ramrod, breathing heavily and leaning against the truck as he strode along with it, now cried out in an agonized appeal: 'But what must we understand from this? Do hate and death rule the cosmos, even among the most high?'

Rama Joan, her eyes on the sky as she pulled Ann along, called back to him in a swift, bell-like voice: 'The gods spend the wealth the universe gathers, they scan the wonders and

336

fling them to nothingness. That's why they're the gods! I told you they were devils.'

Ann said accusingly: 'Oh, Mommy.'

True to McHeath's guess, the five white points had swollen to the pale hemispheres of explosion fronts, through which the steely surface of the Stranger showed unbroken.

Hixon said: 'I don't know about devils, but I know now there'll always be war.' He waved a hand at the zenith. 'What more proof could you ask than *that?*'

Mrs Hixon shouted cryptically from the cab: 'Now you're talking sense, Bill, and what good is it?'

The Ramrod gasped: 'But when the highest . . . and the wisest . . . *Is there no cure?*'

Young Harry McHeath's imagination took fire from the tragedy of that question, and for a moment he saw himself in an almost all-powerful, one-man spaceship poised midway between the Wanderer and the Stranger, turning back their bolts from each other, somehow healing their sanity.

The Little Man said, not in a loud voice, almost as if to himself: 'Maybe the cure always has to come from below. And keep coming from below. For ever.'

But Wojtowicz heard him and without looking away from the sky asked: 'How do you mean from below, Doddsy? Not from *us?*'

The Little Man looked at him. 'Yes, Wojtowicz,' he said with a chuckle at the ridiculousness of it, 'from little nothing guys like you and me.'

Wojtowicz shook his head. 'Wow,' he laughed. 'I'm punch-drunk.'

Moving steadily forward all the time, the cars and the walkers were almost to the floodlit walls. A young man in a sweatshirt rushed by Margo and grabbed a major and yelled in his ear: 'Opperly says douse those goddamn floodlights. They're spoiling our observations!'

Hunter, hearing that, had to think of Archimedes saying to the enemy soldier treading on his sand-diagram: 'Don't spoil my circle!'

The soldier in the legend had killed Archimedes, but this major was violently nodding his head as he turned around.

Hunter recognized Buford Humphreys from two nights back. At the same time Humphreys saw him, saw Rama Joan and Ann, saw the whole lot of the 'saucer bugs' he had kept out of Vandenberg. He goggled wildly, then with a shrug of incomprehension and a quick glance at the sky, raced off, calling: 'Goddamn it, corporal, kill those floods!'

Meanwhile Margo had grabbed the young man by his sweatshirt before he could dart away. 'Take us to Professor Opperly!' she ordered. 'We've got to make a report. Look, I've got a note from him.'

'O.K.,' he agreed without glancing at the dirty, crumpled sheet. 'Follow me.' He pointed a hand at the cars. 'But douse those headlights!'

The Corvette's and the truck's beams winked out a moment before the white wall went dark, but Margo held on to the young man. His pale sweatshirt made it easy for Hunter to follow them. Beyond them Hunter saw now the loom of radar screens and the white barrel of a field telescope.

Overhead the blue beams flashed off along their length, and the mist-curtain around the Wanderer faded, to be instantly replaced by a hundred points of white light, stabbingly bright.

But even as McHeath, squinting his eyes, called: 'Implosion globe!' it was to be seen that the Wanderer had slipped aside twice her diameter up the sky, with the dizzying feeling of the foundations of the universe shifting. The implosion globe brightened as the white blasts that had been on the other side of the Wanderer shone through and the globe now had a wide ragged neck where the Wanderer had burst out.

'They've gone inertialess – the whole planet,' Clarence Dodd cried.

There were a half-dozen ragged holes in the Wanderer's skin now, black but glowing dull red towards their central depths – so many of them that the mandala was barely identifiable.

Tangentially from the ravaged planet's side there shot out towards the Stranger a violet beam thicker and many times brighter than any of the earlier ones.

But before it was half-way to the Stranger, the bigger planet moved as swiftly as one of its beams – a rhinoceros rush across the sky, destroying all feelings of stability – to a position along-

338

side the Wanderer. There was not a moon's width between them.

The Wanderer vanished.

A blue broadside burst from the Stranger and laced through the space where the Wanderer had been.

'Goddamn, they blew her to bits!' Pop screamed ecstatically.

'No, she disappeared a fraction of a second earlier,' the Little Man contradicted. 'You've got to *observe*!'

The Stranger, her steely surface unholed, though streaked with brown and greenish scars, hung there three, four, five seconds, then she vanished too – like a big dim electric globe, the solar highlight its filament, switched off.

The sheaf of blue laser beams and the single thicker violet one crawled away from each other, dimming and shortening but ruler-straight, into the astronomic distance, while the pear-like implosion globe from which the Wanderer had first burst grew momently paler, bigger, and ghostlier.

'The Wanderer escaped into hyperspace,' McHeath said.

'Maybe, but she was a goner,' Hixon said. 'She'd been knocked to bits, and the Stranger's gone in after her. She's done.'

'But we can't be sure,' Hunter said. 'She might go on escaping for ever.' In his thoughts he added, *Like the Flying Dutchman*.

'We can't even be sure they're really gone,' Wojtowicz said with a nervous guffaw. 'They might of just jumped to the other side of the earth.'

'That's true,' the Little Man said, 'but we didn't see them even start to move . . . they just vanished. And I've got a feeling . . .'

Only then, as the bright yellow and orange after-images faded from their retinas, did the saucer students begin to realize, one by one, that they were all standing quite still in inky darkness. Hunter had switched off the Corvette's ignition. Behind him he heard the truck's motor die. By twos and threes the stars began to wink on in the black heavens – the old familiar stars that the slate sky had masked for three nights.

Don and Paul gazed up through the spacescreen of the Baba Yaga at the empty starfields and the blue and violet laser beams straight-lining off towards infinity.

They were both strapped down. Paul held a reddened handkerchief to his cheek. Don kept an eye on the skin temperature gauge and on the green-glowing aft radar picture of Southern California and the Pacific below. Although all but a trace of Earth's atmosphere was still under them, he'd already braked once, mostly to assure himself that the main jet would fire.

'Well, they're gone,' Don said.

'Into the storm,' Paul finished the thought. 'The Wanderer was a wreck.'

'Nothing's a wreck that can boost into hyperspace,' Don assured him quite cheerily. The stars began to crawl across the screen, and he tripped a vernier or two and they steadied.

'Maybe the Wanderer will *drift* to another cosmos,' Paul muttered thoughtfully. 'Maybe that's the way: don't try to force it, just drift like a wrecked ship with the hyperspatial currents, surrender to the storm.'

Don glanced at him sharply. 'She told you quite a bit, didn't she? I wonder if she got back aboard in time.'

'Of course,' Paul said shortly. 'I think even those little ships can move as fast as light, or faster.'

'That was quite a clawing she gave you,' Don remarked casually, then rapidly added: 'Me, I didn't have any big romances up there.' He rippled the verniers again and frowned at the skin temperature gauge. He continued briskly: 'And I don't think I got any left down below, either. Margo's really serious about this Hunter character, I'd say.'

Paul shrugged. 'What do you care? You always liked loneliness better than you liked people. No offence – liking yourself's the beginning of all love.'

Again Don gave him a quick glance. 'I bet you loved Margo more than I did,' he said. 'I think I always knew that.'

'Of course I did,' Paul said dully. 'She'll be angry I lost Miaow.'

Don chuckled. 'What things that cat'll see.' Then his voice changed. 'You wanted to go with Tigerishka, too, didn't you? You stayed behind to ask her.'

Paul nodded. 'And she wouldn't have me on any terms. When I asked her what she felt towards me, she gave me this.' He hugged his cheek against the bloody rag.

Don chuckled. 'You're a glutton for punishment, aren't you?' Then, quite lightly: 'I don't know, Paul, but if I were in love with a cat-lady, that clawing would be the one thing that would convince me she did love me back. Grab hold of the barrel now – here we go over Niagara Falls.'

The saucer students stood in inky darkness roofed with stars. Then, so near at hand it seemed for a moment they were in a room, a small low light went on, showing a cluttered table and behind it a man with the ageless, thin, sharp-featured face of a pharaoh. Margo moved towards him, following the young man in the sweatshirt, and Hunter got out of the car and came up after her.

The man behind the table looked to one side. Someone there said: 'The magnetic fields of both planets are gone, Oppie. We're back to Earth-normal.'

Margo said loudly: 'Professor Opperly, we've been hunting you for two days. I have here a gun that dropped from a saucer. It puts momentum in things. We thought you should be entrusted with it. Unfortunately we've used up all its charge, getting here.'

He glanced quickly into her face, then down at the grey pistol she had taken from her jacket. His lips thinned in a small, quite nasty smile.

'It looks to me a great deal more like something from a dime store toy counter,' he told her briskly. Then, turning again to the man beside him: 'How about the radio sky, Denison? Is it clearing, or –'

Margo had quickly turned the arrow on top of the gun away from the muzzle, then pointed it across the table and pressed the trigger button. Both Opperly and the young man in the sweatshirt started to grab her, then stopped. Some papers drifted towards the gun and then along with them three paper clips and a metal pencil that had been holding some of the papers down. For a second they all clung to the gun's muzzle, then dropped off.

'It must be electrostatic,' the young man in the sweatshirt said curiously, watching the papers as they fluttered down.

'It works on metal objects, too,' the one addressed as Denison pointed out, seeing the paper clips as they fell. 'Induction?'

'It pulled my hand! I distinctly felt that,' Opperly himself said, spreading the fingers of the hand he had reached across the table towards the gun. He looked at Margo again. 'Did you say it actually fell from a saucer?'

She smiled as she handed it to him.

Hunter said: 'We also bring you a message from Lieutenant Donald Merriam of the Space Force. He'll be landing here –'

Opperly had turned to someone else beside him. 'Wasn't there a Merriam among those lost at Moonbase?'

'He wasn't lost,' Margo cut in. 'He got away in one of the moon-ships. He was on the new planet He'll be trying to land here – maybe he's already coming in.'

'And he had a special message for you, Professor Opperly,' Hunter added. 'The new planet has Earth-radius linear accelerators and an Earth-circumference cyclotron.'

Opperly grinned. 'We just had a demonstration of that, didn't we?'

None of them noticed a star wink belatedly on very close to Mars. An escaping laser beam had struck Deimos, the tiny outer moon of Mars, heating it white hot – to the considerable excitement of Tigran Biryuzov and his comrades.

Opperly put down the grey gun and moved around the desk. 'Come with me, please,' he told Margo and Hunter. 'We should alert the landing field to this possibility.'

'Wait a minute,' Margo said. 'Are you just going to leave the momentum pistol lying there?'

'Oh,' Opperly said apologetically. He reached for it, and handed it to Margo. 'You'd better look after it for me.'

Richard Hillary and Vera Carlisle tramped along a little road that wended south near the crests of the Malvern Hills. Once more there were other trampers with them, dotting the little road.

They had discovered that not even sex and companionship can still the lemming urge, at least by day. Richard was thinking once more of the Black Mountains. It might be possible to reach them without leaving high ground.

The morning sun was hidden by a grey overcast that had come in from the west just as the Wanderer had been setting at a quarter to its *D* face. There had been a weird phenomenon then. Just as the Wanderer had vanished in the cloud curtain, it had seemed to be reborn, all silver grey and bigger than itself, an hour above its vanishing spot. They had speculated as to whether this was a mirage of the Wanderer or a second strange planet. Then the mirage or the strange planet had vanished in the overcast.

Vera stopped and turned on her transistor wireless. Richard stopped beside her with a sigh of resignation. Two nearby walkers had stopped too, out of curiosity.

Vera slowly turned the dial. There was no static. She turned up the volume full and turned the dial again. Still only silence.

'Maybe it's broken, Miss,' one of the people suggested.

'You've worn it out,' Richard told her unsympathetically. 'And a good thing.'

Then the voice came, tiny and whistling at first, but then, as she tuned it, clear and loud in the grey-roofed silence of the hills:

'Repeat. A report, cabled from Toronto and confirmed by Buenos Aires and New Zealand, definitely states that the two strange planets have vanished as they came. This does not mean an immediate end to tidal reverberations, but . . .'

They went on listening. From up and down the road people were gathering, gathering. . . .

Bagong Bung decided the waves had gone down enough to make it safe, so he took the stout cloth sack out from under him, where he'd been sitting on it for safety, along with the lashed-down little bags of coin from the *Sumatra Queen*, and he opened it so that he and Cobber-Hume could peer in.

The wild waters, washing again and again across the orange life raft, had carried away all the mud and scoured clean all the tiny objects in the sack. Along with bits of coral and pebble and shell, there was the dark glow of old gold and the small, dark red flames of three – no, four! – rubies.

Wolf Loner stopped feeding soup to the Italian girl, because she had turned away to look at the rim of the rising sun over-topping the grey Atlantic. '*Il sole*,' she whispered.

She touched the wood of the *Endurance*. '*Una nave*.'

She put her hand against the wrist of the hand holding the spoon and looked up into his face. '*Noi siamo qui*.'

'Yes, we're here,' he said.

Captain Sithwise looked down from the bridge of the *Prince Charles* at the leagues of mud-filmed green jungle beginning to steam in the low red sunlight.

The purser said: 'Extrapolating from the casualties in view, sir, we have eight hundred broken limbs and four hundred fractured skulls to deal with.'

The executive officer said: 'Brazil has for herself the core of an atomic jungle city. I fancy that's the way it might turn out in the end, sir, though it should be quite a case in the inter-national courts!'

Captain Sithwise nodded, but continued to study the strange green sea in which his ship had come to harbour.

Barbara Katz looked at the blue waters around the *Albatross*. Hardly one wave in ten was even white-crested. The sun was rising over a coast of broken and bedraggled palms barely two miles away. Hester sat in the hatchway, holding the baby.

'Benjy,' Barbara said, 'there's a spare boom below, and the blankets, at any rate, if there isn't canvas. Do you think you could rig up a little mast and sail and –'

'Yes, Miss Barbara, I'm sure I could,' he told her. He stretched and yawned widely, pushing his chest at the sun. 'But this time I'm going to take a rest first.'

Sally Harris said to Jake Lesher: 'Oh, Christ, now the excite-ment's all over.'

'Jesus, Sal, don't you ever want to sleep?' Jake protested.

'Who could sleep now?' she demanded. 'Let's start signalling people. Or better yet, now we got all the material, let's really work on the play!'

Pierre Rambouillet-Lacepède regretfully pushed aside his three-body calculations, which could never now be fully verified, and gave ear to François Michaud.

The young astronomer said excitedly: 'We have pinned it down beyond the possibility of doubt! The sidereal day has been lengthened by three seconds a year! The intrusive planets have had a measurable effect upon the earth!'

Margo and Hunter stood in the dark arm in arm on the edge of the landing field towards the north end of the plateau of Vandenberg Two.

'Are you bothered about meeting Don and Paul?' he whispered to her. 'I shouldn't ask that, of course, when we're all keyed up over whether they'll even make it.'

'No,' she told him, putting her other hand over his. 'I'll just be glad to greet them. I've got you.'

Yes, she has, he reflected, not altogether happily. And now he had to fit his life to his conquest. Could he give up Wilma and the boys? Not altogether, he was sure.

Then something else occurred to him.

'And now you've got Morton Opperly,' he whispered.

Margo grinned, then asked: 'Just what do you mean by that, Ross?'

'Nothing in particular, I think,' he told her.

Around them were gathered the rest of the saucer students. The truck and the Corvette stood just behind them.

To one side were Opperly and a few members of his section. Radio contact with the Baba Yaga had been reported from the tower a few moments ago.

Over their heads the old familiar stars of the northern sky spread between the two constellations of Scorpio and the Dipper, but high in the west there lay among them a spindle-shaped scattering of new stars, some faint, some brighter than Sirius – the glittering remnants of Luna.

'It's going to be funny, not having a moon any more,' Hixon said.

'A hundred gods sponged out of mythology at one sweep,' Rama Joan remarked.

'I'm more sorry to lose the Wanderer,' Ann piped up. 'Oh, I hope they got away.'

'More than the moon gods are gone,' the Ramrod said gloomily.

'Never mind, Charlie,' Wanda told him. 'You've seen great things come to pass. All your predictions –'

'All my dreams,' he corrected her. He frowned, but pressed her hand.

Hunter said: 'We'll get two gods back for every one we lost. That's my prediction.'

Pop said grumpily: 'I don't give a damn about the moon going. She never did a thing for me.'

'She never even softened up one pretty girl, Pop?' Margo asked him.

McHeath said, as if he'd just worked it out: 'No moon – no tides.'

'Yes, there'll still be solar tides,' the Little Man corrected. 'Small ones, of course, like they have at Tahiti.'

'I wonder what'll happen to what's left of the moon?' Margo asked, looking towards the west. 'Will it just keep going in a ring?'

Opperly heard that and said in explanation: 'No, now that its gravitational centre has gone with the Wanderer, the fragments will spread out at the velocity they had in orbit – five miles a second, about. Some of them will strike Earth's atmosphere in approximately ten hours. There'll be a meteor shower, but not too destructive, I imagine. The ring lay in a plane passing above our North Pole. Most of the fragments should miss us. Many of them will take up long, elliptical orbits around Earth.'

'Gee,' Wojtowicz remarked rather cheerily, 'it's like having Doc back to explain things.'

'Who's Doc?' Opperly asked.

The group was silent for a moment. Then Rama Joan said: 'Oh . . . a man.'

At that moment a yellow flare shone in the zenith, became a lemon flame pointing and dropping earthward. There was a softly mounting roar, such as comes from a fireplace when all the wood catches. The Baba Yaga touched down, its yellow jets dying, to a perfect landing.